✝ VIRGIN
OF THE
WIND ROSE

GLEN CRANEY

BRIGID'S FIRE PRESS

Copyright 2014 by Glen Craney

Art by Glen Craney
Design by Glen Craney

This book is a work of fiction. Apart from the historical figures, any resemblance to actual persons, living or dead, is entirely coincidental.

All rights reserved. No part of this book may be reproduced in any form or by electronic or mechanical means, including information storage and retrieval systems, without permission in writing from the publisher, except by a reviewer, who may quote brief passages in a review. Any members of educational institutions wishing to photocopy part or all of the work for classroom use, or publishers who would like to obtain permission to include the work in an anthology, should send their inquiries to Brigid's Fire Press at www.brigidsfire.com.

Published in the United States

FIRST EDITION

Library of Congress Cataloging-in-Publication Data
Craney, Glen
The Virgin of the Wind Rose: A Mystery-Thriller of the End Times/Glen Craney

ISBN 978-0-9816484-2-2

1. Suspense Fiction 2. Historical Fiction. 3. Columbus, Christopher-Fiction. 4. Rapture (Christian eschatology)-Fiction. 5. Quests (Expeditions)-Fiction. 6. Treasure troves-Fiction. 7. Age of Discovery-Fiction. 8. Henry, Infante of Portugal (1394-1460)- Fiction. 10. Spanish Inquisition-Fiction. 11. Cryptography-Fiction. 12. Spain-History-Ferdinand and Isabella, 1479-1516-Fiction.

Brigid's Fire Press
www.brigidsfire.com

The explorers who opened the New World operated from a master plan and were agents of rediscovery rather than discoverers. Very little is "known" about the origin, lives, characters and policies of these intrepid adventurers. Although they lived in a century amply provided with historians and biographers, these saw fit either to remain silent or invent plausible accounts without substance. ... If there was a mystery, that which was hidden must have been regarded as valuable.

Manly P. Hall
America's Assignment With Destiny

[Newton] looked on the whole universe and all that is in it as a riddle, as a secret which could be read by applying pure thought to certain evidence, certain mystic clues which God had laid about the world to allow a sort of philosopher's treasure hunt to the esoteric brotherhood. He believed that these clues were to be found partly in the evidence of the heavens and in the constitution of elements (and that is what gives the false suggestion of his being an experimental natural philosopher), but also partly in certain papers and traditions handed down by the brethren in an unbroken chain back to the original cryptic revelation in Babylonia. He regarded the universe as a cryptogram set by the Almighty. ...

John Maynard Keynes
Newton the Man

In 1921, laborers discovered a large circle with radiating spokes etched into the ground near an old church in the Algarve region of southwestern Portugal. The ring had remained hidden for centuries below the overgrowth of the wind-swept peninsula known as Sagres Point.

The ancient Greeks knew this hinterland as *Ophiussa*, where the native Serpent People worshipped a snake goddess who revealed lost treasures. Centuries later, the Romans built a temple on its cliffs to stand guard over the edge of the world. They named the place *Sacrum Promontorium*, the holy promontory, where their sun god slithered hissing into the sea each night.

Today, the origin and purpose of this excavated circle remain a mystery.

The Portuguese call it their *Rosa dos Ventos*, the Wind Rose.

ONE

SATOR
APERO
TENET
OPERA
ROTAS

LALIBELA, ETHIOPIA
JANUARY 20, PRESENT DAY

Sopped in sweat, the ten-year-old Ethiopian boy prayed to St. Georgis the Dragonslayer for protection as he wormed his way toward the tomb of the first man on Earth.

The tunnel's gritty sandstone, stained red from the blood of Satan's serpents, punished his hands and knees. To preserve the precious air, he slowed his breaths as he crawled. The settling night had cooled the mountain village above him, but here, sixty meters below the surface, the trapped midday heat could roast a chicken. Faint from hunger, he stopped and pulled a crust of bread from his pocket. He chewed the morsel slowly, taking care to muzzle its aroma with his tunic's sleeve to avoid being swarmed by the bees that hived in the crevices.

His dizziness eased, and he resumed his quest, groping blindly on all fours along the narrowing walls. At last, he came to the Armory of the Shining Ones, the long notch in the floor where the angels had once stored their lances.

"*Mäqäraräb*," he whispered. *Not far now.*

He knew every bend and cranny in this secret passage by memory, having accompanied the priests on their daily inspections of the subterranean churches. *That* was the only godsend from his miserable duties. His father, the High Priest of Lalibela, had marked him at birth for religious service by tattooing a blue cross on his right temple. As a result, he was forbidden to play football or chase tourists for candy, and he would have to slave six more years carrying sandals just to become a deacon. Everyone said he should be grateful for the honor, but he had no desire to waste away his life mumbling incantations. Tomorrow he planned to stow away in the cargo bin of the bus to Addis Ababa, where he would find prosperous construction work and a beautiful girlfriend.

Before leaving home, however, he craved an even more exciting escape, one that promised a glimpse of Paradise. In a few hours, at dawn, his fellow villagers would celebrate Timkat, the holiest of their many religious festivals. The elders of the monastery had retired early to their cloisters to fast and prepare themselves with chants. This night, the tenth of Terr, was the only time of the year that Bet Golgota—the underground church of the Crucifixion—was left unguarded. It would also be his last chance to pierce the veil that shrouded Heaven's wisdom and delights.

He came hovering over the yawning trench that protected the entrance to the nave, and ran a finger across an inscription on a stone carved in *Ge'ez*:

The opening verse of Genesis.

He kissed the ground that covered the bones of the biblical Adam. Then, he reached up and inserted the stolen key into the lock just beyond the grave. After several turns of the rusty tumbler, the pitted door squealed open.

He slithered inside the trapezoidal cavern. Overhead, lit by ambient moonlight from the fissures in the ceiling, faded frescoes of the martyred saints stared down at him. Turning away from their accusing glares, he climbed to his feet and approached the Selassie Chapel. The sanctuary was so sacred that for ages only the head priest had been allowed to enter it. With a shaking hand, he drew aside a ratty curtain that covered the burial vault of King Lalibela, the monarch who had ruled Ethiopia during the time of the White Knights.

Yes, it was here, in this very vault, where he had spied his father hide the precious Leaves of Eden. How long he had dreamed of the ecstasy now so near his grasp. He heard a whisper of warning from his soul: *He who gazes upon the hidden treasures of Lalibela will be struck blind and mute for eternity.*

That ancient curse gave him pause, but only for a moment. He wasn't fooled. The priests spread such tales to scare off grave robbers. He pushed hard against the slab. Finally, after several attempts, the adhesions of centuries gave way. He took a deep breath and reached blindly into the sarcophagus. His palm brushed against the trove.

"*Egziabhiyär Ymäsgn*," he said softly. *May God be praised.*

Clutching his discovery to his chest, he shoved the heavy lid back into place with his shoulder and spread dust over it to conceal the—

A bolt of light radiated through the chapel.

The foundations shook and buckled the ceiling. He ran through the arches to avoid being buried alive—a second flash blinded him. He covered his face and screamed, "*Abba!*"

Seconds passed, and he took another shallow breath, then opened his eyes. His mouth gaped in horror—he tried again to call for his father, but this time he couldn't force a sound past his quivering lips.

Washington, D.C.
January 20, Present Day

Jaqueline Quartermane—'Jaq' to her friends and fellow lawyers at the State Department—dashed through the doors of the agency's Foggy Bottom headquarters. She slid into a waiting taxi and gave her destination: "EEOB."

As the cabbie sped off, she congratulated herself for remembering the inside-the-Beltway lingo for the Eisenhower Executive Office Building. She was a player now, one of the chosen charged with spreading Freedom and Christ around the world, and she had learned the importance of the shorthand code used by Washington's power elite. To save money, she usually walked the half-mile to her weekly prayer breakfast, but today she didn't want to be late. Her mentor, Rev. Calvin Merry, founder of her *alma mater*, John Darby School of Law, would be speaking. The televangelist had flown up from Knoxville that morning to lobby for a faith-based initiative that would earmark federal funds to bring the Gospel to Third World countries. She hadn't seen the reverend since graduation and was eager to thank him in person for greasing the wheels on her new job at the Office of Legal Advisor.

The taxi turned east onto G Street, and on both sides of her, sleepy students trudged down the sidewalks to their early classes at George Washington University. She smiled and sighed with relief, so glad to be done with school. She had been working in D.C. for six months, but there were still times she couldn't quite believe a poor farm girl from eastern Kentucky had really made it to—

The cab screeched to a jolting stop. The gnomish driver, whose copper skin looked to have the texture of a cigar's binding, grinned at her through the rear-view mirror. "*Temos chegado.*"

Sent flying across the back seat, she came back upright. "Excuse me?"

"We arrive. ... You are from Brasilia, no? *Muito bonito*. Like our *senhoras*."

Flustered by the creepy compliment, she paid the fare and bolted the taxi. She often got that sort of reaction here because of her lithe Caribbean figure, black olive eyes, and luscious sable hair tangled with wild Medusa curls. Many in this city of embassies and consulates simply assumed she was from South America or the Middle East.

She climbed the EEOB steps still muttering to herself. She'd always had dark skin with light patches splotched across her back. Growing up, she had suffered such merciless teasing about this oddity from the other kids that she still reacted defensively when anyone, even a homesick cabbie, perceived her as different. She finally made it past the security guards, who scanned her a second time with their leers. Hearing Rev. Merry's booming drawl echoing down the hall, she rushed up to the conference room and, smiling, opened the door.

Fifty pairs of interrogating eyes turned on her.

Mary Magdalene emerging from the Holy Sepulcher couldn't have been met with a more skeptical reception. She saw at once that this wasn't the usual gathering of low-level staffers. Today's invitation-only guests were middle-aged men and older, Republicans mostly, with the typical Washington mask of placid authority etched into their pasty jowls. She recognized a couple of senators, a few representatives and cabinet members, all being served eggs and grits around a long mahogany table lit in amber by a Georgian chandelier.

"Press room's on the first floor," mumbled one of the grayheads while he stuffed his mouth with toast.

For once, she was thankful for her dark complexion, to hide the blush of embarrassment. Being branded a member of the media was a Washington insult comparable to being born into the lowest caste in India. She was about to retreat to the hallway when a command froze her.

"Please stand, gentlemen," Rev. Merry ordered.

She locked eyes with him. The pastor looked more tired than usual, she thought, and there was a little less gold in his thinning hair. But his round face, a bit liverish from too much fried food, still featured that famous forbearing smile that channeled God's forgiveness. His ample girth, as always, was immaculately draped in a charcoal merino suit, fitted by the same Nashville haberdashery that had tailored General Pat Cleburne's butternut uniform before both wool and wearer were ripped to shreds by Union lead at Franklin.

Rev. Merry abandoned the head of the table and, in more of a demand than a request, boomed: "Would you captains of government join me here on this side of the room?"

The men traded vexed glances, but they slowly stood and gathered as ordered. None of them dared disobey the most prolific GOP fundraiser in the country, for even a gentle scolding sent out across the airwaves of the reverend's Glorious Resurrection Network could bring a penitent congressman crawling to Knoxville for absolution.

Surrounded now by his disciples, Rev. Merry thumbed opened his well-worn bible like a casino dealer who could stop a shuffle and identify a card without peeking. "'And He shall separate them from one another, as the shepherd separates the sheep from the goats.' Who knows the verse?"

When no one risked a guess, Jaq sheepishly offered: "Matthew Twenty-Five: Thirty-two."

The reverend broke a gold-capped grin and threw open his arms in welcome. "Jaqie, darling, come bless me with a hug. And don't give a moment's thought to these old billies. They've forgotten the manners their mamas taught them. I suspect some have a deficient Northern upbringing to blame."

Wrapped in the pastor's loving embrace, Jaq saw a distinguished-looking man with cropped silver hair and penetrating cobalt eyes come forward and extend his hand to her.

"I'm the damned Yankee he just slandered."

She was shocked that anyone would use an expletive in the pastor's presence, but Rev. Merry merely chuckled at her nonplussed reaction.

"This is Josiah Mayfield," the pastor said. "Deputy Director of the National Security Agency. His Indiana forefathers probably shot at our kinfolk, so don't trust him with any of our Confederate secrets."

Informed of the powerful pastor's affection for Jaq, the other men came up and gathered around her as if she were Scarlett O'Hara at the cotillion ball.

"Quartermane is Scottish, isn't it?" Mayfield asked her.

She was a little unsettled to learn that the NSA official knew her last name. "I'm embarrassed to admit, I don't know. I was always told my kin came west through the Cumberland Gap."

Mayfield curled a discerning smile at her discomfort. "Don't worry. We haven't started a dossier on you yet. Actually, we have something more in common than hailing from bordering states. The Reverend here has parted the waters many times during my exodus through the desert of public service."

She was anxious to divert the attention. "We should give him the pulpit."

"Amen to that." Mayfield finally broke off his wilting scrutiny on her and turned to fire a quip at the pastor. "Cal, I trust there's no commandment against me finishing my oatmeal while you save our souls?"

"Just don't ask me to multiply the loaves." Amid the chuckles, Rev. Merry saw Jaq trying to escape to the corner. He caught her hand to delay her. "But first, I have an announcement. In a few weeks, I'm going to have the honor of marrying off our lovely guest here."

Over the applause, Mayfield asked the pastor: "Who's the lucky guy?"

"Paul Merion," Rev. Merry said. "A fine young man doing God's work in Kenya. Y'all can send your generous gifts to my office."

Jaq squeezed his forearm in a plea to move on. "That's not necessary."

The pastor laughed. "They have so much PAC money in their war chests, darling, you'll be doing them a favor by taking some off their hands."

Signaling for all to return to their seats, Rev. Merry took his place again at the head of the table and bowed his head in prayer. After nearly a minute of this inward contemplation, he looked up and bore down on his audience with his eyes blazing holy fire. "Now, y'all are here today because you live the Word of God. I'm not going to sugarcoat the situation in the world today for men and women who have front row seats." He paused to underscore the gravity of what he would next reveal. "The Rapture, my good friends in Christ, is imminent.

It will be sudden and it will be shocking. Mothers will be separated from their children and husbands from their wives. There will be seven years of Tribulation before we are taken up to abide with the Almighty and His saints."

Jaq marveled at how swiftly the eloquent minister had captured the attention of men not easily impressed—of all except the NSA guy, who seemed more interested in waving down the waiter for more coffee.

"How do I know this?" Rev. Merry asked rhetorically. "I read the signs prophesied in the Bible. The nations have unified their currencies with the global markets and the Zionists have brought peace to Israel. With the United Nations and the European Union, we are nearing a one-world government. There is only one condition left to fulfill. ... Anyone?"

Jaq saw him glance at her, but she didn't dare upstage the room again.

"The Temple," Josh Mayfield finally answered, as matter-of-factly as if he had just ordered another item off the menu.

Nodding pensively, Rev. Merry turned toward the window to gaze at the columns of the Lincoln Memorial on the mall. "The Jewish Temple must be rebuilt and the Holy of Holies restored. Only then will the Antichrist be revealed and the Kingdom of God installed on Earth."

Senator Barkin from Arizona cleared his throat. "Cal, let's cut to the chase. We can all read about the Rapture in those dime-store novels they sell at the airport. What is it you want from us?"

After stealing a glance at Mayfield, Rev. Merry stepped closer to the senator and towered over him. "John, my duty is to proclaim God's commandments. Yours is to see that they're not ignored by the secularists who have infiltrated this government like a plague of Massachusetts boll weevils."

"Meaning what, exactly?" Sen. Barkin asked.

"I received a call this week from Jerusalem," Rev. Merry said. "Prime Minister Aronowitz says you've been dragging your feet on the foreign-aid bill."

His appetite ruined, Sen. Barkin shoved his plate away. "The Israelis are asking for another five hundred million. Aronowitz won't tell us why he needs it. We're already giving him three billion a year. Is he planning to use the money to build more West Bank settlements? I can't justify this to the Dems on Appropriations unless Aronowitz and his Likudniks come clean."

The pastor glared sternly at the senator. "We Americans have been given a biblical mandate to stand by our Jewish brethren."

Sen. Barkin shrugged. "Why even worry about Israel if the Jews are going to be left behind at the end of it all anyway?"

"God placed the sons and daughters of the Old Testament on Earth to fulfill a vital purpose," Rev. Merry said. "The Second Coming cannot unfold until the Jews first prepare the way."

Jaq had heard the reverend talk many times from the pulpit about the destiny of the Jews, and still his passion on the subject never failed to stir her. She was about to murmur an "amen" when the door opened.

A female aide stuck her head inside. With a worried look, she glanced at Rev. Merry, then at Jaq. "Miss Quartermane, Under Secretary Darden needs you back at State immediately."

Sana'a, Yemen
January 20, Present Day

Jamaal al-Sourouri dragged his crippled right leg down a trash-littered alley, taking his usual route through the slums to avoid being recognized. In front of him, three barefoot boys stopped kicking a soccer ball and laughed at how he was forced to crouch to ease the excruciating pain caused by the infidel beatings. He reached for the dagger in his thwab belt to chase them away.

Fools! Their mortification was fast approaching. Could they not see the signs? The televisions in the coffee houses showed Iran's Al Quds militia waving their black flags in triumph. People chattered about the strange weather, ninety degrees in winter, and homosexuals now walked openly in the streets, dancing while demonic American music played on radios. Women were even making themselves barren with potions. All of it had been prophesied long ago.

The Time of Trials was at hand.

He winced from the aching in his bones. The memories of his wasted life dogged him with each agonizing limp. He too had once been blind to Allah's will. The stench of vomit in that Saudi prison still filled his nostrils. After torturing him for a week, the Riyadh police had shipped him to Guantanamo on the false charge of being a soldier for Al Qaeda. Even after the Americans discovered that he had been delivered up as a scapegoat for a nephew of the Royal Family, they'd kept him locked away for five more years. He had tried to hang himself, but the devils had built the cage ceiling too low.

His nightmare should have ended with his release, but it had only just begun. Dumped into an Albanian refugee camp, he had been forced to beg his way back home to Yemen. It was only then that he discovered his wife, thinking him dead, had married another man. Now, even his old friends shunned him, convinced that the Americans had recruited him for a spy.

He tried to calm himself by thinking back to that night three months ago when he had climbed to the roof of his tenement to jump to his death. Before he could launch himself over the edge, an old man sneaking a cigarette in the shadows of the stairwell had whispered, *You are persecuted for your faith.*

Let me die!

Do not waste your life. The Awaited One requires your service.

On that fateful night, his intercessor revealed himself to be Yahya the New Baptist, the advance lieutenant for the Mahdi. In truth, he could still not be certain if Yahya had been an angel or mortal, for he had not seen him since. A week after his salvation, masked fighters had taken him away to be initiated into the Mahdi's *mujahideen*, tattooing his biceps with the secret hadith. His suffering, he had been promised, was ordained from above to harden him for the coming apocalyptic battles.

Now, as a servant of the Islamic messiah who would defeat the Great Deceiver and rule the world, he received his orders every Sunday by email.

He lived only for these communications.

He turned a corner and levered his useless leg up the steps of an Internet café. When the clerk at the front desk, a lazy Iranian student, refused to look up, he threw four coins on the counter and snatched the access code. Careening down the row of computers, he landed on an empty chair and began pecking furiously on the keyboard. Waiting and waiting, he cursed the slow processor. Finally, the browser popped up. He inserted his password, concealing it with his jittery hand. One email. Yes, it was from Yahya.

Inspired by Allah, he had spent those many months in prison learning English, vowing to turn the vile language against its users. Now, he quickly converted the message from Arabic, having been instructed that the American intelligence agents placed a lower priority on emails in English: *The Awaited One offers His blessings, my son. He wishes to know if His will is done.*

He tapped a reply: *I have obeyed His command.*

Several seconds passed. Where was the response? Was the infidel machine going to crash? He was about to kick it when another email arrived:

Do you return from your journey with God's Mercy?

He lowered his head in shame. Finally, he found the courage to type: *No.*

Seconds later, Yahya's reply appeared on the screen: *The Awaited One will be disappointed.*

Distraught, he frantically typed the reason for his failure: *The Ethiopian would not surrender it.*

At last, more words from Yahya—these cold in their brevity—scrolled before his eyes: *Go to Cairo. Wait for instructions.*

The clerk at the desk shouted down the aisle, "Time is up!"

His cheeks hot with tears of shame, Jamaal angrily yanked the computer's cord from its socket. He limped back down the row of cubicles and grinned at the haughty clerk with a vision of him being incinerated in the coming holocaust. Showing off his English, he whispered to the student's ear: "For once, Persian monkey, you speak the truth. Soon—very soon—*your* time is up."

two

Cold and weary, Pero da Covilha struggled to keep up with his father as they led their two Lusitano stallions through the drifting snow. If the storm did not let up soon, they risked becoming trapped on this desolate shepherd's path along the foothills of the Serra da Estrela, a range of crags that divided Portugal like a scabbed wound across the chest. Holy Mother Church deemed travel on Good Friday disrespectful, but Pero knew his father, the king's procurer of military mounts for the Monhantas province, was determined to reach Belmonte before dusk to find shelter for the animals.

"*Pai*, can we ride?" he begged.

Diogo da Covilha, short and bald with a lugubrious face set like a shriveled apple upon a hairy wreath of double chins, increased their pace to punish his eleven-year-old son for the shameful plea. He glanced over his shoulder to ensure that the thistles were not gouging the fetlocks of his new purchases. "We are merchants, not *cavaleiros*. We live by our feet."

Pero grudgingly resumed his battle with the iced needles. He had walked this path across the border at least a dozen times to the equestrian market at Ciudad Rodrigo, where his dark African features, suspicious Levantine eyes, and talent for picking up the Arabic tongue caused the Castilians to mistake him for a Morisco. He hated being treated like a converted Moor. But his father, aware that Andalusians were renowned for judging horses, had turned the ignominy into prosperity by tutoring him to play a breeder's son. The ploy never failed to fool the sellers into abandoning their schemes of preening their nags to resemble El Cid's Babieca. Then, after Covilha's high altitude worked its disciplining effect, he and his father would take their bargains to Castelo Branco, where the horses with their enlarged lungs would outperform the pampered garrons from the Algarve.

They made a good living at the horse trading, but Pero found the work humiliating, and he dreamed instead of one day becoming a famous mariner. Risking his father's wrath again, he asked, "How long do you think it will take the Admiral Cadamosto to reach the Boiling Waters below Africa?"

Diogo huffed. "Why do you fill your head with such nonsense? The king will have no use for our services if he wastes his coin on sails instead of purchases for his cavalry."

"Emilio says if Cadamosto falls off the earth's disc, the admiral will be dragged away by Antipodian savages and roasted for meat."

Diogo rolled his eyes at that wild tale. "Have you ever climbed a tree to see down a road?"

"Of course."

"If the world *is* flat, why then can you see farther from atop the tree?" Receiving only a shrug in reply, Diogo kept boring in on his son. "If two sticks are driven into the ground, one in Coimbra and the other in Lisbon, why are their shadows at different angles during the same hour of the day? Why do the sails of a ship appear to rise up from below the ocean?"

That last question stung Pero, for he had never even seen the ocean, a negligence considered a perverse abomination in Portugal. "Padre Dinis says that the Devil took Christ to a high mountain and showed Him all the kingdoms of the world. He said such a feat was possible only because the earth is flat."

His father took out his anger by kicking a limb from his path. "Padre Dinis would be hard pressed to find his own shadow on a cloudless day."

"But the priest is educated."

"Educated in the art of licking a chalice dry! Only once did I meet a truly learned man, and that was in Cordoba. He devoted his life to proving it impossible for truths arrived at by the intellect to contradict God's revelations."

"Who was this philosopher?"

His father suddenly turned guarded. "His name is of no consequence. You must never speak of what I just told you."

"But why?"

His father seemed to search for a reason. "The priest might become jealous of the Cordoban teacher's wisdom."

"What then *is* the shape of the earth?"

"We can only arrive at the deepest truth concerning an object of reflection only by asking what is *not* true about it." His father surveyed the wilds to make certain no creature was within earshot, then he asked, "Is God multiple?"

"You mean like the Trinity?"

His father hissed for him to lower his voice. "Can the Ultimate of all that exists be divided?"

Pero knew from the Creed that such an assertion was contrary to Church teachings. "Are you saying that God is only One?"

"I said no such thing," Diogo insisted. "I am only indicating what God is *not*. You must approach every object you encounter with this same test. I cannot tell you what form the Earth takes. But I can tell you with all certainty that it is not flat. And that is the first step to enlightenment."

Pero never failed to be impressed by his father's knowledge of cosmology. After his mother died from the bloody flux three years ago, his father had given him the best education possible. Yet it was the other path of discovery that he truly yearned to blaze. Timidly, he asked, "Have you ever sailed the seas?"

Exasperated, Diogo snapped the reins in his hands. "A wish to leave one's home is more baneful than the pestilence. Our forefathers …" He stopped, and then insisted sharply, "I'll hear no more talk of this."

Pero noticed that his father always saddened whenever their family's past was mentioned. All Pero knew was that his grandfather, Aben, a saddler, had migrated to Covilha from an unknown land and had died from the flux before Diogo had been old enough to marry. A raven cawed overhead, yanking Pero from his thoughts. He had become so engrossed in their discussion that only now did he see the tower of Belmonte castle rising over the peak. His father led him down into the village, where they found the windows shuttered and the clanking of the hooves of their stallions the only sounds to be heard.

Somewhere in the distance, a woman's scream pierced the eerie calm, and nesting pigeons flapped loudly in response. A low roar from the far end of the village erupted and became louder.

His father halted their approach. "We must leave at once."

"But you promised we would eat and—"

Diogo glared a silent demand for his son's obedience.

As they hurried their retreat, Pero caught a glimpse through a window of a family dressed in black and sitting around a table. The mother met his eyes briefly; she quickly extinguished the lone candle on the table and hid it. He saw her children bring out playing cards from their pockets, and they began trading them, but appeared to be having no fun at the game. He wanted to linger there, trying to understand what he had just witnessed, but his father dragged him away toward the outskirts of the village.

They were nearly past the boundaries stones when a mob armed with cudgels turned the corner. A constable and two black-robed friars leading the pack prodded forward a disheveled and distraught woman who wore a yellow cross on her chest. Her face was bruised and bloodied. She stared at Pero with eyes so helpless and forlorn that it caused him to shudder.

"You there!" the constable shouted at his father. "Halt!"

Diogo froze. After a hesitation, he handed the reins to his son and bowed to the constable and friars. "Our Lord's peace be with you."

One of the friars came closer to examine their faces. "You violate the day of Christ's death."

Pero saw his father's hand shaking as he produced the letter of agency.

The friar seemed disappointed as he read and returned the royal document. "Be quick about your business. Even the king owes contrition to God."

Pero's father bowed again. "We will not impose on you further. My apprentice and I are on our way to Covilha."

Apprentice? Why did he not call me his son?

The constable answered the obsequious bowing by spitting a wad of bile at Diogo's boots. "Covilha is a pig sty. Be gone with you."

Diogo paled. Rather than defend the reputation of their home village, he led Pero away in silence.

When they reached the safety of the foothills, out of sight of the village, Diogo tied the stallions to a tree. Without a word of explanation for their cowardly retreat, he staggered over to a boulder and retched.

Pero rushed to his side. "*Pai*, are you ill?" When his father did not answer him, he risked asking the question that had been plaguing him for the last hour. "What crime did that woman in the street commit?"

Diogo wiped his mouth. "She was caught preparing to celebrate the eve of the Sabbath."

"But the Sabbath is not until Sunday."

"For them, it is Saturday."

Now Pero was even more confused. "Why did we not livery the horses there?"

In a sudden surge of violence, Diogo drove Pero against a tree and tore open his son's shirt. Drawing his dagger, he dug its sharp edge into Pero's upper arm and cut a slender chevron of flesh. When Pero finally stopped struggling and screaming, his father staunched the bleeding with his sleeve.

Terrified, Pero looked down at the blood dripping on his bare chest. "I asked only—"

His father silenced him by opening his own shirt, revealing an old scar in the same shape as the incision he had just made. "We are Jews. ... as was that woman in the town."

Pero feared his father had become unhinged. "Jews? I was baptized! You take me to Mass every Sunday!"

Diogo rubbed his hand over his own scar, as if remembering the day it was inflicted. "I was marked like this by my father, and he by his. The Church forbids circumcision. We do this in its stead to preserve our tradition."

"But you pray the Creed!"

His father held his silence in a shameful admission that their adherence to the Church commandments had been a ruse.

"You lied to the *priests*?"

Diogo looked east, toward the border. "When I was a *menino* growing up in Valencia, a madness swept across Iberia. Thousands of our people were massacred. My own brothers and sisters were butchered before my eyes. A *converso* family took me in and forced me to be baptized for my survival."

"You mean … you don't believe in Christ?"

Diogo cast his eyes down. "I've kept the rituals of the true faith in secret, as have many in our country."

"That family in the window …"

"They were playing a game called *barajas*. After the friars conduct their Friday inspections, our people study Torah lessons written on the back of the cards."

Several moments passed before Pero found his voice again. "Why did you not tell me of this until now?"

Diogo blinked back tears. "I thought it best to raise you as a Christian. But seeing that brave woman suffer, I can no longer stand by and allow our family's faith to expire for all eternity. You must never reveal what I am about to tell you, not even to those you believe you can trust with your life. Do you understand?"

"*Sim, Pai.*"

His father grasped him by the shoulders to drive home the gravity of what he would next reveal. "There is One God, not three in one. The Messiah has yet to come. Do not allow the friars to convince you otherwise. Their writings have not superseded the Law of Moses. And, above all, you must always remember this: Our faith will be restored to its former glory only when the Temple of Solomon is rebuilt in Jerusalem."

Pero felt unsteady, as if the world had suddenly collapsed under him. What *was* he now, a Christian or a Jew? Only that morning he had joined in the traditional Good Friday ritual asking that the veil of faithlessness be removed from the eyes of the perfidious Jews.

Had he been praying all along for his own damnation?

THREE

Sped toward Foggy Bottom in a State Department limo, Jaq checked her appointments calendar, baffled by the summons back to the office. Had she screwed up a case? As the newest lawyer on the foreign-assistance staff, she was assigned only minor projects, such as reviewing trade contracts and handling consular traffic violations, and those rarely raised a blip on the radar of Fred Darden. Although the Under Secretary of Political Affairs hadn't attended the prayer breakfast that morning, he was a fellow Merryonette, the media's moniker for the Rev. Merry's many political friends. She had spoken to Darden only once, during her interview rounds, and had found him to be a cold fish, calculating and a bit hostile, with leaden eyes and a cadaverous pallor. Sometimes she got an odd vibe when passing him in the building, as if he considered her a rival because of her closeness to the pastor. But that was ridiculous. How could she, a rookie attorney, possibly threaten one of the most seasoned diplomats in Washington?

Her worry lines gave way to a grin. Of course. This had all the fingerprints of one of Paul's pranks. Yeah, she'd bet a month's salary that her fiancé had returned home from Africa early. He probably convinced his buddies at State to whisk her back for his grand entrance.

She couldn't wait to be in Paul's arms again. In law school, she had given up hope of ever finding love, but the Lord worked in mysterious ways—with a little help from Rev. Merry.

Only a year ago, during one of the pastor's Sunday services at the Good News Cathedral, she had been seated next to a handsome man with shocks of tawny hair and a lantern jaw. Rev. Merry's sermon that morning had been on Ephesians 5:21-33 and God's holy covenant between husband and wife. *Wives, submit to your husbands*, another Paul had written two thousand years earlier. Her pew mate that day had leaned over to her and whispered: *St. Paul never found a woman who would marry him. I wonder why?*

She had laughed so loudly at his irreverence that half the congregation turned on them. The reverend, she later discovered, had conspired with the ushers to bring them together. Paul had been impressed enough with her potential for obedience—or was it the way she enjoyed his jokes?—that he had invited her to join him for banana pancakes at the IHOP that morning. Two months later, she was waving goodbye to him with an engagement ring on her finger.

Now, three weeks before the wedding, he was returning to become the new executive director of the reverend's foundation on K Street. Maybe they'd sneak out early today to search for a larger apartment.

As the limo wheeled up to the Truman Building, she saw Bart Ochley, the agency's chief legal advisor and her immediate boss, waiting under the canopied entrance. Rail thin, he had the forlorn eyes of a bureaucrat who long ago had given up the idealism of youth. A news crew with a camera was tailing him. She chuckled, seeing how Paul was really pulling out all the stops on this little escapade of his. Climbing out, she decided to play along. "Who called the paparazzi, Bart?"

Ochley didn't break even a smile as he hurried her through security.

Strange. Why would Paul call his journalist cronies down here if they weren't meant to be a part of the act?

He dug an energy bar from his pocket and pushed it on her. "Take a bite."

She looked around, confused. Was he on some new jag against low blood sugar? She had barely gotten the first chew down when they reached Secretary of State Ben McCrozier's office.

Inside, Darden and McCrozier stood and shepherded her to a couch.

It slowly dawned on her from their somber faces that this was no prank. "Am I being fired?"

McCrozier brought her a glass of water. "Ms. Quartermane, I'm afraid we have some bad news."

She glanced at Darden, suspecting him of ratting her out. "I had permission to attend the EEOB breakfast and—"

"Paul Merion is dead."

Nausea seized at her throat. Dazed, she tried to stand and nearly staggered into the curio. McCrozier eased her back to the couch, supporting her hand with the glass. Praying for a mistake, she coughed out, "Are you sure?"

McCrozier removed his jacket and poured two drams of Glenfiddich from the half-full bottle on his credenza. He offered her one before remembering she didn't drink, then sighed heavily. "Mr. Merion's body was found last night in the northern Ethiopian village of Lalibela. He was shot several times in the head and chest. The Ethiopian authorities confirmed his fingerprints with the duplicates on record at the embassy in Addis Ababa."

Sobbing, Jaq finally managed to ask how Paul's death had happened.

Darden held a dispatch marked with a classified stamp. "The Ethiopians aren't releasing many details. There's been a recent surge in violence on the border. This is their holy week. Busloads of tourists were in Lalibela. Eritrean rebels apparently seized the opportunity to cross the border and stir up some bad publicity. He probably got caught in their crossfire."

McCrozier offered her his kerchief. He remained frozen in helpless silence over her until finally managing to mumble something about having been told of their engagement.

Jaq dabbed at her mascara while a hundred jagged thoughts pounded at her brain. She would have to tell Paul's mother and sisters. *God, that will be horrible! And they'll need help making the funeral arrangements.* She would have to be the strong one. *Keep it together, Jaq.* She looked up and realized that the men were staring at her, waiting for her to say something more. She coughed to regain her voice. "When will his body be returned?"

McCrozier returned to his desk. His bloodshot eyes bagged with exhaustion, he sank into his chair and took another bracing sip of his scotch. "We're sending Lawrence Barrington over to expedite the paperwork. Even though Mr. Merion was a civilian, we've put in a call to the Pentagon requesting a waiver for transport."

"What about the investigation?"

The three men stared blankly at her.

Finally, Darden asked, "What investigation?"

Confused, Jaq blinked through the tears. "Aren't you going to track down the killers?"

"We'll let the Ethiopians handle it," Darden said. "Internal police matter."

"What if Paul was murdered because he was a Christian? There are Muslim radicals in Africa, aren't there?"

"Some of the Eritrean rebels are *jihadists*," McCrozier admitted. "But it's very unlikely they launched this raid because of Mr. Merion's missionary work."

After taking a moment to gather her thoughts, she looked up at them through her filmed eyes. "I want to go over there and bring him home."

"That's out of the question," Darden insisted. "The region isn't secure. Besides, you're emotionally involved. We need to get this behind us quickly. The press is already sniffing around. We don't want another problem."

"How could my going over there create a problem?"

"Ethiopia is the only Christian government in east Africa," Darden said. "And a vital source for intelligence on Al Qaeda in the Horn. The Ethiopians are very sensitive about any breakdown in their domestic security. This needs to be handled by an experienced diplomat."

Turning away from Darden, she pressed her case with McCrozier. "Larry Barrington has his hands full with the Hague conference next week. I want to do this instead of taking bereavement leave. I sacrificed my time with Paul so he could go spread Christ's message in Africa."

Moved by her tearful plea, McCrozier relented. "Let her do it, Fred."

Darden reddened. "Ben, in my judgment, that's not wise."

McCrozier stood abruptly, his face pinched with anger. "Hell, I've about had my fill of your judgment! You convinced me to authorize Merion's extended visa in the first place. Give him consulate protection to feed and proselytize African Muslims, you insisted. Now, damn it! Let her go bring back the man she loved!"

Woodshedded in front of his subordinates, Darden glared a silent promise of retribution at Jaq.

Too late, she realized that she had just committed one of Washington's unforgivable sins. She had launched her end-run right under Darden's nose, not behind his back, as was the usual *modus operandi* employed by the hordes of Judases in suits who populated this city.

Jerusalem
January 20, Present Day

Courbet Renan, the director of the Israel Museum, pointed out every neglected detail as he strode through the galleries ahead of his staff and security detail. Within minutes, the cultural *cognoscenti* of France and Israel would be arriving for the evening premiere of "The Lost Treasures of the Holocaust," an exhibition that had been diplomatically impossible just a year ago.

And he alone, the son of French Jews, had made this miracle happen.

After months of negotiations, he had obtained from the Louvre and the Musée d'Orsay a loan of those works once owned by the exterminated Jews of Europe. Museum boards on the Continent had always rejected such collaborations because of draconian laws allowing descendants to sue in Tel Aviv for the return of stolen art. But he had successfully lobbied the Knesset to require Israeli citizens to now bring these claims in the country where the pieces were held, an expensive and time-consuming ordeal.

He ran a manicured hand through his lustrous black hair and filled with preening triumph as he took in the breathtaking fruits of his accomplishment. Assured that all was in order, he nodded the signal.

The doors swung open amid a blast of symphonic fanfare.

He mingled with the first black-tie arrivals, accepting their congratulations and engaging in small talk. Among the masterpieces surrounding him were a magnificent Renoir stolen from Lazare Wildenstein, several sculptures confiscated from the Hamburger family, and a Matisse ripped from the home of the German socialite Sarah Rosenstein. He stopped to admire his exhibition's crown jewel: A Delacroix painting of Christian Crusaders surging over the battlements of Caesarea. The work had once hung in the lodge of Hermann Goering, who had seen in it a prophetic allegory of the Nazi occupation of Paris.

He surveyed the gallery and took a quick head count. Determined to put the nervous French dignitaries at ease with a show of force, he turned to his security chief behind him and whispered: "Get four more guards in here now."

The security officer delayed relaying the order. "I need them at the doors. We're understaffed as it is."

Renan grimaced with irritation. "We've been over this. The guests have been prescreened with fingerprint IDs to speed the lines. Just do a quick body scan on every tenth arrival."

The security officer looked skeptical. "That will leave us vulnerable."

Renan pulled the insubordinate officer aside and got into his face. "I'm not going to turn this museum into Ben Gurion airport. Now do as I say or—" His Bluetooth earpiece crackled with a report that the most important guest of the evening was waiting at the front entrance.

He rushed into the lobby and was relieved to see that the Chief Rabbi of Jerusalem had not yet been taken in his wheelchair through the security arch. The bent septuagenarian was a living icon of Israel, having survived three Palestinian attempts on his life, the last one requiring the amputation of his legs. Although the rabbi had led the opposition to the new art-recovery law, Renan was confident that he could win over the cantankerous codger with charm and flattery. "Shalom, Rabbi Halevi! There is no need for you to be subjected to such an intrusion."

The rabbi growled something in Yiddish, his words becoming lost in his wild whiskers.

Renan wheeled the rabbi around the magnetic scanner and into the gallery wing. Amid thunderous applause, the director positioned his honored guest in front of the Delacroix. "Justice has triumphed, Rabbi. This masterpiece was recovered from the Nazis."

The rabbi scowled at the painting. "Who owned it?"

Renan whispered into the rabbi's hairy ear in an effort to coax him to lower his voice. "It's on loan from the Louvre."

The rabbi became even more agitated. "I asked who *owns* it!"

Renan tried to calm him. "Great art belongs to the world."

"One law shall be to him that is to the home born! So sayeth Exodus!"

Ignoring the rabbi's senile rant, Renan turned to the gathered guests and began his own prepared speech. "It is my pleasure, ladies and gentlemen, to stand before you and—"

The lights went out.

Moments later, film footage from World War II appeared high on one of the white walls. Scenes of Nazi brutality were be projected from a lens hidden somewhere in the chamber. Edward R. Murrow's voice narrated news clips of S.S. thugs ransacking Jewish homes in Germany and storm troopers loading stolen paintings onto Paris rail cars.

Fuming, Renan nearly spat into his microphone. "What the hell's going on?"

"A fuse is missing from the switchbox," the security chief reported into Renan's earpiece. "Wherever the projector is hidden, it has its own power source."

The blinded guests began bumping into each other and spilling drinks.

Renan groped and whispered for his honored guest, but the rabbi was nowhere to be found. "No need to be alarmed!" he shouted to the stumbling crowds. "A temporary power outage! The lights will be back up soon!"

After a few minutes that seemed an eternity, the halogens flashed back on. Renan smoothed back his gel-slicked hair to compose himself as he looked around. The rabbi had apparently wheeled himself into the lobby to use the facilities. Not wishing to delay his speech further, Renan cleared his throat and announced: "It is my great honor to welcome to Israel one of the great works of art. This painting by Euguène Delacroix behind me is a superb example of—"

"Are you sure that's a Delacroix?" a guest asked.

Interrupted yet again, Renan calmed and met the challenge to his expertise with a condescending smile. "My good man, I was trained at the University of Paris. You don't think I'd mistake a Delacroix?"

A lady standing next to the questioner insisted, "It's *The Pillage of a Village* by Sebastian Vrancx."

Renan spun toward the wall behind him—the Delacroix was gone. In its place hung a Baroque painting of Napoleon's army ransacking a town in Flanders. Crimson-faced, he examined the substitute installed in the Delacroix's frame. How had such a delicate transfer been accomplished during those few minutes the lights were down? The intended message was not lost on him: This scene of Napoleon's thievery was meant as a reminder of the Nazi crimes against European Jews. He whispered with gritted teeth into his wire for the doors to be secured. As the restless guests began dispersing to the coat checks, he rushed from the gallery and was met by his guards running through the lobby.

"The exit alarms didn't go off," his security officer reported under his breath. "The thief has to be inside the building."

Renan squinted at a dark object gliding off toward the restroom. The rabbi, he remembered, hadn't been in the exhibition wing when the lights came back on. And *he* was the only invitee who had not been prescreened.

The director took off after the escaping imposter, the heels of his spit-shined Gucci oxfords percussing the travertine floor. He captured the con man from behind and dragged him thrashing from the wheelchair. "You aren't Halevi!"

Reporters and photographers circled the manhandled imposter, who was screaming in Hebrew that terrorists were attacking him.

Renan uncovered the scoundrel's knees to expose his calves, which had obviously been tied under the seat to mimic an amputee. In the scuffle, he felt two scarred stubs. Horrified by the discovery, he backed away and sputtered: "Where were *you* during the blackout?"

"What blackout?" Rabbi Halevi—the real one—flung his invitation at the director. "The least you could do is have someone meet me at the door!"

Renan inspected the invitation. The embossed card had been reprinted to indicate the exhibition time for an hour later than scheduled.

That babbling fool he wheeled in earlier must have been the thief!

A guard stuck his head around the corner. "Sir, you'd better have a look at this in here."

Renan rushed back into the gallery.

Above the space on the wall where the Delacroix had hung, strange images had materialized in delayed-action ink.

"What is *that*?" he asked.

Brought back to his wheelchair by the other guests, Rabbi Halevi snorted Yiddish curses as he rolled himself into the wing. He glared up at the symbols and curled a spiteful smirk. "Glyphs from the Proto-Sinaitic script. Those marks were the forerunner of ancient Hebrew."

A reporter in the crowd flipped open his notebook. "What do they say?"

The rabbi's bearded grin glowed brighter than the Burning Bush. "Elymas."

"Does that name have some significance?" Renan asked.

The rabbi was barely able to contain his glee. "Elymas was a first-century Jewish magician. The Christians vilified him as an evil sorcerer. The glyph in the middle of his name is the all-seeing Eye of Providence."

Renan was incensed to find the rabbi enjoying his humiliation. "What is so amusing, if I may ask?"

The rabbi spun his wheelchair—rolling over Renan's toes—and raised his voice so that all the guests could hear. "The Christians claimed that Saul of Tarsus struck Elymas blind when the two men debated the power of Jesus before a Roman proconsul. The All-Seeing Eye is a clever message."

Renan looked up from stooping to brush the tread marks on his shoes. "Saying what?"

"Elymas was never blinded," the rabbi explained. "Saul and his proselytizers spread such slander to destroy his reputation."

Renan reddened. "What does any of this have to do with *me?*"

The rabbi snorted with delight. "A modern Elymas has outwitted you, Mr. Museum *Groyseh Macher*. I have received letters from many families expressing gratitude for the work of this righteous magus. I wish him eternal blessings on his quest to return such stolen properties to their true owners." He wheeled toward the reporters again and, as if delivering a message from Yahweh Himself, ordered them: "You will quote me on that!"

FOUR

SATOR
APERO
TENET
OPERA
ROTAS

ALMOUROL CASTLE, PORTUGAL
JULY 1455

"**C**ease your mumbling, *menino*! You'll scare the ghosts dead again!"
That command from across the darkness startled Pero out of a
fevered sleep. He staggered to his elbows and searched the window-
less dungeon. At the far end of the cell, in the flickering shadows, sat a white-
bearded man in dirty rags. His bony frame was hung with weathered skin the
texture of a worn-out saddle, and he leered through narrow eye slits that wrapped
around his bald skull; if perched in a tree, he might have been mistaken for a
giant lizard. Disoriented, Pero rubbed his swollen eyes. "Where am I?"

"In the Old Man's Hell."

"What old man?"

"Neptune's nemesis. The fisher prince who baits the hook with human flesh.
He who, denied the kingship by cruel birth order, schemes to seize sovereignty
over all the briny waves."

Pero wondered if he had been thrown into this pit with a lunatic. "You
mean ... the Navigator?"

The prisoner leapt to his spindly legs to protest the use of that honorific.
"What did that bilious windbag ever navigate but the worn path from his
feather bed to the chamber pot?"

Pero prayed the guards would not overhear these traitorous ravings. No
man in Portugal was more feared than Prince Henry, the 61-year-old patriarch
of the royal house of Aviz. Consumed with turning the kingdom into a maritime power, the Infante—as the younger brother of the deceased King João was
known—had for thirty-five years been the grand master of the Order of Christ,
an elite brotherhood of warrior-monks. Secretive and reclusive, Henry had never
married, preferring the austere life of a lay monk. Brilliant, moody, shy, impul-
sive, and eccentric, he was either worshipped or despised by his countrymen.

Pero's own father was convinced that the Old Man—the nickname used behind the prince's back—would drive Portugal to ruin with his costly sea voyages.

Yet Pero had declared Henry his hero the first time he had heard how the prince's mariners discovered the isle of Madeira. Now, fists balled, he climbed to his feet to defend the Navigator again. "Mind your tongue, you batty fool!"

The crazed inmate flailed his arms as if set upon by demons. "The Old Man never in his mollycoddled life stepped foot on a caravel! But he holds no qualms about sending men off to their gurgling deaths! Have you, *menino*, sat dead in irons in the foggy webs of the Green Sea? You wouldn't know the Borius wind from a Castilian's fart! You have that in common with him, too!"

Pero took a threatening step closer. "I don't care if you are *louco* in the *cabeça!* Speak basely of the prince again and I'll split your lip!"

"You can't even split your babe-ass cheeks to wipe them."

Pero charged at the mouthy prisoner, but a forearm sent him reeling. Concussed, he looked up from his knees at an outstretched hand. He slapped away the offer of assistance.

"The rock of the damned."

"What?" Pero muttered, rubbing his jaw.

"You asked where you were. The Templars built this formidable keep during the *Reconquista.* Now the King uses it as a dump for refuse like us."

Pero buckled to his haunches, unable to make any sense of his sudden turn of misfortune. While on their way to Castro Marim to deliver the stallions, he and his father had been arrested and brought in chains to this gloomy tower. Had his father cheated the king in a transaction?

"You took a sharp blow there for the Old Man," the old prisoner said. "Why defend him so gallantly?"

"The Navigator will make Portugal the envy of the world! I hope one day to command a caravel in his fleet."

The dotty prisoner laughed so loud that he sent a rat scampering off along the wall. "How many sea voyages have you made, my eager young admiral?"

Pero turned aside to blunt the admission. "None."

"You've at least apprenticed as a fisherman's gutter." The interrogator in rags narrowed his eyes in suspicion. "Have you even *seen* the Mediterranean?" When Pero could not bring himself to speak the truth, the old prisoner broke a yellow-toothed grin. "Blessed Sancha, I'm holed up with the only lad in all Lusitania who's never been properly baptized."

"I *will* sail the seas one day! I swear it!"

"Ah, you must give up that fancy," the pestering prisoner insisted. "No one has ever escaped this salted hole alive. Perhaps I can offer you a small consolation by describing my own adventures along Cape Bojador."

"*Your* adventures?" Pero scoffed. "You think me a fool? Prince Henry sent his own shield bearer to conquer those waters. Gil Eannes would never have taken a mouth-flapping degenerate like you."

"Eannes is a liar and a coward!"

Indignant, Pero leapt to his feet. "Ignorant foreigner! Eannes is the finest mariner in all of Christendom!"

"Spare me your fairy tales about the great Eannes. I was aboard the *Santa Iria* when he set off from the Canaries. That old goatherd clung to the coast like a suckling to its mother's teat."

"A dozen men failed to reach the Cape before Eannes made it!"

The insolent codger persisted in spinning his tale of woe. "The night we reached Bojador, the sea turned redder than that blood on your chin."

An easy mark for any sea story, Pero came to his hands and knees in rapt attention. "I've heard it said that another set of temperate and frigid environs are to be found below the earth."

"They are indeed, *menino*. But first one must penetrate the Cauldron of Fire, where no living creature can long survive. Protecting its fringes is the Sea of Darkness. The fog here is so thick that one can barely breathe in it."

"What happened when you entered the Dark Sea?"

The prisoner gazed toward the roof beams as if watching the luffing of imaginary sails. "The windstorms felt like a thousand daggers scraping our faces. Eannes was forced to tack between the wreckages of those who had reefed before us. Some swore they saw the bloodless face of Goncalo Velho in the watery depths begging us to go back."

"But Eannes pushed on."

As he told his tale, the old prisoner's neck muscles became taut as rigging rope. "He had no choice. The Old Man had provisioned us with only enough fresh water to reach the Cape."

Pero tried to imagine the fear spreading among the crew that horrid day. "I have heard it said that Eannes was never the same after his return."

"Every mariner has one great voyage in him. That is why the Old Man sends out a new *capitan* each time to push beyond where the one before him has gone. The moorings of Eannes's soul broke that day." The old prisoner's voice dropped. "Bojador is Hell's moat."

"If you gave such fealt service to the crown," Pero asked, "what crime did you commit to warrant—"

The grille swung open.

Guards entered the dungeon and dragged Pero and his mouthy cellmate up the stairwell and into the bailey. Helpless to fight them off, Pero was suddenly attacked by the blinding sun. He required several moments to focus his eyes, and then saw, on the ground before him, two naked men splayed on their backs and tied to stakes, surround by a circle of helmeted knights. Prodded closer, he realized that one of the staked victims was his father, bloodied and terrified. The poor wretch lying next to his father had been slathered in honey to increase the agony of roasting.

On the tower's balustrade, a tall man in robes stood with his face occulted. The drape of his cowl suggested a long head and a proud jaw shaded by a heavy growth of stubble. A flabby paunch hung over the cords at his waist and his ankles, swollen and red with gout, bulged against his sandal straps.

"Take a good look, *menino*," whispered Pero's cellmate. "That pigeon's perch is as close as your *Navigadas* has ever come to manning a mast watch."

Stunned, Pero swung around for another inspection of the balustrade. *That sagging bag of adipose was Prince Henry the Navigator?*

The Old Man signaled for the ordeal to proceed.

His seneschal straddled the staked man smeared with honey. "Rodrigo de Sintra! Sworn to the Order of Christ, you have been found guilty of treason!"

The frightened man on the ground fought against the cords. "*Nao! Nao!* I left it in Sevilla by mistake! My aging memory failed me!"

"Let this be a warning!" the seneschal shouted to the ranks. "Any mariner provisioned with a chart from the royal depository must guard it with his life! The cartography and logbooks are the realm's treasure!"

The condemned man cried out, "My Lord! Mercy!"

Unmoved, the Old Man on high raised his hand and dropped it in a signal.

A nervous attendant walked out of the granary carrying a large crock jar. As the knights placed logs end to end to form a rectangular buffer around the doomed prisoner, the seneschal took the jar from the attendant and poured an army of red fire ants onto the enclosed ground.

Pero watched, horrified, as the ants climbed the condemned man's honey-slicked limbs and attacked his eyelids and genitals. This form of execution was designed to delay death for an hour until the lungs finally clogged. Their bites were so vicious that the ants would be pulled in half before releasing their jaws. Pero turned and retched, but his stomach held nothing to expel.

While the ordeal took its slow, agonizing course, the Old Man slouched as if weighed down by a momentous burden. He studied Pero intently, and then, inexplicably, his vengeful demeanor eased. The Navigator angled his head at his officer to order the matter be brought to an end.

The seneschal glared at Pero, as if questioning what the boy had done to soften the gruff grand master. Reluctantly, the officer ended the traitor's suffering by decapitating him. Then, he turned and, forcing Pero to stand over his father, demanded, "Is this man at your feet a Jew?"

Pero's face drained. Had these knights discovered his family's damning lineage? He had sworn an oath to his father never to reveal the truth about their Jewish roots. What was he to say?

"I will ask but once more," the seneschal said. "Is your father, Diogo da Covilha, a secret Hebrew?"

The knights tightened their cordon of intimidation as the royal attendant carefully scooped up the ants in the dirt for another feeding.

On his loft, the Old Man adjusted his hood to better hear Pero's answer.

"Lie to us," the seneschal warned, "and you will forfeit both your life *and* your father's. We have evidence of his guilt. You need not take on the stain of his crime."

Numb with terror, Pero confronted a cruel choice: Break his oath, or die a miserable death.

"*Menino!*" pleaded the berserker who had been sharing his cell. "Tell the *cavalerios* the truth and save yourself!"

The knights closed in on Pero with threat. Forced to answer, he braced for the inevitable assault. He looked up at the tower and shouted his answer at the prince who had once been his hero, "My *Pai* attends the Mass every Sunday! He is not a Jew!"

The Navigator paced behind the banister of his eyrie. Suddenly, after nearly a minute of private debate, he came to a halt and pointed at the ground where the traitor's beheaded body had just been removed.

Pero stared down at the blood-soaked pit until rough hands seized him. Stripped and dragged to the stakes, he prayed that the knights would not notice the ritual scars that he and his father had carved on their arms. He shouted to his father, "*Pai*, I love you! Let me die first! The ants will be less hungry for you!" He closed his eyes to prepare for the shock of a thousand bites. He prayed that if he showed courage, the Navigator might be merciful and end his suffering quickly.

A sting attacked his wrists—he coiled in anticipation.

"Pull anchor, *menino!*" shouted his cellmate.

Pero opened his eyes, confused. Hovering over him—with grins—were his father and the pestering cellmate.

The knights cut the cords and lifted him to his feet.

For the first time, the Old Man on high deigned to speak. "What say you on this, Eannes?"

Pero's cellmate came to attention and lifted his gaze toward the balustrade. "The *menino* defended your good name against every slander, my lord."

Stunned, Pero spun on the devious dungeon spy. "*You* are Gil Eannes?"

Eannes bowed to him in mock courtesy.

"You deceived me!"

Eannes laughed, unrepentant. "I told you the great Eannes was a coward and a liar. There are many who would swear to the first charge, and I have just proven the second. Every knight here has undergone a similar test. We had to be certain you possessed the requisite fortitude and honor. We take only those few who are willing to give their lives for a greater cause."

"Take? For what?"

"To serve as a squire in the Order of Christ."

Pero turned with disbelief to his released father, wondering how the son of a crypto-Jew could allow himself to be enlisted for a Christian duty like this. "And you, *Pai*, were part of this trickery?"

His father embraced him and nodded contritely for having participated in the cruel ruse. "I learned only yesterday that the Prince and his knights have known of our secret for two years. Their spies have been watching us in the border horse markets. The Prince petitioned my agreement to this trial of your honor. I could not deny him. In time, you will come to understand."

Eannes walked into the tower. Moments later, the mariner escorted out two men who wore the robes and turbans of scholars and brought the strangers before Pero. "Allow me to introduce Masters Jehuda Cresques and Abraham Guedelha. Our cartographer and astrologer."

"But those are …"

"Hebrew names," Eannes confirmed. "Jews have been welcomed into our ranks for years. We serve the same God. And the same quest."

"What quest?"

"That will be revealed to you in due time."

"But I told you," Pero said quietly, forced to reveal his shame again, this time in the presence of the Old Man. "I have never stepped foot on a boat."

"Any fishmonger can be taught to sail," Eannes said. "You have another talent that may one day be of use to us."

Pero no longer knew what to believe. First, he discovers that he is a Jew, and now these knights arrange the execution of a traitor to test his loyalty. Was there no devilry from which they would abstain to further their designs? What of any value could he, a Jewish boy from a small mountain village, possibly offer to the most powerful maritime brotherhood in all Christendom? He looked up at the balustrade for confirmation of Eannes's outlandish assertion, but the reclusive prince had disappeared.

FIVE

Glancing at her watch through a haze of tears, Jaq realized she had lost all track of time. She had been walking the streets of Georgetown for hours. It was now past midnight and the restaurants were closing, but she couldn't bring herself to go home alone. Exhausted, she decided to head toward the campus to search for a student lounge.

Earlier that night, her best friend, Alyssa, had left a text message saying she had just purchased her maid-of-honor dress. Great timing, Paul. Alyssa couldn't afford such an extravagance on her Hill staffer's salary. Damn him! Why did he have to go to Africa, anyway?

I don't deserve to be happy.

Even on the day she got engaged, she had known deep down it was an affront against the biblical warning against pride. Some people were just born to suffer. She learned that lesson early on, when her boozing father would take out his rage on her with his fists. She hadn't spoken to him in five years. Who knew where he was now? Probably tottering shit-faced on some bar stool.

She wandered across the university grounds and came to the white columns of the Holy Trinity Church. A priest nodded to her before disappearing into the rectory. She hadn't stepped into a Catholic church since Rev. Merry baptized her into the evangelical faith four years ago. Childhood memories came flooding back: Her first confession in that upright coffin that smelled of Lemon Glade and candle smoke. *Forgive me, Father, for I've had evil thoughts about killing my papa.* She had gotten off easy that day with ten Hail Marys for penance, but the priest never looked her in the eye again.

A siren behind her wailed.

She froze with the door ajar as a police car pulled up. A searchlight aimed its beam at her face, and a voice on a bullhorn ordered her to step down. She approached the car slowly with her hands raised. She had heard too many stories about the District cops here shooting first and asking questions later. She couldn't see their faces behind the harsh light.

"Are you Quartermane?"

"I was just going in to sit down and—"

"You're coming with us."

She knew better than to play the lawyer card. One of the officers opened the back door and made it clear that she had no choice but to climb in. She asked as politely as she could: "Is there a curfew in Georgetown?"

The cop behind the wheel looked put out. "Get in. We've been looking for you all night."

She obeyed the order, and the patrolmen sped her several blocks south.

Minutes later, they pulled up with bubbles flashing to the entrance of the Hay-Adams Hotel. The officers got out, slamming their doors, and escorted her to the door as if perp-walking a scofflaw to the slammer.

Rev. Merry rushed toward her through the lobby. "Praise God you're okay."

"Why didn't you just call me?" she asked.

One of the officers tossed over her phone. "You left it at Chadwick's."

She convulsed with sobs as she sank into the reverend's embrace. "I thought you'd gone back to Tennessee."

The reverend nodded the officers back to their cruiser, and they got in and squealed off. Alone with Jaq, he firmed his embrace and wiped a tear from her cheek. "We must believe the Almighty has a greater purpose in this."

"Why would God bring us together, only to take Paul away?"

"Paul must be needed in Heaven, my love. We *will* see him again. Sooner than you know." The reverend waited for an inebriated couple to stagger past them, then he hailed a cab and opened the back door for her to get in. "There's something I want to show you."

Ten minutes later, they were let out in front of a massive graystone building that resembled drawings Jaq had seen of the ancient Greek mausoleum of Halicarnassus, one of the ancient Seven Wonders of the World. Two stone sphinxes—miniature copies of the famous original in Egypt—guarded the pyramid-crowned edifice.

The reverend glanced down 16th Street to make certain no one had followed them, and then he hurried her up the steps. Two towering bronze doors with frieze-carved panels swung open. When they were inside, a uniformed guard pulled the doors shut and checked a bay of television monitors that provided surveillance from every angle.

"All in order, Marcus?" Rev. Merry asked.

"Very quiet tonight, sir."

"We shouldn't be more than an hour."

As the pastor led her down a marble concourse, Jaq gazed around in awe at an atrium that resembled the initiation hall of an Egyptian priesthood. "Don't tell me you've gone pagan."

His expansive girth rippled with a naughty chuckle. "Sorry for the cloak and dagger act. I have to keep the news under wraps for now. I purchased this building six months ago."

"What is it?"

"The Scottish Rite Temple."

"You're going to put your lobbying offices in *here*?"

"No, no. I have much grander plans for this little gem. I love the irony, though. The local Masons were strapped for cash. They had no choice but to sell it to me, their avowed enemy."

They passed under an arch inscribed with an inversion of Dante's warning: *Expect ye hope, all who enter here.* On the walls, a panoramic mural depicted people from all countries going about their work: Flying planes, driving cars, serving customers in restaurants, and attending church. The display reminded her of one of those WPA paintings she had seen in the courthouses in Kentucky. The dome had been painted to mimic the sky, complete with clouds and stars.

The reverend pushed a button. "Don't move."

The recessed floor lights disappeared, leaving them in darkness. Moments later, the room shook and rolled as if hit by an earthquake.

Jaq dropped to her knees. A deafening crash of thunder split her ears and she heard thousands of screams followed by moans and cries for help. Slowly the lights came back up, imitating a rising sun. She climbed to her feet, squatting low in case of another jolt. The first panorama had been replaced by another depicting the devastating results of a nuclear holocaust: Burned children, charred homes, armies fighting with tanks and bomber planes. Above her, on the dome, humans were being lifted up to the sky.

"What do you think?" the reverend asked her with a sly grin.

She finally found her breath. "Are you trying to send me over the edge?"

"In six weeks, my fondest dream will finally become a reality. The Museum of the Millennium. I've had to keep it under tight wraps. The liberal media will try to destroy it."

"I don't understand."

"I'm going to recreate the Rapture and Tribulation times for unbelievers. When they see firsthand what the End of Days will be like, they'll run into the arms of the Lord."

She followed him through a long gallery as he explained each episode of the virtual End Times. In an adjacent room, a red horse ambled past walls of flames. The temperature was so hot that her skin felt seared. Next, a pale horse dragged victims of a famine marred by seeping plague sores.

The pastor was moved to tears by his creation. "The Seven Seals of Revelation will be opened in here. The Tribulation Years will take about a half-hour to walk through, provided there's no fainting or pleas for expedited baptisms. It's going to be followed by the Second Coming exhibit. We'll have Christ in full armor lowered from Heaven to fight the Antichrist."

"Where will the spectators watch from?"

"Watch? No, no. They're going to be part of the battle. We'll arm them with mock weapons so they can learn what it'll be like to serve as Tribulation Saints. The kids are my greatest hope. They'll abandon their Play Stations after they've conquered a dozen live demons."

She squeezed his palm to congratulate him on the amazing exhibit. "You've been inspired by the Holy Spirit."

"You haven't seen the finale." He led her up a circular staircase to an auditorium painted in white and gold. In its center sat a spacious baptismal pool. "This is where visitors will be reborn. If I can run two thousand through a day, I can get an eighty-percent conversion rate."

Suddenly feeling weak, she took a seat on the bleachers to rest.

The reverend gave her an apologetic pat on the hand, realizing that he had momentarily forgotten about her grief. "I didn't bring you here to show off. I wanted you to understand why you and I will be with Paul again very soon." He stole a glance at the door and then lowered his voice. "A few months ago, I had a dream of the Lord holding Paul in His arms. I didn't know what the vision meant until I heard the news of Paul's death. The Lord has told me not much time is left. The warning signs are being witnessed as we speak. We must strengthen our faith in preparation."

She became alarmed. "What's going to happen?"

The pastor's eyes lifted toward the ceiling. "The Bible promises that the Lord shall descend from heaven with a shout. The living believers shall be caught up in the clouds to meet him in the air."

"The Lord took Paul to spare him from the suffering?"

He nodded. "He was blessed for his faith."

Comforted, she smiled wistfully through the tears. "How long will we have to wait?"

"Certain events will unfold in precise order. If we should ever become separated, you must watch for the signs. First, the Church will be taken up in the Rapture. It will happen so quickly that a person may be next to you and then you'll see only their jewelry on the ground. Some believers, however, will remain behind as Tribulation Saints to save others."

She took a deep breath, bracing for the possibility that she might at any hour now be called to make such a sacrifice. "How will I know if I'm meant to stay?"

"Jesus will give you the opportunity to make that choice," he promised. "If you know any Jews, you must do all in your power to convert them in the days ahead. One hundred and forty-four thousand Jews must first become witnesses. They will play a vital role in heralding the Day of Judgment."

The Jews, again.

In the many sermons that she had heard him deliver, he had always demonstrated a selfless devotion to saving as many of them as possible. She squeezed his hand again, this time in admiration. "What will they do to further God's work?"

"Our Hebrew brothers and sisters must rebuild the Third Temple. Until the Holy of Holies is restored on its original site in Jerusalem, the Antichrist cannot rear his head to desecrate it."

"Is that why you lobby for military aid to Israel?"

He nodded. "The revival of the Jewish state was divinely foretold, and its survival must be assured. I'll never forget sitting at my father's side as a boy while we listened to radio reports of the Israelis retaking the Temple Mount during the Six Days War. He told me, 'Son, this will be the most important day in your life.'"

She hugged him, grateful for such intimacies. "I'm so blessed to have you in my life."

"That our daughters may be as cornerstones," the pastor said, quoting from Psalms. "Polished after the similitude of a palace."

She was touched that he had remembered her favorite verse from their Scripture lessons. "You've always made me feel like I'm your daughter."

Aglow with pride, the reverend pulled a small volume from the inner pocket of his jacket. "My beloved Sarah was taken to her reward before we could have children. I want you to have this. It's the bible my father gave me when I graduated from ministry school. A Scofield study edition. I'm afraid I've been marked it up with a lot of notes over the years."

She took the precious gift into her hands. As she pressed the bible to her heart, an ache of foreboding struck her. Fearful of what lay ahead during the time of trials, she prayed for the courage to prove worthy of the reverend's trust should the Lord call on her to join the Tribulation Saints.

SIX

RIBATEJO, PORTUGAL
AUGUST 1455

Pero awoke with the bitter taste of cowbane salve on his tongue. He knew the smell of the narcotic flower, for his father had often applied it to the nostrils of wild horses. He looked around, confused, and slowly realized that he had been deposited in an underground pit with no light.

His curse echoed in the black void.

After two grueling weeks in this service, he was already regretting his decision to accept the apprenticeship with the Order of Christ. He had expected to spend his days learning the mysteries of the seas. Instead, these sadistic knights had subjected him to all manner of abuse, forcing him to launder their garb and carry out their piss buckets.

This time, they had gone too far with their demented pranks.

He felt around his legs and found a gourd filled with water sitting at his side. Evidently his tormentors did not want him to die of thirst before he could go mad. Clad only in a tunic and pantaloons, he crawled to his knees. The floor felt smooth and the air was cold. He refused to call for help, determined not to give that degenerate Eannes the satisfaction. He coughed from thick incense, and the echo spawned a distant shuffling of feet. Was some beast stalking him in here? He growled loudly to chase it off.

A rock caromed off the wall near his ear.

That was no animal.

"Who's there? Reveal yourself, or I'll cut you to shreds with this sword."

"Who are you?" answered a tremulous voice.

Pero peered into the darkness. "I asked first!"

After a pause, the same voice—that of a boy about his own age, Pero calculated—blustered with a false bravado, "Put the blade down and I'll tell you." The voice inched closer. "I am Salvador Fernandes Zarco."

"What are you doing down here?"

"We don't know."

"*We?*"

"I have an *amigo* with me. He doesn't talk much."

"What's his name?"

"Bartholomeu Dias. We've had nothing to eat for two days."

Reaching for their hands, and finally finding them, Pero offered the two parched boys water from his gourd. "Somebody must want us dead."

"Whose toes did *you* step on?" Zarco asked.

"The Order of Christ has it in for me," Pero said. "It could be any one of a hundred in that den of scoundrels."

Zarco sounded skeptical. "You're attached to the Tomar knights?"

"I shovel their shit."

"That's how they start you."

"How would *you* know?"

"My grandfather was a Knight of Christ."

Pero couldn't believe his ears. "You're of the Zarco family that discovered Madeira? The *banditos* who did this to you will have Hell to pay!"

"I'd say we're already in Hell," Dias said.

Pero sized up the smaller shadow hovering next to Zarco. "So, this one does speak. What's his story?"

"His father serves in the king's chancery," Zarco said.

Pero pondered that revelation. Why would cutthroats take the chance of losing their heads just to abuse two boys from important families? Suddenly, he came up with a theory for why they had been left here. "Don't you see what has happened? You two have been taken for ransom and thrown in here until the royals pay up."

Zarco wasn't convinced. "What about you? You're not of noble birth."

Pero mulled over that hole in his explanation. "The knights must be planning an attempt on the king's life. If his plot goes awry, they put me down here to take the blame for your kidnapping."

"What should we do?" Dias asked Pero.

Zarco bristled at this new threat to his authority. "I say we stay put."

"The knights will expect us to do just that. We have to find a way out."

Zarco protested: "We could break our necks in a hole!"

Pero kept feeling for the cold wall as he cautiously walked into the blackness. When his hand found an opening, he called back over his shoulder. "Then go back where you came from."

"Wait!" Dias yelled at Pero. "I'm coming with you."

Overruled, Zarco grudgingly followed them, not wanting to be left alone.

As he stepped deeper into the darkness, Pero tore his own sleeves into ribbons and handed them to his two new friends. "Tie these to your loops. If we feel a pull, we'll know one of us is straying off."

"Which way should we head?" Dias asked.

Pero felt the disturbed dirt under his toes. "The knights brought me from over there. You two came from that direction. I say we go the opposite way and keep the wall close to our left."

"Dead reckoning," Zarco said.

Pero stopped. "Dead *what?*"

"It was the navigation technique my grandfather used to find the Blessed Isle. He kept land in sight for as long as possible and ciphered the distance he sailed from the coast."

"How did he manage that?"

"Course and time," Dias muttered. "Course and time."

Baffled, Pero turned to Zarco. "What's he babbling about?"

"His father makes him repeat those words every morning, noon, and night."

Pero told Dias, "Your father must be a deranged tyrant."

"Distance on the seas cannot be gauged as on land," Dias explained. "Water flows in one direction and the caravel another. There is no fixed point. A mariner must rely on other measurements."

"What other measurements are there?"

"We were taught a chant," Dias said. "On voyages, a piece of flotsam is tied to a rope. When the log passes the hull, the admiral signals for us to start singing until it reaches the aft mark. That's how the speed of caravel is calculated."

"What if you forget the words?"

Dias found Pero's hand and placed it under Zarco's tunic to feel the scars on his friend's back, remnants of a flogging inflicted for similar negligence. "He got off light," Dias said. "Last month, the Old Man ordered any coxswain who loses the count to be thrown overboard."

Pero swallowed hard. "For an innocent mistake?"

Zarco sounded as if he held no grudge against the punishment. "Survival at sea depends upon the count."

Pero's dream of going to sea no longer seemed so romantic.

"Dias and I can sing the chant," Zarco said. "But you'll have to calculate and remember the number of steps we take."

Pero sighed in defeat. "That won't do us any good, unless we know the precise direction we take."

"Direction is impossible. We have no sun or stars to use for guides."

Hearing Zarco's lament, Dias slid off a necklace that held a small pouch stitched with squares of silk. Working without light, he carefully removed a sewing needle from the pouch, rubbed it against the silk, and allowed it to float in the gourd of water that the Tomar knights had left for Pero. After waiting several seconds, Dias felt for the needle's tip and announced with an extended finger: "North is that direction."

Pero groped the darkness until he found Dias's pointing finger. "You expect us to rely on a juggler's trick?"

"It is God's law," Dias insisted. "When the needle takes on the character of the silk, which is soft like a Moor's wife, the tip always points north, away from the Devil's abode in Arabia."

Pero had no other ideas, so he reluctantly agreed to give the conjuring trick a try. Tethered by the strips, the boys made their way blindly in the direction indicated by the needle. While Dias and Zarco chanted the mariner's song, Pero took the lead, groping the wall as he edged forward.

Several minutes into their dark sojourn, Pero's palm brushed up against an intricate carving that felt like a knight in effigy. He took a step back and whispered, "I think it's a tomb."

Dias cowered behind Pero. "Can you make out the inscription?"

Pero took a deep breath to calm his racing heart; then, he traced his index finger down the bevels that formed the letters. He whispered his discovery, "*Sanctus … Spiritus … Salvator.*"

"That's Latin for 'Holy Spirit save us'," Zarco said.

Dias gasped. "The motto of the Knights Templar."

Pero backed away. "They dropped us into a Templar necropolis?"

"This prayer was written on the graves of all Temple grand masters," Zarco said. "My great-grandfather's resting stone has the same inscription. The Order of Christ gave refuge to those Templars that survived the persecutions."

Pero felt a raised Templar cross atop one of the sarcophagi, confirming Zarco's suspicion. "That means the Tomar knights are really Templars in disguise."

Zarco hissed for Pero to avoid uttering that dangerous claim. "If the Old Man finds out you know, he'll cut out your tongue and use it to strangle me."

Pero tried to make sense of this shattering discovery. Why had they been thrown into a cavern once deemed sacred and inviolate? "The Templars built commanderies all over the kingdom. We could be anywhere in Portugal."

"But the monks buried their masters in one place only," Zarco said.

Pero was annoyed with Zarco for milking the suspense. "Are you going to tell us or wait until we faint from hunger?"

"Santa Maria do Olival in Tomar. The church sits across the river from the fortress monastery of the Order."

"You think we're in Santa Maria's crypt?"

"My ancestors came from Tomar," Zarco said. "I visited that church with my father. A blind man charged with its care told me that a well under the apse once offered nourishing water."

Pero shrugged. "So?"

"When I begged a drink," Zarco revealed, "he winked at me and said it was not really a well."

Pero scoffed at the queer tale. "A blind man who winks? Sounds like a fool who's really a fool."

Zarco dropped his voice even lower. "I've heard it said that the Templars always built escape routes from their churches in case of an attack."

"Where would they go?" Dias asked.

"Where would *you* go if surrounded by infidels?"

"The fortress," Pero and Dias answered together.

Zarco shook his head. "Hercules himself couldn't manage such a feat. The Templars would have had to burrow under the river."

"Unless," Dias said, "a natural passage already existed."

Weary and half-frozen, Pero was now finding it more and more difficult to marshal his thoughts. He sat down for a moment to try and regain his bearings. When the dizziness eased, he blinked hard and asked, "Which direction did the church face?"

"West," Zarco said. "Toward the river."

Pero weighed the risks. If they, three boys with no military training, could stumble onto the Templar retreat tunnel to the old monastery, then those infidel invaders from Africa would likely have found it, too. A thought suddenly occurred to him: Had the Templars excavated this passage to seduce the Mohammedans into a blind end ... and a slow death?

He chose not to reveal this suspicion to his new comrades, preferring to chance starvation rather than return to the misery of living among those cruel Tomar knights. He tossed several pebbles until drawing a yelp. "Dias, wake up and give that sorcerer's needle of yours another spin."

SEVEN

SATOR
APERO
TENET
OPERA
ROTAS

NORTHERN ETHIOPIA
JANUARY 23, PRESENT DAY

Green from the bus fumes, Jaq slogged down another Dramamine with the sludge in her coffee cup. Earlier that morning, at the station, she had eaten a small slice of the grainy pancake so popular with the locals here. She had ordered it fried in grease to kill the parasites, but a worrisome aftertaste of cow dung lingered in her mouth. Fred Darden was probably laughing at her that very moment, having taken his revenge by canceling the usual State Department driver and ordering her booked on this chugging double-decker relic.

Desperate for fresh air, she stood and tried to pry open the window, until the other passengers shouted her down. The glassy-eyed man sitting next to her explained in broken English that these flayed plains were haunted by *jinns*. She shook her head in exasperation, aghast that these Ethiopians preferred splitting headaches to being set upon by imaginary ancestral spirits. The man offered her a sprig of a shrubby leaf and rubbed his stomach to indicate that chewing it would make her feel better. She nodded reluctantly and accepted the herb, hiding it in her pocket when he wasn't looking.

She tried to take her mind off her misery by reviewing her briefing binder. The summary began with the usual diplomatic verbiage, but on the third page the reading became more interesting: *Prime Minister Meles Zenawi's government is under pressure from radical Islamists on his borders. Our policy is to provide assistance to prevent Ethiopia from being overrun by Al Qaeda.* She saw that Ochley had scribbled a handwritten addendum: *Zenawi is creating a police state. Morale in the army is low. Civilians are being drafted without training. Widespread dissatisfaction and prolonged droughts have created instability. Transfer Paul's remains and get out ASAP.*

The bus lurched to a stop, and the Ethiopians trilled loudly as they leapt into the aisle and swayed in a line dance toward the door.

"What's happening?" Jaq asked her seatmate as she leaned down to recover her fallen binder from the floor.

The man flashed her an ecstatic grin. "The Holy City!"

Freed at last from the window vigilantes, she wedged opened the pane and made out a jag of pink-hued mountains through the haze in the distance. She wrangled her bag off the bus and, following the others out, walked a few steps closer for a better view of the giant eruption of red volcanic tuff. Dozens of people wielding brocaded umbrellas were moving in and out of the earth near a village that looked to be at least another half-mile away. She couldn't imagine lugging her carry-on up that hill. "Why is the bus stopping here?"

"It is our tradition to walk to the churches," the man explained.

She looked around. "Churches? I don't see anything larger than a hut."

"The holy sanctuaries are below ground. We have no trees for lumber, so the angels carved the churches into our earth.

She hurried to keep up, barely able to hear him over the joyful shouting. "Why is everyone so excited?"

The Ethiopian man heaved for breath in the arid air as he tried to catch the other passengers running ahead. "God made a promise to us. He who comes here to Lalibela to live, he who comes to Lalibela to pray, and he who comes to Lalibela to die, all will be saved."

"You mean ... some of them came here to die?"

He nodded. "If they are blessed, within a few days."

"You seem healthy enough," she said. "Why did you come?"

The man turned a beatific smile over his shoulder. "I have tumor of the brain. Here I will walk into the arms of Our Lord."

She stopped, aghast at her insensitivity. "I'm so sorry."

He waved off her embarrassment. "Be happy for me. I am but a few steps from Heaven."

"Wait!" she shouted. "Where is the police station here?"

Hearing that question, the man suddenly lost his smile and shook his head sternly at her as he staggered away.

Puzzled by that last reaction, she dragged her luggage up the gullied path toward the shuttered village. She tiptoed along the cracked hardpan sidewalk, careful not to step on the half-starved dogs that sat curled in what shade they could find. Across the street, she saw an iron awning that held a sign: *Constabulary*. She walked over and opened a fly-spattered screen door that led into a cramped office. The thatched ceiling sagged and chickens were roosting on the sill.

"The tour buses load at the Roha Hotel," said a voice behind her.

Startled, she spun back toward the door and found a tall black man in a white linen suit staring at her with evasive eyes under high cheekbones. "I'm not a tourist," she told him with irritation in her voice. "Can you please tell me where I might find Abebe Bogale?"

The man kicked away a pack of boys who were trying to shine his Italian shoes. Reclaiming his unsettling calm, he turned back to her. "And you are?"

"Jaqueline Quartermane. I'm with the U.S. Department of State. A communication was cabled to Mr. Bogale."

"We were told this matter was of some importance to your government."

"It most certainly is."

"And yet they send a *demoiselle* from the typing pool?"

She was taken aback. Was that a hint of a French accent in his haughty, educated English? "Sir, if you will please tell me where I could find Constable Bogale, I won't take up any more of your time."

"Abebe Bogale has been reassigned for reasons of health. The prime minister has placed me in temporary charge of the judicial administration for this district. I am Brehane Dese. Inspector for the National Directorate."

Flustered at not being informed of this change, she handed him her letter of introduction, allowing the extended silence to underscore her pique.

His condescending smile vanished as he read it. "I am sorry for your loss."

"I've made arrangements to fly the body back through Addis Ababa," she said. "I'd like to get the identification finished quickly."

He refolded the letter and handed it back. "There is nothing to identify."

"What do you mean?"

"Mr. Merion's corpse was cremated."

The blood rose in her temples. "You destroyed his ..." She couldn't utter the word. Seeing the man nod without even a flicker of emotion in his eyes, she insisted, "No one from my government authorized you to do that!"

Dese strolled into a back room. Moments later, he returned with a shoebox and handed over Paul's ashes and belongings, wiping his hands with a kerchief. "We are a poor nation. No air conditioning. Ice is scarce. The nearest morgue is five hundred kilometers away."

She teared up as she cradled the moldy cardboard stamped with a faded Nike emblem. She knew Paul would have wanted his body intact for Judgment Day. Her voice cracked as she asked, "What did the autopsy reveal?"

Dese snorted, slightly amused by her expectation. "A coroner is even more of a luxury here than a morgue."

"His wounds weren't examined?"

Dese pulled a folder from a rusted file cabinet. "We are poor, not uncivilized. Five gunshots. Four in the chest. One in the head." He produced a photograph of the victim's head and upper torso. "Fired by Kalishnakovs."

She held her stomach as she stared at the black hole just above the bridge of Paul's nose. She saw a green stain ringing his distended mouth. "What is this discoloration?"

"The heat here decays the flesh very quickly."

She braced against the counter. "Who did this to him?"

Dese lowered himself into a squeaking swivel chair and propped his feet on a wastebasket, careful not to scuff the back of his heels. "Eritrean commandos. Funded by Islamic jihadists."

"How can you be sure they were Eritreans?"

"The murders—"

"There were other victims?"

"The terrorists also killed the head priest of Lalibela." With an air of smugness, as if suggesting that Americans were pampered even in death, Dese produced another photograph. "Mr. Merion was fortunate. The priest was tortured before being executed."

She saw from the photograph that the priest's forehead had been carved with a knife and his left lid sliced to droop over his eye. His right eye looked to have been splashed with acid, forming red streaks across the retina. "Are those words above his brows?"

"Kaa Faa Raa."

"What does that mean?"

"It is a jihadist calling card," Dese said. "The terrorists believe that a false prophet named Dajjal will appear a few days before the end of the world. They claim that Allah's true believers will know Dajjal's identity by these words branded on his forehead. His left eye will be squinted and his right eye webbed. Unfortunately, that was not the extent of their demented poetry."

"They wrote more?"

"Words were also gouged into the priest's buttocks. Those photos I will not show to a woman."

"What did they say?"

Dese penned two lines on a paper and handed it to her to read:

A Jew hides behind me. Seven Judgments now.

"In English?" she asked. "Why not Amharic?"

"Perhaps the riddle was meant to reach America."

"What did any of this have to do with Paul Merion?"

"The Eritreans knew there would be many tourists in the village that night. Terrorism spawns bad publicity. Mr. Merion must have come here for the festival. The Eritreans no doubt discovered his passport and capitalized on their good fortune by executing him."

"Where was he found?"

"In Bet Golgota, one of our underground churches."

Feeling queasy again, she closed her eyes to chase the dizziness. "I need to see the crime scene."

"I am sorry, but that is impossible. No woman has ever been allowed entry into the Selassie Chapel of Golgota."

"I have an obligation to investigate this matter fully."

"In *my* country, religion takes precedent over secular legalities. Riots would erupt if the sanctuary were to be violated. Now, I will escort you to your hotel. I can offer you transport back to Addis Ababa in the morning."

She was too exhausted to protest further, and she certainly needed no encouragement to avoid the return bus ride. As she walked out of the office with the Ethiopian cop and accompanied him down the street, the local residents scurried away as if frightened. When she and Dese reached the hotel, she thought of another question. "Inspector, who found the bodies?"

Dese masked a flash of annoyance with an officious smile. "The son of the mutilated priest."

"A boy? What did he say of the discovery?"

Dese shrugged. "The trauma of finding his father in such a condition has caused him to lose the ability to communicate."

Astonished, she walked back down the steps. "I'd like to see him."

Dese shook his head with a peremptory glare. "The boy was admitted to the sanitarium in Addis Ababa. His doctors have ordered that he is to have no visitors. Should he recover, God willing, I will certainly advise you of the blessed miracle. Now, I must bid you *bonsoir*, Miss Quartermane."

In the middle of the night, Jaq bolted up from a panic attack, convinced that she had heard Paul screaming. She flipped the switch under the moldy lamp shade.

The bulb flickered and snapped, returning her into eerie darkness.

Her head felt on the verge of exploding. What time was it?

She searched the bed stand for her watch: 3:30 AM. She'd have to lie awake four more hours in this blistering Hell. Her tongue was inflamed from the red Berber powder slathered on everything eaten here. She'd pay a king's ransom right now for a couple of Ativans to knock her out. She found the prescription bottle in her purse, but it was empty. She threw it against the wall.

Wait … the numbing weed.

Using her phone for light, she dug into her pants for the stash and wadded a few leaves of the Ethiopian aspirin substitute into her mouth. They had a bitter taste, like fir needles. Her sinuses expanded and a bolt of pleasure skyrocketed to the center of her head. In just minutes, she felt downright euphoric. *So this is why the locals chew it.* She hadn't smoked a cigarette since law school, but she really needed one now to seal the deal. But where could she find …

Paul's wallet.

He had sworn off tobacco. The Devil's temptation, he called it. But she knew he always hid one for emergencies. She rifled through her bag and found the envelope with his possessions. She had vowed not to go through them until she got home for fear of spiraling into a depression. None of that mattered now. She broke open the clasp and dumped the contents on the bed.

His college fraternity ring. Wallet. Empty money clip. His passport.

She searched the wallet. Several receipts fell out, but no cigarette. He probably threw it away before going through customs. Just to be sure, she checked the inner pocket, even though she knew any cigarette there would be crushed. The pocket was stuffed with two thousand dollars in crisp hundreds. She stared at it in confusion. He never carried that kind of cash. If the Eritreans had intended to rob him, why did they leave this? And why didn't they take his passport?

She parsed through his travel stubs. One was dated two weeks ago for the La Foresteria del Monastero hotel in Subiaco, Italy. She stifled a gasp, stung with hurt. They were supposed to see Italy together for the first time on their honeymoon. Didn't Paul care about that? She found a news clipping torn from the Rome edition of the *International Herald Tribune*:

> JERUSALEM - *Israel's chief rabbis will meet Pope Benedict XVI on Friday and seek permission to search the Vatican storerooms for artifacts such as the golden menorah that stood in the Jewish Temple 2,000 years ago.*
>
> *Vatican officials declined to comment on the request.*
>
> *The Vatican audience will be the first by Israel's chief rabbis. The late Pope John Paul II met Israel's previous rabbis in the Holy Land during his visit in 2000.*
>
> *Chaim Metain, leader of Israel's Jews of North African origin, told Radio Italia that he had received the invitation. The menorah was the most important symbol of the Temple after the Ark of the Covenant. Some believe its restoration with other holy vessels will be the first step in rebuilding the Temple in Jerusalem.*

She stared at the clipping, trying to make sense of it. Paul had never mentioned an interest in ancient Jewish relics. First, he goes to Rome without her, and then he shows up in this Ethiopian backwater.

Something didn't add up.

She unfolded a map the hotel clerk had loaned her. Ten of the subterranean churches were segregated with the sacred tombs of Lalibela and Adam into two clusters. The thirteenth holy site, Bet Giorgis, was set apart from the others:

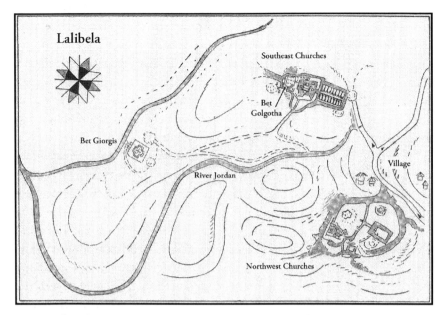

The churches appeared to be connected by a maze of passageways. She traced a finger to Bet Golgota, where Paul's body had been found. That church sat in the southeastern complex, not far from the hotel. She'd have to navigate through several other churches to reach it. But she'd never forgive herself if she returned home without learning why Paul had risked his life to come here.

And besides, she was feeling much better now.

This Ethiopian herb was a wonder drug.

She searched the closet and found a red serape provided for festivals. The perfect accessory stood in the corner: a dula staff. She opened the mirror in her makeup kit. In the dark, she would have mistaken herself for a local priest. She blew out the candle and stuffed it into the folds of her shawl as she slithered out the back door to avoid the lobby.

A trickling stream ran through the village and edged down the hill past the cross-shaped baptismal pools, where a lone priest, half-asleep, sat slumped on his haunches under a roped-off entrance. She'd have to find another way to get inside. She remembered from the map that Bet Giorgis was the one church that sat apart from the others. Maybe they hadn't posted a guard at its entrance, confident that trespassers would be more interested in the main churches.

She descended the winding incline and stayed along the shadows. A chasm surrounded the submerged cruciform church like an empty moat. There were no steps, so she had to slide down a narrow trench. The door was unguarded, just as she had hoped, but the walls appeared held together only by the roots of olive trees. The slightest quake would bring tons of dirt crashing down on her.

Reaching the interior of Bet Giorgis, she lit her candle with a match from an offertory niche. The chamber glowed, revealing snarling gargoyles and saints spearing dragons all around her. These were motifs that one would expect to find in France, not Africa. In the courtyard of the holy of holies, an iron rod crowned by a cross stood against a blocked tunnel.

Had the priests left it there to scare off intruders?

She protected the candle's flame as she crawled into the narrow chute that angled up through the red earth toward the direction of Bet Golgota.

She tossed off the serape and pulled the fractured door shut behind her. After several more minutes of climbing, she found the passageway widening enough to allow her to stand. She groped the jagged limestone for support—and dropped the candle down the incline.

She cursed her clumsiness. Blanketed in darkness, she had no choice but to keep moving forward. Her head pounded. The analgesic effect of the weed was wearing off. Her fingers brushed across icons in niches. They felt like the Stations of the Cross. Behind her, she heard a rumbling, followed by a shriek. Wild hyenas ran through the village at night, she'd been warned. Had one of those nasty creatures stalked her into the tunnel? She found another carved cross, this one with a nailed Christ. She had to be getting close. More confident of her bearings, she increased the pace of her steps and—

Two hands grabbed her shoulders.

"Don't move," a man whispered to her ear.

She froze, terrified. She couldn't place the voice, but it was definitely not American. She expected at any moment to feel a knife against her throat. Were Paul's murderers still here? At all costs, she had to prevent them from finding her State Department identification. A flashlight flicked on. She looked down and saw that she stood inches from a deep trench. Another step and she'd have fallen to her death.

The flashlight clicked off. "Stay still," ordered the voice behind her. "If you step back, the edge will give way."

What was his accent? British maybe? She couldn't quite place it.

Granules of soil began crumbling around her sandals.

"Take off your shirt."

"I will *not!*"

He firmed his grip on her shoulders. "I don't have time to argue. I'll tie it to mine."

She angled slightly to confront him, and nearly slipped. Convinced, she unbuttoned her blouse and removed it, leaving herself exposed in a black bra.

"Roll it lengthwise." He gave her one end of his shirt. "Quickly."

She fixed the knot and—the ground gave way.

Dangling, she screamed, "Help me!"

Inch by inch, the obscured man leveraged her to safety. She rushed into his arms, and the flashlight clicked back on.

She was caught in the bare embrace of a fortyish man with curly black hair, broad shoulders, and dark European features suffused with a provocative mischievousness. His burnished eyes leapt at her like talons. If cleaned up a bit, he could be cast in a beer commercial as the ne'er-do-well son of the Most Interesting Man in the World. Remembering that she was wearing only a bra, she struggled from his clutches. "My shirt!"

Her rescuer smoothed out the wrinkles in the blouse, extending the delicious moment. He chivalrously offered to help her into its sleeves and flipped up her collar to imitate the fashion of the Parisian ladies. "A scarf would improve the look, but this will have to do for now."

She turned the collar back down in defiance. "Who are you?"

The man dusted off his boots. "You're welcome."

She saw that the boards laid across the trench had been notched to weaken their strength. "I'm sorry. I don't know who to trust in this place. I'm Jaqueline Quartermane. From the—"

"U.S. State Department."

"How did you know that?"

"Word gets around fast in the bush. I'd love to trade travel stories, but we've got twenty minutes before those priests show up for their morning lauds."

"What are *you* doing here?" she demanded. When he refused to answer her, she bored in on him. "Aren't you at least going to tell me your name?"

"I *do* know who to trust in this place," he said. "And it's not the American government."

"Why was that trap door placed here?"

The man searched the walls for a way around the trench, but found none. "The priests have hidden them in all the churches."

"Why? To maim tourists?"

"They've had a few thefts lately. Our best bet is to backtrack down that tunnel."

"I'm not leaving until I see the church called Golgota."

"Have you ever spent time in an Ethiopian jail?"

"No, but I'm guessing you have."

"Here's some free advice. Get out of this hole into Hell tonight."

Despite the warning, she refused to budge. "I wonder if that Ethiopian cop would be interested to know that a white man was grubbing around in his church? I hear they cut off the hands of thieves here."

The man debated the threat, and decided against testing her. "I'll get you into Bet Golgota. After that, you're on your own. Understood?"

She begrudged him a noncommittal half-nod, refusing to make an oral contract. He retreated several steps and sprinted toward the crevice. He leapt the deep cleft and landed with barely a foot to spare.

Her jaw dropped. "You don't expect me to do *that?*"

"Of course not," he said with a smirk. "You're just a pampered American mall princess."

She desperately wanted to take a swing at him, but the gap was too wide. "You're just going to leave me here?"

The infuriating cad glanced at her over his shoulder as he scurried off. "The priests start their inspection in Bet Giorgis, behind you. They should find you in, oh, I'd say about fifteen minutes. By the time they get done shaving your head and parading you through the streets as a witch, I'll be long gone." He took off on a run. Disappearing into the blackness, he stopped and added, "I nearly forgot. If you're ever in Paris, stop by *Quelle Belle* and ask for Veronique. She'll put a new blouse on my account."

"You promised!"

"And *you* didn't." He ran into the darkness, leaving her on the far side of the precipice. "*Au revoir!*"

She heard the faint thrum of approaching sistrums. Given no choice, she backed away three steps, then broke into a run and timed her blind jump from memory. She landed with the most welcoming thud she'd ever suffered. Recovering from the jolt, she staggered to her feet muttering curses. She turned the corner of the tunnel and ran straight into the man who had abandoned her.

"*Bravo!* I knew you could do it!"

Regaining her breath, she found the smooth-talking intruder watching her from around a corner. "Asshole!"

He laughed. "That fanny fit you threw back there gave you an extra boost. You should thank me for the motivation." The diffused light from a narrow opening in the ceiling fell on her tormentor, revealing him for the first time from head to foot.

Her eyes bugged at a coil of rope tied to his belt. "What ... why did you need my shirt?"

He grinned. "I couldn't take the chance of losing you. You can't get reliable hemp these days. This new synthetic rayon they now make is the mutt's nuts."

Before she could slap him, he grabbed her hand and led her through an angling cut of underground passages. Minutes later, she and her mysterious rescuer arrived at a cavernous crypt that held three altars carved whole from stone and hollowed on top to allow the draining of blood. The slabs resembled drawings she'd seen of the four-legged blocks used for sacrifices by the Israelites. Behind them lay a sealed vault protected by an iron grate.

"The Selassie Chapel," he whispered to her ear. "You're probably the first woman to see it."

She was fascinated by the sanctuary's medieval gothic architecture. "It must have taken them centuries to excavate."

"These churches were built in the twelfth century by King Lalibela. The Ethiopian prince had been exiled to the Holy Land. When Lalibela returned to claim the throne from his half-brother, he brought a bodyguard of Christian Crusaders. Some people think those French knights helped Lalibela design this underground amusement park."

She examined a carved cross radiating with flared flanges. "Where have I seen this before?"

"It's the insignia of the Knights Templar. The king who built these churches is supposed to be buried under one of these slabs."

"Why *did* this Lalibela guy build these churches?"

The man shrugged. "Seems like a perfect place to hide something important, don't you think? Or maybe the Ethiopian king just knew how to milk a good mystery to draw people to his new capital. Next door, in the church called Bet Maryam, there's a shrouded pillar that the Ethiopians have long believed holds the secret name of God. That kind of nonsense is like crack to tourists. Now can we get out of here?"

She stood there trying to imagine how Paul had stumbled onto the terrorists. Had he put up a fight? One of the steps near the altars had a stain. Was it his blood? Her eyes teared up.

"I heard about the raid," said the man. "Someone you knew?"

"My fiancé."

His rascally eyes softened. "What was he doing in here?"

"The police think he came to see the festival."

"Timkat? Not likely. A tourist wouldn't be able to just stumble into the Selassie Chapel. The head priest is the only one allowed inside."

She turned, confused. "I was told women only were banned."

The man shook his head, insistent. "If your fiancé was murdered here, I can assure you he didn't just wander off from the crowd. He bribed or stole his way in."

Her head was spinning. Bribing? Stealing? It didn't sound like the Paul she knew. But then, she was beginning to wonder if the Paul she'd known was all there was to him. She spied a narrow opening in the far corner that led to a smaller room. "What's in there?

"The ossuary. The priests store the bones of their dead brothers inside it."

"How come you know so much about this place?"

He wouldn't look at her directly. "Old churches are a hobby of mine."

She cracked open the door and found thousands of femurs and skulls piled high on shelves. "There must be skeletons in here going back a thousand years." Noticing a small wooden door with a knobbed handle, she walked over and opened the tabernacle.

"Don't touch that!" the man shouted, too late.

An army of buzzing bees swarmed out, and Jaq fell to her knees, curling into a ball. The man rolled his flashlight into the chapel to draw the raging bees toward its tumbling beam. When the ossuary was finally cleared of the pests, she climbed from the floor—something on the bone pile next to her caught her eye. Some of the bees had become stuck in a viscous substance. A strong aroma of smoky musk wafted up from the slathered bones. She flared her nostrils. "Do you smell that?"

The man scooped up a dollop and brought it to his nose. "It's myrrh. The priests use it in their ceremonies. They probably broke a jar of it in here."

One of the bees escaped the sticky myrrh and circled Jaq's head. She swatted it away and kicked at the bones in anger, only agitating more bees. She danced around cursing them. "Why don't they exterminate these pests?"

The man laughed at her skittishness. "Lalibela in Amharic means 'chosen by the sacred bees'. The locals here believe that the bees anointed their kings in ancient times. These hives are hundreds of years old."

She inched her eyes a little closer. "These drippings don't look random. The bees seem to be forming some sort of—" She heard voices.

He put a finger to his lips. "The priests are coming."

She pulled out her cell phone and shot a digital photo of the zigzagging congregation of bees on the bones. The drumbeats became louder. Her impatient accomplice grabbed her hand and rushed her into the nave, causing her to drop the phone. She broke free from him and backtracked into the ossuary to retrieve the phone. Crawling in the dark, she finally found it. She tucked the phone into her back pocket and—

"You disappoint me, Miss Quartermane."

The police inspector, accompanied by a posse of priests armed with torches, stood at the entrance to the ossuary. The Ethiopians looked angry enough to stone her. She glanced around for her new friend—if such an unreliable cad could be called a friend—but he had escaped without her.

"This is how you repay our hospitality?" Dese asked.

"I can explain." She stalled for time, keeping the phone hidden behind her back while turning off the ringer and dialing 001 for the United States.

Dese motioned her forward. "No explanation can justify the sacrilege of holy ground."

She prayed for a few seconds more. Estimating the time required to connect the call, she dialed Alyssa's number in Washington and pressed the SEND key to forward the last photo she'd taken. Her skill at texting behind her back, perfected during months of boring staff meetings, was finally proving useful. She tried to put the cop on the defensive. "You lied to me!"

Unaccustomed to being challenged, especially by a woman, Dese tugged at his starched sleeves in rising anger. "I will not be slandered."

She tried to focus on two tasks at once. "Women aren't the only ones banned from this chapel. How was it that *you* were allowed to investigate the murders here?" While talking, she pressed the Text Message key and tapped the letters: DNT ERAZ! She hit ENTER and dropped the phone, coughing to blunt the sound of the impact. She nudged it into a gutter with her heel.

Dese came closer. "I am afraid your return to the United States will be delayed. Perhaps for quite a long time. You will be taken to Addis Ababa in the morning to face prosecution."

"On what charge?"

Dese curled a thin smile of satisfaction. "Conspiring to remove holy relics. Your consort is a notorious thief who goes by the name of Elymas."

She rolled her eyes, not surprised that the guy who had been tailing her was a criminal. After all, he had impressed her as having the moral constitution of a grifter. She huffed with faked indifference and tried to walk past the inspector. "I'm protected by diplomatic immunity."

Dese blocked her path. "And being a barrister trained in diplomacy, you should know that our government recently obtained an exception to the Vienna Conventions for crimes against state religion. A few years ago, our most precious treasure, the silver Cross of Lalibela, was stolen from this very church. And your accomplice was a suspect in that crime. Our constitution was amended to make it a capital offense for anyone, even a foreign *chargé d'affaires*, to steal a holy icon from our country."

Capital offense?

She swallowed hard and wondered which would be worse: a firing squad, or the call she'd have to make to her bosses at State.

EIGHT

TOMAR, PORTUGAL
AUGUST 1455

The three Portuguese boys dropped to their knees to gather their waning strength. With each staggering step deeper into the blackness, they were becoming more despairing of finding a tunnel that connected the crypt of Santa Maria do Olival to the old Templar fortress.

Pero slapped his cheeks to stay awake. "How long have we been walking?"

"Four hundred and ten chants," Zarco said hoarsely. "Ninety paces for each verso. That's five hours."

Pero felt water seeping from the ceiling. He stuck out his tongue to collect the precious drops and swallowed with difficulty, soothing his strafed throat. "We have to be close."

"Only if we have been walking in a straight line," Zarco reminded him. "And only if Dias's magical needle is accurate."

"Even if we find our way out," Dias warned, "the knights will flog us for trying to escape."

Pero stubbed his toe, and cursed. He picked up the offending rock and angrily flung it into the void. "To Hell with those old crows! I'm running off to Lisbon to sign on with a merchant galley."

Zarco laughed off that plan. "The Order will hunt you down. No caravel leaves the harbor without the Old Man's blessing."

After another ten minutes of blind staggering, Pero sniffed a pungent aroma and felt a wet trickle wash over his bleeding feet. He ran his hand along the ground and found a sluice chute. He scooped up a handful of the slop and thrust his dirtied finger under Zarco's nose.

Zarco gagged from the stench. "Smells like shit!"

Pero grinned at their discovery. "Not just any shit. Shit of high standing. There's beef and mutton in it. Some nutmeg and ginger, too."

Dias shook his head in disbelief, as if convinced that Pero had finally lost his mind. "When did you become such an expert on shit?"

"My father taught me to judge horses by their chips," Pero said. "I can tell where a stallion is bred by the grass it eats. There's only one table in Tomar that dines this well."

Intrigued, the other two boys followed Pero as he stalked the flow of excrement. They came to a small orifice where the sewage drained. Just as Pero had feared, the tunnel led to a dead end. Dias and Zarco slid to their haunches in defeat, too exhausted to berate him.

Pero kept staring at the sluice drain, which was barely large enough to fit his foot through. Struck with an idea, he ordered: "Take off your pantaloons."

Zarco, half-conscious, muttered: "What did you say?"

Pero began removing his own breeches. "Hurry up!"

Dias refused. "If I'm going to die, I won't be found naked."

Pero grabbed Dias's cuffs and stripped them off him. He rolled their three pantaloons into a ball and tied them with the cord belts, then stuffed them into the drain orifice, arranging the makeshift cork so that the belts served as a seal around the edges of the hole. Zarco and Dias watched in befuddlement as the streaming sewage reduced to a trickle and finally stopped.

Shivering, Zarco curled into a ball for warmth. "What do we do now?"

Pero monitored the tunnel behind them. "We wait."

Five minutes passed, and when nothing happened, Zarco blew a dry ball of spittle at the ground in disgust. "Give back my pantaloons."

Pero tackled Zarco before he could remove the plug. They wrestled and pummeled each other with fists. Dias tried to break them up when a groaning from above stopped him short.

The ceiling was rumbling.

The boys scrambled away just in time to avoid being crushed by a large falling stone. Water surged down the opened hole. Within seconds, the tunnel was flooded, several feet deep. Zarco and Dias paddled to the surface, but Pero, unable to swim, had to be pulled up.

After several minutes, the water line finally receded into the tunnel.

Wet as ducks, the boys looked up at the fissure. Just as Pero had hoped, the pressure from the sewage backup had dislodged the escape stone. He raised his fist in triumph. Those Templars were cunning, but he had matched them in wits. He grinned from ear to ear as Dias and Zarco hoisted him into the breach.

The light from a hundred candles blinded him. Where was he? When his sight finally returned, he found himself surrounded by knights mounted on caparisoned horses. He was standing naked in the Templar charola of Tomar, the most secretive place in all Portugal.

One of the knights cantered up and removed his helmet.

"What took you so long, Master Pero?" Gil Eannes asked with a smirk. "You are late for Mass. And a bit underdressed."

The next morning, the boys, still exhausted from their previous day's ordeal in the tunnel, were roused from their pallets by a rotund little man crowned with a white turban and shrouded in maroon robes. The noisy intruder waved a flame over their heads. "You think we keep pampered Dominican hours? We have work before breakfast!"

Pero lifted to his elbows and winced from the ache in his overtaxed muscles. When his unidentified tormentor brought the lamp closer, Pero saw, in the full light for the first time, his fellow squires lying aside him. They looked nothing like what he had imagined from their voices. Zarco was the taller of the two; he had blondish-red hair, a freckled face, thin determined lips, and amber eyes whose heavy lids made one think of a spotted owl peering through the slats of a crate. Dias was as thickset as Zarco was slender, and his red skin was so burnt from his time on the sea that it resembled a lobster's carapace. He wore his raven hair pulled back in a ponytail and his frog-like face featured protruding brown eyes and a snub nose that looked pounded with a mallet.

The curmudgeon poked at the boys with the end of his staff. His doughy face, weighed down by a wild gray beard and thick lenses that magnified his watery blue eyes, looked vaguely familiar. "Up! Up! Up!"

Pero fended off the annoying prodding. "Who are you?"

"Abraham Guedelha."

That name sparked Pero's memory. *Sim*, he had seen this Jew on the day of his recruitment at Almoural castle. "You're the Old Man's astrologer."

"I have just cast the pitiful charts of you donkey brains." Guedelha turned his contemptuous stare on Pero with a warning. "Neptune shadowed *your* midheaven at birth. You will prove a difficult one to bridle and break."

"Horoscopes?" protested Pero. "When are we going to be taught to sail?"

The astrologer loosed a laugh of ridicule. "You think Prince Henry allows rock urchins like you to step foot on a caravel before learning the ways of the stars? I have been given the thankless task of disciplining you three sod brains on the mysteries of the heavens. After your sorry performance in Santa Maria's crypt, I am certain it will be a waste of my time."

Trading confused glances with Dias and Zarco, Pero asked the pestering old Jew. "How could *you* know what happened to us in that tunnel?"

The astrologer chortled. "Eannes amused us with hourly reports of your unsurpassed ineptitude. Had it not been for that lodestone needle, you three bait worms would now be pickings for the scorpions."

Outraged, Zarco leapt up from his straw bedding in hot protest. "That madman Eannes was stalking us the whole time?"

The astrologer wailed his staff at their buttocks to herd them out of the room. "Caravels are too valuable to waste on training squires, so the prince devised a less risky method for culling those with the necessary skill and fortitude for navigating under blind conditions. I would have failed the lot of you, but Eannes vouched you another chance. Now, to the stars!"

Groggy, the boys staggered down the hall and stumbled into a dusty chamber filled with strange devices: An armillary with iron rings rotated in haphazard angles around a globe; a bronze disc with a flanged arm that spun from center bolt; and a cauldron filled with sand for drawing planetary symbols. Titles such as the *Tetrabiblos* by and *Speculum astronomiae* by Albertus Magnus lined the shelves. All three of them were drawn to a frame with a thick iron screw piercing its center like a wine press. On its base sat a tray with miniature Latin letters that could be interchanged.

The astrologer placed a parchment on the tray and rubbed black liquid over rows of moveable blocks with raised letters. When the ink had settled, he turned the screw and produced a blank chart. "The Germans are using such a mechanism to produce twenty Bibles a week. The scriptoriums will soon be out of business. Mark my word, lads. The world is about to reverse on its axis."

Pero was intrigued by one prominently displayed parchment that featured a circle with a cluster of planets in one of its twelve pie sections. "Whose chart is this one?"

The astrologer used his staff for a pointer. "The Moon conjuncts Venus in the first house. This chart depicts a lover of the unknown. What else do you see?"

"Jupiter in Pisces," Pero said.

"Fortune flourishes in the sign of the fish. Your quotidian seer would pronounce this as revealing the destiny of one who would sail unknown seas. But the true sage always seeks beyond the primary planets. The midheaven is conjunct the North Star. Betelgeuse is also beneficially aspected. Fame and honor are due. But where, lads, is the fly in the ointment?"

Zarco pointed to a lone symbol on the opposite side of the circle. "That one looks ominous."

"Why think you so?" asked the astrologer.

"It opposes the other planets," Zarco said.

"Saturn, the great taskmaster," Guedelha agreed. "Here the planet resides in Libra, on the scales of judgment. It is also in malefic aspect to the Moon, the protector of seamen. The Old Man knew early on that he would never make the discoveries himself. He had to accept his fate as Judge of the Great Enterprise, sending others out to accomplish what he could not."

Dias gazed awestruck at the chart. "This is the Old Man's birth casting?"

The astrologer enjoyed their admiration of his work. "Tell anyone I have allowed you to see it, and I will flay your skins for palimpsests."

Pero would never have pegged the irascible Old Man as one who would readily surrender his will to such impersonal astrological forces. "Did the Navigator ever rebel against his stars?"

"In the vigor of their youth, all kings and princes resist the limitations placed upon them by Fate. But the wisest eventually come to accept the dictates of the heavens."

Zarco studied the clustering of the Old Man's planets. "When did he give up his dream of sailing?"

"Thirty years ago, the prince ordered me to assess the prospects for an assault on Tangier. His aspects were in a malefic angle that year. I begged him to abandon the attempt, but he was flush with the confidence of youth. His brother Fernando, then only eleven years old, was allowed to join the assault to gain his spurs."

"The Old Man was defeated in that crusade," Dias remembered.

"Defeat alone would have been endurable," Guedelha lamented. "But the heavenly orbs that year were bent on teaching the prince a painful lesson. Forty thousand infidels surrounded him and his army in the grilling African desert. Forced to capitulate, he was offered the choice of leaving either himself or young Fernando as a hostage to the Sultan."

Pero was appalled. "The Old Man gave up his own brother?"

The astrologer nodded dolefully. "Fernando lingered in a Moorish prison for five years. The infidels hung his corpse from the walls of Tangier to be eaten by the vultures."

Pero lingered his thoughts a moment more on the harrowing story. "If the Old Man *had* heeded your warning, he would have saved his brother. But then he would not have suffered the shame that now drives him to seek unknown lands. Does that mean his desire to conquer the seas is also contrary to the stars?"

The astrologer glared at Pero with a slack jaw, as if questioning whether his own natal stars had condemned him to suffer the disquietude and annoyance of such brainless urchins during his few remaining years.

ΠΙΠΕ

A couple of bones in the underground ossuary shifted.

Terrified, Jaq retreated to the corner of the claustrophobic grotto and watched the jumble of femurs and skulls for movement. After several seconds of silence, she enjoyed a nervous laugh on herself. The bones were so old and brittle that one probably broke from the weight and caused this grotesque pyramid of Lincoln logs to resettle. Still, she was more than a little frazzled, having been kept isolated for six hours overnight here because this outback was too poor to afford a jail. The three priests stationed in the adjacent Selassie Chapel were making sure that no one entered. She knew the drill. That control freak of an inspector was trying to break her down before he—

A skull with a fracture gash tumbled down and rolled toward her feet.

She screamed—was there a giant rat under the bones? She grabbed a thigh-bone and waited for the culprit. The bones erupted like a calcified volcano.

She pounded at the burrowing fiend.

"Hold off!" a muffled voice shouted from under the pile.

She held up the crucifix on her necklace for protection.

A dark head pierced through the lattice of bones. "You've got Him upside down. And that won't work on me anyway. I'm Jewish."

"*You!*" Her eyes widened in anger. "You hung me out to dry last night!"

Elymas rubbed his bruised scalp. "You're welcome again."

She searched the ossuary floor for a hole. "How did you get in here?"

"A cistern connects the River Jordan to these churches. But we'll have to leave through the front door. There was an unfortunate accident back there with a cave-in and one of the priests."

"So now I'm running with a thief *and* a murderer? I'll take my chances with a phone call to the U.S. Embassy."

"I'd strongly advise against that. You're the second American to be trapped in this pit. Your fiancé didn't fare so well, did he? I wouldn't push the odds."

She wasn't sure if she should trust him. "That detective is on to you."

"Dese? He's an old friend."

She considered her options and quickly calculated that she didn't have much negotiating leverage. "I'll go with you on one condition."

"I came back to help you. And *you're* making demands?"

"Tell me the truth," she said. "Why are you in Ethiopia?"

Elymas nudged the door to peer into the chapel, but he couldn't get enough of an angle to see the priests who were guarding the nave. "You're a lawyer. What I tell you is confidential, right?"

He wasn't a client, Jaq said to herself, but she fibbed anyway. "I suppose."

"Those monks out there guard an eight-hundred-year-old relic called the Cross of Lalibela. A few years ago, it ended up in the hands of a Belgian antiques collector before it was recovered."

"You stole it from this church?"

"I don't work for small-time dealers. And I don't botch jobs."

"So, you're trying to steal it now."

Refusing to answer her cross-examination, Elymas reached into his backpack and pulled out what appeared to be a leather-bound square about the size of a wallet. With a flick of his thumb, he expanded the square into a three-dimensional box that held mirrors on its inside panels. Jaq could barely keep up with his quickness as he collapsed and manipulated the box to form an extended series of panels, placing all of the mirrors on one side. He slid the makeshift periscope through the door's slender opening and looked around the corner at the priests. He whispered, "We'll have to wait until they change shifts."

The clever mirror impressed her. "You take accessorizing seriously."

"You should see my cosmetics compact."

"I would have thought that in your business, you'd wear a gun."

"I prefer an understated look. Besides, a reflection is much more lethal than a bullet. Archimedes destroyed an entire Roman navy with one of these."

Jaq caught a glimpse of her face in one of the panels. She brushed her hair, dismayed by her tired and disheveled appearance. Determined not to spend another minute in this Halloween chamber, she hit on an idea. "Give me your cell phone." He reluctantly handed it over, and she dialed her own number. "You're going to have a big bill this month."

Her Loretta Lynn ring tone played somewhere in the chapel. She waited for two more verses of "As Soon As I Hang Up the Phone," then opened the door and led Elymas past the priests while they searched for the phone that she had kicked into the shadows during her arrest.

The monks scurried around the chapel, desperate to locate the source of the blasphemous Western music. One of them finally pounced on the phone and answered it. "*Salam?*"

"*Dese ezih,*" Elymas whispered into his phone as he hurried Jaq through Bet Golgotha's dark nave. "*Ay tawa tsalo bet.*"

The monks stared at Jaq's phone in confusion.

She finally reached the tunnel, a step ahead of Elymas, and bent down to catch her breath. "What did you tell them back there?"

"I imitated Dese and told them to sit tight. Their relief was coming late."

Grinning at him, she had to admit this guy might not be so bad to have around. She rushed him into the outer court of the underground church, stopping only to check her watch. "It'll be sunrise soon."

He took the lead. "We'll have to hurry to reach the airstrip."

She froze. "There's an airport here? How will we get past security?"

"How much cash do you have on you?"

She avoided his expectant look. "That creep detective took it all."

He didn't buy the flimsy excuse. "I've had more than a few encounters with the *femmes* of the diplomatic corps. Hand it over."

Cornered in the lie, she sheepishly reached under her blouse and pulled out five hundred-dollar bills from her left cup.

He snatched the money from her grasp. "Now that's what I call a Wonder Bra."

On the outskirts of the village, Jaq crouched with Elymas behind an oil drum near an empty hangar. Nearby, a packed dirt runway was cracking and snapping from the morning's rising heat. A siren went off in the village, nearly a kilometer away. She figured Dese had probably discovered the empty ossuary. She looked around the dilapidated airport. "Is there a daily charter flight?"

Elymas kept his eyes fixed on the distant mountains. "You could call it that. ... Do exactly as I say. And keep your mouth shut."

Before she could protest that misogynistic order, a sputtering turboprop coughing a trail of gray plume dived over the peaks and came toward them. Buffeted by the wind, the plane bounced and heaved in an effort to line up with the short runway. Suddenly, a train of Jeeps and SUVs dashed out from behind the hangar and sped toward the end of the field. Confused by the frenzy of activity, she observed, "That doesn't look like a commercial flight."

Elymas leapt up and began walking toward the runway. As the turboprop touched down, he approached the vehicles, which were filled with armed militiamen preparing to unload cargo from the plane. He pulled her hundred-dollar bills from his pocket and shouted: "Two kilos!"

The Ethiopian gunmen laughed and peppered him with insults.

As the plane screeched to a rubber-burning halt a few feet away, Elymas dropped his demand. "One kilo."

The head Ethiopian thug fixed his eye on Jaq while showing off his English. "The money *and* your whore!"

Elymas signaled with a palm behind his back for her to remain calm. "The whore is worth two kilos alone."

Horrified, Jaq backed away, now questioning if she had put her life in the hands of a modern slave trader. The only thing she really knew about this Elymas character was that the Ethiopian government considered him a criminal. She sniffed a strange aroma in the air. While the pilot kept his propellers spinning for a quick getaway, the mercenaries flung down white sacks from the cargo bay into the SUVs as if their lives depended on finishing the task in breakneck speed.

Elymas asked his negotiating rival, "Where is the pilot from?"

"Yemen," the warlord said.

"Yemenites are fair people. I will ask him to decide a price for us."

The warlord kept one eye fixed on the cargo bay, apparently more concerned about his own men stealing from him than with selling a bag of his contraband to this Caucasian junkie. "Yes, go ask your Yemenite judge. He will cut off your balls for a good deal." When Elymas turned to go barter with the pilot, the warlord called him back. "*Faranji!* The woman stays with me."

Shrugging, Elymas climbed into the cockpit. Seeing the warlord return to his loot, he glared a warning at Jaq to accept the condition.

Two Ethiopians prodded her toward the warlord with their rifles.

The hideous thug grinned and thrust his pelvis at her. "Egyptian whores do it like monkeys."

She stared dumbfounded at the scumbag, who had apparently mistaken her for an Arab. She was about to correct him when the henchmen around him began shouting and running like maniacs. The pilot fell lifeless from the cockpit door—and the plane taxied off with its cargo bay still open. The Ethiopians stared at the apparition, not believing their eyes, until the plane turned and began picking up speed down the runway.

"*Qoma! Qoma!*" the warlord yelled at the cockpit.

"Lying bastard!" Jaq shouted at Elymas over the warlord's ranting.

Now she had been twice fooled by this con man.

She watched in numbed disbelief as the bush gangsters fired at the turbo-prop sputtering into the sky. The plane banked tightly and sent several unloaded sacks tumbling to the bush. As Elymas disappeared over the mountains, the Ethiopians abandoned her on the airstrip, jumped into their SUVs, and raced off to retrieve their precious sacks.

Jaq cut loose with every curse she had learned in the hills of Appalachia. Not only did the thief steal her money, he had left her to these thugs to be auctioned off—if Dese didn't catch her first. She ran for the hanger and heard the buzz of the turboprop coming up from behind. The plane landed and bounced on the dust with its cargo flap hinging wildly. She threw herself off the taxiway to avoid being diced and sliced by the propellers.

As the plane raced past, she risked looking up.

Elymas had swung the plane around on the ground. He stuck his head out of the cockpit window with an insufferable grin. "First class or coach?"

Sheer anger shot Jaq upright. Looking over her shoulder, she saw the Ethiopians in their SUVs speeding back toward the plane. She crawled up the bay ramp a split second before Elymas flipped the switch to raise it.

"Hold tight!" He took dead aim at the onrushing convoy.

The cursing Ethiopians were forced to split off to avoid colliding with the nose of the fuselage. Bullets peppered the plane as it chugged skyward and cleared the Lasta Mountains by only a few feet.

Safely airborne, Elymas relaxed at the controls and enjoyed a laugh—until the rear cockpit door flew open and a boot slammed his head. The plane lurched and dived, but he finally managed to regain control and level it out.

Jaq knocked off his hat and shouted into his ear, "You stupid son-of-a-bitch! I could have been passed around and raped by those brutes!"

Elymas rubbed his scalp, which had really taken a beating that morning. "You're selling yourself short. The head warlock would have kept you for himself."

She closed her eyes a moment, trying to stop her heart from racing. "What was in those sacks?"

"A weed called *qat*. The Ethiopians chew it to get stoned. It's a national pastime. I'm surprised you haven't heard of it, being the high-flying international legal hack that you are."

Her nostrils flared from the familiar aroma wafting in from the cargo bay. "I may have come across a reference."

"They'd give up sex before missing their daily qat sessions. That's how I knew they'd forget about you. If they don't get the qat to their buyers within five hours, it loses potency."

She didn't need convincing. "Now that we have half the country chasing us, where do you plan to land this thing?"

"Any requests?"

As Lalibela receded into the red haze below, Jaq slumped, depressed and ashamed at how she had let Paul down. Not only had she failed to solve his murder, she had left his ashes behind. How could she live with the nagging doubt about what really happened to him? There was only one person who might provide a clue. "How well do you know Addis Ababa?"

"Well enough to stay away."

"I need to make a stop at the psychiatric hospital there."

Elymas nodded. "Finally decide to get some help?"

Ravenous from not having eaten since dinner the night before, she searched the cockpit for something to snack on. "I'm hurdling three thousand feet in the air at the mercy of a stranger who steals religious relics for a living. I've also managed to piss off the Ethiopian police and a gang of drug smugglers. You tell me if I need my head examined."

The *merkato* bazaar in Addis Ababa was so chaotic that none of the shoppers seemed to notice when Elymas landed the stolen plane on a deserted soccer field atop a terraced hill overlooking the capital. Bringing it to a stop, he scanned the trashed environs below. "You sure we're in the right place?"

In the hazy distance, Jaq saw an expanse of red clay enclosed by a wire fence that surrounded a lugubrious gray edifice with barred windows. People in pajamas were walking the grounds like zombies, and attendants dunked patients into pools in a ritual that seemed designed to cleanse them of evil spirits. "Amanuel Hospital must be that monstrosity over there."

"Just out of curiosity," Elymas asked. "How do you expect to get inside?"

"You speak Amharic, don't you?"

"Enough to order a beer."

"You talked to those priests and druggies just fine." She took a deep breath for courage. "Don't wander off on me like you did last time." She leapt from the cockpit and, followed by Elymas, walked with authority toward the security kiosk. The lone guard reached for his pistol and blocked their path.

"Sorry we're late." She flapped her arms like a bird and nodded for Elymas to translate for her. "That glider the UN gave us has a scooter motor for an engine. Slower than geese."

The guard and Elymas stared at her as if *she* should be a patient there.

"You weren't informed?" She leaned into the guard. "Can I confide in you?" When the confused guard surrendered a reluctant nod, she whispered: "We're from the World Health Organization." The guard reached for his radio to warn his superiors of the unannounced inspection, but she pressed his end-call button. "We conduct our reviews anonymously. Your name?"

"Demeke."

In an aside to Elymas, she ordered: "Remind me to bring up Mr. Demeke's exemplary work at the review." Seeing the sketchy translation draw a smile from the guard, she whisked Elymas onto the hospital grounds while the guard was still mentally counting the *birrs* in his future raise.

Rushed upon by dozens of mental patients who babbled at them in Amharic, she pulled aside an elderly man whose eyes seemed a little more focused than the others. "A boy was brought here from Lalibela. What room is he in?"

The old man shouted at her. *"Sayt'an!"*

She turned to Elymas. "What did he call me?"

"The Devil. I think he's sane enough to be released."

"Ay gobana!" the agitated patient growled. *"T'abaqis."*

"No visitors," Elymas translated. "Guards are posted."

She told him to ask the elderly patient which nurse took care of the boy. When the man pointed toward a large Ethiopian woman in a green uniform who was trying to restrain two patients in a shoving match, she rushed over to help the nurse break up the altercation.

"Who are you?" the nurse demanded.

"You speak English?"

"I trained two years at Cornell Nursing College."

"I need some information. The boy here from Lalibela."

The nurse moved to call security. "I have nothing to say."

Jaq slid out three of the five hundred-dollar bills that she had gotten back from Elymas. She slipped them into the nurse's hand.

The nurse stared at the bribe, nearly a month's salary. "They watch me."

"What's wrong with the boy?"

The nurse kept her eyes pinned on the ground. "The doctors say he suffers from catatonia. They claim it is a latent genetic disorder set off by his trauma."

"You don't believe them?" Jaq studied every blink and flicker of emotion.

The nurse shook her head slightly, trying not to be seen by her superiors.

"But if he hasn't spoken since that night?"

"He *has* spoken," the nurse insisted, looking directly at her for the first time. "The night he was brought here, I heard him mumble one word over and over. I was the only staff in the room. When the others arrived, the boy became silent. He has shown no signs of consciousness since then. The doctors won't believe me. They ordered my report stricken from his chart."

"You don't think seeing his father dead caused his trauma?"

The nurse made a dismissive snorting sound.

"What did the boy say that night?"

The nurse kept glancing nervously at the hospital entrance.

Jaq flashed the last two of the hundred-dollar bills under her palm.

The nurse pulled a prescription pad from her pocket and wrote: *Egziabher.*

Jaq stared at the Ethiopian word. "What does *that* mean?"

The hospital director, followed by his security men, burst through the entrance doors and made a beeline for them.

The nurse hurried away.

Jaq whistled for Elymas, who was being hounded by begging patients. She took his arm and walked quickly with him toward the gate. When the hospital director shouted for them to stop, they broke into a run. They darted past the startled guard and high-tailed it for the plane.

Airborne just in the nick of time, Jaq felt her pulse finally go back to normal. She took a deep breath in relief. "Where are we headed?"

Elymas banked the plane over Addis Ababa while setting the instrument dials for the northeast sector of the country. "We've got just enough petrol to make it to Djibouti. That five hundred bucks you've got should get us on a cargo barge to Cairo."

She chose not to reveal that she was flat broke.

Elymas glanced back at the hazy black cloud of pollution hovering over Addis Ababa. "Well, that was a waste of time."

"Maybe not." She spelled out '*Egziabher*' aloud. "What does it mean?"

He turned on her, startled. "Where did you hear *that*?"

"That nurse said the boy was muttering it the night he was brought in."

He shook his head. "She must have heard wrong."

"Why?"

"That's the *Ge'ez* substitute code word for 'the Name of God.' No son of the head priest would ever talk about the name of God."

"Why not?"

"It's prohibited on penalty of death."

She wondered why the priest's son had taken such a risk. Something must have frightened him terribly in that underground church. "Didn't you tell me there's a pillar in Lalibela that contains the name of God?"

"It's just a legend," Elymas said. "In Bet Maryam."

"The church dedicated to the Virgin?"

"Yeah. A shroud covers the inscription there. The priests claim that the secret message has never been displayed. I told you, they make up stories like that to bring in the tourists."

"I need to see that pillar."

His jaw dropped. "Do you have a death wish? We barely got out of that snake pit alive. And now you want to go back?"

"Dese will be long gone," she assured him. "Lalibela is the last place the Ethiopian police will be looking for us."

He didn't look convinced. "And just how do you expect us to get past those *qat* heads whose plane we borrowed?"

When she told him her plan, he shook his head, but finally he dialed in the coordinates. He was being oddly compliant, she thought. Did he expect to get her into bed as a reward? Or did he have a more sinister motive?

A bus blazoned with the banner *Sacred Sites Tours* pulled into Lalibela and disgorged fifty New Age devotees chanting mantras given to them by their bearded guru, a golden-robed Caucasian hippie who resembled a reincarnated fusion of Obi Wan Kenobi and John Lennon.

"Look, dear!" exclaimed one of the tourists, a portly matriarch who wore large, wrap-around sunglasses and a white scarf. "There's a market here!"

Her husband, a stooped codger with a fluffy gray beard, chased away a swarm of pestering children with his cane. "Get off of me! I'll have to send these chinos out for dry cleaning!"

Their half-stoned guru herded his complaining Americans into the entrance of Bet Maryam, where an Ethiopian priest tailed them to prevent stragglers from touching the icons. As the gaggle of tourists departed Bet Maryam for the next church on the chain of underground sites, the corpulent woman in sunglasses turned to the priest guarding them. "Where is the restroom?"

The priest, having heard that English word a thousand times, glared at her with disgust. *"Yalam!"* he barked. "None!"

"No toilet?" she cried. "But I *have* to go!"

When the priest remained adamant in his refusal, the woman's husband intervened. "My wife has an infection. Caught from your water, I might add!"

Fearful of losing out on tips, the priest anxiously watched the rest of the Americans depart through the far exit.

"I *will* take my wife back to the entrance!" the husband bellowed.

The priest figured he'd see no *baksheesh* from this annoying couple anyway, so he waved the two pampered Americans off toward the crude lavatory near the entry gate and scurried ahead to catch up with other *faranji*.

Left alone, the elderly couple ducked behind a colonnade.

Jaq removed the pillows from under her dress while Elymas tore off his fake beard and drooping safari hat. They found a slender column in the corner of the church. It was wrapped with a frayed shawl that appeared old enough to have been Eve's first garment.

Elymas just stared at it.

"Well?" Jaq said. "What are you waiting for?"

"Me? You're the one who wants to see it."

She was baffled by his sudden loss of nerve. "Is there something about this pillar you haven't told me?"

Elymas hesitated. "The Ethiopians say an eternal curse will be cast on anyone who unveils Lalibela's secret."

"What's supposed to happen?"

"You go blind and mute."

She thought a moment. "That's what the doctors claim happened to that murdered priest's son. Whatever he saw in these tunnels that night must have caused him to lose his senses."

"Or made him *think* he lost them."

She dug in on him with her narrowed eyes. "You said the curse was a foolish legend. Go ahead. Uncover it. You're already going to Hell for all those thefts."

Shamed by her challenge, Elymas slowly drew back the covering that hadn't been removed for centuries. He aimed his flashlight at the exposed section, which was lighter in hue because of the years of protection. He barely made out a faint line of indented letters.

"What does it say?" she whispered anxiously.

"Looks like ... ROTA."

"English letters?"

"Probably Latin." Elymas ran his fingers across the inscription. "There were other lines above it, but they've been eroded."

"How many lines?"

"Maybe five. I can't tell in this light. Wait, maybe it's not ROTA. This village was called Roha before King Lalibela renamed it for himself. The 'h' may have been partially effaced."

Jaq frowned, perplexed. "Why would medieval Ethiopians go to all this trouble to hide the old name of their own village?"

"Rota ... Roha. It's all probably just nonsense anyway."

"Isn't 'rota' the Latin root for—"

"To rotate," Elymas whispered, now even more intrigued.

Struck simultaneously by the same thought, they both turned toward the door behind them. On its arch was carved a medieval knight, mounted and spearing a serpent monster.

Jaq glanced at Elymas and wondered: Could the ancient Ethiopian name for God—and whatever the hospitalized boy saw on the night of the murders— have something to do with this strange warrior etched in stone above them?

TEN

SATOR
APERO
TENET
OPERA
ROTAS

TOMAR, PORTUGAL
SEPTEMBER, 1455

D rilled for weeks on the many possible combinations in a natal horoscope, Pero and his fellow squires now knew, for example, that having
Saturn and Mercury within two degrees in the Seventh House warned
of betrayal, but if the angle were accompanied by a trine with Jupiter in Libra,
the traitor could be persuaded to serve as a double agent. Yet the Order's astrologer, Abraham Guedelha, still had not told them why such knowledge was
essential for a mariner.

On this night, rather than dismiss them for Vespers, Guedelha commanded
the boys to climb to the roof of the old Templar charola with him. There, on
the tower's deck, they found a tripod supporting a wooden tube that had
been fitted on each end with lenses thicker than the astrologer's spectacles.
Motioned forward to peer through the cylinder, Pero saw a kaleidoscope of stars
come into focus around the moon. He let out a gasp of disbelief. The orb's pale
surface appeared to have rivers and continents.

After Dias and Zarco took their turns, Guedelha unrolled several scrolls
and fired the tapers for light. "It was not in whimsy that Prince Henry ordered
me to teach you the secrets of the cosmos. To conquer and rule men, one must
first learn the forces that shape their hearts and minds. One day, God save us,
each of you may be given command of a caravel."

"Perhaps even an armada?" Pero piped.

The astrologer puffed up like an angry blowfish. "Only if all the other witless
dolts in Lusitania have first been tried and found wanting!" He required a
moment to reclaim his composure. "You may one day find yourself cast adrift
with no land in sight. Your crew will be illiterate men, superstitious and sworn
only to their own survival. You will encounter strange lands populated with
savages. To survive, you must become a swift and certain judge of character."

"All of that is possible from knowing the stars?" Zarco asked.

The astrologer gazed up at the heavens like a proud father observing his progeny. "The powers and influences of those luminaries above us have been imprinted into the soul of every mortal. The edge of the cosmos is demarked by a celestial sphere that holds the stars and planets in place, and the twelve zodiacal constellations travel around the Earth each year in a band called the ecliptic. If you had no calendar to consult, how would you go about confirming that we are in the month of September?" Seeing that the conundrum had stumped the boys, he pointed to a cluster of stars. "What does *that* resemble?"

Pero offered a guess. "An overturned jar?"

Guedelha flailed his sleeves. "Is an overturned jar one of the zodiacal signs?"

"No," Dias answered, admittedly uncertain.

"That beauty up there is the home of the Virgin," Guedelha said. "Do you see how she lays upon her back giving birth to Our Lord? And there, the farthest star to the South, is her head." He ordered the boys, "Draw two lines from that point through the stars. What next do you see?"

"Her legs?" Zarco asked.

Pero pointed to the brightest star in the cluster. "That one looks like it forms the Virgin's ass."

Guedelha swung his staff, barely missing Pero's head. "Blasphemous cretin! That is the Madonna's womb! The most brilliant star carries the God child."

Pero could not fathom why a Jewish sage would identify a constellation with a Christian story from the New Testament.

The astrologer detected Pero's skepticism. "Did you think there was only one virgin who gave birth to a god? The Greeks and Romans gave identity to those same stars. That constellation was first named for Persephone, the virgin daughter of the harvest goddess Demeter. Persephone was abducted by Hades and taken hostage into the underworld. Why do you suppose the stars of the Virgin arise on the highest point of the ecliptic during the month of September?"

"Winter approaches in September," Dias suggested.

When the astrologer did not gainsay that explanation, Pero followed up Dias's conjecture with his own idea. "Perhaps September was the month when Persephone was taken. Darkness and sadness follow."

"Indeed." Guedelha surrendered a rare wink in admiration at their progress. "All secrets of God's cosmos can be unlocked by the application of such deductive reasoning."

"So, if we find ourselves lost," Zarco asked, "we can determine the month, even the day, by measuring which sign of the zodiac is highest in the heavens?"

Guedelha sighed heavily. "Ah, Master Zarco, if it were only that simple. The Almighty, in His infinite wisdom, embedded a hidden key into the Universe to thwart usurpers of the gnosis." The instructor produced an apple and pierced its core with a stick, leaving the makeshift axis exposed at each end. He gave the stick a spin, and the apple twirled for several revolutions before wobbling to a fall. "What did you just observe?"

"A good apple ruined," Pero proposed, having missed the evening meal.

"Idiot! What happened to the apple before it tumbled from its axis?"

"The stick began gyrating in larger circles," Zarco offered.

Guedelha nodded. "What now do you deduce about the earth's rotation?"

Dias tried: "The world is going to fall?"

Before the old sage could explode with another torrent of invectives, Pero blurted out his guess. "The earth spins on an axis! And the axis is not fixed! The path of the zodiac must therefore alter its course as the earth teeters."

Dias circled in growing frustration, bewildered by the lesson. "But that would mean the months and constellations do not line up! Have we wasted weeks memorizing stars whose arrival is never constant?"

Guedelha reached into his knapsack and pulled out a leather-bound ephemeris. "Not wasted, if you possess one of *these*. The Alfonsine tables take into account the uneven rotation of the earth and reveal the positions of the planets and constellations for the future years and seasons."

Zarco studied the book. "How did you come by such rare knowledge?"

"My forefathers on Mallorca made maps for the Moors."

Dias was stunned that the Old Man would hire a Jew once employed by evil Mohammedans. "Where did these Mallorcans gain such secrets?"

"Their liege, King James of Aragon, was raised by the Knights Templar. Those crusader monks learned their astrology from infidel scholars in the Holy Land. The Arabs are much more learned than the fools who teach in the universities at Paris and London. When the pope and the king of France disbanded the Templars for trumped-up crimes against the Church, some of the monks loaded their ships with what documents they could save from their libraries and sailed to Palma. They retained my family to copy their maps and codices."

"Why then did you come to Portugal?" Pero asked.

"Prince Henry brought me here to instruct him on the arcana of the Levant. Look around you. What strikes you as unusual about this monastery?"

Zarco turned on his heels. "The design is round."

"Easier to defend?" Dias suggested.

"To the contrary," Guedelha admonished. "Without angles, there are no enveloping points of cross-fire."

Zarco risked another guess. "My grandfather once told me the Templars built their sanctuaries in the shape of a circle to imitate the domed edifice that served as their headquarters in Jerusalem."

"João Goncalves Zarco was a brilliant and courageous man," Guedelha said. "But on this matter, your grandfather was mistaken. Not all Templar churches were built in the round. Only those meant for a particular purpose."

Pero peered down over the curving wall. The buttresses and crenellated teeth, he realized, were spaced like the lines that divided the houses in the circular chart of a horoscope. This tower resembled a giant astrolabe or casting circle. "We are standing on an observatory. The Templars must have mapped the stars from here."

"And the winds," Guedelha said. "Each position of the planets across the zodiac produces its own potent zephyrs and climactic conditions. The inner winds give birth to the outer winds, just as thought gives birth to action. The Templars discovered this truth from a Mohammedan astrologer named Abu Mashar."

"Can the winds also bring evil?" Pero asked.

The astrologer pointed to an entry in his ephemeris. "In 1345, Saturn, Mars and Jupiter were conjoined in Aquarius. What tragedy commenced that year?"

"The Black Death," Zarco said, remembering the stories that his grandfather had told of that horrible plague.

Guedelha nodded. "When the planets crowd together, their effects are intensified. Mars turned retrograde that fateful year, and the malignant vapors corrupted the air."

Zarco looked shaken by that revelation. "What can we expect from the stars and their effects this month?"

"Saturn is in Libra," Guedelha warned. "The winds will be raging and muddy. Kings will be volatile and turgid in their thinking."

Pero now regarded Tomar and its surroundings in a new light. "Does the Old Man really make his decisions on the expeditions based on the approach of these zodiacal winds?"

"Without deviation," Guedelha said. "The Prince wrote a treatise on the effects of the stars. You will be required to learn it."

"There is something I still don't understand about this science of yours," Pero said. "You say that the stars compel—"

"Incline," Guedelha corrected. "God has blessed us with free will, however influenced by the stars it may be."

"The stars *incline* men to act in certain ways," Pero continued. "But how can an object so far away, one that is not in contact with me, act upon my desires and thoughts?" When the astrologer glared at him in unbearable silence, Pero quickly apologized for his impertinent question. "I meant no disrespect."

Guedelha gloated at having gained Pero's quick capitulation. "What caused you to lose resolve just now?"

"You were scowling at me with evident loathing."

"And yet I made no physical contact with you. How was I able to influence you so forcefully from a distance?"

The boys marveled at the demonstration.

"Is it like prayer?" Zarco asked. "Do the angels not prosecute the Almighty's bidding without touching our flesh?"

Guedelha tapped the squire on the head in praise. "You, Master Zarco, could have been an acolyte in the service of St. Aquinas. The great doctor conceded that while the stars do not cause events, they do indeed influence them, as do prayers. Do the tides not rise with the fullness of the Moon? Where is the physical contact there? Stellar rays, undetectable by the mortal eye, flow down from the heavens without cease."

Pero was a little jealous of Zarco, who always seemed to come up with the right answer. He reminded the astrologer: "But on his deathbed, the saint was also said to cry out that the true secrets of God's Universe had at last been revealed to him in a rapturous vision. He insisted that all the works that he had written in his life were no longer of any value."

Guedelha turned apoplectic. "Where were you schooled? In a coven of foul-tongued witches?"

"My father taught me from his own books."

The astrologer stomped his sandals against the stones in exasperation. "A miracle twice conjured by the angels will be required to turn you into boat-swain, let alone a serviceable mariner!"

Pero negated that prediction with an inaudible mumble. "You'll be long rotting under sod while I'm on the high seas."

Finally calming, the astrologer bade the boys sit down around him. "Now, *meninos*, the task I will now perform is deemed a sacred duty in our Order. The most difficult obligation a man faces in life is to stare unflinchingly at his own fate. The Old Man requires every aspirant to know his own weaknesses and celestial influences. Are you prepared to hear yours?"

The boys, unsure, nodded slightly.

The astrologer brought out Zarco's chart first, and he regarded the grandson of the famous Madeira discoverer with a look of compassion. "This is a rare confluence indeed, Salvador. Your Sun and Moon are both exalted in Gemini, the sign of the twins. You will have two lives. And two deaths."

Zarco was unnerved by the strange prediction. "Two lives and two deaths? How is that possible?"

"The ways of the Almighty are mysterious," Guedelha said. "The purpose of your twin destiny will be revealed in time. But you must prepare to give up the life you cherish to serve a higher cause."

The three boys traded skeptical glances, unsure about this star conjuring.

The astrologer next brought Dias's chart out and held it under the flickering light of the tapers. "Master Bartholomeu, do you see how all of your planets are gathered below the horizon?"

"*Sim.*"

"South will be your destiny. You must always seek your fortune below the equator. Do you see Saturn covered by Mercury the Messenger? You will pave the way, but others will bring the word back. There are disappointment and sacrifice in these stars. You must take solace in knowing that you will be forearmed."

The blood drained from Dias's face.

With cruel anticipation, Guedelha turned next to Pero, having saved the chart of his most difficult student for last. "Master Pero, the thorn in my side. Your Mercury is exalted in Leo. That explains your cleverness with languages and your impious proclivities. Your Jupiter is also in opposition to the north node. You will be drawn to foreign lands."

Exultant, Pero clapped his hands. "I am to be a mariner, after all!"

Guedelha remained somber. "Saturn also shadows your moon in Capricorn."

"What does that bode?"

The astrologer sighed heavily. "The Capricorn goat is an animal of burden. When exalted, it leads to freedom. When poorly aspected, as it is here, it signifies being tethered, separated from the flock and shepherd. The goat thrives in mountains. Not on water."

Pero blinked hard. "But you said the stars only influence."

"There is always hope," Guedelha conceded.

The boys turned inward, trying to come to terms with their forecasts.

After allowing them a moment, Guedelha rolled up the charts and stored them in tubes for safekeeping. "This night concludes my work with you, *meninos*. I always leave my students with the story of Ascletario, the royal astrologer who served Domitian. When the Roman emperor persisted in demanding to know the details of his death, Ascletario reluctantly told him that it would occur four hours after sunrise on the day that blood stained the Moon in Aquarius. That fearful aspect finally arrived, and although Domitian tried to stay awake all night, he dozed off. Awakened hours later, the emperor asked his trusted servant for the time. Relieved to learn that the fateful moment had passed, he scratched a mole on his forehead to fulfill the prophecy in a harmless manner. He then accepted a visitor, who promptly assassinated him. Under torture, the servant admitted lying about the wrong hour because his master had been so fearful of it. ... Remember always: Fate leads the willing and drags the unwilling."

Pero pondered the strange story. *Fate are the stars be damned*, he silently vowed. *No aerie constellation will ever deny me my dream.*

ELEVEΠ

SATOR
APERO
TENET
OPERA
ROTAS

Sitting in front of the empty casket, Jaq shivered from an icy wind that whistled down the rows of slumping colonial gravestones. Three days ago, she had been broiling under the Africa sun. Now, here in Paul's hometown cemetery, the ground was so frozen that the funeral had to be postponed a day until a stronger backhoe could be brought over from Portsmouth to dig the grave. She tightened her collar, stifling painful coughs. Near exhaustion, she prayed for Rev. Merry to finish his long, impassioned eulogy.

"Paul Merion died a good Christian," he preached. "Despite the outrage inflicted on his body with the pagan cremation, we must continue to believe that the Almighty will resurrect him in the flesh on the Day of Judgment."

Still queasy from her Ethiopian ordeal, Jaq gripped the chair arms to steady herself. After leaving Lalibela, she had made her way to Cairo with the mystery man who went by the name of Elymas, but he had slipped off without leaving a number while she waited for her clearance at the embassy. She didn't even know what country he called home. He was a slime ball, for sure, but she owed him a letter of thanks at least for twice coming to her rescue. He probably knew it was best that a State Department lawyer not be seen with a notorious smuggler.

Standing at the head of the casket, Rev. Merry quivered with righteous anger. "We pray that the heathens who took his life and dealt with his body so flagrantly come to know the forgiveness of the Lord."

Jaq caught Paul's mother and sisters glaring at her from across the grave. They quickly averted their eyes. She knew they blamed her for leaving his ashes in the Lalibela hotel room. To remind everyone of the negligence, Mrs. Merion had insisted a casket be buried with only Paul's photo inside. His family had always looked down on her as nothing but Kentucky trailer trash.

As the service ended and the mourners began leaving, Jaq allowed the Merion women to pay their last respects before she approached the casket. After they drove off in the limousine, she stepped closer to peer down into the snow-dusted grave, coughing back the grief.

Rev. Merry came up and braced her with a hand on her arm. "You look paler than Martha at the empty tomb. Come warm yourself in my car."

"I'm okay. A little tired, is all." Out of the corner of her eye, she saw Bart Ochley and Fred Darden waiting just beyond the service tent. They finally stepped forward to offer their condolences. She avoided meeting eyes with Darden, refusing him the satisfaction of gloating over the disastrous results of her trip.

Rev. Merry tried to soothe her with a reassuring hug. "You did right by our dear Paul. You must commend him to Our Lord and move on with your life."

Despite his counsel to let go, she couldn't keep her suspicions to herself any longer. "We're not being told the truth."

"By whom, darling?"

"That Ethiopian police inspector I dealt with over there. He knows more about Paul's murder than he would tell me."

Darden frowned at her accusation. He glanced around the cemetery to make sure there were no eavesdroppers. "This is not the time or place."

"Who told the Ethiopians to cremate his body?" she demanded to know. "They wouldn't do that without our authorization."

Ochley tried to diffuse the tension. "You're too emotional right now, Jaq. Take the rest of the weekend to recover. We'll go over your report on Monday."

She kept edging in on Darden. "*You* ordered it, didn't you?"

Darden sneered at Ochley. "I warned you she should have been kept out of this. If McCrozier hadn't stuck his nose into—"

"Gentlemen!" Rev. Merry interjected. "Ms. Quartermane is grieving."

Darden tried to stare her down. "Drop the entire matter. ... *Now.*"

She wouldn't back off. "You didn't want me over there because you were afraid of what I'd find. Paul wasn't spending his time saving nonbelievers." She opened her purse and produced the clipping she had found in his wallet.

The reverend looked increasingly distraught as he read the newspaper story about the possibility of Jewish Temple relics being kept in the Vatican. "Paul never told me of this."

"Me either," Jaq said. "Why would he keep it a secret?" She thought Darden and Ochley seemed oddly unsurprised by the contents of the article.

Darden stepped closer and loomed over her in a challenge. "How well did you know your fiancé?"

"Well enough to know he had no interest in tramping through filthy African ruins. What was he looking for over there?"

"Drugs." Darden's pleasure in delivering that slamming revelation was all too evident.

Jaq stammered that horrid word. "Drugs?" She waited for Rev. Merry to condemn the slander, but he was too astonished to form a response.

Darden didn't give her time to recover from the revelation. "And that green ring around his mouth in the photo wasn't decay."

She realized that somehow he had learned about her questions to Dese that day in Lalibela. "How do you know about the photo?"

"The Ethiopians wired us a full report of your antics," Darden said.

"Paul never touched drugs!" she insisted.

Denied in his effort to mediate their clash, Ochley reluctantly walked to his car, pulled a file from his briefcase in the passenger seat, and returned. "I was hoping we could do this back in Washington. The Ethiopians had Merion under surveillance. He was running a smuggling operation for a *qat* ring in Yemen. It's a psychedelic weed. Half the Horn of Africa is addicted to it."

"I know what it is!" she snapped.

Rev. Merry kept staring at the clipping, trying to make sense of it. "Why would the Africans offer an American missionary a cut of their illicit profits?"

"The demand for *qat* here in the States is exploding," Ochley said. "Ethiopian émigré populations in Detroit and Portland pay top dollar for it. Problem was, nobody had a way to get it past customs … until Merion came along."

"We were tipped off by Customs three months ago," Darden told her. "Merion was moving the qat through the Port of Galveston under the cover of the Reverend's food program."

Jaq traded horrified looks with the pastor. Then, she nearly shouted at the two government officials. "I don't believe you!"

Ochley opened the file and displayed to her a report of an autopsy performed by the Ethiopians. She grabbed the document and read it. Significant amounts of cathinone, the amphetamine-like alkaloid contained in *qat*, had been found in Paul's bloodstream. Sickened, she slung the report to the ground.

Rev. Merry retrieved the document from the snow and examined it. "Lord in Heaven."

Jaq was furious that Dese had also lied to her about the autopsy. "What was Paul doing in that underground church?"

"The Lalibela priests were his middlemen," Darden explained. "Their tunnels offered the perfect depot for the *qat* flown in from Yemen and shipped to Djibouti. The murdered priest was providing him cover in exchange for a cut."

"*Qat* isn't illegal in Ethiopia," she reminded him.

"But it *is* here in the States," Darden said. "Two weeks ago, we informed the Ethiopian ambassador that foreign aid to his country will be cut if his government refuses to assist us in countermanding the *qat* trade."

Jaq needed a moment to make sense of it all. Then, it dawned on her. She locked eyes with her two State Department bosses. "Paul wasn't executed by Eritrean rebels."

Ochley shuffled with a downcast look of guilt. "The Ethiopians put that story out to protect their informants. A rival gang murdered Paul and the priest in a *qat* exchange that went bad. The message carved into the priest's flesh was a ploy to shift the blame to the Eritreans."

"And Paul's trip to Rome?" she asked. "How do you explain that?"

Darden answered her before Ochley could sugarcoat it. "We suspect Merion was using the Italian Mafia to repackage the *qat* and haul it across the Atlantic."

Suddenly lightheaded, Jaq stumbled, and the pastor caught her. Recovering, she shook off Ochley's attempt to help her. "Why didn't you tell me about this before I left for Africa?"

Ochley looked genuinely pained. "We wanted to spare you the humiliation. What good could come of being told the man you loved was dead because of criminal activity? We ordered the Ethiopians to shred the report and cremate the body to destroy all evidence of his involvement. We can't let this get out to the press."

It all made sense to her now: Paul's failure to call as often; the hostility of that Ethiopian inspector; Ochley's warning in his briefing memo that she should get out of the country quickly. Horrible as such a drug addiction was, she could understand how the devilish weed had seduced Paul. She now realized that she had mistaken Darden's circumspection for animosity. She had to do the Christian thing and make amends. "I owe you an apology," she told him. "I went over your head because I thought I couldn't trust you."

"Water under the bridge," Darden said. "But I want you to do something for me. Take two weeks leave. Get your mind straight, come back and give us the best you have."

Rev. Merry asked her, "You still have those airline tickets that you and Paul purchased for your honeymoon, don't you? Where were you planning to go?"

"Italy," she muttered, stung by the bitter irony.

The pastor embraced her again. "Come now, darling. Take someone with you. What about your friend? What's her name? Allison?"

"Alyssa," she said. "I'm sure she couldn't get time off."

"Where does she work?"

"Congressman Yardley's office."

The reverend punched in a number on his cell phone. "Cal Merry calling for Bill Yardley. Tell him I'm collecting on a favor."

Jaq stared at the overstuffed suitcase on the couch in her apartment, trying to choose which sweater to leave behind to make room for the new Grisham novel.

Anxious to get to the airport, her friend Alyssa—a cute, sassy brunette with a Wisconsin attitude sharper than cheddar—huffed in exasperation. "They have bookstores in Rome. It's not like we're going on *Survivor* in New Guinea."

"What's the weather forecast there?"

Alyssa rolled her eyes. "Who cares? Just bring a jacket and scarf. We'll dress up like Audrey Hepburn in *Roman Holiday.*"

"Are you sure Toby's okay with this?"

"Actually," Alyssa said, fussing with her bag, "we had a fight last night."

"Over this trip?"

"That and a hundred other things. It's probably good we're taking a break. The relationship's been shaky for a while."

"I'm sorry."

Alyssa pressed her elbows into Jaq's carry-on with the gentle finesse of a Turkish bath masseuse. "Don't be. As they say in a Roma, there's a more thana one mushroom ona the pizza."

"They really say that?"

"Probably not. Speaking of big mushrooms, that pastor of yours must be one powerful dude. Not only did Yardley insist I go with you, he gave me five hundred bucks from his campaign fund for spending money."

"Is that legal?"

"Hey, I just answer the phones. If somebody wants to give me a bonus, I'm not going to complain to the Supreme Court."

Jaq pulled her new phone from her purse and tossed it on the desk. "If I lose another Blackberry, Ochley will dock my pay."

"You can use my phone over there," Alyssa said. "The new GPS feature comes with a SIM card that works in Europe."

Jaq shrugged. "The GAO has probably suspended my international account for going over my allotted minutes anyway."

Alyssa spun on her. "Hey, that reminds me! You cost me twenty-four bucks with that text from Africa last week."

"What are you talking about?"

"The one telling me not to erase the photo you sent. Were you drunk on Ethiopian beer sending it on the international rate? It looked like you hit the camera button by mistake."

Jaq had tried to put those frenetic moments in the ossuary out of her mind. "I forgot all about that. I thought I'd found something important in a church. Turns out it was nothing."

Alyssa shoved her toward the door. "You're being pretty mum about this Indiana Jones guy. Did he have a big whip?"

"Stop it! I just buried Paul!"

"Yeah, and Paul was being real honest with you. He treated you like some veiled harem slave from the Old Testament."

Jaq dug in her heels. "You're mocking my faith now? I don't ride you about going to Mass every Sunday just because half the priests in your Church are running around molesting boys!"

"Paul was selling drugs for thousands of bucks while whining every chance he got about how much you spent. Don't you even wonder what else he was doing over there that he didn't tell you about?"

"You mean women?"

"I mean women, men, animals. I know I shouldn't be talking like this, but the sooner you get over that lying scumbag and back into the dating scene, the better off you'll be. Maybe in Rome we'll run into ... what was his name?"

Jaq acted uninterested. "I think he called himself Elymas."

Alyssa honed in on her. "Now there's a name to whisper on a pillow late at night." She moaned each syllable, "El—*eee*—mas."

"Mention him again and I'll tear up the tickets!"

Alyssa pranced around her, thoroughly pleased at having elicited such an intense reaction. She thumbed through the dozens of photos saved on her cell phone. "You could've at least sent me a picture of him." She finally found the photo she was looking for. "Here it is. You might as well keep this one for the memory."

"Why would I want to remember the worst week of my life?"

Alyssa studied the photo. "Are those bees?"

Jaq nodded with disgust. "I'm lucky I don't have stings on every inch of my body. Those idiots over there think bees are sacred."

Alyssa brought the phone's screen closer to her eyes. "They look like they're forming a word."

"I said they were sacred," Jaq scoffed. "Not educated."

"Aren't those Latin letters?"

Jaq took the phone from her and examined the digital photo up close. "This screen's too small. Can you print it out?"

Alyssa connected her cell phone to the USB port on Jaq's computer and sent the file to the printer. "Are those bones?"

"Yeah, and you wonder why I can't hold any food down?"

Alyssa flipped the printout upside down for a different angle. "I swear that's a Latin 'S'. This was how the Romans shaped it in their alphabet. They drew sharp corners instead of curves."

Jaq waved her off. "You're just seeing patterns where none exist. It's like a Rorschach test. You read the Congressional Record and see letters. I starve myself all day and see French fries."

Alyssa spelled aloud the letters that looked formed by the bees stuck in the myrrh spilled on the jumble of bones. "S … A … T … O … R."

"SATOR? You took Latin in school. What does that mean?"

Alyssa shrugged. "There's no such word that I know of. You're right. It's probably just a random arrangement. Anyway, let's stop by the liquor store on the way to the airport. I need a couple of those midget vodkas to sneak onto the flight. I'm not paying those airline extortion prices."

As they walked out the door of the apartment, Jaq took another look at Alyssa's butt. "Have you been working out?"

Alyssa arched her bottom. "Give it a smack."

Jaq let fly and hit something gelatinous under Alyssa's blue jeans. "Are you wearing *padding?*"

Alyssa did her best imitation of Sophia Loren walking down the runway. "I ordered it from a Conde Nast ad. Latin men love a big ass. And it's guaranteed to prevent bruises from pinching."

Rolling her eyes, Jaq wondered what she was getting herself into with this trip.

TWELVE

LISBON
NOVEMBER 1455

Pero had to stop and catch his breath as he followed Eannes up the steep path that led to the Castle of St. George. Below them, along the Tagus river, the fishmongers were lighting their torches to welcome in the morning haul, and mobbing gulls serenaded the wash hags shuffling with their laundry baskets toward the communal basins. He remembered once hearing a bard describe the city of Lisbon at dawn as a beautiful *senhora* awakening after a long night of wine and lovemaking; she appeared a bit disheveled and languorous, which only made her that much more alluring.

"The Old Man will have us thrown off these cliffs if we keep him waiting!"

Eannes's shrill complaint punctured Pero's daydream. He wasn't fooled by the absurd claim that the Old Man wished to see him. Having reached his fill of such lies, he balled his fists and prepared to fight. "I've had enough of your damnable tests and trials!"

"This is no trial."

Pero held his ground. "I'll not take another step until you tell me why you woke me in the middle of the night and dragged me here from Tomar."

"Keep climbing with me. I will tell you on the way up."

He suspected the promise was merely a ploy. If he came closer to the walls, Eannes would just call the guards and have him arrested. "Tell me now!"

The mariner finally relented. "An envoy from the East arrived last night."

"Where in the East?"

"The Kingdom of Prester John."

"Who is Prester John?"

"Have you lived under a rock? Prester John is the virtuous Christian patriarch who has ruled for centuries over a lost Christian nation in the Indies."

"For centuries? How old *is* this king?"

"No one knows. Some say he is immortal and descended from the Three Magi, who taught him the secrets of escaping death."

"And you call *me* a fool?"

"Mind your tongue," Eannes ordered. "The Old Man has devoted forty years of his life to searching for Prester John."

"What does the arrival of this emissary have to do with me?"

"We require a translator. The African legate carries a communiqué from the Prester. Fortunately, the envoy had the foresight to bring a slave from the Prester's court who speaks Arabic. Did you think we chose you for the Order because of your fearsome skill with the sword?"

Pero now regretted having acceded to his father's insistence that he learn the infidel tongue. He had discovered to his dismay that these Tomar knights were bent on using him as a scribe rather than training him to become a mariner. He fantasized each night about escaping; he would do anything to avoid being locked in some dusty scriptorium to waste away his life copying manuscripts. "Why would the Old Man care about a monarch on the far side of the world?"

"We suspect it involves Jerusalem."

Pero stopped climbing again. "The infidels have governed Palestine for decades. They would never allow a Christian prince to visit the Holy City."

"Who said anything about visiting? Was Moses not denied the privilege of accompanying the Israelites to the Promised Land?"

"Does the Old Man intend to wage another crusade?"

"I have not been informed of his intent."

Pero hurried to catch up. "What if this envoy is an imposter? The Moors could have sent him to seduce the Old Man to cross the sea and lose another army below the walls of Tangier."

"There are many in our Order who fear just such a catastrophe. And there is only one among us who can prevent it."

"Who, pray tell?

"You."

Pero cocked his ear, not sure he had heard correctly. "How could *I* possibly dissuade the Old Man from such a folly?"

"You will be the first to hear this message from Prester John and test its authenticity. The words of diplomats are often gilded with duplicity and clever ambiguities. You must be on your guard. Marry the meaning of the word to the facial betrayals of the deliverer. Your interpretation will be of vital importance."

Pero was stunned. "Then you must tell me more about this Indies king."

Eannes forced their pace. "His existence was first hinted at in Scripture. A disciple named John the Presbyter wrote the Second and Third Epistles. Some foreigners call that assignation 'Prester' as the term for a priest."

"Are you saying this Prester John walked with Christ?"

"Some churchmen assert that he did. In the Gospel of St. Mark, Christ told St. John that there were some among His disciples who would not taste death until they saw the Kingdom of God come to power. And in the Gospel of Saint John, Christ promised that his disciple John would not die."

Pero's jaw dropped. "Saint John who wrote the Gospel and this Prester John are the same man?"

"Perhaps."

"Then the Prester *is* immortal."

"The Old Man believes it is possible."

"Why has it taken so long for the Prester to communicate with us?"

"His kingdom is under infidel siege. He has sent many couriers, but until now only two have survived the perilous journey. Three centuries ago, the Byzantine emperor received a letter from the Prester begging assistance in his war against the unbelievers. We have a copy of this letter in our archives. The Old Man reads it every fortnight and on holy days."

"And did the Greek emperor send an army as requested?"

Eannes shook his head. "The letter gave no directions for reaching the Prester's kingdom. Twelve years later, Pope Alexander III deployed his physician into the darkest reaches of India to find the Prester and gain more information. The physician was never heard from again."

"That's it?" Pero was incredulous that so much was being risked on so little. "That's all the Old Man knows about this lost Christian king?"

Eannes hesitated as if debating the wisdom of revealing the last bit of information he had withheld. "The first letter warned the Holy Father to avoid a cabal of treacherous Frenchmen around him. In it, the Prester also pleaded with the Byzantines to put to death those knights called Templars."

Pero's eyes rounded. "That means the Templars must have found the Prester."

"The Old Man may be a dreamer, but even he would not launch an armada based on two suspicious letters. Do you not remember that the Templars were given refuge with our Order?"

"Of course I remember! And do *you* not remember that Templar shit tunnel that you dragged me through that night?"

Eannes snorted, bemused by the memory of that cruel test. "Our Order also took possession of the hunted Templar archives. Neither Rome nor the Castilians have ever been allowed to know that these records exist."

"But why would Prester John want the Templars killed?"

"He did *not* want them killed. That letter purported to be from the Prester was obviously a forgery. An unidentified enemy had tried to scheme the demise of the Templars."

"How then do we know this newly arrived emissary hasn't been sent by the same knaves who schemed against the crusader monks in the first place?"

Eannes fixed a stern gaze on Pero to drive home that very point. "The fate of our Order may well depend on your instincts for the truth. God save us."

Nobles from as far away as Évora and Sintra had crowded into the palace, eager to see the new envoy from the East. In the center of the hall, the Old Man circled a tall Nubian whose spine was as straight as a rod. Wrapped in purple robes and armed with a staff crowned by a silver cross, the black emissary seemed detached from the buzz of interest swirling around him. Next to him stood a dwarfish dark creature whose slovenly attire suggested that he was spawned from a tribe of lesser rank. Unable to communicate with the two foreigners, the Portuguese stood observing them in expectant silence, as if ogling exotic beasts.

The Old Man caught sight of Pero, and a flash of excitement filled his baggy eyes. He eagerly motioned the squire to him. "It is time you earned your keep, *menino*. Ask our guest here to grace us with his name and purpose."

Nervous from the hundreds of eyes now on him, Pero cleared his throat and directed the question to the ambassador's slave, who relayed it in a language that sounded similar to Hebrew. Receiving the reply, Pero duly translated, "He says his name is Jorge. He is a trusted councilor of the king you call Prester John. He has traveled many years and suffered great hardships to bring salutations from the Monarch of the Indies to the great Father of the Western Seas."

The chamber hummed with thrilled whispers.

The Old Man grasped the ambassador's slender palms in welcome.

Seeing that the Nubian did not understand the gesture, Pero whispered an explanation. Informed of its intent, the ambassador bowed in gratitude.

Impatient to proceed with matters of state secrecy, the Old Man waved the disappointed courtiers and ladies from the hall. Then, he led the Nubian envoy into his private study, followed by Eannes, Pero, the Seneschal, and the envoy's translator. As the doors closed, the Old Man ordered up two goblets of wine and offered one to his guest. "Our finest from the Douro Valley. I think you will find it much preferable to the French vintages."

The Nubian ambassador stared at the cup. Advised of its contents by Pero, the envoy graciously declined the offer and spoke an apology.

Pero explained to the Old Man, "He says his vows do not allow him to partake of the nectar of the vine."

The Old Man was even more intrigued. "What vows are those?"

Pero posed that question, and conveyed the envoy's reply. "The spiritual discipline known as the Qadosh."

The Old Man nodded, impressed by the envoy's pedigree. He whispered to Pero, "He is a member of the Therapeutae from the Theban desert."

The taller Nubian uttered what sounded like an ominous warning.

Pero stole a reluctant glance at Eannes, but finally he was driven to the task by the Old Man's insistent stare. "He says, my lord, that you will not live much longer unless you drink from the miraculous waters of India. His king, whom you call Prester John, wishes to join forces with yours to subdue the infidels."

Hearing that dire prophecy, the Old Man's mouth quivered slightly. "May God grant your good king's wish for me. Tell us more about him."

"My master's robes are woven by salamanders and washed each day in fire," Pero translated. "He is as ancient as the mountains and yet appears younger than you and me."

"How is that possible?" the Old Man inquired.

Pero translated: "He begs that you come to bathe in his Fountain of Youth and discover this miracle of Christ for yourself."

Time retrograded in the Old Man's lined face with each of the Nubian's astonishing claims. "Your homeland ... you called it India?"

"My liege's domain is so vast that it covers all three Indias," Pero translated.

These marvelous descriptions seemed to transform the Old Man into a guileless young dreamer who had already been immersed in the Prester's magical waters. "*Three* Indias?" When that assertion was confirmed with a nod, the Old Man asked hopefully: "From which India do you come?"

Pero felt a great burden of responsibility, for on this matter he sensed the Old Man required his protection. "The Middle India," he translated, uncertain if the emissary was being entirely truthful. "The greatest India of them all."

The Old Man's voice lifted in anticipation. "What route did you take to find us? Land or sea?"

Pero translated: "By land."

The Old Man turned toward the window and stole a glance at the Tagus. "Is there a way to reach your master's kingdom by water?"

Despite his qualms, Pero conveyed the envoy's answer. "He says vast sweeps of water surround his kingdom, but he can only attest to the land route that brought him here. He followed the setting sun. He had no maps or other means of finding you."

"Ask him how long his journey took."

"Ten years," Pero reported.

The Old Man was visibly shaken by the report of the journey's prohibitive length. After a moment of deep thought, he motioned for Eannes and the Seneschal to leave the room.

Eannes became alarmed. "My lord, these foreigners have been searched for weapons, but they may be trained to kill with their hands."

"The *menino* will stay with me."

"The squire is not capable of defending you should—"

"I said give me leave!" the Old Man shouted. "I stormed the walls of Ceuta! Do you think me incapable of defending my own quarters?"

Eannes bowed in contrition. Before departing with the seneschal, he glared a reminder at Pero of the high stakes at hand.

The Old Man locked the door and poured another cup of port to steel his nerves. He took pains to set the goblet firmly on the table so as not to betray his affliction. After several moments of troubled contemplation, he asked the Nubian, "Does your king hail from the lineage of St. Anthony?"

Informed of the question, the taller Nubian brought a necklace from under his robe. He displayed, hanging on it, a silver Tau cross engraved with a rose at the meeting point of its beams.

The Old Man seemed to recognize the icon. "Do your fellow Thebans still protect the mysteries of the Egyptian artificers?"

"It is so," Pero translated the reply.

As the Old Man asked the next question, he grasped Pero's forearm in rising hope. "And the mystic dimensions of Solomon's Temple?"

For the first time, the Nubian displayed a moment of mental disruption.

Pero sensed that he had not expected that question.

The Nubian raised his staff.

Pero jumped in front of the Old Man to defend him. But instead of striking, the Nubian smiled to reassure Pero, and then drew with his staff an image in the frost on the pane:

The Old Man nodded at the drawing, as if it held some deep significance for him, then he erased its imprint in the frost with his hand. He removed the medallion cross of the Order of Christ from around his neck and gave it to the Nubian as a gift for Prester John. The Nubian's eyes watered with emotion.

Turning to depart, the Old Man glared a silent warning at Pero that he must never speak of what he had just witnessed.

THIRTEEN

Jaq dragged Alyssa away from the flirting gladiator in the short toga who was guarding the tourist entrance to the Colosseum. "Come on, Cleopatra. Enough with the snakes already."

"Will you lighten up!" Alyssa groused as she looked longingly over her shoulder at her Spartacus. "He wanted my number."

Jaq rolled her eyes. "He already had your number. 1-800-ROMANORGY. I've heard of falling for men in uniform, but at least you could make it one from this century."

Alyssa huffed. "If I'm not snuggling up behind an Italian hunk on a scooter before we leave, this'll be the last trip we take together. Just because you don't …" She caught herself.

Jaq turned on her. "Don't what?"

Alyssa threw up her hands in exasperation. "I swear you must have been one of those Vestal Virgins in a previous life. Come on. Let's have some fun. It's been three days and all we've done is climb old rocks. Mario told me—"

"He told you his name was Mario? More likely Alexi or Serg. No Italian man would stand in a clown suit posing for photos. They ship these guys in from Croatia and teach them a few lines to fool naïve American girls."

Alyssa brushed Jaq's hand from her arm. "God, you've turned into such a cynic! Just because Paul's gone doesn't mean you'll never fall in love again!"

"Paul has nothing to do with it. And just because I don't throw myself gaga at every guy doesn't mean I'm cynical."

"You'd change your tune if that grave robber showed up singing under your balcony."

"Don't be ridiculous."

"You haven't tried to find him?"

Jaq wouldn't look at her directly. "Of course not."

Alyssa locked on her until she relented. "A mysterious man swoops down and saves your life, and you brush him off? You are a cold, cold woman."

"What am I supposed to do? Order an INTERPOL search?"

In the brittle silence of a momentary truce, they headed up the Via Di S. Giovanni de Laterano to find a good trattoria for lunch. A few blocks east of the Colosseum, they passed an ancient church whose slender marble columns appeared almost feminine next to the ponderous pillars of the classical era. Jaq veered off the sidewalk to read the inscription: *Basilica di San Clemente: 1ˢᵗ Century foundations.*

"No!" Alyssa cried. "I can't take another stained-glass window of some saint being sliced up like lox!"

"This one's really old."

"I'm starving!"

"Five more minutes. I'll buy lunch."

"And go club-hopping with me tonight."

Jaq caved on the bargain, and they stepped inside. Given the noon hour, there wasn't anyone else in the stunning twelfth-century basilica. The docents were taking their lunch breaks, a Roman ritual more religiously practiced than the Mass. She circled the apse and gazed up at a bronze mosaic featuring a large crucifix that sprouted sprawling vines. All of this effusive Catholic imagery seemed so foreign to her newfound understanding of Christ and His teachings. She peeked inside the sacristy and spied a stairway. "There's another church below us."

Alyssa grunted. "Oh, just great."

Jaq saw that the smoke-stained crypt was much gloomier than the basilica above it. Faded frescoes lined its bricked walls, and a rough-hewn baptismal font sat in the center of a flag-stoned floor that held the tombs of saints.

Revolted, Alyssa reflexively curled her shoulders to her neck. "Ick! Are these the catacombs?"

The cavern reminded Jaq of her horrid experience in those underground churches at Lalibela. She shuddered with a frisson of dread. "I don't think so. I bet this was one of the churches used by the first Christians in Rome." She threaded past several precarious pillars and found another descending stairwell at the end of the aisle.

"No!" Alyssa shouted.

Not to be denied, Jaq descended the narrow corridor of steps. "I'm really getting my money's worth." Down another level, she found a complex of caves and heard water trickling from somewhere deep beyond the walls. Above her head, esoteric symbols and geometric patterns had been carved into the stucco.

"Let's get out of here," Alyssa begged, looking downright spooked.

Jaq gasped with delight. "You've got to see this!"

Alyssa tiptoed over, as if expecting at any moment to encounter a colony of flesh-eating bats. Jaq showed her an elongated cavern with rows of stone seats. The den resembled a small locker room in an old basketball field house. In the middle of the narrow aisle, a rectangular stone altar sat elevated on a marble base. The altar's facing depicted a carved soldier cutting the throat of a bull. Alyssa backed away from the gruesome image. "What *is* this place?"

Jaq ran her hand across a faint red stain. "Maybe sacrifices were performed in here."

"On *humans*? I swear I'm gonna freak!"

Jaq led her back toward the entrance. She was about to ascend the stairs when some words etched into the wall caught her eye. "Do you see what I see?"

"Looks like …" Alyssa slowly turned toward Jaq, convinced that somebody had to be playing a trick on them. "SATOR."

"I thought you said there was no such word."

"Maybe it's not Latin," Alyssa said. "Anyway, it's probably just one of those weird coincidences. You know, like when you break up with a guy and suddenly you think you see him everywhere. The brain creates patterns where none exist."

"Yeah," Jaq said, unconvinced. "Maybe."

Jaq watched with annoyance as Alyssa savored the last of her pistachio gelato and washed it down with another sip of the Brunello di Montalcino wine. When the Diva of Dupont Circle finally let out an orgasmic groan, Jaq summoned the bill, having suffered quite enough of the grand performance. "You sure you don't want to lick the dish?"

Alyssa snuck a look at the total on the check. "Ouch! I hope that little excursion to the Church of Saint Creepy was worth forty-seven euros. The waiter winked at me, so add an extra five to the tip."

Jaq opened her wallet and counted out the cash. "Extortion is one of the seven deadly sins. You should go to confession. You won't have trouble finding a priest around here."

"That's the last must-do on my itinerary. I plan to have a few more sins to atone for by the end of the trip. So, what now? I hear the eye candy at the Trevi Fountain is mandatory."

"I think I'll take a stroll through the Forum."

Alyssa flipped her head back in exasperation. "You're hopeless! You're not going to meet a guy in that garbage pile!"

They paid and walked out. The sun was lost to low winter clouds and the temperature had dropped ten degrees. Shivering in her light dress, Alyssa rubbed her bare shoulders for warmth, until Jaq offered her maroon jacket with the padded shoulders.

Alyssa wrapped herself. "Are you sure you won't need it?"

"Our hotel is on my way,. I'll stop in and get my sweater."

Alyssa donned her new sunglasses and tossed her head sideways, sending shocks of blond hair flowing in the wind. "You know what would really put the cork in the bottle. Could I also borrow your black scarf?"

"How about my panties, too?"

"Don't be moronic." Alyssa sashayed off, imitating a European model on the runway. "You know I don't wear any."

"Wait!" Jaq shouted. "When should we meet up?"

"Eight in the lobby. I'll call if I get lucky."

"I didn't bring my Blackberry."

Alyssa tossed over her phone. "I'll use my Italian lover's."

With the threat of rain, Jaq nearly had the Forum to herself. Alyssa was right, she realized. So many ruins made her feel old, as if the weight of the ages was crushing her shoulders. The men here didn't even glance at her when she walked by. Maybe she *was* sending out the wrong vibes. She tried to fake a seductive saunter, but it just took too much energy.

A young male guide leading a group of coeds caught her eye and smiled.

What the hell, she thought. She gave him the "look-down-because-I'm-shy" treatment. To her surprise, he motioned her over. She was amazed; this positive-thinking stuff worked fast. If nothing else, she'd at least have a story tonight to fend off Alyssa's pestering.

"American?" the guide asked her.

"Is it that obvious? I usually get mistaken for a foreigner."

"Only Americans walk the Forum alone. It is too sad a place to visit without one's family and friends. Please, join us. My name is Gerard. I'm a student here at the American University."

"Looks like you're near the end of your tour."

"I've saved the best for last. This is the Arch of Titus. My favorite monument."

The guide's female students bristled with glares, jealous of the attention that their intended conquest was giving her.

"Gerard," purred one of the coeds, who wore a skimpy tank top despite the dropping temperature. "Will you tell us why you like this ruin so much?"

"Yes," another girl begged. "Tell us, Gerard."

Oblivious to their flirting, the handsome but studious guide pointed to a bas-relief carved on the eastern side of the massive arch that depicted Roman soldiers hauling off loot after a battle. "What does that look like to you?"

"Men moving furniture," said one of the college girls.

"*Jewish* furniture," the guide said. "Furniture owned by my ancestors in Israel. The large object that resembles a candelabrum is called a menorah by my people."

"You're Jewish?" Jaq asked him.

He nodded. "I was raised in New York, but my family came from Rome. Their neighborhood was near the Theatre of Marcellus, along the Tiber. It's still called the Jewish ghetto."

"They let Jews live near the popes?"

"In the fifteenth century, Queen Isabella expelled all Jews from Spain. Nine thousand of my people came here to Rome begging for a place to live. They were offered food if they converted to the Church. Some continued to practice Judaism in secret."

Jaq gazed up at the scenes of pillage sculpted on the arch. "And this memorial has some connection to those Jews?"

He nodded. "In seventy A.D., the Roman general Titus sacked Jerusalem and carried off the Temple treasures to Rome. His brother Domitian erected this arch to commemorate the victory. My ancestors would have been forced to look upon it in humiliation."

The college girls were no longer paying attention to the lecture, but Jaq was suddenly very interested. "Where were these treasures kept?"

"No one knows for sure," the guide said. "Perhaps in the Temple of Saturn. It was that building down there in front of the Capitoline. When the Goths and Vandals overran Rome in the fifth century, the Church tried to save the Imperial Treasury."

"The Vatican took possession of the Jerusalem artifacts?"

The guide swept his arm across the crumbled horizon. "Look around you. Basilicae. Pontiffs. The Curia. All were Roman institutions before being adopted by the Christians. No one has chosen to do as the Romans did with more tenacity or success than has the Catholic Church."

"So, are you're saying that if the Romans protected the Temple relics, then the Vatican would have continued to protect them?"

Instead of answering her question, the guide wrote something on the blank side of a tour brochure and gave it to her. "I have to take my students back to the university now. Perhaps we will meet again."

She thanked him and slipped the brochure into her purse. He was good-looking and smart, but she had no intention of calling a younger man. Still, she had to admit it felt good to be hit on. Alyssa would be impressed. Damn, she should have taken a picture for evidence. Did he include his last name with his phone number? She pulled out the brochure to check what he had written:

The Vatican: Its History—Its Treasures. By Ernesto Begni, James Grey, and Thomas Kennedy. In the Vatican Library.

What did *that* mean?

She didn't know whether to be grateful or insulted.

Jaq entered the lobby of the Vatican Library, and a young priest with cropped red hair and a melancholic Irish face greeted her with a half-hearted *buongiorno*. He led her down a long corridor in silence and escorted her into a spacious office that featured an immense Florentine desk embossed with the Vatican armorial seal and walls hung with a sixteenth-century mural of Herod's massacre of the innocents.

Moments later, a stately *eminence grise* draped in a red cassock entered from a side door. His bald, vein-laced head could have been the model for a bust of Julius Caesar. He offered his chalky hand in a half-hearted welcome. "I am sorry to have kept you waiting, Ms. Quartermane. I am Guissepe Bertolotti, Cardinal Protector of the Vatican Library. You must forgive my insecure English."

Jaq wasn't sure if protocol required her to shake his hand or kiss his ring, so she compromised with a slight bow. "I didn't expect to speak with a cardinal."

The cardinal smiled weakly. "I assure you, the title is more impressive than my duties. If a *gabinetto* here does not flush properly, the problem eventually reaches my desk. You have met my assistant, Father Mulcahey. He is the vice-prefect of the Archives."

"The Secret Archives?"

The cardinal sighed. "If it were in my power, I would posthumously excommunicate the culprit who gave it that name. I am afraid there is very little secretive about them. Scholars from all over the world have access to the collections."

She glanced at the young priest for a confirmation of that claim, but he maintained an inscrutable gaze on his superior. She turned back to the cardinal and apologized, "Forgive me for calling on such short notice."

The cardinal offered her a chair. "We are always pleased to assist our good friend, the U.S. State Department."

"My visit is of a personal nature."

"Do you require spiritual counseling?"

"Some of my friends would say so, but that's another matter. I have a question that involves an investigation into the death of a colleague." She showed him the news clipping from Paul's wallet. "The victim was carrying this on the night of his murder. It indicates that a delegation of rabbis from Israel petitioned the Vatican for permission to search the basements of the Holy See for relics taken from the Temple in Jerusalem."

As the cardinal read the clipping, his possessed demeanor remained fixed, but he removed a kerchief from under his cassock and daubed the beads forming on his upper lip. "Very sad."

"I'm sorry?"

"What now passes for journalism. Whoever wrote this sensationalist story has launched you into, how do you say it in your country, a blind alley? No such meeting or request ever took place. There exist certain organizations with nefarious agendas. They spread lies like this to foment their conspiracy theories."

"But this appeared in the *International Herald Tribune.*"

"All the more lamentable," the cardinal said. "I wish I could be of more help, Miss Quartermane. But we have no such items in our possession."

"Could they have been stored in forgotten vaults?"

He shook his head firmly. "Every box and bone here are inventoried."

She showed him a photocopied page from the book about the Vatican treasures that the cute guide in the Forum had cited in his note to her. She had found the work in the Vatican library while waiting for this meeting and had highlighted a passage:

> *Naturally, one of the duties of the architectural department has been to prepare various plans of the Vatican Palace, and its officers feel always incited to inquire further into the mysteries of the buildings. But, notwithstanding all their past inquiries, it still happens that wherever extensive alterations or repairs are undertaken they stumble across some stairway of whose existence no one had been aware. Consequently, however exact they may be for the main divisions of the palace, none of the plans remains for long entirely reliable in all its details regarding the portions which have been used perhaps for centuries as living rooms or magazines, or perhaps left entirely unoccupied.*

The cardinal removed his spectacles to collect his thoughts. "I suppose anything is possible. All I can tell you is that we have never found such relics. Now, if you will excuse me, I have a delegation from Mexico waiting. Father Mulcahey will show you out."

Jolted by his abrupt retreat into coldness, she stood and thanked him, then walked toward the door. Halfway out, she turned. "This morning, I visited a church near the Lateran."

The cardinal looked up with irritation from the paperwork on his desk. "There are many churches in that part of the city."

"The Basilica of San Clemente."

His mood lightened. "One of my favorites. St. Clemente was our third pope. He was martyred by being tied to an anchor and thrown into the sea."

"There was an unusual chamber deep below the church."

"The Mithraeum."

"I'm not familiar with that term," she said.

"Mithraism was a rival to Christianity during the first two centuries. San Clemente was built atop a private apartment that included a temple to Mithras. We have only a partial understanding of Mithraism's tenets. Adherents passed on their mysteries by word of mouth. They worshipped a sun god called Sol Invictus and sacrificed bulls in a resurrection rite. The cult was popular with the Roman legions. It might have overtaken us but for one flaw."

"Which was?"

"It was an all-male sect."

"In fact, your Eminence," the young priest interjected. "There have been recent studies suggesting that women may have been admitted into some of the Mithraic rites."

The cardinal seemed both surprised and peeved by the correction. "Indeed?" He turned back to Jaq and said coldly, "Perhaps Father Mulcahey here can better instruct you on the subject." He returned to the in-box on his desk, indicating that his offer of hospitality had expired anew.

Escorted back to the main entrance, Jaq apologized to the young priest. "I hope I didn't get you into trouble back there."

He looked shaken. "I shouldn't have spoken."

"Do you know a lot about this Mithraism?"

He seemed hesitant to admit to it. "My order, the Irish Dominicans, was placed in charge of the Basilica of San Clemente and its restoration. I spent three years digging into its foundations."

She drew him from the hall into an alcove for privacy. "On the lowest level there, I saw a word carved near the sacrificial altar. I think it was 'SATOR.'"

The priest became increasingly nervous. "My advice to you is to forget what you saw and preserve your sanity."

The warning confounded her. "I need to know what it means."

The priest glanced around the corner. "SATOR is the first line of an ancient Latin palindrome." He opened his scheduling journal and wrote five lines:

$$
\begin{array}{ccccc}
S & A & T & O & R \\
A & R & E & P & O \\
T & E & N & E & T \\
O & P & E & R & A \\
R & O & T & A & S
\end{array}
$$

He quickly tore the page from his journal and slipped it to her. "The words can be read in any direction. The ancients believed that such word squares possessed magical powers. For centuries, scholars have wasted their careers trying to unlock the secrets of this one. There is something insidious in its hold on the soul."

"But what does this word game have to do with the Mithraeum?"

"The SATOR square has been found inscribed at several sites connected to Mithras. The most noteworthy example is at Herculaneum."

"Near Pompeii?"

He nodded. "The impact of the lava from the Vesuvian eruption was the only reason the word square was preserved there. There were no doubt many other examples in the classical world that have been lost to time."

She looked down and saw that ROTAS was part of the square. Weren't those the letters carved on the Lalibela pillar? She wondered if there could be a connection between the SATOR square and the Ethiopian name for God. If so, what had that dying Ethiopian priest been trying to say with his message scribbled in myrrh on the bones?

"Father, did this religion of Mithras ever reach Africa?"

Footsteps echoed down the hallway, draining the color from the priest's ruddy face. His eyes darted off from her waiting inspection, but finally he managed a last, tremulous whisper. "If you could provide me with a telephone number, Ms. Quartermane, perhaps I can forward more information."

"Yes, of course." She handed him her State Department business card. "Thank you for your help." She walked alone toward the exit and remembered that her home cell number on the card was useless. "Wait!" She hurried back, marked out her number on the card, and wrote Alyssa's cell number on top of it. "This is where I can be reached while I'm in Rome."

The priest slipped the card into his breast pocket, and hurried off.

The skies had cleared, so she decided to take the long way back to the hotel by walking the banks of the Tiber. On the route, she passed the imposing Castel Sant'Angelo, the round mausoleum that once held the remains of the emperor Hadrian and was later converted into a fortress to protect the popes. She spied a cafe across the way. In need of an energy boost, she decided to drop in for a chai latte. Before she could order, Alyssa's phone buzzed with a text message:

SUBIACO A RK.

Subiaco? Why did that name sound familiar?

She checked the sending number—"Restricted." Just great. Alyssa was probably texting from God-knows-where about some hot new club. She didn't even leave an address. Worse, Alyssa had written the message in her usual Internet pidgin of chopped words and anagrams. She didn't have a clue what it meant.

She looked around for a tech-savvy American student who might be able to translate the slang. A ditzy girl hanging onto her boyfriend's arm seemed the best bet. "Excuse me. *Parla* English?"

"Sure," the girl said, chomping on gum.

She showed the girl her phone screen. "My friend left me a text message. Can you tell me what this means?"

The girl stared at Jaq as if she were dense. "Subiaco."

"Is that a dance place or a restaurant?"

The Italian boy hugging the gum-happy girl broke away long enough to explain, "It is a town outside Rome. About an hour away."

Jaq cursed under her breath. Alyssa must have sweet-talked her way into a motorcycle ride to the outskirts of the city with some hot-to-trot guy. Now she was probably stranded. "What about the rest of the message?"

The girl read it aloud, cracking her chewing gum. "'*Subiaco a rk*' ... Subiaco's a wreck."

"What does *that* mean?"

The girl was half listening, more interested in getting another kiss from the boy. "Sounds like it's a cool scene there. Free drinks and dancing, maybe. Is this your daughter texting you?"

Jaq scowled. "We're the same age. And why would calling something a wreck mean a good thing?"

The Roman boy-toy chimed in with his opinion. "You know. It's like when you Americans say, 'Jon Stewart is a riot.' He is not really a riot. He is just funny. Or, like that blond over there is nasty. It means she is sexy."

His girlfriend threw an elbow into his side.

Jaq interrupted their spat to ask another question. "Are there lots of bars and clubs in Subiaco?"

"No," said the boy, rubbing his thumped ribs. "Just monks."

"Monks?"

The boy moved in on his girlfriend for a makeup kiss. Surfacing to find Jaq still waiting for an explanation, he told her, in a polite way, to buzz off. "Take the Metro Line from the Castro Pretorio."

Stepping off the bus, Jaq had to crane her neck to take in the full height of Subiaco's hillside terraces. Near a path that climbed toward a complex of ancient stone buildings, she saw a rotund monk tending tomato plants. She walked over and asked him, "Is this the abbey?"

"If not," the monk said with an Australian accent, "then I've been sleeping in someone else's bed by mistake for forty years. Are you here to see the abbot?"

"To tell you the truth, I'm not sure why I'm here."

Amused, the monk waddled over to the fence to help her. "We get more than our share of young women like you who have been moved by the Holy Spirit. The convent is across town."

"I've not come to become a nun, although I could easily qualify in certain departments." She showed him the text message on the phone. "Is there any place here that might attract a frisky young woman looking for a good time?"

The monk studied the message, and laughed. "Ah, Lord in Heaven. I fear you've been the victim of a cruel hoax."

"What do you mean?"

"The Subiaco Ark. Not a week goes by that we don't get some harebrain coming here convinced that the Ark of the Covenant is secreted away in our caves. A few days ago, we even had a burglary."

She realized that Alyssa had mistakenly typed a space between A and RK in haste. She would wring her neck for sending her off on this little scavenger hunt. Alyssa must have read about the burglary in the paper and sent the message as a joke. "Why would anyone think the Ark of the Covenant was brought *here*?"

The monk launched himself over the fence with a wobbly leap and landed with a thud. "I'll show you." He led her up an ancient path called the Via de Monasteri and toward a cluster of religious buildings built into the face of the mountain. "At one time, there were twelve monasteries here. Now we have only two. This one was the home of St. Benedict."

"The founder of the Benedictines?"

The monk nodded. "He and his twin sister lived in these mountains. Western monasticism was born on the very spot where you're walking. The area is riddled with caverns and underground streams." He led her inside a chapel built over Benedict's cave, the *Sacra Speco*. "This is as far as we can go, for now. The other caves haven't been excavated."

"And the Ark?"

"One of our brothers moved to the States several years ago. He created a stir by telling a researcher that he had once been taken to a cave four stories below this monastery and shown the disassembled pieces of the Tabernacle and Ark."

"You don't believe him?"

"I have never seen such relics. What others claim as the truth can only be judged by God."

"If someone *was* lying about the Ark, why would they promote Subiaco as the site for its storage?"

The monk pointed to the surrounding heights. "The Emperor Nero built a summer home here. When the Empire collapsed, the popes used Subiaco as one of their retreats. During the barbarian invasions, some of Rome's most valuable possessions were hidden in those caves above us. Many have never been explored. If someone wanted to spread a wild tale, I suppose this would be the perfect place to set it."

It was already 8:30 p.m. when the bus from Subiaco pulled back into Rome. Dead tired and a half-hour late for her rendezvous with Alyssa, Jaq hurried up the Via Novembre IV. She turned the corner and saw Alyssa pacing impatiently at the entrance to the hotel. Scooters threaded the traffic on the busy street. She was about to wave at Alyssa when her phone buzzed. She looked down at the text message: EMBASSY NOW!

Strange. Alyssa had no phone in her hand. So who was texting her?

A black Mercedes sedan sped around the corner and swerved across the curb onto the sidewalk. The car slammed into Alyssa and sent her airborne.

My God!

She tried to rush to Alyssa, but the heavy traffic prevented her from crossing the street. The black sedan squealed off before she could make out its license number. Alyssa, in sunglasses, lay motionless, bleeding and contorted. She was still wearing the borrowed coat and scarf.

Jaq gasped. *The driver of that car meant to hit me!*

She dodged several motorcycles and finally made it across the street to fight through the hovering crowd. She pressed '118' on Alyssa's phone for the Italian emergency number. When a voice answered, she begged for an ambulance, but the operator couldn't understand her.

She looked up. The black Mercedes was coming toward her from the opposite direction. The driver slowed down as he passed. She tried to identify him, but sunglasses hid his features. He looked directly at her and turned quickly for a second glance, as if not believing what he had just seen. Then, he spoke into a mobile phone as he sped off.

She shuddered—the murderer now knew he had hit the wrong woman. She quickly cancelled the emergency call before it could be traced. But who had texted her to go to the U.S. Embassy? The compound was on Via Veneto in the modern section of the city, too far to run. If she waited here or tried to take Alyssa to the hospital, they would both be killed. She couldn't bring herself to abandon her.

A cab sitting on a far corner wheeled a U-turn and beat two other taxis to the curb. The driver rolled down his window and shouted, "Taxi?"

Panicking, she squeezed Alyssa's limp hand and whispered to her bleeding ear, "I'm going for help." Circling in despair, she pleaded with the Italians crowding around. "Somebody please call an ambulance!"

As the crowds converged, she climbed into the cab, shaking with terror.

The driver slid back a small window in the Plexiglas pane that separated the front and back seats. "*Dove, signora?*"

"U.S. Embassy!"

The cabbie clicked the doors locked. "Much crime here." He kept watching her in the rear-view mirror. "Better to be safe."

"Please hurry!" She looked back at the sidewalk, praying that Alyssa was still alive. An ambulance rushed past, weaving through cars and changing lanes. When the cab turned the corner, an Italian-looking man rushed after it, yelling and shaking his fist.

The cabbie ignored the irate man, who came up pounding on his window. "Very busy today," the cabbie said casually. "Many people want ride."

She noticed that her driver pressed the accelerator with his left foot.

Was he crippled?

They were heading south. But the embassy was in the Quirinale neighborhood, in the other direction. She knocked on the Plexiglas. "The United States Embassy."

"Yes, yes. Two embassies here." He slid the slot shut and locked it.

She tried to focus. There was another embassy for the Vatican? But then shouldn't he be heading for the Tiber? She studied the license photo. The picture wasn't of the man behind the wheel—it was the man who had been chasing them on foot! This driver looked Middle-Eastern and had a tattoo with Arabic calligraphy on his arm. And he hadn't turned on the meter. She shouted through the glass, trying to hide the fright in her voice, "I'll get out here and walk!"

The driver refused to slow down. "Bad neighborhood."

She tried the door latch, but it was locked. He was picking up speed and heading toward the outskirts of the city, past the Aurelian walls. The route turned into a cobblestone road lined with trees and the ruins of tombs overgrown with weeds. This was the only cab in Rome she'd seen with a seat divider. She tried to slide open the small window. It wouldn't budge. She was trapped.

He's taking me into the countryside to kill me.

She gasped in recognition—*this* cabbie was the same man who had been driving the black Mercedes.

He must have stolen the cab while she was tending to Alyssa.

She searched for a way to reach him. The only entry into the front was the space under the driver's seat, but the distance was too far to reach his foot.

She opened her purse, careful to keep it hidden. The mace was useless. She rifled through her make-up kit. A small pair of scissors. No good. Needles. Lipstick. Coins. ...

The retractable umbrella.

It was a long shot, but she had no other option.

She punched the dispatch calling number shown on the cab's license into Alyssa's cell phone. Then she quietly slid the umbrella under the driver's seat and aimed its top end at the accelerator. Her eyes darted from the driver's right foot to the road as she waited for the next turn when he would have to brake.

A tight bend was coming up.

She cradled the phone in her lap and pressed 'ENTER' to send the call.

A second later, the taxi dispatch radio squawked.

The driver reached for the receiver just as the turn approached. His foot slid off the accelerator and touched the brake.

She dropped to the floor, shoved the umbrella under the seat, and pressed the button on the handle.

The umbrella's retractable arm shot forward.

They skidded off the road—she went flying into the Plexiglas. The cab rolled and came to a smoking halt. Tasting blood, she revived and saw the driver slumped over the wheel. She kicked at the door and the latch gave way. She crawled out and stumbled to her knees. The driver stirred and moaned.

She ran down rows of ancient tombs and looked back. The driver, bloodied and cursing, was limping after her. Dozens of tourists poured out of an old church. She threaded into the throngs and glanced over her shoulder. The driver shoved the tourists aside and yelled at them in a desperate attempt to find her. She tried to sneak over the turnstile.

A female guard stopped her. "*Chiuso!*"

"I have to get in!"

The guard, suspicious, stared at her. "We are closing."

Jaq stole another glance behind her. The departing crowd had swallowed up the man chasing her. She ducked behind a pillar and was forced to cool her heels while a lecturing professor led a gaggle of British tourists from the church.

"There are twenty miles of galleries on four levels," the professor told his group. "One hundred and seventy thousand burial places have been unearthed, including the tombs of six popes."

An old Brit biddy on the tour asked the professor, "Why did the Christians want to be buried in there?"

The professor explained, "The Romans would not allow them to be interred within the city's walls. They practiced cremation and thought the Christian obsession with burial and resurrection quite bizarre." Hearing that, Jaq closed her eyes in shame, reminded of Paul's cruel end as the professor went on, "The catacombs are so numerous that many have never been explored. I suspect more than a few poor souls hiding down here never found their way out. Many probably went mad."

As the last of the tourists trickled out, the guard began locking the doors.

Jaq glanced toward the portico steps.

The taxi driver had spotted her again and was closing on her fast.

Frantic, she turned to the guard and, pointing to her own eyes, begged, "My sunglasses. I left them in the church. I'll only be a second."

The exasperated guard finally waved her through.

Jaq rushed into the nave, passing a sign that said: *This way to the Catacombs of St. Sebastiono.* She hurried down the stairs and came to a maze of narrow passages slotted by burial niches. The place looked like a giant honeycomb. Voices echoed down the stairwell. The halogens, fed by ceiling wires, began turning off. What if she became trapped down here? She pulled out the phone and used its monitor for light, shutting it on and off to save the battery.

Italian voices came closer.

Blind and lost, she knew she couldn't outrun them. She climbed up the wall slots and slithered inside the highest burial niche. Three shadows passed by with flashlights. The beam stopped at the niche below her. She said a prayer in relief that the searcher of this row had been too lazy to climb the platform.

Slowly, the voices receded. A door was bolted.

She released a held breath—and began to hyperventilate. She wiggled out of the niche and leapt down. She tried to retrace her steps, clinging close to the pocked walls, and after several minutes of groping the walls, she saw a distance flicker of light. She edged closer and saw a homeless woman in a frayed shawl sitting near a kindling fire.

The woman clutched a bundle of clothes against her chest. She shouted to defend her spot, "*La mia casa!*"

Jaq raised her palms to calm the woman. "Is there another way out?" Seeing that the woman did not understand her question, she mimicked the motion of a climber ascending a rope.

The old woman shook her head and pointed up. "*La Basilica.*"

Jaq figured the guy chasing her would probably stake out the entrance. She pulled twenty euros from her pocket and offered to buy the bundle of clothes.

The next morning, Jaq remained hidden behind a tomb until the day's first group of tourists entered the catacombs. Disguised in one of the homeless woman's ankle-length dress, she wrapped her head in the shawl and fell in with a group of chattering Sicilian women who had come to Rome on a pilgrimage trip. As the women climbed the steps into the upper basilica and surfaced into the sunlight, she kept her head bowed and her back hunched.

She saw three sedans with darkened windows parked on the street opposite the public entrance to the catacombs.

The minutes seemed like hours as she waited at the stop with the other women. Finally, the public bus for downtown Rome came chugging up the hill. She merged into the boarding line and stole a glance back at the sedans.

When the door closed, she released a sigh of relief.

After an hour's ride into the city, she got off the bus near the U.S. Embassy in the Quirrinale and rushed to the guard station. She looked around for her pursuer while whispering to the Marine on duty. "My name's Quartermane. I work for the Office of Legal Advisor in Washington."

The Marine stared at her as if confronting a destitute American bag lady stranded overseas. She fished out her passport from the security pouch hanging under her blouse and flashed her photo ID page to him. Skeptical, he picked up the phone to confirm the unlikely claim. Astounded to discover that she was telling the truth, he buzzed her in.

A female consular officer came running down the hall. She was stopped in her tracks by Jaq's smelly disguise. "Ms. Quartermane?"

"Yes."

"We've been trying to reach you!"

Jaq threw her ratty shawl into a trashcan. "I got that from your message."

"Message?"

Jaq was perplexed by the woman's surprise. "Yes. Someone from this embassy sent a text to my friend's phone yesterday telling me to come here."

The consular officer acted equally puzzled. "We had no number for you."

Jaq struggled to fix her thoughts. Then who *did* send her that text message? No one else knew that she had Alyssa's phone.

"Mr. Ochley wants you to call him at once."

"Is there a secure office I can use?"

"Of course." The consular officer led her into a conference room.

Jaq locked the door and punched in Ochley's direct number on the phone. She put him on the speaker. "Bart, it's Jaq."

"Where the hell have you been?" he snapped. "I've been calling your hotel room all night."

She didn't know where to begin. "I've got a problem. My friend—"

"It'll have to wait. There was a bombing in France last night. Ten American citizens are dead, maybe more."

"Where?"

"Chartres."

She took a moment before responding; the last thing she needed right now was to betray her ignorance of international geography, but she had no choice. "Where is that?"

Ochley let out a groan of exasperation. "A goddamn tourist town south of Paris! Al Qaeda hit the cathedral there. We're short-handed at the Paris embassy. You need to get to Chartres today and handhold the injured. The French are taking the lead on the investigation. See what you can find out about the explosion without getting their noses bent out of shape. It may be part of a larger operation targeting Americans worldwide."

"But I can't just leave my friend here alone without—"

"Get to Chartres now, damn it! That's an order direct from McCrozier! Call me as soon as you arrive."

Ochley hung up before she could tell him about Alyssa.

Shaken, she tried to calm down. After several deep breaths, she dialed Rev. Merry's church office in Knoxville, and his secretary answered. "It's Jaqueline Quartermane. Is the Reverend available?"

"I'm sorry, no. He's on his annual spiritual retreat in Dallas. Rev. Haskins is handling all emergencies. Is there something he can help you with?"

"No. Thanks anyway." As she hung up, her eyes flooded with tears. She didn't know anyone in Rome to ask for help. She had no choice but to leave Alyssa behind at least for a day. She checked her wallet to see if she had enough euros for a ticket to France and a return ticket back. The journal page containing the five lines of the magical SATOR square dropped out of the money pocket.

She stared at it.

The Vatican priest … *he* must have sent her that text message. She had written Alyssa's number on the business card she gave him. But why would he tell her to come to the Embassy?

Wait … Had he also sent her the text about the Ark in Subiaco?

She buzzed the receptionist. "Could you please connect me with the Vatican Archives?" When the call light blinked seconds later, she picked up. "Father Mulcahey, please."

After a pause, the Vatican operator replied, "Father Mulcahey no longer works here."

"But I saw him there yesterday. Where he can be reached?"

"*Mi dispiace*. We have no forwarding information."

FOURTEEN

SATOR
APERO
TENET
OPERA
ROTAS

THE ALGARVE, PORTUGAL
AUGUST, 1456

Pero could barely contain his excitement as he lashed his pony across the rocky Barrocal headlands. Eannes had decided to reward the squires for finishing their first apprenticeship year with a journey south to tour the royal shipyards. Anxious to fulfill his dream of seeing the Atlantic, Pero kept pestering the mariner with the same question. "Will we reach Lagos before nightfall?"

Riding at Pero's side, the old mariner ignored that question and posed one of his own. "What signs do you see in the sky?"

Pero reined up and shrugged as he gazed at a clump of passing clouds.

"Perhaps if that gull up there shat its load on your head," Eannes barked, "you would take more notice of it."

"There must be a thousand of them up there. Are you telling us that one gull, among all the others, is a portent of something important?"

"I should send all three of you brainless weasels back for another year of scrubbing bedpans. Why do you suppose those birds are called *sea* gulls?"

Dias tried solving the mystery. "Because they live near the sea?"

"Brilliant!" Eannes mocked. "We have a scholar in our midst! How far can a gull fly before it must return to land?" When the boys shook their heads in ignorance, the mariner bored in on them. "If you were dying of thirst on the Sea of Darkness, would you find my question of more interest?"

"Gulls mean land," Zarco offered.

Eannes corrected him. "Gulls mean land *and* sea."

Pero suddenly connected the relevance of the lesson to his immediate concern. "How far can they fly?"

"That depends on a gull's age," Eannes said. "That one stalking us has the plumage of four years. An adult can manage only two leagues from land. Gulls never venture far from home."

Pero stood in his stirrups for a better view. "You mean … we are only two leagues from the sea?"

"Close your eyes." Eannes took the reins of Pero's pony and circled it several times. "Now point me toward the sea."

Coming to a jangled halt, Pero opened his eyes to find his finger aimed at the mountains. He heard Zarco and Dias laughing at him.

"A gull reveals range, not direction," Eannes explained. "You land mites take for granted the changing horizon to calibrate your bearings. One day you will be surrounded by an endless circle of nothingness."

Pero had a better idea. "I'll just consult a compass."

Eannes slapped the reins from Pero's haphazard grip to demonstrate a point. "And what if some half-wit drops the compass overboard, as was the fate dealt to Cadamosto?"

Pero shuddered at the thought. "How did the admiral regain his direction?"

"His skies were obscured for four nights," Eannes said. "He could not locate the Pole Star, so he had to rely on his knowledge of clouds."

Pero was appalled. "Now we have to learn different species of clouds?"

"You will learn hundreds of them, if you wish to sail one of the Old Man's caravels. During Cadamosto's ordeal, with the lives of his crew hanging in the balance, he searched for high, puffy clouds turning vertical and dark."

"Why those?" Dias asked.

Eannes slammed a fist into his palm to make a loud sound. "Because he knew the clash of earth and water creates such thunderheads."

Pero was becoming more adept at divining the direction Eannes would take when applying his Socratic method for teaching navigation, and he rushed ahead to the conclusion of the long-winded lesson. "I'm guessing the sea also has its own clouds."

Eannes nodded. "And yet another breed of cloud forms over the limen where Neptune's kingdom crashes onto *terra firma.*"

Pero searched the horizon. "What do such coastal clouds look like?"

"Something akin to that low marine layer just ahead."

Several moments passed before Pero fathomed what had just been revealed. Lagos and the sea lay just over those bluffs ahead. His heart pounded as he led Zarco and Dias in a dash across the grassy knolls. There, below them, lay a natural port with quays filled by caravels in various stages of completion, and beyond the harbor the Atlantic's angry chops hurdled against the escarpments. The squires were about to descend the angling path into Lagos when two sentries on horses intercepted them at the defile.

The sergeant of the patrol circled the three boys. "You barnacle maggots can return to the dung pit you crawled out from."

"We've been sent by Prince Henry," Pero insisted.

"You must be the three Magi. Which one of you comes bearing gold?"

"Perhaps they are hiding it in their ass cracks," the second soldier suggested.

The sergeant aimed his blade at Pero's throat. "Take off those breeches and we'll have a look."

Pero braced to be roughly abused when his tormentor took a rock to his head and catapulted from the saddle. The second soldier's horse spooked and sent him tumbling, too. The grounded sentries looked up to find Eannes, mounted, hovering over them.

Recognizing the famous mariner, the sergeant bolted to his knees. "We thought the whelps were trespassing. We've had a spate of magpies recently."

"Get up, you fools!" Eannes ordered the two grounded soldiers. "These are squires from Tomar. They will be working in the shipyards for the next year."

Pero traded stunned glances with his mates. "Working?"

"Did I fail to mention that?" Eannes asked with a devilish grin. "You three urchins are going to be building a new caravel from the keel up."

"That's yeoman duty!" Zarco cried, indignant.

Eannes slapped the back of Zarco's head to punish the squire's high opinion of himself. "One day you could end up being the lone carpenter on a voyage. You'll need to know your ship from bolt to caulk line."

Before the boys could prosecute their protest, Eannes herded them down the bluffs and into the harbor.

As they neared the first pier, the mariner spied a crusty old salt. "Adoa Gaspar, you cross-eyed mast crow! That bulkhead tilts askew!"

Hearing his name abused, an aged shipwright poked his sunburned head through the crease between two hull planks. He came bobbing up through the boards with fists balled. "Eannes the Caravel Wrecker! You wouldn't know a bulkhead from a rudder, you lime-brained minnow for a cod!"

Eannes dismounted and taunted the cursing shipwright toward him for a clash of fisticuffs. "That rudder you built for me on the *Sao Marcos* broke in half before I reached Bojador."

The shipwright growled like a trapped dog as he squeezed up through two ribbings and came charging at Eannes. "The cog was built for coastal scudding! You took it to the deeps and crushed it into kindling!"

Pero leapt from his pony to defend Eannes—only to be roughly repulsed for his gallantry. Dazed, he looked up from his knees to see the two old codgers breaking into wide grins and hugging each other.

"Blind *bastardo*!" Eannes howled in the friendly clench. "Your guild license should have been confiscated years ago!"

"Did you come all the way from Tomar to bobstay my *cajones*?"

Eannes kicked at the calves of the three wide-eyed squires to shoo them forward. "I've brought you another bevy of chicks to hatch."

Gaspar glared at the squires as if taking delivery of a cartload of steaming dung. "Ah, for the mercy of St. Gabriel, what have I done to deserve such Purgatory before death?"

Eannes slapped Gaspar on the shoulders in mock commiseration. "How goes the latest order for caravels?"

Gaspar shook his head wearily as he led his guests down the busy pier for a tour of the works in progress. "We'll have four finished by winter, God and weather willing. Always more tonnage! The Old Man expects the impossible!"

Behind Gaspar's back, Eannes imitated the shipwright's gyrations and expressions of outrage for the squires's amusement. "The Prince expects the impossible from all of us."

Gaspar would not be denied his rant. "The caravels must be swift and easily steered in shallow coastal waters, he orders me! Point them fifty degrees to the wind to reduce leeway! But they must also have hulls large enough to carry back fifty tons of cargo! I am not a fodering miracle worker!"

Grinning, Eannes nodded to the passing dockworkers and was welcomed with good-natured curses and seamen's taunts. As he strode down the pier, he asked Gaspar, "What sails has the Old Man commissioned?"

Gaspar scowled as if having been asked to give up a state secret. Finally, he revealed, "Lanteens mostly."

Pero had never heard of that description. "What is a lanteen?"

Eannes enjoyed Gaspar's leer of consternation at the naive question. "The lad has never sailed."

Gaspar made the sign of the cross to blunt what all within hearing distance considered the equivalent of a mortal sin. "Mary, Jesus, and Joseph! Has Portugal lost so many mariners that we must now scour the mountains for latrine rats to man our crews?"

"The lanteen," Pero reminded the two men, eager to change the subject.

While the two old sea comrades fell to exchanging insults again, Zarco explained to Pero the purpose of the lanteen. "The three-cornered sail is better for tacking on returns up the African coast."

"But if the caravel is too large," Dias reminded Zarcos, "the lanteen becomes difficult to handle."

Finished for the moment with upbraiding Eannes for his past wreckages, Gaspar turned to the squires and took over the instruction. "The lanteen always whispers a warning to inexperienced whelps: 'If you do not know me, do not touch me.'"

Pero tried to imagine another shape of sail. "What is the alternative?"

"The square-rigged," Gaspar said. "Navigation is always a trade-off. For coastal waters with hidden reefs and unknown rivers, a shallow hull with a single lanteen is advised. On the high seas, a deep hull with square sails on two masts offers the best chance to return with the prevailing trade winds. The Old Man expects me to build a caravel that serves both purposes."

Eannes led the boys toward a hull that was still being fitted with planks. "What strikes you unusual about this one, Master Pero?"

When Pero remained silent, unable to offer a guess, Zarco answered for his mystified friend. "Flush planking. If the boards are not clinked—"

"Overlapped," Dias explained for Pero's benefit.

"With nail cinches," Zarco continued, "water could leak through the caulking. But if these seals hold, the caravel will meet less drag, like poop sliding down a babe's bottom."

Gaspar whistled, impressed. "The lad knows his draughts."

Eannes took rare pity on Pero, who could not hide his shame at growing up landlocked. "This one hails from the Serra da Estrela forests. He understands timber."

"Is that so?" Gaspar decided to test Pero. "Which tree makes the best planking for a watertight hull, lad?"

"I would use oak," Pero said, straightening to enhance his authority on the matter. "The farther north it is timbered, the better its quality."

"Oak, eh?" Gaspar rubbed his chin, noncommittal. "Pray, tell us why."

"Oak produces long, straighter logs with few knots. It's good for splitting. Ash and elm wedge poorly. The best wood comes from colder climes."

Gaspar pressed his inquisition. "What about pine?"

Pero shook his head. "Pine has less tannin and dry rots faster."

Gaspar's eyes narrowed. "Do you know what timber we use here?"

Pero glanced at the split planks being hoisted to the caravel's ribbing. "Looks like pine."

Gaspar turned a shade darker at that declaration. "And if pine is inferior, lad, why then do you suppose we use it?"

Pero would not hazard a guess, suspecting it to be a trick question.

Gaspar's face suddenly purpled with anger. "Because King Dinis—"

"Furl that luffing tongue, Adao," Eannes warned.

But Gaspar was already running with the wind. "—chose to plant the royal forest in pines! The king reasoned that because pines grew faster than oaks, he would have his ships sooner! He didn't give a holy damn that his ships would last only half as long!"

While Gaspar bellowed on about the incompetence of the royal court, Pero searched the yard and saw that one of the caravels under construction had a darker hue with planks being nailed to a skeleton frame, a costly technique. Its aft castle rose so high that the vessel appeared to be unstable. "You're using oak for that one."

Gaspar suddenly quieted, impressed by the astute observation. "Indeed. Oak imported from the Argonne."

Pero was fascinated by the half-built behemoth that resembled a miniature city with separate quarters below deck. Caulkers lathered its seams with a double layer of resin while carpenters drove curved nails into its hull at intervals half the normal distance apart. The beak jutting from the bow held a latrine to prevent the fouling of the decks. On the mariner's platform, a mahogany *bussola* casing was fitted to protect its large compass against the elements.

Confirming Pero's insight, Eannes turned on Gaspar with a glower of suspicion. "The *menino* speaks true. This caravel has three masts and a length-to-beam ratio that has to be five-to-one. A deep draught, and by the breadth of its cargo hold, a seventy tonner at least."

"Built for a very long voyage," Zarco predicted. "It will be at the mercy of trade winds."

Gaspar slapped Pero's back, conspiring with his irritating of Eannes. "Perhaps the Old Man has something more in mind than dead reckoning by old shore monkeys like Eannes, eh lad?"

Eannes watched in rising disbelief as a third beam was hammered into a slot near the stern. "That mast is too small for a square sail. Tell me you're not matching it with a mizzen lanteen?"

Gaspar had a twinkle in his brine-scarred eye. "Such a combination has never been attempted." He winked at Pero and predicted, "It will take the finest sailor in Portugal to man its station."

Eannes was aghast at the engineering arrogance. "In the name of all that is holy! This abomination will violate every law of God's creation!"

"The Old Man's mathematicians have tested the calculations." Gaspar said, sounding less than convinced. "The Jews promise it won't heel ass over bow."

Sea lust filled Eannes's heart. "Who has been assigned its command?"

Gaspar affected outrage at the blatant attempt to wheedle the secret from him. "You ask me to divulge royal orders? That is a capital offense."

Pero stared longingly at the magnificent caravel in progress. In only two decades, the Old Man's armada had evolved from a few fishing barinels to include what would become the most impressive ship in all of Christendom. Was this the caravel the Prince would send to find Prester John? Turning to Eannes with a suspecting glint in his eye, Pero pleaded his new heart's desire. "I want to work on *this* one."

FIFTEEN

CHARTRES, FRANCE
FEBRUARY, PRESENT DAY

Iaq stepped off the train into chaos.

Hundreds of panicked tourists shoved and fought to speed the queues in the small station, where they had been waiting hours for the delayed northbound SNCF. With the European airports shut down because of the bombing scare, she had been forced to take the overnight train from Roma Termini and connect to this small town ninety kilometers south of Paris. After discarding Alyssa's phone in a trash bin at the embassy to avoid being tracked, she had called every hospital in Rome from pay phones, but none showed a record of Alyssa being admitted. She had agonized over leaving Italy without her friend, but Ochley had ordered her to get to France immediately. And besides, if she had stayed in Rome, she would have been looking around every corner and wondering if the next person she met would put a gun to her head.

What had she done to cause someone to want to kill her? Was she just imagining it all?

Exhausted from lack of sleep, she weaved past the jostling throngs and climbed the hill that led to the main square from the north. A low fog shrouded the town with a Gothic foreboding, and she braced for a bloody scene of mayhem as she angled up a dark warren of medieval side streets.

Then, suddenly, the cathedral appeared through the mists, looming over her and taking her breath away.

Overwhelmed by its majestic delicacy, she mouthed a prayer of relief that bombing hadn't brought down its magnificent rose window with its thousands of stained-glass pedals. Rev. Merry's voice whispered a warning in her ear against the lure of such graven imagery. Yet she found it difficult to break away from the gaunt Old Testament prophets who stood frozen in stone, glaring down on her as if in judgment. On one bay, an African servant cowered at the feet of a queen with Negroid features. Why were Africans depicted on a French cathedral? She circled the column and saw a tableau of a chest being hauled away in a cart drawn by oxen. Two Latin words were carved below the baffling scene:

ARCHA CEDERIS

She walked to the far side of the column and discovered the sculpture of a robed priest bending over another box. Below it was a second inscription:

HIC AMICUTR ARCHA CEDERIS

She was about to reach up and touch the engraved Latin letters when she heard a voice over her shoulder.

"*Chartres n'est pas le place pour un athée.*"

She turned, startled. Behind her stood a refined-looking Frenchman of perhaps sixty, with wavy silver hair and steely eyes of royal blue. His arrival had spawned a rush of *gendarmes* chastened by the discovery that an intruder––an American, no less—had somehow pierced their cordoned perimeter.

Detecting her confusion at his greeting, the man translated it with a smile as thin as his mustache. "Chartres is no place for an atheist."

He thinks I'm an atheist? She was about to disabuse him of that notion when he explained his observation.

"That is what Napoleon said when he first saw our beloved cathedral."

She looked up at some nicks in the buttresses. Thinking back to her history classes, she asked him, "Didn't the revolutionaries blow up churches in France?"

"Not Chartres, *grâce à Dieu*. Robespierre and the other members of the Committee on Public Safety rightfully sensed a power greater than Reason resided here. The cathedral has been burned down several times, but it is our phoenix, always rising anew. These Islamic ruffians cannot destroy it."

"Are you the curator here?"

He gave a condescending little laugh. "I am the curator of all France, in a sense." He extended his hand in a half-hearted gesture. "Jean Roban. Deputy Director of the *Direction de la Surveillance du Territoire.*"

She realized that she was speaking to one of the higher-ups in France's version of the FBI. She looked around for broken glass. "Where did the bomb go off?"

He ignored the question, his arched brows making no effort to hide his opinion that she was overstepping her limited brief. "Your citizens are being treated at the hospital here. I will escort you there now."

"Was there much damage inside the cathedral?"

"Some."

"May I take a look?"

"The interior is closed until we complete our inquiry."

"My superiors will have questions."

"Do you know, Ms. Quartermane, how many French nationals were killed in the terrorist attack on your World Trade Center towers?"

"I'm afraid I don't."

The official met that concession with a dismissive snort. "How would your government have reacted if my president had demanded that I be allowed to trample through that debris?"

He had a point, she conceded. Led around the cathedral to the west entrance, she saw, on the front façade over the doors, a tympanum of Jesus, who was framed by the cross with the splayed flanges similar to the one she had seen in the Lalibela churches. "Does that cross have any significance?"

"Only the salvation of the world," the snooty Frenchman muttered.

At the small, overcrowded Chartres hospital, Jaq walked down the aisle of a lobby that had been converted into a communal recovery room. Introducing herself to the American patients, she came to an elderly couple holding hands across their beds. "Where are you folks from?"

"Toledo," said the woman as her bruised eyes teared up. "Harry didn't want to come. I promised him it would be safe."

Jaq glanced at their charts, looking for information on their condition that she might need to forward to her superiors. "You're going to be fine. We'll get you home soon as you're well enough to fly."

The husband picked at the bandage on his head. "We were lucky. The couple with us yesterday didn't make it."

"Where were you when the bomb went off?"

"In the crypt. We came to see the Black Madonna."

She was unfamiliar with the reference. "I'm sorry?"

"The holy statue of the Blessed Virgin," the man's wife explained. "She's been in Chartres for centuries. They keep Her below the main church. She grants miracles to those on pilgrimage. Our son was diagnosed with cancer. Now he has to deal with this."

As an evangelical, Jaq didn't approve of this unbiblical Catholic worship of Mary, but she hoped Rev. Merry would forgive her this one instance of leniency for the comfort of the poor woman. "I'm certain the Holy Mother will help him. Look how she saved her own cathedral."

The husband lurched up onto his elbows. "Those bastards weren't trying to destroy the church!"

"Why do you say that?"

The man's wife tried to calm him. "Harry was in the construction business. He knows about these things."

"Maybe they just miscalculated."

The man shook his battered head. "Those Arabs may be nuts when it comes to religion, but they damn well know how to raise a building and how to bring one down. You think those bums didn't know where to hit the Trade Center towers? The blast last night went off near one of the transepts, several yards from the foundations."

The nurses, alerted by the raised voices, glanced over.

Jaq whispered to the man, "But the force of the propulsion—"

"If they really wanted to crash it, they'd have set off the detonation near the buttresses. The masons didn't put those supports there for show. Hell, the French learned how to build these things from the Arabs in the first place."

"Did you see anything suspicious in the crypt?"

"There was one Egyptian-looking fellow who seemed kind of jumpy," he said. "I just thought he was one of the custodians. I told the Frogs about him, but they just shrugged it off."

She contemplated that oddity as she signed the charts to indicate that a U.S. government official had reviewed them.

"Oh, and one more thing." The husband rubbed his bandaged scalp to spur his memory. "The tours to the crypt usually close at four in the afternoon. Yesterday the guide agreed to extend the hours because our bus was late arriving from Paris."

"And?"

"Those sonsabitches wouldn't have any way of knowing there'd be tourists down there at that time, now would they?"

"Unless your guide tipped them off."

The man waved off that possibility. "He was killed in the blast. Standing damn near in the center of it. And if the bastards *were* targeting tourists, they could have killed a lot more of us during the day."

Jaq broke off their conversation when one of the French nurses, looking put out, began marching down the aisle.

After checking into her hotel that evening, she placed several calls on the lobby pay phone in an attempt to locate Alyssa, but Ochley's voicemail said he was in meetings all day, and the manager of the Rep. Yardley's office had heard nothing. Alyssa's on-again-off-again boyfriend, Toby, wasn't returning messages, probably out of spite. So much for that.

Feeling helpless, she decided to take a walk to clear her mind. That retired contractor at the hospital had a point. Chartres was a tourist spot, true, but it was relatively isolated compared to more-populated places in France. Why *would* Al Qaeda pick such a small town to target and then botch the bombing? It wasn't their typical method. Until he was killed, Bin Laden had always preached getting the biggest bang for the bombing buck by hitting large cities. Wouldn't Notre Dame in Paris have been more effective?

After taking another circuit around the outskirts of the town, she walked back south along the river and decided to check on the injured Americans again before turning in. Unfamiliar with the streets, she asked a woman leaving a bakery for directions. "Hospital?"

The woman pointed down the Rue St. Brice, and Jaq followed the street a few more blocks until she came to an old Romanesque building crowned by a cross. She shook her head in exasperation. How many churches does one town need? And, of course, there was no hospital in sight. These condescending French apparently enjoyed confusing Americans. She tried the iron-bracketed door, hoping to find someone inside to ask. It was open. She walked inside and saw an elfish old man sweeping the flagstones.

"The hospital, *si vous plais?*"

The janitor came to attention. "*Oui! C'est l'hôpital.*"

Confused, she scanned the empty church. "The *main* hospital?"

"*Non, l'hôpital de Saint-Brice.*"

"You have two churches *and* two hospitals here?"

The janitor flashed a toothless grin. "You are American, no? *Il arrive tout le temps.*" Seeing her grimace, frustrated at having understood only the French word for time, the janitor struggled for the correct rendition. "*L'erreur* occurs quite often. This is Eglise of St. Brice. Once called Eglise Saint-Martin-au-Val. The adjacent buildings were converted into, how do you say, a hospice? My English is not so good. A place for the dying? We now use it for our *chapelle.*"

She realized that the woman at the bakery had merely misunderstood her question. Exhausted, she began to leave. The little man kept walking aside her, determined to regale her on the importance on his prized patch of Gallic rubble. "Now that you are here," he insisted, "you must see it."

She tried to escape, but visitors were apparently, and understandably, so rare to his church that the janitor had locked onto her like a missionary. "I appreciate your offer, but—"

He arched his gray brow. "Older than the cathedral."

She halted her retreat. "Really?"

"*Oui*, once a Roman temple and cemetery." The janitor nearly dragged her into the crypt. "Here the Roman soldiers worshipped their god."

"Mithras?"

"And before them, the Druids." The janitor showed her several crumbling tombs. "The bishops were buried here, not in the cathedral. The night before their vows, they lay in darkness here. And *voila!* Now they spend darkness of Eternity with me."

"Why here?"

The janitor pointed to her feet. "The Druids initiated their magicians where you stand. The Christians were *beaucoup savant*, no? They stole the power." He pointed to a depiction of Christ nailed to the cross on one of the tombs. "Here are two things you will never find in the cathedral. Tombs and crucifixes."

"But I saw crosses on the outside of the cathedral."

"Crosses, *oui*, but no tortures or executions. The cross is a symbol more ancient that Christ. The Companions who built the cathedral did not believe in the salvation of the crucifixion."

"The priests allow you talk heresy like that?"

He hissed his disgust. "Priests! *Imbéciles!* Chartres is the womb of the Blessed Mother, a place of birth. The Brotherhood has never allowed it to be defiled by death."

"What brotherhood?"

This time, the janitor didn't answer her. She studied him, wondering if he was just pulling her leg. She really needed to get some photos of the blast scene. If she returned home without inspecting the crypt, Darden would have another reason to dismiss her as incompetent. That asshole despised the French, she knew, probably because he was so much like them. If she could prove the retired foreman's theory with evidence overlooked by that candy-ass Paris detective, she might redeem herself for the Ethiopia debacle. This curious little droll didn't seem much of a threat to rat her out. The local gendarmes probably humored him as being a bit soft in the head. So, she risked the question: "Do you know a way into the cathedral?"

The janitor stared at her for an extended moment. "The doors."

She saw that he was trying to be coy. "I mean *other* than the doors."

"I might."

"I need to see that crypt tonight."

"And I need a thick beefsteak and a bottle of Beaujolais."

This gnome was more cunning than he had first posed. She pulled out fifty euros and yanked the bills back from his reach. "I'll leave it in the donation slot *after* I've returned."

After debating her proposal, the janitor revealed, "I have dug most of the septic tanks in this *ville*. The cathedral sits over several subterranean streams and passages. The earth's power swirls here like a water snake."

"Do any of those passages lead to the cathedral?"

He nodded. "Bishop Fulbert ordered sluices cut below the foundations of the first cathedral here to harness the currents. This church once sat outside the city walls. The monks would never have stayed here without an underground evasion route."

"Do you know where it starts?"

He flicked on his flashlight and led her to the entrance to a passage. Offering the flashlight to her, he warned, "I have never tried it."

She peered inside. "How far is it to the crypt?"

"I once walked it off on the rue above us. One thousand and twenty paces. Perhaps a few more for a *petite femme* like you."

She followed the faint gurgle of water overhead and, after twenty minutes or so, came to a door with half-rotted planks. She slammed the boards with her shoulder and finally managed to open a crack wide enough to reach through and turn the latch. The entry led to a large gallery that could have passed for a bomb shelter. Yellow barricade tape circled the blast hole. Was that a footprint? It looked as if someone had tried to climb down the shaft.

When she came nearer, the edges threatened to cave. Whoever set off the explosion must have known a cavity rested under this section of the floor. A few broken pews were stained with blood, but this wasn't the catastrophic scene that she'd expected. The terrorists had apparently been trying for depth with the bomb, not lateral coverage. A small altar, unharmed by the blast, held a statue of the Holy Mother cradling the Christ child. The figurine appeared to have been carved from a block of shellacked wood. She remembered the American woman's claim of a miracle granted by the Black Madonna. Violating her evangelical beliefs, she offered up a prayer for Alyssa's safety and reached to touch the statue—

"*Vous deux sont des jumeaux.*"

Stalked by a voice, she recoiled into the shadows. Had the assassin followed her here from Rome? Unable to endure the uncertainty, she drew up a false courage and demanded, "What did you say?"

"I said you two are regular twins."

This man trailing her spoke both French and English. It was that condescending Parisian cop again! She turned on the flashlight and marched out to confront him. "I have every right—"

Elymas's smirking face came into the beam's path.

Her heart quickened, and she felt fluttery as a schoolgirl. Wait, what was that wisecrack he'd just made? *Twins? With the Virgin?* Crimson with embarrassment, she swung a hand to slap him, but he ducked and she landed on her rump. "Who told you I was a vir—" The perplexed twist of his face alerted her, too late.

Elymas caught her stealing an incriminating glance at the Black Madonna. He broke a wide grin of discovery. "You're a *virgin?*"

She leapt to her feet. "What did you mean to say?"

Elymas sized her up as if for the first time. "The Black Madonna is called the Lady of the Underground. You both seem to spend a lot of time below the surface. I was about to award *you* that title, but this virgin thing is even better. So, you and that guy …"

"Paul."

"Never slept together?"

"That's none of your business."

"No wonder you're always so wound up."

"I am *not* wound up!" She launched a kick at his shin, but missed and fell again. "I was saving myself for marriage. Go ahead. Make fun of my faith! The Bible says—"

"Spare me the sermon."

When he pulled her, thrashing, to her feet, his lips hovered near hers—until she broke from his grasp. *Who is this guy?* She tried to recall the features of the driver of that hit-and-run car in Rome. She had gotten only a quick glimpse, but she remembered the man had black hair and the same dark complexion. She was, after all, the only witness to his attempted theft of the Lalibela Cross, a crime punishable by death if he were to be arrested and extradited. Was he trying to get rid of her as a witness? She dredged up as much false courage as she could manage and confronted him with the glare of a cross-examiner. "What did you do with my friend you ran down? Is she still alive?"

He came closer and pinned her with a questioning glower. "What are you talking about?"

"Are you following me?"

"Don't flatter yourself. I'm here on business."

"What could possibly be of interest to …" She did a double take at the icon on the altar. "Not even someone of your low morals would steal a statue of the Blessed Mother."

"You mean *that* damn thing? It isn't worth the block of wormwood it was hacked from. It's a copy of a copy of the real one."

"Where's the first copy?"

"In the nave," he said. "It's called the Black Madonna of the Pillar."

"Then where's the real one?"

He walked the perimeter of the horseshoe-shaped crypt, searching for crevices and cracks. He stopped at a crude well near the altar and peered down into it. "My guess is somewhere right below us."

She stared down at her feet. "There's another crypt under this one?"

He nodded. "The first cathedral here was set atop an older Carolingian dolmen sanctuary known as St. Lubin's cavern. We're standing on the floor of a Romanesque church built by a bishop who was a magician. This well was called the Abyss of the Strong."

She took a guarded step closer. "Do I want to know why?"

He dropped a pebble into the well, listening for the plunk. "The Druids worshipped a mysterious relic they kept hidden down there. Viking raiders threw the monks down this hole to Hell when they wouldn't deliver it up."

She forced herself to look into the depths of the well. "I thought no one was allowed to be buried in the cathedral."

"Not voluntarily. The Carolingians converted a Druid dolmen below us into their crypt. The Roman soldiers who camped here used it for their rituals."

"What rituals?"

He shrugged. "No clue. The lower level has never been excavated. The engineers are afraid these walls above us would come down. I'm hoping our terrorist friends scattered up a few nuggets of interest."

"You think the real Black Madonna was hidden under the dolmen?"

"I get paid to find, not think."

"Paid by whom?"

"People with lots of money and an obsession for privacy."

She glared an accusation of betrayal at the *faux* Madonna on the altar. "I can't believe the Church allows people to believe this is a real miracle relic."

He lowered his shoulders into the blast shaft and continued talking while he conducted his inspection. "The priests put up with the superstition for the donations." He unknotted a coil of rope at his belt and, tying an iron weight to its end, lowered the depth tester into the chasm. When the weight clanked on hardpan, he shook his head. "Looks like they hit a dry hole."

"How did you get in here?"

"I made a generous monetary gift to the local bishop." Denied the trove he had hoped to find, he began walking up the stairs to the main church.

She rushed after him. "Don't you want to know how I got in?"

"No."

She had no desire for a return trip down that slimy tunnel to St. Brice's. Besides, if that batty janitor forgot to leave the door unlocked, she'd be trapped. And if she tried to walk out of the cathedral alone through the doors, those French cops would arrest her and blab to the media about the American diplomat who was making a career of trespassing on crime scenes. The last thing she needed right now was another international screw-up on her employment record. "How do you plan to get past the *gendarmes*?"

Elymas broke into the sacristy and began removing his clothes with no concern for modesty. When he stripped to his skivvies, she averted her eyes, then snuck a glance at his bare chest and was impressed. The guy was really in shape.

He opened the sacerdotal closet and put on a priest's smock. "Would you like me to hear your confession, *mademoiselle?*"

She was incredulous, and a little hurt. "You're just going to leave me here?"

"Of course not. The Church saves all." Elymas reached to the highest shelf and found a nun's habit that smelled as if it hadn't been worn in thirty years. "Here you go, Sister of the Untapped Treasure. You should have no problem pulling off the performance."

"We're just going to walk out together?"

He armed himself with a chalice. "The bishop has told the French police that one of his priests will be retrieving the Holy Sacrament for Mass this evening in the rectory."

"How do I know if I can even trust you? You left me hanging in Cairo."

"I don't care if you trust me or not, ye of little faith and even less sex."

She stayed on his heels. "Won't the cops be suspicious of a priest and a nun walking out of an empty church together in the middle of the night?"

He hid the coil of rope under his cassock. "If anyone asks, I'll tell them I was instructing you in the Ecstasy of the Holy Rapture. The French appreciate *that* religious impulse."

Given no choice, she swallowed her pride and accepted the bitter fact that she would have to rely on his help again. She traded her clothes for the wedding gown of a bride of Christ, which fortunately, for present purposes, was of the old style with a bonnet and tight collar.

As they tiptoed down the nave in their robes, she stopped at a series of intertwined circles scored into the floor. She began feeling a little disoriented from a ringing in her ears. Her body tingled, and she had the odd impression that this cathedral was a giant stone tuning fork. Although it was night, a luminous blue light suffused the nave. What was the source of this strange radiance?

SOUTH TRANSEPT

WINDOW

Near the south transept, she stepped on a flagstone that was several shades lighter than the others and had been set askew. A gold-plated tenon was driven into its core. She looked up. Above this unique stone stood a stained-glass window of a praying saint with stones crashing around him. A small hole had been drilled into one of the window's panes.

At the door, Elymas turned. "What's wrong?"

She pointed at the floor. "Every stone is the same except this one."

He backtracked to examine her discovery. "Probably marks the spot where some saint had his head lopped off."

She looked up again and saw that the Christ of the Apocalypse was glaring down at her from the center of the large rose window. She couldn't shake the feeling that she was missing a clue to the bombing here. Craning her neck, she swept her eyes across the high walls and studied the intricate images in the smaller window that stood directly above this spot in the wing. The stones shown falling around the saint looked to be from a temple that was being destroyed.

A *pagan* temple.

Could the bomber of the crypt be connected to the men who had tried to kill her in Rome? Now that she thought about it, every underground location that she had been led to since Paul's death had one thing in common.

Maybe if she followed *that* thread.

She glanced at Elymas again. She was about to share her new theory with him, but then it occurred to her: If he had no qualms about being a mercenary thief, would it be that much of a stretch to sign on as a hired gun for terrorists? She decided to smoke him out with the old lawyer's trick of asking an unexpected question and then watching his body language for tells of deceit. "What do you know about Mithras?"

"Who?"

"The god worshipped by the Roman soldiers."

His blank look seemed authentic enough. "Nothing."

"You know anybody who might?"

He thought a moment. "Maybe, but he's a little eccentric."

"What do you mean?"

He lifted her nun's wimple and whispered to her ear.

She stared at him in disbelief. Either he took her to be very gullible, or he had been reading way too many Harry Potter novels.

SIXTEEN

SATOR
APERO
TENET
OPERA
ROTAS

SAGRES, PORTUGAL
NOVEMBER, 1456

The maritime academy where the Old Man trained his admirals looked nothing like what Pero had imagined. He had expected to find an opulent palace ringed with gardens, but the sages who stayed behind here to plan the sea voyages were required to endure conditions no less ascetic than those suffered by the sailors on the waves. Known as the *Vila do Infante*, the heavily guarded compound sat perched atop sheer tawny cliffs above the Bay of Sagres, bordered by a jagged finger of hardscrabble so desolate and wind-sheared that only the scratchiest of gorse could survive on it. Below the whitewashed fortress, blowholes sprayed a rocky coastline where bloated corpses from shipwrecks had been washing ashore for centuries. So frequently were these gruesome deposits found that the Old Man had sanctified a cemetery in their honor.

He followed Eannes and the other squires through the eastern gate. They passed the *Nossa Senhora da Graça,* the revered chapel dedicated to the Virgin, where the mariners always spent their nights fasting in vigil before challenging the Sea of Darkness. He longed to peek inside the sanctuary, but he decided against tempting the curse of misfortune promised to any seaman who committed such a trespass before his maiden departure. The door to the chapel creaked opened, and out walked an apparition of a stooped old man wasted to the bone. He saw the penitent nod grimly to Eannes before limping off into the mists. He wondered what he had just seen. "Was that a shade?"

"He damn well should be," Eannes said. "The Venetian Lion has reconnoitered the gates into Hades more times than any man alive."

Pero gasped. *That* pitiful wraith was the famous explorer, Alvise Cadamasto? He exchanged bewildered looks with Dias and Zarco, questioning if Eannes was toying with them again. "But I thought the admiral was away testing the limits of the African coast?"

"He returned last night," Eannes said. "Did you think I brought you poop barnacles from Lagos because I missed your erudite conversation?"

"Why *did* you bring us?" Zarco asked.

"The Old Man wishes you to hear the Venetian's defense of his voyage. Do not ask me why. Perhaps he requires three fools for jestering."

Led up the steps of the ramparts and across the allures, Pero looked down and saw a giant wheel carved into the ground near the bluffs. The strange sculpture, marked with small stones, possessed thirty-six spokes radiating from its center. Its cyclopean size and mysterious symmetry stirred his senses, but just why he could not explain. Across its expanse lay dozens of haphazard footprints. "What is the purpose of that circle down there?"

Eannes played hard of hearing. "Go douse your sorry asses in lye and change into your doublets. The Old Man convenes the disputation at sunset."

That night, the great hall of Sagres was filled with the Order's most renowned mariners, cartographers, astrologers, and mathematicians, all sitting below the Old Man, who held court on a raised platform. Flanking the prince were his two most trusted advisors, Jehuda Cresques, known as the Jew of the Needle because of his invention of the compass, and Master Rodrigo, the academy's physician and cosmic philosopher. Between the high-backed stalls, a long trestle table held the kingdom's priceless collection of maps and charts.

Pero gawked at the precious documents from a distance. He had thought some of these maps to be mere legend, but here before him lay a copy of the Greek Ptolemy's rendition of the world; a Venetian drawing by the cartographer De Canistris that depicted continents in the form of humans and beasts; a chart bearing the Templar cross and revealing lands west of Scotland; and a drawing with Arabic letters that suggested the existence of a western continent beyond the Atlantic. He tried to angle for a closer examination, but before he could do so, the doors flew open and the chamberlain announced an arrival.

"Admiral Cadamosto!"

The Venetian mariner who only a few hours ago appeared half-dead now strode into the hall as if resurrected by a miracle of healing. Behind him came a procession that included his grizzled captain, three aboriginals in flowing white robes, and a dozen scullions carrying ivory tusks and cages filled with chattering parrots and writhing snakes.

Pero applauded loudly, until he saw the other mariners remaining silent, their jealousy and disappointment at the Venetian's survival all too evident.

Bemused by the admiral's grandiose entrance, the Old Man waved Cadamosto forward and observed dryly, "I trust that, with such a swift and rousing return, Venetian, you found the ends of Africa?"

Cadamosto swiveled his head from side to side so that his rivals could hear every word of his triumphant report. "No, my lord. But I did witness a marvel so astonishing that I felt duty bound to bring it to your attention with all due speed."

"I grow older by the hour," the Old Man groused. "Are you going to tell me, or stand there fluttering like a peacock?"

Cadamosto swept his hand to his feet in a bow so florid that only an Italian could have pulled it off without looking ridiculous. "I have discovered, in your honor, prosperous new isles below Cape Blanco. So lush is the vegetation there that I named them Cape Verde. I then pushed south and turned inland on the Gambia. There I encountered friendly Negroes who believed my caravel to be a living creature. Their king, a Mohammedan, challenged me to a debate on the superiority of Islam."

The Old Man suppressed a smile. "You prevailed in this battle of wits, else you would not be here regaling me with details of the encounter."

Cadamosto waved forward the Africans for the Old Man's inspection. "As always, you are prescient, my lord! So forceful were my arguments that the Mohammedan sent these members of his family as a gift. They have offered to learn our language and serve as translators."

Intrigued, the Old Man touched the necks of the Africans and examined his fingers, testing if their blackness rubbed off. "Does the sun char them so?"

The admiral shook his head. "Their infants emerge like this from the womb."

The Old Man turned and punished the physician at his side with a judicial glance. "So, it seems the southerly sun does *not* incinerate the flesh."

Master Rodrigo shot to his feet to defend his long-held thesis that Africa could not be circumvented by water. "My lord, this Venetian has offered no evidence proving that he reached the limits of the sun's descent!"

Cadamosto came up fast to confront the bilious physician who had predicted his failure from the start. "My lord, I pray you avoid the ministrations of this ignorant blood-letter!"

Rodrigo's reddening neck nearly burst its collar. "I shall sever that impertinent Italian tongue and sew it to the throat of a deaf mute!"

While the two antagonists and their defenders hurled charges, the Old Man returned to his chair and shot Pero a private smile full of mischief. Pero returned the smile, knowing that one of the few pleasures his master allowed himself was the pitting of his counselors in battles over cosmology.

At last, having heard enough of the boisterous argument, the Old Man rapped his knuckles sharply on the table aside him, causing everyone in the hall to fall silent. "The physician speaks true, Venetian. I require incontestable proof before the maps are allowed to be revised."

Cadamosto motioned forward his pilot to give testimony. "Tell them what we saw below the Gambia River."

The nervous pilot hawed, searching for his voice. "My lord, the last clear night before we turned back north, I could not find the Pole Star to read the latitude." That assertion was met with hoots, but the captain would not be cowed into a retraction. "I swear by St. George, what appeared in its stead was a constellation of six new stars in the form of a cross!"

Cadamosto presented the Old Man with a drawing on parchment of this Southern Cross of stars that had dazzled the sky. "My lord, this omen clearly means that God was welcoming you into His unexplored Creation."

The Old Man turned to his mapmaker for an assessment of the shocking possibility that another sky existed below the known aspects of the earth.

"If they saw what they now claim," Cresques conceded, "then they passed the equator without falling into the abyss."

Rodrigo refused to accept this upheaval of his cosmos. He bounded out of his chair and came up to challenge Cadamosto, nose to nose. "This Venetian and his trained birds saw only what their eyes wished to see! Many of your men fell ill as you approached Gambia, is that not so?"

Cadamosto was rocked to his heels. "They did, but—"

Rodrigo spun toward the Old Man to drive home the dagger of rebuttal. "There is your proof, my lord, that evil lurks in those waters!"

The council members again fell to arguing over whether Cadamosto had demonstrated the safety of venturing farther south along the coast.

"Enough!" The Old Man stood so swiftly that he required a moment to reclaim his precarious balance. "Did Herodotus not record that the Phoenicians sailed through the Pillars of Hercules?"

Cadamosto preened at the classical comparison. "He did indeed, my lord!"

The Old Man glared down at them all. "And each time I have sent a caravel south, have I not been met with the same objection? That the ends of the earth lurk ahead! And each time, have my mariners not come back to report that they have gone further than these self-proclaimed wise men said was possible?"

"They have indeed!" Cresques cried, acting as the Old Man's chorus.

"You cannot find a peril so great that the hope of reward will not be greater!" The Old Man lapsed into a spasm of coughing from the exertion. Recovering his breath, he lifted his chin again and challenged the assembled mariners. "Who among you will push beyond the Gambia and find the ends of Africa for me?"

The hall became shamefully silent, as each seaman waited for another to take up the mission of suicide. Pero knew from his studies at Tomar that the Old Man had formed his conception of Africa from the writings of infidel geographers, who were considered untrustworthy by most Christian scholars.

According to the Arab chronicler Ibn Said, a large central lake in the middle of Africa gave source to the Nile. The Old Man was convinced that Prester John had established his capital on the banks of this great lake, but most of his councilors believed that Africa had no southern boundary. The sea below the equator, they had always insisted, boiled from its proximity to the sun, a fact proven by the withered coastline below the Gambia. Moreover, the Earth's slope at the equator was so steep that the water would threaten to cascade over its edge and prevent the caravels from sailing back home.

Disappointed by the response to his call, the Old Man slumped into his chair. After nearly a minute of meditation on the maps below him, he beckoned up one of his servants, whispered to him, and sent him out.

Pero watched as the knights and seamen waited tensely, conferring in hushed tones. He had heard the vile gossip that the Old Man pushed his mariners to the very shoals of death while he remained safe here in Sagres. Yet now he saw that the prince suffered more than any in the Order, for he was forced to endure the expeditions vicariously while placing his fortune at risk.

"*Grand Pai!*"

Startled by young Zarco's cry, the councilors and mariners turned toward the door. They gasped at what they saw: clinging to the royal servant's arm for support stood an aged gentleman. Seven years had passed since Salvador had last spoken to his grandfather, João Goncalves Zarco. In a tearful reunion, the squire rushed to hug the legendary discoverer of the Madeira Islands, who was nearly blind from the wound he had suffered decades ago at the conquest of Moorish Ceuta. Pero now realized that the Old Man had secretly summoned his aged comrade from his retirement lair for support during this crucial night of decision.

"Tell them, *hidalgo*," the Old Man ordered the elder Zarco. "Tell them what the priests vowed before you set sail thirty years ago."

João straightened in obedience to his prince. "On the night of my vigil, the friars gave me the last rites, for they assured me that any man who tempts the limits of God's realm was doomed to find only Hell."

The Old Man edged up on his chair. "Tell them of the blessed isle."

The celebrated hero of Madeira turned his glassy eyes toward the rafters, as if reliving that fateful day. "We tacked within sight of an ominous cloud blacker than these Africans before you."

All eyes turned on the Ethiops.

"My caravel heaved from a violent churning in the depths."

Salvador knelt at his grandfather's feet and hung on every word. "Was the sea boiling?"

The elder Zarco clinched fists from the memory. "My sailors begged me to turn back lest the planks dissolve. But I ordered the pilot to maintain our course. An hour into our ordeal, the sun finally broke through the blackness. It was then that we first saw the emerald paradise."

Pero saw tears welling up the Old Man's bagged eyes.

With his grandson's assistance, the elder Zarco limped down the aisle and glared an indictment at each mariner he passed. "I would have preferred death that day over living to see a Venetian venture where no son of Portugal dared to go." With his weathered face seamed in sadness, João turned to the squires, who were watching him raptly. "You *meninos* are our only hope now. When the hour of your service comes, I pray you do not retreat from duty, as these cowards before me have done this night."

The mariners around him lowered their heads in disgrace.

After another nettled silence, Diogo Gomes, a young knight in the royal household, stood and came forward. In a low but determined voice, he told the Old Man, "With my lord's permission, I will make the attempt."

Weary from having made too many such pleas for volunteers over the years, the Old Man managed only a tremulous nod and, with the assistance of his servant, arose and shuffled toward the portal to retire to his quarters. As the hobbling prince passed the squires, he pinned them with a fearsome glare.

Pero shuddered from an inexplicable premonition of loneliness.

SEVENTEEN

SATOR
APERO
TENET
OPERA
ROTAS

CHAMPAGNE, FRANCE
FEBRUARY 5, PRESENT DAY

Two hours out of Chartres and with no sign of the French cops in pursuit, Jaq cranked back her plush seat in Elymas's Alfa Romero Spider and let down her guard for the first time in two days. She still hadn't figured out this guy next to her, though. As he sped down a country road a few miles south of Verdun, he punched the roof-retraction button on the dash and folded the top behind them. Watching him closely, she caught him sneaking another smirk at her discarded nun's habit in the rear seat. She stuck out her tongue at him.

Why did I just do that? Real professional, Jaq.

Was Satan tempting her? She was taking a big risk trusting a notorious thief who, by the way, might very well be the murderer stalking her. Yet with each passing hour, she was becoming more desperate to find Alyssa. She knew she'd be summoned back to Washington any time now. Her only lead to solving Alyssa's disappearance, admittedly a thin one, was the possibility that her attacker in Rome had some connection to the bombing in Chartres.

Which begged the real question: Why was *she* caught in the middle of it all? She resisted the urge to phone Rev. Merry again. She had to stop using the pastor for a crutch every time the Lord put a challenge in her path. He had once told her that God drafts unbelievers for His glorious purpose, and she could think of many such examples from the Bible. Rahab the prostitute had given aid to the Israelite spies, and surely Rahab had been no less sinful than this mysterious guy sitting next to her.

She decided she simply had to trust that God kept sending Elymas to her for a reason. After all, he *had* agreed to introduce her to the only person in France who might explain the anomalies in the cathedral and any connection to the Roman god Mithras. She inched a little closer to him. "So, this friend of yours we're going to see. What'd he do? Discover the elixir of youth?"

He downshifted to take a sharp turn, sending her against the door. "Thomas Aquinas, greatest thinker in Church history. Francis Bacon, greatest thinker in English history. Isaac Newton, wise guy with falling apples."

She recovered her breath from the hairpin maneuver. "What about them?"

"All were alchemists."

The more she thought about it, this mystery friend of his sounded like some medieval Gulliver reawakened in modern times. "I didn't think you believed in all that spiritual mumbo-jumbo?"

"I don't. But I can't help but notice you Christians always make a big show of condemning magic. Unless, of course, it's the magic *you* conjure up."

Her glare sharpened. "Hey, Catholics built that cathedral in Chartres, in case you forgot. We Protestants kicked them to the curb during the Reformation. We had enough of their relic-filled altars and miracle-dispensing Virgins." Winking, she added, "Though you never know, I could be one of the latter, right?"

"Well isn't that plummy. So, you Protestants don't speak in tongues? You don't believe that God waves his wand of death and destruction over sinful cities like New Orleans when the homosexuals and perverts flout the Bible?"

"If you think so little of my religion, why are you helping me?"

He did a poor job of hiding a mischievous grin. "This promises to offer the most entertainment I've had in a while. Just to give you a fighting chance, there are a couple of things I should tell you about Monsignor Guilbert."

"Monsignor? You mean he's a priest?"

"Used to be. He was defrocked for heresy fifty years ago when the local bishop discovered he was studying occult magic with a man named Fulcanelli."

Fifty years ago? The guy must be a real geezer. And playing the Ouija board with some Rasputin-like charlatan? That name sounded downright demonic. What was she getting herself into here? She asked him, "Was this Fulcan fellow some kind of New Age guru?"

"Fulcanelli, and he was a master occultist. Some say he lived for two hundred years. Lots of people claim to have known him, but nobody agrees on what he was really up to. He wrote a book called *Le Mystere des Cathedrales.* The monsignor continues his work near Resson. And he rarely accepts visitors."

"But you can just drop in any time on this gold-spinning priest."

"I make a few deliveries for him from time to time. Here are the ground rules. Twenty minutes. And no lights."

"What?"

"He lives in complete darkness."

"Is he some kind of werewolf?"

"He believes that radiation from the sun suppresses pineal gland secretions that spawn a spiritual sun inside his head."

She cackled. "Uh, beam me up, Scotty."

"Sure, go ahead and laugh. But tell me something. How come we were able to see well enough to walk through that cathedral last night?"

"There must have been *some* ambient light."

"There was a new moon, and it was overcast. Scientists still haven't figured out what chemicals those medieval glassworkers used to generate primal light."

"So, how does this alchemist of yours see to get around?"

"His eyes have adjusted to the dark. He'll see you, but you won't catch even a glimpse of his face. He also tends to slip in and out of a strange language."

"You mean foreign?"

"No, I mean *strange*. He knows a secret code of argot called *Langue Verte*. Alchemists and heretics once used it for communication to avoid being arrested by the Inquisition. Just don't react to him like Jodie Foster meeting Hannibal Lecter. And one more thing."

"Yeah?"

"He'll probably put you to a test."

"You mean an exam of some sort?"

"More like a hazing. He doesn't particularly like women. Especially those who stick their noses into his business. Other than that, he's a charming fellow."

Jaq braced for battle with the occult while accompanying Elymas on foot up an isolated hillock overgrown with weeds. After a strenuous hike, they came to an ancient chapel weaved in vines and on the verge of collapse. Elymas hammered the iron clapper against the oak door.

"*Solvitur ambulando!*" a gravelly voice shouted from inside.

She clung to Elymas's arm as they entered and clomped over strewn books and broken pews clotted with spider webs. Graffiti scratched into the baptismal font warned that Pope Pius XI had desanctified this ground in 1937. Shell fragments and empty cartridge boxes lay scattered, evidence that the converted church had once been used as a refuge by retreating German armies.

A hatch panel in the middle of the floor suddenly flew open.

She followed Elymas down a dark stairwell and made out the faint silhouette of a trollish man sitting at a desk against the far wall. He wore a head stocking with its point draped to the side. Hadn't she seen such a cap on the sculptured gnomes at Chartres? She searched for bubbling athanors and beakers, but all she saw were shelves stacked with ribbed tomes.

Leaving the hatch cracked, Elymas he deftly positioned his folding mirror on a basin, allowing just enough invasive light to create a reflection.

"You bring a temptress into my temple?" growled their obscured host. "Do you wish me to go the perfidious way of Abelard?"

"I heard you were taking on new students," Elymas said.

The floor reverberated with a crash of ceramic jars.

"Who told you such a lie? SSSSSSSSS!" Riled, the priest made buzzing noises between sentences, sounding as if he suffered from some kind of hissing Tourette's Syndrome. "Those flap-tongued village clods? ZZZZZZZZZ! You know I have not found an acolyte worthy of my time in twenty years! SSSSSSSS! I would teach an ass to talk before throwing pearls to female swine!"

Elymas squeezed her hand playfully, as if to prepare her for more stoking of the priest's fiery temper. "She wants to know the secrets of Chartres."

Now doubly furious, the old heretic thrashed about in the darkness. "Fulcanelli devoted a hundred years to deciphering the Book of Stone! And this frivolous feline thinks she is entitled to the mysteries of the greatest crucible of the soul?"

"Test her with a question. If she gets it wrong, I won't charge you for the next shipment. But if she answers correctly, you'll grant her a hearing."

She spun on Elymas—he was just using her for a bet?

The monsignor delayed an answer, weighing the offer. Finally, he asked Jaq: "Upon what side of the cathedral, distaff, did you first make your approach?"

Elymas jabbed an elbow into her side to spur her on.

"The north porch," she said.

"The Door of the Initiates." The priest sounded surprised; he asked her another question: "What was the name of the château that guarded the *San Graal*?"

She shot an exasperated look at Elymas. What did *that* have to do with anything? She was finding it difficult to focus. Maybe this claim about light's absence altering the brain wasn't so crazy, after all. *Come on, Jaq. Concentrate.* What did *San Graal* even mean? *Graal* sounded like Grail. Did he mean the Holy Grail? The only thing she knew about Christ's Cup at the Last Supper came from the few bits and pieces she'd come across in the Arthurian legends. Wait a minute. Hadn't she read something in World Literature about Parsifal? Where *was* it those Grail queens lived? She blurted the only name that came to mind. "Sarras."

After a few grumbled curses, the priest conceded: "A fortuitous conjecture."

Elymas chortled. "Looks like she wins, *padre.*"

The hunched little priest sounded peeved at having been outwitted. "That was *not* the dispositive interrogatory. Now, for the true test: What does Sarras have in common with Chartres?"

Jaq set her teeth, angered that this creepy night crawler wasn't playing fair. A Grail castle and a French cathedral? What could *they* have in common?

The priest taunted her. "Do you need the riddle repeated?"

She shushed him for silence. *Sarras and Chartres.* She whispered those names several times. Both had an 'a' and an 's' and two 'r's. Technically that would be a similarity, but he had to be expecting something more significant.

She spelled the words in her mind's eye and searched for anything else in common. Their first syllables, 'Char' and 'Sar', and their last three letters were nearly identical. She decided to wing it. "When the first and last syllables are pronounced as they appear visually, they sound the same."

The monsignor sighed and signaled for her to take the chair in front of his workbench. "The answer was incomplete. First rule of esoteric interpretation: Apply the phonetic cabala. The masters cloaked the true meanings of their art with intellectual façades. The ignorant seek evidence of heresy in the denotation, not in a word's sound or shape."

"I don't understand," she said.

"An adept would perceive that 'Char' and 'Sar' derive from the same origin. And a word or part of a word that repeats itself in reverse carries even deeper spiritual import. Phonetically, 'Res' and 'ras' are the reversals of 'Char' and 'Sar.'"

"What do those syllables mean?"

"Think like an occultist," the priest said. "What word uses 'char' as a root?"

"Charisma?"

"And what does 'charisma' mean?"

"I guess, maybe possessing a special gift for inspiring others?"

In the dim haze, the priest appeared to nod. "A gift, indeed. For conjuring the Spirit. What words carry the root 'res'?"

She thought for a moment. "Congress … Digress."

"A meeting point," he confirmed. "For coming or leaving."

She was starting to get the hang of this cryptic stuff. "So, both Chartres and Sarras are places for coming together and receiving spiritual gifts. But there's one difference. The name for the cathedral has a 'T' in it."

"In esoteric codes, variances become even more revealing," the priest said. "What strikes you about the letter 'T'?"

She formed it with her fingers. "Looks like a cross without the top half."

"The Tau cross," the priest said. "The gate between Heaven and Earth stands at the intersection of the vertical and horizontal beams, where one undergoes the death of the old life and obtains the Heaven of spiritual awakening. The Romans called it the Cross of Mithras."

Amazed, she angled a triumphant glance on Elymas, convinced that *had* to be more than just coincidence. She told the priest: "I keep coming across a word that seems connected to this Mithras. It's spelled S-A-T-O-R."

She heard him carving letters into a slender block of wood. When finished, he pushed his crude palimpsest across the desk for her inspection.

She brushed her fingers across the board and felt five engraved letters: R-O-T-A-S. "No, the word I mean is SATOR."

"*Sic,*" said the priest. "SATOR."

Elymas whispered into her ear. "He reads and writes like the ancient Hebrews, from right to left."

She gasped. "ROTAS was the word on the pillar in Lalibela."

Now even Elymas sounded intrigued. "It's also SATOR in reverse."

She fingered the letters on the board again. How had she failed to see this? The inscription on the Lalibela pillar must have contained the other lines of the square. Did the ancient Ethiopians believe that this word game held the Name of God? She revealed: "A Vatican priest told me that SATOR was part of a magical square found where Roman soldiers worshipped Mithras."

"Vatican? Fools and sodomites!" The priest lowered his voice, as if to impart a key revelation. "SATOR is the first word of the Templar Square."

"Templars?" she said. "Why is it named for them?"

"The square has been found carved at several Templar sites."

"What do its words mean?" she asked.

The priest groaned at her presumption that the arcana could be so easily understood. "I have spent half of my life trying to unlock that secret."

"But wait," she protested. "The Mithras cult was centuries older than the Templar order. Why would Christian knights embrace a word game that had been used to summon a pagan god?"

"Solve *that* mystery," the priest told her, "and Zeus himself will bow at your command. There are many levels of revelation within the square, of that I am certain. Apply the principles that I have just taught you and perhaps you will succeed where I have failed. You might start with this question: What did the initiates of Mithras and the Templars have in common?"

Truth was, she didn't know much about them at all. She looked to Elymas, wondering if he had come across any information on secret societies during his thieving sojourns around the world, but he just shrugged.

"Both were military brotherhoods that recognized degrees of advancement," Elymas said. "Both were also accused of being infected by Eastern religions."

She turned back to the priest. "What else could there be?"

"What was kept at Chartres that both orders might have treasured?"

"The Black Madonna?"

"Ah, the *Prima Materia*. Perhaps. Both orders did worship a virgin mother goddess who gave birth to a solar hero."

She remembered the splayed cross behind Christ's head on Chartres's west portal, the one that resembled the rays of the sun. "The Templars had a connection to Chartres?"

"Those monks all but built the architectural masterpiece," the priest said. "They financed the Compagnions."

"Who?"

"The French masons. The Templars oversaw the quarrying for the cathedral near their commandery at Sours. They also brought back the sacred geometry from the Moslems and applied the special cubit of measurement used for Solomon's Temple in Jerusalem. Like the Templars, the Compagnions were hounded by the Church."

"What was this Chartres unit of measure?" she asked.

The priest carved *0.738 meters* into the board. "The first cathedral was destroyed by fire in 1194. The Templars returned from the Crusades about that time."

"What are you suggesting?" she asked.

"The Templars suddenly need an expensive new cathedral. By stroke of luck, the old cathedral at Chartres burns down under mysterious circumstances. Perhaps the Templars brought back something from the Holy Land that required safekeeping in a sanctum built with mystical dimensions."

She felt a tap on her shoulder, the signal from Elymas that they had overstayed their time. She arose, but at the stairwell she turned back toward the darkness and told the priest: "In the south transept at Chartres, I saw a stone in the floor that was different from the others."

"Did you observe anything unusual near it?"

"A window with a tiny hole in one of its panes. It depicted a saint praying for the destruction of a pagan temple."

"How do you know *that* was what the saint was praying for?"

"I just assumed."

"And did you see the statue of St. Peter on the north porch?"

She thought back to her inspection of the bay. "Yes, near the central doorway."

"On what was he standing?"

"A small man with a large purse hanging from his neck," she said. "St. Peter was crushing the poor elf's shoulders."

"That elf, as you call him, was Simon Magus, a Gnostic heretic condemned by the Church fathers in the First Century. Is another interpretation of the tableau possible?" When she offered no alternative, the priest followed up with another question. "Why would a heretic magician be shown wearing a purse?"

She thought for a moment. "A purse holds money. Maybe he was being shamed for selling his evil tricks."

"Publicans in the time of Christ wore purses to protect the treasury of their kings. St. Matthew was a publican."

"So, a purse was a mark of honor."

The priest nodded. "In which direction was the Magus's face turned?"

"Upward," she said. "As if he were admiring St. Peter."

"Like an admiring father, perhaps?" the priest asked.

She pondered these pieces to his puzzle: A purse containing a treasury ... a *treasure*? If St. Peter stood on Simon Magus's shoulders ... Wait, he was standing *on his shoulders!* What was that old saying: Standing on the shoulders of giants? "Were the builders telling future initiates that the foundations of true wisdom had been taught by the heretic Simon, not by St. Peter, the founder of the Roman Catholic Church?"

"Now, distaff, apply that same mode of analysis to your pierced glass and aberrant flagstone."

"The saint in the window."

"Apollonaire. The first bishop of Ravenna."

"Maybe Apollonaire was grieving for the temple's loss."

"Another ambiguity," the priest confirmed. "Chartres is full of them. What hint can you derive from the saint's name?"

She whispered the names again. "Apollonaire and Apollo ... The saint was named for the Greek god?"

The monsignor answered her by posing more conundrums. "Why would a Christian bishop take the name of a pagan sun god? Why would he kneel near a pagan temple? Why would French Templars devote a window to an obscure Italian saint? Why was the cathedral aligned northeast when all other churches at that time were set facing east toward Jerusalem? And why—"

She finished his thought. "—would a hole be cut in *that* window to allow in a sun ray?"

"A ray that strikes your variant stone every year on the same day," the priest added. "The day of the summer solstice."

She allowed the silence to extend. Here, she realized, was another arcane message camouflaged inside a Christian story. She retreated to the door again, and the priest sent her off with what sounded like a Latin epigram.

"*Quod est Inferius est sicut quod est Superius, et quod est Superius est sicut quod est Inferius. Ad perpetranda Miracula Rei Unius.*"

She failed to grasp its meaning. "I'm sorry?"

"The great Fulcanelli once told me that every flute and image in Chartres was placed in proximity to its neighbor to serve a master design. The Book of Stone is to be read over and again. Every return to its pages offers new revelations. Therein resides the key to your quest, my young Hypatia. May Hermes guide you. ..." His voice receded into the darkness.

"He called me Hypatia," Jaq said. "What did he mean by that?"

Preoccupied with the news ticker scrolling across his phone screen, Elymas ignored her question and kept a heavy foot on the accelerator, eager to make the hundred kilometers to Paris before dark. "They've reopened the airports. I have to fly to Brussels tonight. Anywhere I can drop you?"

She felt a pit in her stomach at the thought of being left alone. Reluctantly, she decided to book a flight back to Washington in the morning. She had to accept the hard reality that she'd probably have more luck getting the wheels of government turning to find Alyssa if she were back at State pounding the phones and pestering Darden and McCrozier. "I haven't even made a hotel reservation in Paris. Any recommendations?"

"Try the Maison Chantal in the Marais."

She wrote down the name of the hotel in her journal. "Ochley's going to skin me alive. I haven't checked in with him for two days."

"Ochley?"

"My boss. I was already in hot water for that little escapade in Ethiopia. I haven't exactly been Mother Theresa to those injured at Chartres." She studied him, trying to determine if he was sorry to see her go. "You have a girlfriend?"

"No."

"Ever married?"

"My line of work isn't exactly conducive to settling down."

"Elymas is an unusual name. Is it a family name?"

"What is this? A Customs interrogation?"

She reached into her handbag and began sharpening her nails with an emery file. "I have ways of making you talk. How well do you know the monsignor?"

"He's a client."

She inched a little closer to him. "He seemed to take a liking to me. Maybe I'll give him a call and dig up some dirt on you."

Elymas froze her with an icy glare.

She was taken aback by how swiftly his mood turned serious; some things about his life were clearly off limits. Had the Lord brought him back to her for another reason? She remembered what Rev. Merry told her: *You must attempt to save every Jew you meet before the Rapture.* She drew a deep breath. "Have you read the New Testament?"

Elymas rolled his eyes. "Here we go."

"I want to tell you how the Lord changed my life."

"Not interested."

"Will you at least pray with me for my friend Alyssa?"

"No."

"Just hear me out," she begged. "The time is fast coming when only those who accept the Lord Jesus as their Savior will be taken up with His Chosen Ones before the Tribulations begin."

"My Chosen Ones have been getting that *spiel* from your Chosen Ones for two thousand years. And my Chosen Ones always get the blame when the big finale doesn't arrive."

"How can you be so cynical? Don't you believe in *anything?*"

"My people have a saying. Beware the man who reads only one book."

"Every religion can't be true."

"I agree. They're all false."

"You're an atheist? A Jewish atheist and a professional thief to boot?"

He swerved the car, causing her to lurch toward him. "Better not get too close. One mortal sin is bad enough, but I've hit the damnation jackpot."

"My pastor sends money to Israel to help against your enemies."

"*My* enemies? Are those the ones who want to blow us up? Or the ones like you who befriend us to usher in Kingdom Come and then, with unconditional love in your hearts, cast us off to Hell to roast with the other unbelievers?"

"It's not like that at all. We're all Yahweh's children."

"Let me give you a real preview of the Rapture." He cupped the back of her head and brought her lips to his, locking onto her for several delicious seconds.

She surfaced from the kiss—and slapped him.

The car skidded off the shoulder. Elymas regained control of the wheel in time to avoid an oncoming Renault with horn blaring.

She fussed with her hair, acting as if she'd just been ravished by a Viking raider. "Are you trying to kill us both?"

"Why wait for the Apocalypse?"

"I just lost my fiancé! Do you stalk funeral homes?"

"When the infidels proselytize, they promise forty virgins, not one. That seems a better bargain than what you're offering."

"I am *not* offering—"

"Don't you ever worry that the end credits will start rolling and you'll be taken up with the trumpets blasting before you've experienced physical love with a man?"

"You think salvation is some sort of *quid pro*—" Those Latin words fired a synapse in her memory. "What'd the monsignor say to me just before we left?"

Elymas looked at her hard, baffled by her abrupt shift of interest. "That Latin gibberish? Who knows? He tends to go off into the ethers."

"I think he may have wanted me to know something else without telling me directly."

"All I heard was '*quod est inferius*' or something like that. Didn't he mention Hermes? Maybe he thinks you need a new purse."

"Can you get on the net with your phone?"

"Surf at the hotel."

"Hand it over."

When he reluctantly complied, she typed the three Latin words from the monsignor's enigmatic farewell into the search engine. The results came back with a page titled *The Emerald Tablet* and the following: *Quod est Inferius est sicut quod est Superius, et quod est Superius est sicut quod est Inferius, ad perpetranda Miracula Rei Unius.* She switched to iGoogle to get a translation: *That which is Below corresponds to that which is Above, and that which is Above corresponds to that which is Below, in the accomplishment of the Miracle of the One Thing.*

What did *that* mean?

The priest was obviously one pew shy of a full congregation. Above. Below. What an abracadabra crock of … She was suddenly struck with an idea. "Do you still have that rope you used to plumb the blast hole?"

"It's in the trunk. Why?"

"Stop the car and get it out."

Elymas grumbled as he pulled over. "Wouldn't a gun be easier?"

"What was that unit of measurement he said the Templars used to build the cathedral?"

He flipped open the trunk lid with his remote key. "About three-quarters of a meter."

She inspected the rope. "I don't want approximately."

"Point seven-three-eight meters, if my memory wasn't irreparably damaged by the beating I took on my head back there."

"You got a calculator on this phone?"

"Yeah, why?"

She tossed him the phone and began unrolling the rope. "Convert the meters into feet."

Elymas ran the numbers and displayed the results: 2.42125 feet.

She walked the length of the extended rope on the ground. Reaching its end, she pulled out a map of the cathedral's crypt. She kicked at the ground in anger. "Why didn't I see it before now?"

"See what?"

"As above, so *below*," she said. "That slanted stone and the sun window in the cathedral were directly above that blast hole in the crypt."

"Probably just a coincidence. I've seen holes like that in several European churches. Renaissance astronomers drilled them to create sun meridians. The cathedrals were the only buildings tall enough to provide the angles needed."

"We're not talking about just *any* cathedral," she reminded him. "That janitor in St. Brice's told me a brotherhood watches over Chartres. They won't even allow crucifixes and tombs inside. And you think they're going to let some stargazer mar the Virgin's sanctuary with holes in Her windows?"

"You got a better explanation?"

Trying to think, she watched the red sun sink slowly into the horizon. "Maybe preserving the Virgin's purity wasn't the real reason the Templars banned crucifixes and burials inside the cathedral. Maybe they were preserving and concealing a message that the Church wanted suppressed."

"Which was?"

"I don't know. But if that beam through St. Apollonaire's window hits the same place every year on the solstice, why would anyone go to the trouble of marking the spot? They could just wait and find it on the first day of summer."

"They were probably just too lazy to go there each year."

She thought back to what little she had learned in high school astronomy class. "Or maybe they knew the precession of the Earth's axis would eventually shift the beam's location." She suddenly stopped pacing, hit by a brainstorm. "That mismatched stone wasn't placed there to remember the beam!"

"What are you talking about?"

"The beam was placed there to remember the *stone!*"

He tapped on his watch, signaling for her to get to the point.

She stood with the sun behind her and began angling her body in a circle, moving her shadow like the hand on a sundial. "Centuries after the Templars were destroyed, somebody must have become worried the sun's marking point would be lost. They put that stone with the gold tenon there to memorialize it forever."

"You're saying the bombers set off the explosion under that sun stone on purpose? There's one flaw in your theory, counselor."

"And that would be?"

"Even if they possessed the linear coordinates, they wouldn't know how far down to drill below the crypt."

She pulled the rope taut. "How many rings were in that labyrinth?"

"Twelve. But what does that have to do with anything?"

"You really think the Templars built a labyrinth just so peasants could stroll on it?"

"You know what the monsignor yelled in Latin when I knocked?" When she shrugged, he told her: "St. Augustine's famous admonition: It is solved by walking."

"What does *that* mean?"

"Medieval people were obsessive walkers. They walked halfway across Europe just to ogle St. James's bones."

"Yeah, but the monsignor would reject *your* conclusion as being too apparent. There has to be another reason the Templars ordered the masons to build that labyrinth."

"Such as?"

She took Augustine's advice and started walking up and down the length of the rope. "In Kentucky, shovel rigs dig coal by driving around a large hole in concentric circles. Each ring goes one level deeper until the miners locate the veins."

"Wait a minute. You're saying that labyrinth is a secret depth chart?"

She nodded. "It's not even a true labyrinth. There's no way to get lost in it because there's only one trail. The Templars conned the Vatican into believing it was a harmless meditation ritual, but they knew it was a reverse elevation map. Twelve rings and the vault below equals …"

"Thirteen." His hesitant tone was a concession that her theory didn't seem so far-fetched now. "The Virgin and Twelve Apostles."

She was walking now in ever-tightening circles, rehearsing what it might feel like to navigate the labyrinth. "Each ring could have meant one Chartres cubit in depth. To find what was hidden under the cathedral, one would have to know the purposes of both the sunstone *and* the labyrinth. It's like a double blind. If I'm right, whatever those bombers were looking for was buried thirteen Temple cubits below the crypt directly under that sunstone in the South Transept. Twelve cubits represented by the labyrinth rings and the thirteenth cubit would have been the hidden vault itself."

Elymas shrugged. "We'll never know. Those French cops have probably refilled the hole by now."

She stared at his car. "How's your oil?"

"You think my engine might be a portal into the fourth dimension?"

"Pull the dipstick."

Elymas shook his head as he unlatched the hood, no doubt wondering where this next cockeyed idea of hers was headed.

She wiped the dipstick on the grass and examined its notches. "Calibrated in meters. Perfect. Measure the length of your rope. And don't exaggerate. I hear men tend to do that."

He muttered something about wishing he had left her in Lalibela as he crawled across the grass, flipping the dipstick end-to-end and adding up the sums. He came to a spot on the rope where she was holding her finger.

"See that discoloration?" she asked.

"Yeah, so?"

"That's the rub stain where the rope stopped going down the blast shaft when you lowered it. Now multiply the Chartres cubit in feet by thirteen."

Elymas hit the calculator button on his phone and came up with 31.476 feet—the exact length of the stained section on the rope. From his knees, he stared up at her in amazement.

"Gee!" She slapped her cheeks in mock surprise. "Who'da thought?"

EIGHTEEN

SATOR
APERO
TENET
OPERA
ROTAS

LISBON
APRIL, 1457

"We could hire a bark for the day and sail it down the river!" Pero pleaded. "How else am I going to learn to tack?"

Zarco motioned for him to pick up the pace. "Will you for just one hour stop pining for the sea? There are other hidden treasures to explore."

Dias winked at Zarco. "Treasures more precious than gold."

"What are you two bleating about?" Pero demanded.

Zarco continued to play coy. "Just come along and keep a tight rudder."

Pero groused and crabbed as he followed them down the steps that cut through the old Moorish quarter of the Alfama and led to the busy docks along the Tagus. Eannes had given them a rare Easter leave from their instruction, and Zarco was insisting that they, three Marranos no less, don their pleated coats and spend their free day in the city attending Mass. Zarco took them along the riverbank until they came to the Recolhimento da Encarnacção, an imposing edifice where the Order's wives and families kept residence while their husbands were away on voyages for the Crown.

Removing their split-brim wool hats, they entered the Santos Chapel and drew scandalized glances and murmurs as they took seats in the rear pew. Pero saw to his dismay that they were the only males in attendance. He searched for an excuse to escape, but he was trapped in the pew between his two mates. He whispered to Zarco through gritted teeth: "If Eannes finds out we invaded a Mass reserved for virgins and widows, he'll use our skins for deck mops."

Zarco hid a grin as he replied *sub rosa* without turning. "Then we'll all just have to take a vow of silence, won't we?"

The Introit bell rang, and the priest appeared from the sacristy. After glaring at his new worshippers, he turned his back to commence the Mass.

Pero watched, appalled, as Zarco pulled a walnut shell from his pocket and tossed it at the head of a *menina* sitting five rows ahead. The young lady turned with lifted veil and smiled as if having expected their arrival. She was stunningly beautiful, with eyes as black as basalt and thin lips the hue of ripe plums. He elbowed Zarco in a signal to cease the foolery. The *menina* turned again, but this time she shifted her penetrating gaze one seat over. Taken aback by such boldness, Pero saw her sharing giggled whispers with another female novice sitting next to her. The two girls, he realized, were talking about *him* now.

Zarco whispered to his ear. "What do you think of the shorter one?"

Pero stole another glance at her. "Who is she?"

"Filipa Moniz, the daughter of Bartholomeu Perestrello."

"The Captain of Port Santos?"

Zarco couldn't take his pining eyes off Filipa. "Her father and my grandfather discovered Madeira together. I've known her since childhood. We're in love."

Pero turned sharply on Dias, informed that his fellow squire had helped Zarco trick him into becoming an unwitting conspirator in this tryst.

Dias shrugged to indicate that he was powerless to stop it. "Our friend has a passion. He is determined to marry her."

"Does her father approve?" Pero asked.

Zarco waved furtively at his beloved, drawing more giggles. "He died three months ago and left her mother deep in debt. The *senhora* had to sell Santos and move here. I'm going to offer my hand to Filipa this afternoon."

Pero was mortified. His head swam with the implications of such a reckless plan. Would the Order really permit Zarco to marry at such a young age? Surely the Old Man would take umbrage at not being consulted on the betrothal. Still, if Zarco carried through with the outlandish plan, at least he would be marrying into the lineage of the Order. Both the Perestrello and Moniz families were steeped in service to Tomar, and he remembered hearing rumors in the dockyards that Captain Perestrello had compiled a collection of books and portolans rivaled only by the Old Man's own archives.

When Mass ended, Zarco stationed himself near the cloister, and as the mother superior led her female charges past him, he launched forward and bowed. "Gracious Mother, my brothers and I wish to offer our gratitude for being permitted to attend Mass in your magnificent chapel."

The abbess had been prepared to deliver a swift scolding, but Zarco's unctuous charm softened her ire. "Had you submitted a prior request—"

"Profuse apologies, Holy Mother!" Zarco left the abbess momentarily speechless by bending to a knee in a performance of contrition worthy of a flagellant. "We are squires from the Order of Christ. We were permitted a day of prayer on short notice. My father told me I should never pass up the opportunity to take communion in the Chapel of Santos."

The abbess's scowl transformed into a beam of pride. "Any member of the Order of Christ is of course welcome in my chapel."

Behind the abbess, the female novices raised their veils and smiled, aware that she was being played like a lute.

Zarco pressed his hands together in a fervent appeal. "I was advised that a dear friend from my youth has recently taken up residence in your house. I pray it not be true, but I fear her father may have passed to his heavenly reward."

"You must mean our Filipa," the abbess said.

Zarco affected a near swoon. "Oh, cruel world! The mere annunciation of her sweet name causes my heart to bleed. Would it be possible to offer my condolences to her in private?"

Filipa supported his unctuous theatrics by keeping her tearful eyes lowered in modesty.

After weighing the risks, the unsuspecting abbess finally acquiesced. "I suppose a few minutes in the presence of a chaperone would do no harm."

Wincing at that condition, Zarco glanced at Pero in a pointed plea for assistance. With little enthusiasm, Pero nodded his willingness to accept the responsibility. Zarco remained bent, hiding a smirk of anticipation until the abbess confirmed the appointment.

"And a second lady must also be present."

Filipa leapt to her cue. "Mother, I pray you chose anyone but Catrina. She is a terrible gossip."

The abbess took the bait. "Catrina it is. One hour in the garden."

A lithe girl with mournful, smoky eyes stepped forward. Several moments passed before Pero realized that he had been holding his breath, so forceful was this tall co-chaperone's effect on him. Attired from head to toe in black, Catrina was not as beautiful as Filipa, and some might even suggest her features were gangly and overly common, but there was a glow about her that made him feel both exhilarated and strangely at ease.

Wait. … Wasn't she the one who had been sitting next to Filipa during the Mass? He realized that Filipa had schemed all along to have Catrina chosen. Zarco had clearly found his female equal in cleverness and deception.

With the precious minutes flying by, the two couples walked the grounds in awkward silence. Rather than fall into the animated conversation expected of two old friends who had not seen each other for months, Filipa surveyed the walls, as if intrigued by the construction, while Zarco turned uncharacteristically reticent. They wouldn't even look at each other.

Why does he not get on with the courting?

As the walking foursome reached the far corner of the garden, Filipa repeatedly glanced back at Catrina, sending inscrutable messages to her friend with her hooded eyes. Suddenly, obscured from view of the convent windows by the trees, Filipa fell into Zarco's embrace, and hand-in-hand they dashed for a stone urn that had been placed at the crease between the two wall panels.

Pero stood frozen in disbelief as Zarco jumped atop the urn, hoisted Filipa across the wall, and then followed her over. The entire escape operation had been performed with such swift and practiced precision that it was accomplished before Pero could even mount a protest. He was about to shout them back when a soft hand came over his lips.

"Love must not be denied its due," Catrina whispered to his ear.

"But—"

Catrina firmed the clasp of her fragranced palm over his mouth, and he finally surrendered to her insistence on silence. He could not be certain what discombobulated him more: the likelihood of his being marshaled out of the Order for allowing Zarco to flaunt the rules of chivalry, or the tingling sensation now being aroused in him by this girl's touch.

She tested him by removing her hand. "What is your name?"

"Pero," he heaved, catching his breath.

"What does it mean?"

He blinked hard. Such a strange *menina*. What does *any* name mean? And how can she be so calm? Surely she would face expulsion if discovered abetting her friend's insubordination.

Before he could respond, Catrina answered her own question. "*Aspero* means harsh and rough, but you are neither. *Desespero* means despair. You seem happy enough. Ah, I know. *Perola*. Your mother must have named you for a pearl."

"Why do you say that?"

"A pearl is formed in the sea, but only on land does it fulfill its destiny by drawing attention away from what its master seeks to hide." She stared into his eyes. "You love the sea, but I see you on land. And just like the pearl, you protect yourself with a shell of secrecy."

He was unnerved by her apparent power to peer into his soul's deepest desires. "Why do you live here?"

Her smile vanished. "Three years ago, my father was sent by Prince Henry into the Sea of Darkness. He never returned. My mother died of grief. I have no family. This is where they send the survivors of the mariners who perish."

"You'll get out when you marry."

"There is no hope of that," she said. "I have no dowry. My father spent what little he owned to provision his caravel. I will end my days in this cold *tumulo*. And you? Do you intend to leave another widow to the world?"

"A seaman does not make a good husband."

She smiled sadly, impressed by his concession to hard reality. "Show me your palm."

Alarmed, he scanned the grounds to make certain that no one was watching. "They teach you to practice the Romani witchery here?"

She stole his hand from behind his back and turned it toward her eyes. "My grandmother bequeathed the art to me." She studied his lines. "You say you want to be a mariner?"

"With all my heart."

She reluctantly released his hand, and said nothing more.

"What did you see in it?"

"Palm reading is a foolish diversion," she insisted. "I play with it to take my mind off the boredom here."

He sensed that she possessed wisdom rare for one so young. "Please, I want to know."

Approving of his brave insistence, she opened his right hand again and pointed to a calloused section of raised flesh just below his little finger. "This mound is the Isle of Neptune. Your heart line approaches it, but ..." She averted her eyes.

"But what?"

"It does not reach the Isle."

"What does that mean?"

She tarried a moment before offering the revelation. "The Isle of Neptune represents the kingdom of the sea. I have never read the palm of a mariner who did not have his heart line on the Isle." She squeezed his hand to chase off the gloom of the prophecy. "But there is always a first time. And if the sea is truly your wish, I am certain you will one day attain it."

ΠΙΠΕΤΕΕΠ

SATOR
APERO
TENET
OPERA
ROTAS

PARIS
FEBRUARY 6, PRESENT DAY

Drunken soccer fans below Jaq's hotel window belted out another chorus of the *Marseillaise*. Unable to sleep, she glanced at the room phone again, but the message light remained dark. Last time she had checked, just before midnight, Rep. Yardley's office still had not heard from Alyssa.

The bedside clock clicked three a.m.

She drove her face into the pillow. Her flight to Washington was in just a few hours, and it was going to be brutal now. She wanted to blame her insomnia on the noise and the guilt over abandoning Alyssa, but she knew better.

She couldn't get *him* out of her mind.

What did he think he was doing, anyway, kissing her like that and dropping her off without even leaving a number? Good riddance! He probably had a woman in every city. She knew the type. No morals. She caught herself snuggling with the pillow. She threw it aside and banged her head against the mattress. *He's a rake and a thief! For God's sake, forget him!*

Desperate for a diversion, she decided to turn to her list of other current obsessions: Paul's murder, her abduction in Rome, that Vatican priest's text messages and disappearance, and the Chartres bombing. They all seemed to have one thing in common: A connection to Mithras.

Was the answer to these mysteries locked inside that SATOR square—or the Templar square, or whatever the heck the damn thing was? Did those medieval Ethiopians really believe that a magical word square held the secret Name of God? Why had that priest murdered in Lalibela spent his last agonizing moments scribbling the first word SATOR in myrrh?

And why was this Elymas guy always showing up at these Mithras sites?

She unpacked the Latin-English dictionary she had purchased at Shakespeare & Company, and turned to the word square written in her journal:

```
S A T O R
A R E P O
T E N E T
O P E R A
R O T A S
```

She jotted down some notes on the Latin definitions she found:

SATOR: A sower, planter, begetter, or father (Alyssa was wrong— there is *this word in Latin!)*

AREPO: No such word.

TENET: To hold, to gain mastery over, to reach an object striven for, to hold fast and defend.

OPERA: works or makes effort; trouble, pains, service, exertion, labor, strive.

ROTAS: wheels, the sun's orb, the Wheel of Fortune.

She tried creating some sentences using different combinations:

The sower Arepo holds with effort the wheels.

The father Arepo holds with trouble the wheels.

The father Arepo masters in service the Sun.

None of them made any sense.

Maybe the secret was hidden in the pronunciation of the words. What did SATOR *sound* like? There was the 'T" of the Tau Cross again. SATOR was similar to Satori. Wasn't that Japanese? Yes, the word for enlightenment. A connection between a Japanese word and an ancient European magical square seemed far-fetched. SATOR … SATORI … What about SATURN?

Saturn Arepo masters the service of the sun.

Just more gibberish. Frustrated—in more ways than one—she turned off the light and dived under the covers.

The next morning, she hurried through Charles DeGaulle airport and saw the monitor blinking an advisory that her flight was delayed thirty minutes. That gave her just enough time to purchase some moisturizer, so she checked the directory and found an *L'Occitane en Provence* store two gates down. She hustled over to the small shop and searched the products on the shelves while the saleswoman helped another customer. Scratching at her dry palms, she muttered to herself, "My hands feel like week-old grits."

The clerk and the other customer turned toward her with quizzical looks.

"Sorry," she said. "I'm looking for a good lotion. Something organic."

After finishing her sale, the saleswoman came over and, presenting a royal blue box trimmed in gold, opened its lid to reveal an assortment of creams. "This is our most popular."

Jaq read the box's label: *Arca Archa*. Where had she seen those words before? Wait, hadn't that been part of the inscription she had read on the bay at Chartres Cathedral? She pulled her journal from her bag and found *Hic Amititur Archa Cederis*, the Latin phrase written under the box shown wheeled away in a cart. She asked the sales clerk, "What does *Arca Archa* mean?"

"It is Occitan, of course. From my home region of Provence. How would you say in English? Treasure chest, perhaps?"

Jaq wrote down the Chartres inscription on the back of her receipt and showed it to her. "Can you tell me what this says in English?"

The sales clerk put on her reading glasses and studied what she had written. "This appears to be a mixture of Occitan and Latin. The nearest I can come might be: 'Here you are to work through the chest.'"

At the door, the departing female shopper turned. "I couldn't help overhearing. I'm an exchange student from Boston. I've been studying Romance Languages at the Sorbonne this semester. I hope you don't mind the intrusion, but the Latin word '*archa*' means 'ark.'"

"*Mai oui*," the saleswoman said. "That would make perfect sense."

Jaq took a second look at the label. "'Ark' can also mean chest?"

"An *arca archa* is a special chest," explained the American student. "Similar to a coffin or money coffer. And '*cedere*' means to 'withdraw' or 'take away'. In English, you might say 'secede?'"

"A box like the Ark of the Covenant, no?" the saleswoman suggested. "Our treasure trove of creams is just as potent, but not nearly as expensive. Shall I wrap it for you?"

Lost in thought, Jaq hadn't heard the question.

She knew Ochley would read her the riot act, but she rescheduled her flight for the next day and took a cab back into the city to the *Bibliothèque nationale*. At the reference desk, she was assigned a librarian who spoke English and asked the woman if there was a photographic compilation of Chartres Cathedral's sculptures and art. After several searches, the librarian found an online database.

Jaq scanned the scrolling rows of digital images. "On the central bay along the north porch, I saw a depiction of what looked like a box on a cart."

The librarian clicked through hundreds of photographs until finding one that fit the description.

"Yes, that's it!" Jaq said. "Are those leaves on the base of the column?"

The librarian opened another browser window and scanned a pictorial encyclopedia of fauna. "The leaf has a candle-flame shape with serrated edges. That would be an elm." She read more of the description. "How interesting. It says here that elm wood is used for coffins because of its resistance to water."

Jaq wondered if the box portrayed on the Chartres bay had been some kind of waterproof container. "Does the elm have any symbolic meaning in France?"

Smiling thinly, the librarian explained with a hint of condescension in her voice: "It is our tree of freedom. The most famous elm stood not far from here, in front of the Église of Saints Gervais and Protais. I seem to recall the existence of a drawing of it on one of the stalls there."

Despite the attitude, Jaq thanked the librarian, and she was about to leave to go check out that church when she remembered another aspect of the SATOR-Templar square that she had yet to track down. "I hate to impose further, but could you also find some information for me about the god Saturn?"

The librarian sighed, no doubt wondering what the two topics could possibly have in common, but she punched in the search request and reported the result. "Saturn was the Roman divinity who protected sowing and reaping of harvests."

SATOR in Latin, Jaq remembered, meant 'sower' or 'planter.'

The librarian read on. "In the eastern Roman Empire, Saturn was worshipped as Mithras Helios, the nocturnal sun of the invisible world." She lowered her reading glasses. "Does that have any significance for you?"

Jaq was rushing for the doors.

In the heart of the Marais district, she walked into St. Gervais-et-St. Protais Church and found its nave filled with painting canvases and scaffolding. She threaded past the maze of metal trestles and searched in vain for the picture of the famous elm that the librarian had told her about. Turning a corner in the dusky light, she nearly stumbled over a plasterer who was on his knees, repairing a cracked plinth. Annoyed, the man pointed to a sign indicating that the church was closed and barked, "*Fermé!*"

Startled by his ferocious shout for her to leave, she took a quick step back, as if having stepped on a feral cat. When her heart was back down from her throat, she screwed up the courage to ask him, "The elm tree. Where did it stand?"

The laborer didn't even offer her the courtesy of a glance, but continued slathering dollops of cement mucilage over the base of the ancient column with the expert swiftness of a Michelangelo. "*Orme?* Below the porch! Outside!"

"I was told I'd find a depiction of the most famous elm in France here."

The workman shot to his feet. "*Non!* Not the most famous!"

"But the librarian at the Bibliothèque—"

"Parisians!" The indignant Frenchman flailed his arms and sent plaster flying. "They think their fèces is the most famous fèces in all of France! Go to Gisors in my home of Normandy! There you will see where the *véritable Elm Célèbre* stood before the fools cut it down!"

Her jaw dropped. The damn tree is in *Normandy?* That patronizing librarian had sent her on a wild goose chase. How many sacred elms could there be in one country? Skeptical, she risked his wrath again. "The name Gisors doesn't sound French."

Grudgingly impressed by her persistence, the man seemed to warm up to her. "My hometown was founded as a Roman camp. The French spoken by the soldiers there became mixed with Latin. '*Giser*' in Old French means 'to be buried.'"

She was intrigued by the possibility that Roman soldiers—devotees of Mithras—had buried something there important enough to name the town for it. She waited for the rest of the lesson on etymology. When he did not volunteer it, she kept at him. "And '*ors*'?"

His eyes came alive. "From the Latin '*aurum*.' An object made of gold."

How could a common construction worker become so versed in linguistics? She knew the French were supposed to be well-educated, but come on.

Detecting her doubt about his authority on the subject, he puffed out his chest in a challenge. "You think all they teach us here is how to hold a chisel?"

She was utterly baffled. What else *would* they teach? Then, she remembered seeing a sign on the building next to the church as she entered: *Association des Compagnons du Devoir du Tour de France.* There had to be a good reason why this man was so knowledgeable about mysterious elms and buried gold. She searched the pews, making certain they were still alone. "Are you a member of the brotherhood that protects the cathedrals?" He turned aside, but she wouldn't be denied her answer. "You think gold is buried in Gisors?"

"Maybe something to do with gold," he said cryptically. "I helped build the Eglise St. Gervais-et-St. Protais in Gisors."

Now she was really confused. She picked up a missal in the pew and checked the name. "I thought *this* was the church of Saints Protais and Gervais?"

The plasterer grinned like a man enjoying a secret. "A *singulier* coincidence, no? That I should work on two churches with the same name? Both with famous elms. And both ..." He stopped short.

"What else?"

He stared at her as if debating how much more to reveal. "You are a *beau curieux femme*. You might profit from a *promenade* down the *rue des Barres*. If you happen upon Monsieur Didier in his smoke shoppe, tell him the blooms will be early this spring and ask him to show you his collection of *cigarillos*." He then turned from her and resumed his work.

Why couldn't these French ever speak plainly instead of always dancing around a subject with riddles and innuendos? She was starting to wonder if there was an underground network in this city that guarded its mysteries. As she departed, she looked over her shoulder and saw the plasterer stealing a furtive glance at her. What had been his purpose in telling her such a strange thing? Could she even trust him? She felt as if she was being led deeper and deeper into a black hole. The voice in her head warned her: *Just let it go.*

But she couldn't—not if there was a possibility that this Mithras trail might lead her to the identity of the assassin who wanted her dead.

Afraid she might be walking into a trap, she purchased a blonde wig and sunglasses in a *Bon Marché* before launching her investigation of the street that the plasterer had so obliquely but tantalizingly suggested she check out. She found a busy powder room on the fourth floor of the department store and, after memorizing the faces of the women there with her, slipped into one of the empty stalls. She waited several minutes, time enough for a turnover of the patrons using the room, and then returned to the show floor wearing the disguise.

Once outside again, she circled the block twice before moving in on her target. At first glance, nothing appeared unusual about the rue des Barres, which was lined with the typical Parisian residences and cafes. Only when she passed the Hotel des Barres did a strange architectural feature catch her eye. A cavernous underpass, shaped in the point of a bullet, was crowned by a keystone crest studded with the same splayed cross she had seen behind Christ's head at Chartres. A small rose window circled with leaves decorated one of the bays.

Curious about it, she stopped in at a shop next door. "*Parlez-vous anglais?*"

The proprietor behind the counter could hardly be bothered. "*Un peu.*"

"There is a crest on the door out there."

The shopkeeper nodded wearily, apparently having answered that inquiry many times. "*Ici partition de fortress des la Templiers!*"

She understood two of those French words all too well. If he was being truthful, then these walls must have once been part of a Templar fortress. Was *this* the reason the plasterer at the church had directed her here? She kept digging for information. "And the small rose on the window. What does it signify?"

The shopkeeper shrugged. "Who can say?"

"How large was this fortress?"

"A *ville* unto itself. The monks drained the swamps in the Marais. Their ramparts extended to Saints Protais and Gervais."

"*That* church had a connection to the Templars?"

This time, growing more suspicious of her interest, he barely nodded.

"You wouldn't be Monsieur Didier?" When the man didn't deny that identification, she spoke the coded greeting that she had been given. "I was told to tell you the blooms would be early this year."

The shopkeeper's eyes narrowed. "Are you an *aficionado* of cigars?"

She didn't know what to make of this odd exchange, but she decided to see it through. "No, but I would be pleased to see your *cigarillo* collection."

The merchant looked beyond her shoulder toward his window. Seeing no approaching shoppers, he motioned her into his back office and locked the door behind them. He opened an antique safe with a *fleur-de-lis* emblem on its door and brought forth with great care a leather-bound volume titled *Le Mystere des Cathedrales* by Fulcanelli. "A first edition. Very few survive."

She studied the gold-lettered title on the engraved spine. Hadn't Elymas said that Fulcanelli was the name of the monsignor's long-deceased mentor? She thumbed through the book's fragile pages, looking for anything meaningful. The text was in French, but one word caught her eye: *Rota*. She asked him to translate the paragraph in question for her.

The shopkeeper examined the six lines that had caught her interest. After a moment of debate, he read Fulcanelli's paragraph aloud in English: "'In the Middle Ages, the central rose window of the porches was called Rota, the wheel. Now, the wheel is the alchemical hieroglyph of the time necessary for the coction of the philosophical matter and consequently of the coction itself. The sustained, constant and equal fire, which the artist maintains night and day in the course of this operation, is for this reason called the fire of the wheel.'"

She mentally inserted this new definition for ROTAS into the SATOR square: *Mithras, the sun god ... AREPO ... masters the work on the rose windows.* Was this the third similarity between Gisors and Chartres that the plasterer had been hinting at? She asked him: "Is there a *rota* window in Gisors?"

His glare turned ominous. "If you wish to play with fire, *mademoiselle*, my advice is that you return to America and elevate your cuisine."

That veiled warning, flavored with equal doses of misogyny and French condescension, merely stoked her determination to get to the bottom of the mystery. "How far is Gisors from here?"

He shook his head at her stubbornness. "Seventy kilometers."

"Anything else I should know before going there?"

He returned the Fulcanelli book to the safe and spun the combination lock. With his back still turned, he whispered: "The *Templiers* once governed Gisors."

A chill crawled her spine. Could this Norman town of Gisors, like Chartres, guard a secret connection between Mithras and the Templars?

She reached Gisors by late afternoon and parked the rental car in front of a high Gothic façade that resembled the west portal of Chartres Cathedral. There it was: the rose window. She got out and searched the church grounds for the mysterious elm of freedom, but there was not even a stump in sight. On the frontispiece of the court was a Latin inscription:

TERRIBILIS EST LOCUS ISTE

She walked into the nave and was immediately drawn to a stained glass window of the Virgin Mary whose bright sheen and style appeared too modern for its medieval surroundings.

"If only you could have seen its predecessor."

She looked over at the pews to find the source of that declaration, a heavy-set man with great tufts of whiskers sprouting under his bulbous nose. He arose from the kneeler and, with no small difficulty, trudged over to join her in gazing up at the object of her admiration.

"That window is only sixty years old," he said. "When the Germans bombed us, the original was destroyed and had to be replaced."

"What did the first window here depict?" she asked.

"Our patron saints, Gervais and Protais. They were twin soldiers martyred for their faith. The only other representation of them that survives is in Chartres Cathedral. I keep a photocopy of that one in my office."

She didn't remember seeing such a window at Chartres. "May I take a look?"

As the portly man led her out the church and across the square, he offered his hand to her in a belated welcome. "I am Pierre Lamoy, mayor of Gisors. I supplement my income by serving as a tour guide on weekends. You just missed all the excitement. The film crew left last night."

"Film crew?"

"They were here from London shooting a BBC documentary." He brought her inside his office and found the book on a shelf. He opened it to a page with a photograph of the Chartres window that he had told her about. "Here it is."

She leaned over the bound folio. This copy of the window showed the sainted military brothers side-by-side, one wielding a sword and the other a mace. The description said the window still hung in the clerestory of Chartres's south transept and faced the St. Apollonaire lancet in the bay below. How odd: Two brothers in arms, worshipped in a cathedral that celebrated the peace of the Virgin ... brothers who, like the Templars, had been gruesomely murdered. She looked around the office and saw dozens of histories and travel guides. "You seem quite informed about the cathedrals in your country."

The mayor smiled with pride. "My wife and I take holidays to visit them."

"Outside I saw a Latin description on the church's door frame."

He chuckled. "This place is terrible."

She was taken aback by his harsh assessment of his hometown. "Actually, Gisors seems like a very nice place to live."

His chuckle escalated into a belly laugh. "No, no. I meant that is what the Latin inscription says. 'This place is terrible.'"

"You're kidding, right?"

"No, I am quite serious, *mademoiselle*. And so, I fear, was the anonymous author of that admonition. The scene above the inscription shows Jacob striving for heaven on his ladder. It is identical to the front page of the *Mutus Liber*, a hermetic treatise on alchemy."

She turned and studied the Gisors church through the window. Was this a confirmation that the monsignor's dark art had indeed played a role in crafting the rose windows and crypt depositories in the cathedrals? "But if alchemists had a hand in its construction, why would they call it a terrible place?"

The mayor shrugged. "Maybe they were using the word in its original meaning. Terrible, as inducing a terror in the soul."

She took a closer look at the folio copy of the Chartres window depicting the martyred twin soldiers. "Was it rare for military brothers to be honored like this?"

"I seem to recall other depictions." He searched his crowded shelves and brought down a book titled *Medieval Insignias and Seals*, opening it to a page that held the image of a signet:

"Were the soldiers on this emblem also saints?" she asked.

"*Au contraire*," the mayor said with a sly grin. "They were excommunicates. This was the seal of the Knights Templar."

She borrowed his magnifying glass and honed in on the mysterious knights shown on the insignia. "But I thought the Temple was wealthy. Why would Templars be required to ride two men to a horse?"

"Perhaps there is another meaning to the image."

She tried to make sense of these revelations. Two Chartres windows facing each other; one sun-pierced and depicting Apollo's temple, the other with two martial brothers watching over the temple like an honor guard. Hadn't the monsignor told her that every feature in Chartres was placed next to its neighbor in a grand design? She rechecked the plat of Chartres Cathedral in the mayor's guidebook. The St. Apollonaire window had been set next to another window depicting the miracles of the Virgin. The window with these martyred brothers stood adjacent to a pane showing the Virgin holding the Christ child. Could these proximities to the Virgin really be just a coincidence? These two fighting brothers had been remembered with churches in Paris and Gisors; churches that once possessed a Templar connection and were home to sacred elms destroyed under controversial circumstances. Turning back to the mayor, she said, "I was told that a famous elm grew near this church."

He nodded with unabashed pride. "The elm and the original *église* stood where the old castle now exists. The precise site of the elm is now lost, but a cross was erected in its remembrance. Would you like to see it?"

She took him up on the offer, and even though it was winter, the waddling mayor sweated profusely as he led her on foot down a country road toward the village of Neaufles-Saint-Martin. After several minutes, they came to a lichen-encrusted marker carved with a Templar *cross pattée.* Not far away, the ruins of a round castle crowned a large earthen mound. The medieval tower resembled a stepped wedding cake and seemed more suited for an astronomical observatory than a defensive bastion.

"This tower sat between the French and Norman armies," the mayor explained. "Kings conducted treaty negotiations under the elm here."

"What happened to the tree?"

"It was cut down by a culprit whose identity remains a mystery."

"So, then what did the Templars have to do with Gisors?"

"In the twelfth century, King Louis VII placed the village in the charge of a knight named de Payns. Eventually, England and France agreed to a truce, and Gisors was given to the dowry of the King's daughter, who was offered in marriage to Henry Plantagenet. Because the bride was only three years old, the two kingdoms agreed to place Gisors under Templar rule until she came of age."

"That's the end of the story?"

The mayor grinned at her American impatience. "Only the beginning." He led her down a stairwell into the mound. "This dungeon was called the Prisoner's Tower. One of the Templar founders was a knight named Hugh de Payns."

"The same de Payns who had governed the castle?"

"Very likely. He and other Templar leaders were imprisoned here and at Chinon."

"Were they also executed here?"

"No, most of the monks were burned in Paris. But there is a legend that some of them escaped and brought their treasure on carts to Gisors. This chateau guarded the escape route to the coast."

"Do *you* believe that's what happened?"

"What I believe is that such tales bring us tourists and their dollars."

"Was this story of the treasure only recently discovered?"

He shook his head. "The legend is quite old. I was told of it as a child."

"Then why would the BBC want to do a show about it now?"

"I was not told the reason. But there are many passages below our feet. During the war, a gardener claimed to have found a Roman chapel in one. He said it held Templar crosses and coffers. Many here dismissed him as a liar."

"Why did the gardener think the chapel was Roman?"

"He found markings in Latin." The mayor led her to a hole in the wall that dropped to a shaft. "This is where the gardener went in. He was nearly crushed by a cave-in and suffered two broken legs."

"And yet he kept returning to these tunnels?"

He nodded. "Until the entry was sealed to prevent another catastrophe."

She wondered what had caused the gardener to take such a risk. "He must have truly believed he saw something of great value to keep coming back."

"Or *thought* he saw something," the mayor cautioned. "I am told the allure of the occult can sometimes be stronger even than the lust for gold."

She was beginning to understand *that* warning all too well. She ran a finger down the creases around the blockage and felt fresh mortar. "Has this passage been opened recently?"

"Not in forty years."

Something didn't add up. "What was the name of that film company?"

"Bilqis Media."

"You didn't leave the camera crew in here alone, did you?"

"They filmed only during the day because of the light. I allowed them to store their equipment overnight so that they could …" He became silent, suddenly understanding the possible consequences of his neglectful oversight. "But their permit from the Ministere de la Culture was in good order."

She had a sinking feeling. "May I use the phone in your office?"

Her call to the BBC in London confirmed her fear: No one there knew of a company named Bilqis Media. She next dialed UK directory assistance and was told only one listing existed with Bilqis in its name. She asked to be connected to that number, and when a receptionist with a Middle Eastern accent answered, she inquired: "I'm looking for Bilqis Media. Have you heard of it?"

"I am sorry, no."

"I don't mean to be rude, but what is Bilqis?"

"I should put you through to our publicity director."

Moments later, another woman came on the line. "Yes, I am told you have a question about the name our foundation? We promote tourism to Yemen. We are named for the famous Queen of Bilqis."

Jaq fell silent, perplexed why a company trying to cover its tracks as a television documentary unit would name itself after a queen from Yemen.

The woman on the phone seemed to sense her confusion. "You may know her as Sheba."

Jaq shot a stunned glance at the mayor, repeating the name aloud over the line to make certain. "Sheba of the Bible?"

"We call her kingdom Saba," the woman said. "The Ethiopians call it Sheba."

"The Queen of Sheba ruled *both* Yemen and Ethiopia?"

The woman became suspicious. "May I ask the reason for your call?"

"I'm a U.S. State Department lawyer. Just doing some research."

The woman took a long breath on the line, as if questioning why an American official would have to call a private foundation for such information.

Jaq crossed her fingers. "Our computers are down at the moment."

Finally, the woman explained, "We believe the queen's palace was in Yemen. The Ethiopians insist that she returned from Jerusalem to—"

"I'm sorry. Did you say the queen was once in *Jerusalem?*"

"Yes, it is written in your Old Testament and in the Koran. King Solomon of the Israelites invited her to visit him in Jerusalem. Some say Solomon fell in love with her."

"And she eventually left Jerusalem?"

"This is so. The Ethiopians have a legend that the queen gave birth to a son by King Solomon named Menelik. They believe that when Menelik went back to Ethiopia with his mother, he stole the Ark of the Covenant. In Yemen, of course, we think that story is a myth."

Jaq thanked the woman and hung up. Shaken by what she had just learned, she turned to the mayor. "I have to get into that tunnel."

The mayor's eyes rounded in protest. "I cannot allow it!"

"You may have been the victim of a hoax, or worse. Only you and I will know. I promise to tell no one."

"Such an attempt would be too dangerous!"

Stymied, she tried the only tact that might work on a principled Frenchman: a play on his vanity. "In Paris, a mason told me that Gisors is one of the great jewels of France."

The mayor preened. "A *Compagnion* told you that?"

She threaded her arm around his, drawing him closer in a calculated gesture of comradeship. Not above using a little flirting, she whispered with a smile: "*Monsieur*, in the short time I've spent with you, I can see that you are a dedicated guardian of France's heritage. How would it look if those trespassers went on television and told the world that they found something of great value right under your nose? We have to find out what they were doing in that tunnel and stop them."

Aghast at the possibility of having his reputation besmirched, the mayor finally gave a reluctant nod to her excavation request.

Armed with pick axes, Jaq and the mayor descended the dungeon stairs of the motte tower and chiseled at the blocked entry until the stones finally gave way. She took the lead into the passage, and after several minutes of crawling, she wiggled through a wormhole and assisted her huffing accomplice through the breach. Together they came to their feet and stared at a vaulted chapel that held a stone altar inscribed with Templar crosses and Latin etchings. The place looked just as the gold-crazed gardener had described it decades ago.

The mayor stood awestruck. "This must be the crypt of the old church."

Jaq saw skid marks marring the flagstones, evidence that a large box had been recently dragged out. Following the scored lines to another tunnel, she asked him, "Where do you think this leads?"

"Perhaps to the present church. Or to a cellar in the village."

She shined the light on several carvings on the walls: The SATOR square stood out amid the old drawings. Next to the magical square, several spiraling 'S's with a Tau cross drawn inside a flaming heart had been scratched.

The mayor perched reading glasses on his bulbous nose to examine the wall. "I once saw graffiti like this in the Doudray dungeon at Chinon."

"What do these 'S's mean?"

The mayor opened his knapsack and pulled out a dog-eared pamphlet titled *Gisors et L'Enigme des Templiers*. "If anyone knew, it would have been our country's great detective of ancient mysteries, may he rest in peace. *Oui*, here it is. Jean Markale said that the spiral 'S' shapes left by the Templars at Chinon represented 'the *sol invictus*, the unvanquished sun, symbol of the cyclical divine light that appears to die but then emerges from the darkness.'"

Mithras, again.

She stared at the etchings. Why were these Templars and the Roman god Mithras always showing up together in the same underground vaults? And why did those crusader monks honor the Queen of Sheba at Chartres for carrying off the Ark of the Covenant?

She could think of only one person who might know.

She turned the four-hour drive east to Lorraine into three, but the sun was dying when she arrived at the desolate spot a couple miles outside Resson where she and Elymas had met with Monsignor Guilbert. Armed with her travel journal, she screwed up the courage to walk alone up the overgrown path that led to the alchemist's refuge. Finding no lights on in the converted Romanesque chapel, she banged the rusted knocker against the door. There was no answer.

Maybe the old priest was in the crypt and couldn't hear her. She nudged the unlocked door and called out his name. Only the chirping of a cricket broke the silence. She lifted the floor hatch and inched blindly across the laboratory, crashing into benches. "Is anyone here?"

Even if the monsignor *had* found the elixir of youth, at his advanced age he could be forgiven an occasional nap. She opened the hatch to allow the last gasps of sunlight to enter. Remembering Elymas's trick, she took the mirror from her purse and angled it for diffused light.

There he was, slouched over his table, asleep. She approached him with light steps, intent on waking him gently. Seeing more than his silhouette for the first time, she stifled a gasp. The years of living in darkness with inadequate Vitamin D had deformed his spine with grotesque knobs. She had seen old folks in Kentucky who suffered from such a condition called 'rachitic rosary.' Had God punished the defiant priest by causing him to resemble a human Vatican prayer trinket?

She whispered into his ear. "Monsignor?"

When he didn't rouse, she jostled him lightly. He felt cold and stiff. She raised him up into his chair—and shrieked. A slender incision under his chin was caked with dried blood. His distended mouth was ringed with the white powder and his face was battered with bruises and scratches. His eyes, still open, seemed to hold a frozen warning. She felt his wrist for a pulse.

My God! He's dead!

Had he been force-fed poison? If so, why had the murderers cut his throat? His hand still gripped his writing penknife. Had one of his experiments gone so horribly awry that he took his own life to avoid a painful death?

On the floor, she found his writing tablet. It was spattered with blood.

The hatch slammed shut, shattering glass and casting her into total darkness.

She groped the walls, but there was no window. A sulfuric aroma attacked her nostrils. Unable to breathe, she crawled to the mirror and aimed it at the stairwell to find light.

A beaker lay on its side. Someone had trip-wired the release of a gas when the hatch was opened. She would be asphyxiated in minutes if she couldn't find a way out. On her knees, she felt along the walls and found a jar with debossed labels. The priest had inscribed his chemicals with wax imprints to determine their contents by touch. Desperate, she ran her fingers across the embossed letters: *Magnesia ... Sulfur ... Potassium.*

The noxious miasma was becoming stronger.

If she guessed wrong, she might blow herself up. She decided she'd rather take the chance and die quickly than strangle in agony. She overturned the monsignor's table, sending his body flopping to the floor. Shielded by the planks, she retrieved the Magnesia crock from the shelf and threw it toward the hatch.

Nothing happened.

Eyes burning, she heaved the container of sulfur over the table, but it's sizzling dissipated. She ducked as she launched the last container with the potassium. Several seconds passed, but still nothing happened. She was slipping into blackness. She began praying. *The Lord is my Shepherd—*

The room quaked with a loud explosion.

The recoiling table took the brunt of flying shards and knocked her against the wall. She rubbed her stinging eyes as she peered over the upended table.

The crypt was ablaze. The hatch door had splintered and fallen through.

Coughing and gagging, she ran up the stairwell clutching the palimpsest. When she was clear of the burning chapel, she looked down at the blood-stained board and saw that three lines of letters and symbols had been carved into its grain. She held a sleeve to her mouth as she looked closer at the beveled incisions. The monsignor's blood had been impressed into the wood by his penknife. She realized to her horror that he must have carved the lines *after* his throat had been cut:

TWENTY

LAGOS, PORTUGAL
JULY, 1458

Pero rushed to keep up with Gaspar as the shipwright marched down the jetties barking orders for the finishing preparations. Earlier that morning, a courier had brought news that the Old Man was riding south from Tomar to christen his newest caravel. All around the yards, the carpenters made their last inspections, leaping and swinging from the masts like monkeys, while below them the caulkers lathered on the last coats of pitch and the riggers tightened the rope knots. The maiden launch of a dry-docked ship was fraught with potential disaster; every yard crew's worst fear was to witness its costly creation slide from the rails and capsize to the bottom, never to be salvaged.

Pero was eager to finally set sail on this marvelous caravel that he had helped build. After proving his skill in mathematics, thanks to the private schooling he had received from his father, he had been assigned the duty of confirming the ballast calculations. Yet no matter how stable a new vessel came through in the sums, its seaworthiness remained in doubt until the hull was tested on the waves. The laborers were more apprehensive and short-tempered than usual, for there were rumors that the Old Man had undertaken a burdensome loan to finish his sea behemoth that was surpassed in size only by the legendary *Roccaforte*, a 500-ton Venetian galley. Even though the yard had lost only one launch in thirty years, all knew that there would be severe punishments meted out if the caravel sank in the Old Man's presence.

So much about this grand vessel had been kept a mystery. Why, for example, was it to be named *Nossa Senhora das Estrelas?* No mariner would even speak to him of this mysterious Lady of the Stars for fear of courting bad luck. And why had it been designed with a keel-to-beam ratio of three-to-one and a length of eighty cubits? That would cause it to pull a draught too deep for close navigating along the African inlets, spurring some of the shoremen to lay wagers that the Old Man was planning to take it to the Indies to unite with Prester John on a new crusade against the infidels.

Eannes yearned for its command, Pero knew, but many in the Order considered the veteran mariner too old for another mission. There was also Cadamosto, who had demonstrated courage during the excursions up the Gambia River, but he was a foreigner and sailed only his own ships. Diogo Gomes seemed the most logical choice; he had, after all, converted an African chieftain to the Christian faith and was ingratiating himself by writing a chronicle of the Old Man's accomplishments. After these, the list of suitable candidates was alarmingly short, evidence that the old guard was passing away all too quickly.

For Pero and his fellow squires, the most pressing matter, now that the caravel had been built, was their future assignment. Ever since Zarco had announced his engagement to Filipa, Eannes had been tight-lipped about the next step in their apprenticeships. Still, Pero had no doubt that he and his two fast friends would be assigned to the *Nossa's* crew, for the curmudgeonly Gaspar had been uncharacteristically profuse in his praise of their performance on the docks.

A distant flare of horns announced the Old Man's approach. With a swell of excitement, Pero ran to join Dias, Zarco, and the hundreds of craftsmen who leapt from the riggings and came to attention along the piers. The Grand Master, riding aside Eannes at the head of a column of knights, wore a modest brown frock so frayed that he could have passed for an itinerant hermit. When the prince reached the first pier, two attendants assisted him from the saddle, and he staggered a moment before finding his balance. He now required the use of a cane to walk; the gout had swollen his ankles to the size of oranges and had turned his drawn face to the sickly shade of gruel.

Gaspar came forward and lowered to a knee. "*Bem-vindo*, my lord."

The Old Man looked beyond the bent shipwright and swept every handspan of the new caravel with his hawkish eyes. "The ribbings appear heavily shaved," he complained. "What wood did you use for the rind?"

The shipwright reddened at having his competence questioned. He kept his head bowed, but his astringent tone betrayed a slow burn. "Double-jointed cork oak, as you prescribed, my lord. We had to dovetail and mortise the futtocks to hold the single master frame."

"The caulking was thickened?"

"With hemp soaked in pine pitch and horsehair. The Frieslanders have had great success applying the mixture."

The Old Man turned his acerbic frown toward Eannes. "Has a Dutchman ever sailed the Sea of Darkness?"

"Those tulip tillers would melt in that clime, my lord," Eannes said, relishing his old friend Gaspar's distress.

That jest drew laughter in the ranks, until the Old Man tapped the ground with his cane to command silence. He took a step closer and came hovering over the cowering Gaspar. "And yet my shipwright takes caulking lessons from Frisan cobblers who have never ventured beyond their own canals."

Undone by the prince's ridicule, the shipwright dropped his fretting bow even lower in contrition. "My lord, I meant only—"

"Up with you, Gaspar!" the Old Man ordered, breaking a grin. "Has the brine so pickled your brain that you can no longer tell when I am frying your *cajones* for sport? The caravel appears well forged. You are to be commended. Let us see how it holds the lee."

Restored by the prince's reversal to praise, the shipwright preened and signaled for the mallet yeomen to step forward on the quick. As they prepared to release the wedges, a Jeronomite monk sprinkled the sails with holy water.

The Old Man doused the jutting forespeak with a bottle of Alenjento *vinho* and offered up a prayer, "May the Mother Star of the Sea bless you."

"Amen," affirmed hundreds of choked voices.

The Old Man beckoned forward a tall stranger who had a large egg-shaped head, a foreboding face, and a thick black beard coiffed to a haughty point. "This day, I commission João Corte-Real as captain of this enterprise." He raised the hand of his new officer in a benediction. "May God be your pilot."

These Tomar knights with the prince were trained to remain stoic even in the face of an infidel onslaught, but the dockworkers were not so disciplined, and they rumbled with surprise at the unexpected choice. Pero stole a glance at Eannes, who looked crestfallen at being passed over.

When the Old Man became distracted, Zarco muttered to his mates, "The Corte-Reals have never sailed below the Pillars of Hercules. They learned their navigation from the Danes and Scots."

The decision was a surprise to Pero as well, for Corte-Real was not even a member of the Order of Christ. The Old Man, he realized, must have an expedition in mind for the north seas. He and the other squires had assumed all along that this long-voyage caravel was being built to find Prester John, but that Christian king lived in the East. He made a mental note that he would have to purchase a new set of clothes for the cold climes on the voyage.

Gaspar glared his murmuring charges to silence. After allowing the anticipation to mount, he signaled for the wedges to be knocked from the slats. The hammer blows scattered hundreds of gulls into the slate sky, and the caravel lurched down the sled and sped toward the water like a wild beast released from its cage. Diving into the sea, its prowl reared with a foaming slash and finally came to rest, bobbing gently like a majestic wooden swan. Gaspar made the sign of the cross over his breast in relief. He then signaled the oarsmen to ready a barge to row out the new crew for its maiden run, and the sailors shuffled with anticipation while Corte-Real read off the names of those who would serve on the caravel.

Pero waited with bated breath to hear his summons. After several veterans of the African excursions had been drafted, Dias and Zarco were called to the service. Then, Corte-Real rolled up his list and bowed to the Old Man, indicating that his muster was complete. Pero was certain that there had been a mistake. He looked in pleading at Dias and Zarco, who, seeing him so distraught, tempered their elation.

The Old Man called out: "Translator!"

Pero brushed away tears as he stepped forward and bowed. "My lord."

"Accompany me on a walk."

The knights appeared astonished that a lowly squire was being afforded such a privilege. Ignoring their jealous gazes, Pero placed the Old Man's palsied hand on his shoulder to offer him support, and together they made slow progress toward the beach, where the roar of waves would muffle their words.

The Old Man stopped just above the dunes and gazed longingly toward the azure horizon. "Do you know what the men call me behind my back?"

Pero had heard many unkind descriptions of the elderly prince, but he dared not admit it. "No, my lord."

"*Ratao.* ... I fear you may inherit that accursed nickname from me."

Reddening, Pero vowed to pummel anyone who called him the damnable slang for a land rat, the derogatory term whispered about one who did not pursue a maritime life. "No loyal subject would refer to your lordship as such."

"They think I fear the sea. In truth, I would give what few days I have left in this life to just once accompany Eannes or Cadamosto. But no one could have raised the necessary monies for the quests had I failed to return."

"You could still go, my lord."

The prince, shaded in sadness, shook his head. "The hour to meet my Maker approaches. ... I know you are disappointed at being passed over for the *Nossa*, but I have another need for your service."

"I am at your command," Pero said with no enthusiasm.

Using his cane, the Old Man drew a crude map of Portugal and Castile in the sand. "The Iberian kingdoms to our east are in turmoil. King Henry of Castile is a weakling who wallows in depraved sexual practices instead of siring an heir with his wife, our beautiful Juana."

Pero remembered having once seen Juana, the sister of King Alfonso, at a spring fair in Castro Marim. "She is indeed the flower of Portugal."

"If the Castilian monarch persists in his perversities, his grandees will scheme to have Juana become with child by another man. Her legitimacy as queen will then be called into question, and our influence will be endangered. Worse, Aragon will be free to propose another marital alliance for Henry. A war over the royal succession would be the result. I cannot allow our Indies mission to be thwarted by such a wasteful naval conflict."

Pero could not understand why the prince was confiding in him about such lofty matters of statecraft. "What could I possibly do to avert such a disaster?"

"I have made arrangements for you to join the Duke of Medina-Sidonia's household. You will serve as his squire and courier."

Pero's spirit plummeted to even darker depths. Denied a sea assignment, he would now also be required to reside across the border?

"One of our disaffected counts in Andalusia has recommended you to the Duke. You speak Castilian as well as a native. Medina-Sidonia has been informed only that you are a polyglot whose father is a horse trader. He has extensive dealings in Henry's court. You will accompany him and serve as my eyes and ears."

Pero could barely cough forth the words. "I am to be … a spy?"

The Old Man nodded. "You must reveal this assignment to no one. If you are caught, the Castilians will rack and hang you. I have watched you closely. You have the resourcefulness to succeed in this endeavor."

Pero realized that the Old Man and his knights had planned this assignment for him from the first day of his recruitment. *This* was the special talent they saw in him? The cunning to deceive and hide in the shadows? He cursed his father for making him learn the Castilian tongue. With head hung low, he had no choice but to accept this bitter cup. "When am I to leave?"

"On the morrow. Time sorely presses us."

Pero hesitated. "There is a lady I hope to marry."

The Old Man firmed his grip on his squire's shoulder. "Your Catrina will be cared for in Lisbon. For now, you must give up all contact with her."

Pero turned with a start and searched the Old Man's eyes, informed that the prince had known all along of the trysts with Catrina. "She will think ill of me for abandoning her."

The Old Man fixed his sad gaze on a gaggle of geese flying south. "When I was your age, I too courted a *belissimo senhorita.*"

"What became of her?"

"She passed to the mercy of Our Lord five years ago, in the Convent of St. Clara. I chose to spare her a harsh life on these barren rocks. If your intended is a true lady of Portugal, she will one day come to understand. Your exile will not be forever. I have great plans for you, translator. When the time is ripe, more will be revealed to you. Until then, you must trust me when I tell you that Portugal's future depends on our sacrifices."

Pero could not bear to think of the heartbreak and pain of betrayal that Catrina would suffer. After he disappeared from Portugal, she would not even be told that he was still alive.

Grimacing from his arthritic knees, the Old Man leaned harder on Pero's shoulder. "There are times when I regret … Do you miss your father?"

"*Sim*, my lord."

"And I am certain he misses you." The Old Man hesitated, as if wishing to say something more, but he thought better of it and turned to rejoin his knights.

As they walked back to the docks, Pero dredged the courage to ask one last question. "My lord, are Zarco and Dias going to the northern seas?"

The Old Man broke a faint smile, impressed by his new spy's powers of deduction. "For now, it is best that you know nothing of their commission."

The Northern Seas
July, 1458

After provisioning in Galway, João Corte-Real had turned the *Nossa* west, tacking deep into the Atlantic, but ever since the first draw of anchor in Lagos, he had kept Zarco and Dias uninformed of their ultimate destination.

From his post on the aftcastle, Zarco monitored the man who held their fates in his hands. He had learned from his studies that mariners fell into two camps: Those who were inclined to look down and watch the compass, the draught, and the currents; and those whose instincts led them to look upward and place their fate in the hands of the heavens and the winds. Corte-Real was a down-gazer by training and temperament, a traditionalist who confided only in his two sons. He insisted on sailing solely by dead reckoning, relying upon speed and plotting rather than tracking latitude by the Pole Star. There were also rumors that, when alone in his cabin, the man periodically consulted an ancient sheepskin portolan with a mysterious origin.

During rare moments of privacy, Zarco whispered to Dias of his growing concern that this captain was less proficient than the mariners trained at Sagres. Latitude sailing would have entailed sailing north to a port with a known parallel, then setting a westerly course by calculating the distance between the horizon and the Polestar. Yet many admirals, like Corte-Real, avoided this technique because of the difficulty in taking observations on a rolling deck. And all knew the cloisters at Tomar were filled with old sailors who had gone blind from staring too long into the sun to calculate the distance from the horizon.

Still, the navigational alternative that Corte-Real was now employing—dead reckoning—could prove even more precarious and unreliable. The technique demanded teamwork with intricate precision, and its inaccuracy was so notorious that many a departing crew, taking refuge in gallows humor, would call out to their waving loved ones on the docks: "Reckoning we're dead!"

Zarco kept hearing that warning in his head. He and Dias had been assigned the duty of rolling up the log line, a name derived from the block attached to a rope and cast over the stern. He would count the number of knots passing the stern as the log swept aft, and when the rope reached its full length, Dias would lift the log out to repeat the exercise and then turn a two-minute glass.

Alas, that was only the first step for setting a dead-reckoning course. Informed of the speed and distance gained that day, the captain would then consult his lodestone compass and portolan chart to set a new tacking direction. Dead reckoning required discipline, exacting measurements, and trust in one's mates. One slip in the link of this chain could cause a deviation of several hundred nautical miles, a calamity that might doom a lost crew to an agonizing death by thirst. A caravel bound under dead reckoning was rarely rescued, for the vessel sent to find her would have no knowledge of the course she had set.

Each evening, after Corte-Real retired below deck, Zarco and Dias had been secretly practicing taking celestial measurements with a cross staff. And they had discovered, to their great alarm, that the angle between the Polestar and the water was expanding with each passing day. Although a check of the sun's height at noon would have confirmed these disturbing findings, they dared not risk such daytime measurements for fear of being caught.

On their fourteenth night at sea from Galway, shouts awakened Zarco and Dias in their billets below deck. They rushed up the well stairs to find the captain thrashing the watchman with a rattan.

The sand glass had fallen overboard. The negligent crewman placed in charge of it during the night screamed deliriously while the others watched in panic—not from concern for their mate, but because they were adrift without course. Denied a means for judging speed, Corte-Real could no longer make precise loggings. Worse, the captain had scrimped on expenses by failing to stock a second time glass. There was no way to calculate the return home.

"We are damned!" cried one of the men.

Having beaten the culprit to a bloody pulp, Corte-Real backed away from the rattled crew. He ordered the first mate. "Hang the traitor to the mast!"

The designated executioner balked at the assignment. "He wouldn't have lost the blasted glass if he'd been given an hour of sleep!"

"*Sim*, and how do we know *you* aren't lost?" shouted another sailor.

Corte-Real drew his blade. "I've kept meticulous records on the rhumbs!"

"You won't even tell us where we're going!"

"Show us that chart you've been hiding!"

Corte-Real brought his frightened sons to his side. "You'll all hang!"

"Who is the real traitor?" cried another crewman. "You sailed with Danes and Scots. How do we know you aren't working for them?"

Raising his sword to fend off the rising mutiny, Corte-Real repeated his order to the first mate. "Hang that man! Or I'll run you both through!"

Zarco pushed to the fore. "Hold off!"

Corte-Real, wild-eyed, aimed his blade at Zarco. "I took you two whelps on at the Old Man's insistence! I'll abide no treachery from you!"

"If we're to survive," Zarco insisted, "we'll need every hand."

Dias came to his fellow squire's side. "Let the watchman live. Zarco and I will take responsibility with Prince Henry for the decision."

Corte-Real paled with rage. "That is a fool's bargain!" He spat on the moaning watchman. "Because of this cur's knavery, I cannot get us back to Portugal!"

"Dias and I will get you back."

The crewmen laughed bitterly at the absurd idea that two squires could pilot them across waters never before sailed or plotted.

"What are you two swaddled babes going to do?" the captain snarled at the squires. "Cry for the Old Man to come save you?"

Zarco glanced at Dias, uncertain which was the lesser of evils: Reveal what they had been doing behind the captain's back, or confront certain mutiny. Finally, Zarco admitted, "We've been taking latitude readings."

Corte-Real had to be restrained from thrashing them. "Conniving whoresons! You were sent to spy on me!"

"Hear the lads out!" shouted one of the crew.

Zarco demanded, "You must first tell us where we have been heading."

The captain debated that condition. Left no choice, he grudgingly revealed what he had sworn to keep secret until their arrival. "New Scotland."

The crewmen gasped in disbelief. Most seamen had long dismissed as sheer fantasy such tales of such a land beyond the ends of the world.

Dias challenged the captain, "Do you know its latitude?"

"Forty-five degrees."

Zarco was stunned. "How did you come by that measure?"

"Scot Templars sailed there years ago," Corte-Real admitted. "I have their compass points. Little good they'll do us now."

"Ireland was at fifty-three degrees," Zarco reminded him.

A crewman glared at Zarco. "How could you possibly know that, whelp?"

Zarco lifted a loose board on the deck and revealed the cross-staff that he and Dias had kept hidden. The pole was cut with the notches that they had made to mark the stars each passing night. "We measured the latitude before leaving Galway. We've been steadily drifting south. All we need do is take readings of the Polestar, set our course eight degrees south of fifty-three, and run the latitude by maintaining the tangent angle."

The crew's skepticism gave way to hot anger at the captain for having put them through such needless misery, and one of the men shouted, "I say we let the lads take us to New Scotland!"

When that mutinous call was affirmed with a threatening cheer, Corte-Real could do nothing but glare a promise of revenge at the two squires.

Segovia, Castile
August, 1458

Pero elbowed his way through the chattering market throngs as he climbed the rising street toward the city's imposing Alcazar. He had been in Castile only a month, but already he was homesick for the Algarve's warming zephyrs. These Castilians were a volatile mixture of faith, appearance, and customs. Oddities among them abounded: Black-skinned Christians who spoke Arabic and wore Moorish caftans mingled alongside blond Mujedars and Jewish princesses who attired themselves in the flashy brocaded silks of Moorish harems. Segovia and the Meseta—the geographical core of the kingdom—sat high on a thistle-hounded plateau punished by bone-soaking rains and summer droughts. These weather extremes mirrored the violent tempers of its inhabitants, for whom both Paradise and Eternal Damnation never seemed far from their thoughts. A chronicler's dismissal of the region as nine months of winter with three months of Hell also aptly described the fractious relations between Castile's king and his vassals.

Fate had, however, dealt him one small blessing. His new master, Don Juan Alonzo de Guzman, the Duke of Medina Sidonia, was a rarity among the Castilian nobles, a man of moderation and tolerance who spent much of his time traveling to the royal courts attempting to mediate a solution to the domain's penury caused by King Henry's reckless selling of domains to second and third-born grandees. And yet beneath the duke's veneer of civility lurked a ruthless fighter; the Guzman family had, after all, sired St. Dominic, the hammer of the Languedoc heretics. The duke's infamous great-grandfather had been so hard-bitten that he had allowed one of his own sons to be murdered rather than surrender besieged Tarifa to the Muslims.

Happily, the duke was also so self-sufficient that he rarely required his squire's attendance, a fortunate circumstance that afforded Pero the freedom to disappear for hours and gather surveillance. And as luck would have it, he had recently overheard a bit of news that might prove useful to the Old Man: The prior of the local Dominican monastery, Tomas de Torquemada, had been appointed confessor for the Castilian king's half-sister, Isabella, a precocious girl with the reputation of a sharp mind and a rabid religious devotion.

By all accounts, this ambitious friar strived to excel his tonsured brethren in both mortification and conversions. Tomas and his uncle, John, a powerful cardinal in the Vatican, were rumored to be descended from Jewish *conversos*. Pero's source for this information was a loquacious playmate of Isabella's named Beatriz Bobadilla, who resided in the village of Arevalo, where Isabella had been kept sequestered. Isabella had no chance of attaining her half-brother's throne, for her older brother Alfonso was next in line. Yet so cruelly had the foppish King Henry treated her—even denying her visitations with her insane mother, Isabel of Portugal—that Pero hoped the girl had become sour with the bitterness that often gave birth to a loose tongue.

During his previous explorations of Segovia's foundations, he had discovered a small cave below the monastery with an offshoot that led to a storeroom directly below the prior's chamber. His flirtations with the Bobadilla *senhorita* had also revealed something even more helpful: The Dominican prior always dispensed penance in his private study. It was for this reason that, on this afternoon—a few minutes before Nones, the traditional afternoon hour for dispensing the sacrament of confession—Pero crawled into the cave and ensconced himself in the shadows under the ceiling cracks of the Dominican's chamber. Minutes later, he heard a young woman's voice above him.

"God spoke to me again last night, *padre*."

Pero cocked his ear. Could that truly be Isabella? She sounded much older than her eight tender years. He pressed his head to the boards. The door lock clicked, and sandals strode the planks. The prior sat down and scooted his chair closer to his female penitent.

"Are you certain it was God? We must be on guard against Satan's wiles."

"He said I would be queen," Isabella said. "Just as you promised."

"This is proof indeed of divine revelation," Torquemada said. "If you pray and follow my prescriptions for the elevation of your soul, you will one day herald in the New Jerusalem."

"But I thought Christ would perform that honor."

"Did you read your assignment in the Book of Revelation?"

"*Si, padre. Tres.*"

The prior tested her. "What sign will portend Our Lord's glorious return?"

"A woman clothed in the sun with the moon under her feet."

"*Bien hecho*, you have studied well. You must believe me, child, when I tell you that the Almighty has brought you into this world to fulfill that very prophecy. I have witnessed your destiny in my contemplation. As the *Mujer* of Revelation, you will conquer a powerful nemesis."

"The dragon!"

"*Si*, the dragon with seven heads and ten horns and seven diadems. A dragon that will lust to devour the *Mujer's* son."

"The Christ child!"

"You are wise beyond your years, *niña*. The young Jesus also displayed such wisdom."

Isabella sounded enlivened with spiritual passion, her preternatural voice quickening. "When will the dragon come?"

"The beast slithers amongst us," the friar promised her. "The *Judios* of Castile conspire in a secret Sanhedrin to drive Christ from the hearts of our fellow believers. They cannot be counted upon to defend Christ against the infidels."

"Beatriz says the Hebrews caused the Black Death."

"Your *amiguito* speaks true. The Judios spew blasphemy and secretly practice witchcraft. The Almighty cleansed our kingdom of their sin, but their evil ways have taken root again. Have you been told the story of the first prior who prayed in the cave that sits under this monastery?"

"No, *padre*."

"His name was Dominic de Guzman, my patron saint. Take him as your guiding light. I pray for the day when you follow his example and cauterize Castile of its faithless impurities. ... Now, we must administer to your soul. What sins have you committed since you last confessed?"

"I fell asleep on the Lord's Day without saying my prayers."

"This is Satan's method. What other temptations have you suffered?"

Isabella hesitated. "Sometimes I wish the king were dead."

Torquemada remained silent for several moments. Finally, he lowered his gravelly voice and confided to the girl: "You wish this only because you yearn to see Christ's return hastened. You understand, child, that to reveal communications made during the dispensation of the penitential sacrament is a grave sin?"

"*Si, padre*."

"Your half-brother takes counsel with unbelievers and deviants. Christ will not allow this mockery to abide. You must gird yourself for the momentous task that lies ahead. Now, for your penance, you will say one hundred *Pater Nosters*."

"*Si*."

"You will also make a promise to God with me as His witness. When Christ and His saints set the crown upon your head, you will forever banish the dragon of unbelief from Castile."

"*Lo prometo*," she vowed.

Pero remained absolutely still until the door above him slammed shut. Then, he released a held breath of astonishment. Why was this friar filling the young girl's head with hope of becoming queen? Did the wily Dominican know something the rest of Castile did not? More importantly, was this the kind of intelligence that he should forward to the Old Man? The Order might condemn him for poor judgment if he placed their lines of communication in jeopardy with a frivolous report of an outlandish plot.

He decided it was best, for now, not to risk the wrath of his superiors.

The Northern Seas
August, 1458

For five days, Zarco and Dias had guided the *Nossa* west along the 45th degree latitude under the skeptical watch of Corte-Real. The two squires measured the height of the Polestar during those fleeting moments between day and dusk; at noon on the following day, they would confirm the measurements, taking turns with the cross-staff so that neither would go blind.

They chose not to reveal that the Polestar did not remain stationary at exact North, but made a tight orbit. This was only one of many deviations that they were required to factor into their calculations. They also had to estimate the effect of the currents, the leeway of the ship, and the wind. Eannes had trained them to monitor the turbulence off the bow and to assess the pressure of the wind against their faces. A master mariner, they had been taught, required the clairvoyance of a Cumaen Sybil and the compensating senses of the blind prophet Tiresias.

On this calming afternoon, Zarco held the watch. An hour earlier, he had seen a rare occurrence in the west: a pair of clouds that resembled pinched eyebrows. Such a formation was called the Frown of the Ground because of its tendency to break apart and move together over land. A thickening fog had settled in, thwarting a new Polestar measurement. The crew was uneasy.

Having studied his own personal tendencies, he had concluded that he belonged to that ilk of mariner who preferred to consult the sky. Now, denied such celestial guidance, he had no choice but to watch the wake off the stern and the swell lines below the mists. A ribbon of riffling water streaked along with the flotsam and seaweed. Such sea markings, he knew, appeared at the intersection of major currents and were caused by a change in the bed's depth. He shouted at the crew, "Drop anchor and furl the sails!"

Corte-Real held off giving the order; halting a caravel was an arduous task, and to perform it needlessly the bane of all shipmen. "We'll lose three hours!"

"Heave to!" Zarco demanded. "Or Dias and I will not be held responsible!"

Cowered by the threat to take up the matter with the Old Man, Corte-Real reluctantly signaled for his anchor-keep to comply. Zarco then signaled for Dias to plumb the sounding line. Dias chalked a rope tied with a lead weight and dropped it over the starboard. When the rope stopped descending, he pulled it up and examined the hemp near the lead ballast. The chalk was dirtied with clay mud.

Dias called out his findings. "Twenty knots! The line is silted!"

The fog was so dense that Zarco could not see beyond the stern. Still, his gut told him that land was near. "Release the ravens!"

Corte-Real resisted that plea. "I cannot afford to lose them!"

"If they don't come back," Zarco said, "that means they've flown to land. The waters are too shallow here. We have to be near a coast."

Fearful of grounding the caravel, Corte-Real reluctantly set his harbingers loose into the sky.

Several minutes passed, but the birds did not return. Shaken, the captain ordered Mendoca, his second in command: "Take three men in the bark and paddle sternward. Blow the horn if you find land. We'll blow ours to give you direction for your return."

Mendoca and the chosen scouts stood paralyzed with dread.

"We should wait for morning," Zarco said. "The fog may lift."

Rejecting that counsel, the captain pushed Mendoca to the boat. "We don't have enough provisions to wait."

Dias stepped forward. "Zarco and I will accompany them."

The captain brandished his blade and repulsed the two squires back to their stations. "Nay, both you whelps will stay on board."

Zarco shot a worried glance at Dias, suspecting the captain's insistence was seeded from self-preservation rather than an admiration for their judgment. The man had no doubt calculated by now that the only way he would get back to Portugal was by keeping the two of them alive.

The captain shouted at the conscripted scouts. "Be gone with you!"

Pale with trepidation, Mendoca and his three men lowered their bark into the sea and rowed off into the thick gray soup.

As the minutes passed, their horn blasts became weaker.

After an hour with no report from Mendoca, Zarco feared that the currents had swept the scouts into oblivion. He blew the horn louder, but the fog had turned thicker, forming a soundproof barrier around the caravel. He turned and saw the captain retreating with his sons to their cabin, driven by the vengeful glares of the crew.

Aiming his pistol to hold them off, the captain slipped inside his refuge with his sons and barred the door.

Throughout the night, Zarco and Dias paced the deck, taking turns with the signal horn. Finally, when the sun rose the next morning, the fog burned off, but Mendoca's bark was nowhere in sight.

The captain emerged warily from his cabin. Seeing that his scouts had not returned, he ordered his first mate: "Raise anchor."

"We can't leave them," Zarco protested.

"We have five days of salted pork and water rations left," the captain said. "If we wait longer, we'll all die."

"New Scotland cannot be far," Dias pleaded. "We should continue west—

Corte-Real aimed his firing piece at Dias's forehead to demand his silence. "You and this scheming *cúmplice* of yours will return us to Lagos. Take the reading with that cheat-staff, and set sail *now.* That is an order."

TWENTY-ONE

SATOR
APERO
TENET
OPERA
ROTAS

A cooling desert breeze fluttered the young virgin's diaphanous gown, revealing the luscious curves of her budding breasts and milky hips. She approached him seductively, her mascara-lined eyes as black and beckoning as polished onyx. Dazzled in jewels and perfumed with ambergris, the enchantress untied the drawstrings of her—

"Camel humper! Wake up!"

The butt end of a gnarled shillelagh rousted Jamaal from his snoozing reverie of Paradise. Slumped in a corner while taking a nap, the Yemenite *jihadist*, working covertly as a maintenance employee, grudgingly retrieved his mop and climbed to his feet.

The castle's superintendent complained to the day janitor at his side, a half-wit named Archie. "The whole country's being overrun by these rug-smuggling cuddies."

Archie commiserated with his boss by spitting a jet of tobacco juice at Jamaal's mop. "Aye, the brave Bruce nearly loses his heart to their god-forsaken clutches. And now they're over here tracking up his floors."

The superintendent blew a cloud of pipe smoke into Jamaal's eyes. "You've been on the job less than a day, Jabber, and already you're sleeping your brains to train oil. What'd I tell you?"

Jamaal itched to wrench the whisky-marinated tongue of his tormentor from its throat. But he had promised Yahya he would not to lose his temper again and risk exposing to the British police his purpose for being in the country. This time, he was determined not to disappoint the Awaited One.

The superintendent got into his face. "Answer me, you surly puffin!"

"No slacking," Jamaal groused, chafing under the enforced servility.

"I expect to see these flagstones shining like the crown jewels. Understand?"

Jamaal begrudged a half-nod as he limped off pushing the mop.

The superintendent shook his shaggy head in disgust. "If I had me way, your kind wouldn't be allowed near these ramparts. But that gomeril of a prime minister in Westminster coddles you hashish heads, so I'm forced to hire the sorry likes of you still stinking from the ferry backwash. But there's nothing in the statutes says I can't kick your sorry arse to the bogs if I catch you idling again."

Jamaal mumbled Arabic curses as he wrung out his mop in a bucket.

The superintendent thought he heard his name taken in vain. "What'd you say about me, camel humper?"

"I am praying! The law says I am allowed to pray to Allah three times a day."

"The law? I'll damn well show ye who you'll be praying to in Caledonia!" He turned to his sidekick. "Archie, educate Saladin here on his surroundings."

The bantam janitor snatched Jamaal's collar and drove him toward a window that overlooked Din Eidyn crag. "Out there is where Wallace boxed the ears of the English scum who came raping our women and stealing our bovine!"

Jamaal kept muttering prayers under his breath, forced to endure the ravings of these two mad Scots.

Archie was on such a testifying roll that he didn't notice Jamaal's pointed lack of attention. "Aye, and in that chapel across the bailey is where St. Margaret, our most blessed of saints, passed to Heaven, God rest her unblemished soul."

The superintendent came aside Archie and put a finger into Jamaal's chest. "You'll polish every pane in that sanctuary till the angels sing with joy!"

"We have castles in Yemen that make this look like a Bedouin's goat tent!"

"Sot-brained snail!" the superintendent roared. "Speaking blasphemy in the very chamber where Dark Mary gave birth to King Jamie!"

Archie was hankering to administer an old-fashioned Highland knuckle crunching. "Maybe we should just string him up from the hammer beams and use him to scare off the pigeons."

The superintendent winked wickedly at Archie. "No, I have a more fitting punishment in mind for him." He prodded Jamaal into another hall that held a large block of limestone with rings driven into its side. The stone sat on a viewing base draped in royal purple and was surrounded by a glass encasement protected with sensors. "This may make ye a wee bit homesick, Jabber."

Archie got up in Jamaal's sour face to press the point. "Any idea what this sweet precious is?"

Jamaal suspected the block had been used for chopping off empty British heads, but he kept his silence.

In a hushed tone of reverence, the superintendent revealed: "The *Lia Fáil*. Our blessed Stone of Destiny."

Jamaal snorted, unimpressed. "Our women pound shit stains from their dishdashas on rocks like this!"

The superintendent tremored at the slander. "It just so happens that this came from your shit-hole part of the world. Jacob's Pillar, it is. Sat in the Temple of Jerusalem. You know all about Jerusalem, don't you, Jabber? That's the holy city you feckin' rug smugglers lost to the Israelites a few years ago, remember?"

Jamaal teetered on the edge of an explosion.

"Our kings were crowned on this Stone!" Archie shouted. "You know why it was brought here? Because of all the countries in the world, God loves Scotland the most!"

Jamaal sneered. "Please explain then why Allah has allowed this slag dump to be conquered by the English?"

The superintendent backed him into a corner. "Listen up, you carnaptious-mouthed pip! Archie and I are going over to the pub to savor our evening pints. Come morning, if we don't see our bonnie mugs staring up at us on these floors, you'll be back in Dubai mixing concrete for the sheiks."

The two lunatic Scots finally trudged off.

Left alone in the viewing hall, Jamaal examined the Stone of Destiny for the sacred markings transmitted to him by Yahya. Finding the confirming insignia absent, he dropped his pants and pissed on the lump of limestone.

Heathrow Airport, London
February 8, Present Day

Jaq had expected the monsignor's murderer to be waiting for her at the Paris airport, so she had driven the rental car instead to Calais and, after spending a frazzled night curled up in a corner of the ferry station, took the hovercraft to Dover that morning. Now, before boarding the first flight she could get for Washington, she made another flurry of last-minute calls to the Rome hospitals and police stations. There was still no information about Alyssa.

None of it made any sense.

Hadn't Alyssa been carrying her driver's license or passport?

She paced in front of the airline desk, torn with indecision. Her answering machine at home was filled with irate messages from Ochley ordering her to get back to the States. She thought about telling him to go to hell, but she was flat broke and maxed out on her credit card. She would have swallowed her pride and called Elymas for help, if only she had his number. But he was, as always, a ghost in the wind. She had to accept the bitter fact that she could do more for Alyssa at the office than in Rome with no leads. Reluctantly, she handed the Virgin Atlantic attendant her boarding pass and walked down the runway.

On board, she settled into her window seat and declined the offer of a snack. She'd had no appetite since finding the monsignor dead. Now, only minutes from taking off, she stared through the window at the thickening London haze. Having misplaced her journal in the escape from Resson, she decided to try to take her mind off her anxieties by reconstructing her entries, as best she could, in the new notebook that she had purchased at the gift shop. She suddenly felt another onslaught of nausea coming on, and she dipped her head to her knees.

A man in a business suit came down the aisle and lifted his carry-on to the overhead bin. Armed with a stack of newspapers, he squeezed into the seat next to her. "Are you okay?"

Still bent over, she nodded, her eyes feeling feverish. "Long trip."

"My antidote for that is a good stiff Glenlivet. I'll treat."

"Thanks, but I don't drink."

"Ah, Beelzebub's nectar. I admire your fortitude against temptation." He opened the *London Sun* and began reading the front page.

She looked up and saw the headline on the back page of his paper: SCOTLAND'S PRIZED STONE VANDALIZED. Below the caption was a large photo of Scotland Yard detectives standing around a viewing base in a castle. At their feet lay shards of a stone that appeared to have been smashed. "Looks like you've had some excitement here."

He flipped to the story. "Oh that? Much ado about nothing."

"Apparently the editors didn't think so. That's a pretty big headline."

He curled a disdainful smile. "If the queen drops two crumpets into her tea instead of one, the London tabloids claim it's a covert signal to the Trilateral Commission. The stone was probably smacked about by the usual clack of neo-Nazi skinheads on a wilding. Britain is running amok with crime these days. The mayhem is spreading north."

"I take it you're not from London?"

"Aberdeen." He offered his hand in greeting. "Ian Cloud."

Looking over his shoulder, she read the first paragraph of the vandalism story. "Stone of Destiny. Sounds mysterious."

"It's a fake."

"Why was it being kept in Edinburgh?"

"Did you see *Braveheart*?"

"Who hasn't? I used to have a crush on Mel Gibson."

"A dreadful theatrical," the Scot businessman grumbled. "Painted my ancestors up to look like North American savages. And now all the statues of William Wallace over here resemble that absurd Aussie sot."

"I don't recall anything about a stone in the movie."

"Of course not. Our *Lia Fáil* is too profound a subject to be dealt with by Hollywood. The English king at the time was Edward the First. His subjects called him the Hammer of the Scots. We called him Longshanks and other accursed names. When the ruthless bastard invaded us in the 14th century, he stole what he thought was the Stone of Destiny from Scone. For ages, our Scot kings had been crowned on it. Longshanks took his prized theft to Westminster and set it under his throne to symbolize that Scotland was now firmly under his ass."

"And it was returned all these centuries later?"

He nodded. "After several celebrated thefts and recoveries, those wigged fools in London finally got tired of the hassle and shipped it back to us in 1996. John Major thought the gesture would quell the independence row. Great pomp and circumstance. But most of *my* countrymen, the informed ones anyway, didn't pay much notice. Everyone in Scotland knew the real Stone never left the country"

"How can you be so sure?"

"We're are all taught the story in the secondaries. The history books say that Longshanks sent a second raiding party to ransack the abbeys around Scone. But by then, the real Stone had been taken away for safekeeping. Old Daddy Longlegs probably realized too late that he had been duped with a copy. So, he just acted as if he had the real one."

"What happened to the original?"

"Oh, lots of theories. Some say our monks hid it in the neighboring countryside. The one that catches my fancy suggests that the Knights Templar were rewarded with the governance of the Stone after they came to Robert Bruce's aid at the Battle of Bannockburn."

"Why would the Templars care about an old block of limestone?"

"Legend has it that the Prophet Jeremiah and a lost tribe of Israel brought the Stone to Ireland. For centuries it was kept at Tara, the sacred hill of the Druids. When the Dalradians paddled across the Irish Sea to Scotland, they brought the Stone with them to ensure they'd be recognized as the true kings."

"They lugged it here all the way from Palestine?"

He shrugged. "Not that surprising, really, when you consider that the Old Testament says Jacob laid his head on the Stone when he dreamt of his ladder to Heaven. More to the point, it was used in Solomon's Temple as the base for the Ark."

She blinked hard. "The Ark of the—"

A flight attendant came on the intercom, "Ladies and gentlemen, we're next for takeoff."

Her seatmate buckled in, then folded his paper on the crease and turned to the crime blotter in the back pages. "Oh, begot! Now *here* is a real tragedy."

She was still trying to make sense of the Ark's connection to this vandalized Scot stone as she looked over his shoulder again to see what had caused him such distress. "Someone you know?"

"Dunsinnan House was burglarized."

"A hotel?"

"Aye, it's in an old mansion near Perth. My family used to take holiday there. An eccentric brewing tycoon owned the estate. You might best know the place as the site of Macbeth's castle."

"Macbeth was a real person?"

"Indeed he was. Dunsinnan is a most fascinating place. The hills are honey-combed with caves and tunnels. I used to climb into them as a lad. You must visit the region some day."

As the plane lifted off, she covered her shoulders with a blanket and sank into the seat, hoping for a long hibernation over the Atlantic. "Thanks, but I've already seen enough castles and tunnels for one lifetime."

TWENTY-TWO

SAGRES, PORTUGAL
NOVEMBER, 1460

In the middle of the night, Pero hurried alone down the narrow bottleneck of land that led to Cape St. Vincent. Two years had passed since he had last stepped on Portuguese soil. He prayed that the watch guards would not mistake him for an intruder and fire a lead ball into his head. The coded summons from the Order at Tomar had been terse, and the difficulties in transmitting it across the border could only mean that some development of great importance now demanded his presence. As he neared the fortress, he saw a shadowy presence on the rocks.

"*Quem está aí?*" a voice called out.

He whispered the insulting password—*Ratao*—that had been assigned to him before he left for Castile.

The sentry rushed at him.

He fought off the attack—and found himself embraced by Zarco.

His old friend grasped him by the shoulders to get a better view. "I've been walking this point for three nights. We had all but given up on you."

"You've grown a beard," Pero said. "And three inches in height."

"Considering what I've endured since we parted, I'm fortunate every hair on my head isn't white."

Pero searched the dark headlands. "Where is Dias?"

"We've been taking turns on the watch."

"What has happened?"

Zarco cast his gaze down. "Come. The others are waiting."

Alarmed by Zarco's evasive manner, Pero rushed with him into the Sagres fortress and entered the great hall. Many of his old comrades, including Eannes and Cresques, turned to greet him. Dias grasped his hand in a tearful welcome home and led him in silence to the private quarters.

Inside a spare cell, the Old Man, now but a skeleton hung with gray flesh, lay immobilized on a cot. The oils and purple stole of the last rites sat on a table, and his natal horoscope chart draped the wall above him.

Pero knelt at the prince's bed and dropped his head to hide his grief. Only a few months earlier, the 67-year-old Navigator had felt vigorous enough to lead the assault against the Moorish citadel of Alcacer-Ceguer in Morocco. But the exertions of that battle had taken an irreversible toll on his health. Joining in the deathwatch were the mariner Diogo Gomes; the prince's physician, Rodrigo; and Bor-Domel, the African chieftain who had converted to Christianity.

Sensing a new presence, the dying prince opened his mucous-caked lids and smiled weakly at the face hovering over him. "Translator."

Pero coughed back the emotion. "My lord."

The Old Man angled his glazed eyes up at the horoscope chart and squeezed Pero's hand to instill him with courage. "Saturn squares my Mars in the 12th House. We must accept the judgment of the stars. Heaven has many seas yet to be explored. One day, you and I, the two *rataos*, will sail together."

"I would follow you anywhere, my lord."

The Old Man weakly waved his physician from the room. "Give me leave with the *meninos*." When all but Dias, Zarco, and Pero had been ushered out, the prince gestured the squires closer to ease the agony of his speaking. He whispered weakly to Pero: "What news from Castile?"

"Your niece, my lord, is basely treated by King Henry. His domain seethes with plots."

"Has Juana foaled an heir?"

"No, but she has many ambitious suitors in the shadows."

"If Henry loses the throne, what heights will the young Afonso reach?"

"Nothing in his character portends greatness."

The Old Man's grimace eased. "Then Portugal has nothing to fear."

Pero did not share that optimistic assessment. "My lord, fratricide is becoming a popular sport in Castile. I would give no more than even odds on Afonso reaching the throne."

"On whom would you place your wager?"

"His half-sister Isabella is the most competent of the brood. She may also prove the most dangerous to us. The Dominicans who yap at her heels are bent on seizing influence in the court. They burn to turn Castile into a pyre upon which to ignite the Apocalypse."

"The friars see this child as their means?"

Pero nodded. "A Segovian prior named Torquemada fills Isabella's head with dark visions. He has convinced the girl that she was born to serve as the Almighty's instrument for the Last Judgment."

With difficulty, the Old Man turned his head to make certain the door remained closed. Drawing a painful breath, he warned: "This Dominican lust for fire will not be sated until those rabid dogs have installed their terror over all of Christendom. Years ago, their French brothers conspired with the monarchy in Paris to destroy the Templars."

Dias whispered to Zarco about the secret Templar map that Corte-Real had possessed on that doomed northern quest. Nodding at the reminder, Zarco broached the delicate subject with the prince. "My lord, on our voyage to New Scotland—"

"*Sim*, tell me again of that land," the Old Man begged. "Does it bear strange yellow fruit, as the Templars claimed?"

Zarco glanced helplessly at his comrades, distressed by the Old Man's failing memory. He and Dias had recounted several times to the prince how Corte-Real had lost four crewmen from the *Nossa* on the voyage to New Scotland and how, by the grace of God, they had managed to steer the caravel back home. He reminded the prince: "We never saw this new land, my lord."

Failing to understand, the Old Man persisted. "Did you not find the shaft?"

Zarco and Dias could not fathom what he was asking; Corte-Real had never told them why the attempt to reach New Scotland had been launched.

Pero feared the Old Man's mind was becoming unhinged with each passing minute. "My lord, you must rest."

"I have failed," the dying prince muttered in despair.

Pero tried to reassure him that his regret was unfounded. "Your mariners have reached the ends of the world."

The Old Man was now laboring for each breath. "How far south?"

"Gomes has sailed up the Gambia River," Dias said.

Agitated, the Old Man flailed in a desperate effort to rise. "The East!"

Pero tried to calm him. "But Cadamosto says—"

"The Venetian's time has passed! Eannes! Gomes! Corte-Real! All are prisoners to a frightful world falsely conjured!" The Old Man began heaving and gasping violently. "There *is* a sea route around Africa. I have seen it in my dreams. The coast will trend eastward."

"Who will lead us?" Zarco asked.

The Old Man beckoned them closer to ease his effort to speak. "I have assigned command of the Order to my grandnephew, Fernando. There are those in the royal court who will scheme to abandon all that we have accomplished and instead chase easy riches. You must bide your time until the moment is ripe."

"Ripe for what, my lord?" Pero asked.

The Old Man sucked more air into his failing lungs. "You will all be given your orders soon. Until then, you must remain hidden in the mists." Only when the squires nodded their agreement to this solemn pact did he ease back into his cot. Staring sadly at them for several moments, he rasped: "Do you remember the two exemplars of mariners that inhabit this world?"

The squires nodded through tears, having never forgotten his instruction.

"Those who look to the depths," Pero answered for them all, "and those who look to the heavens."

The Old Man smiled, proud of how far his favorite squire had progressed in the training. "There are also two types of men in general. Believers, who avoid the unknown for fear of destroying their precious beliefs, and Knowers, who risk all to test their doubts."

From the first day of his recruitment into the Order, Pero had harbored one burning question. Now, he resolved to ask it before it was too late. "My lord, you are a fervent servant of Christ. Yet you took Jews like us into your protection and counsel. Why?"

The Old Man gripped Pero's hand as firmly as his waning strength would allow. "Your forefathers were forced to leave their homes and seek survival in unknown lands. I have always recruited men who knew the burden of exile and persecution. They are the ones who challenge the limits of the world for—" He coughed up blood.

Pero moved to call the physician, but the hand on his wrist restrained him. "Take me to the cliffs."

Pero understood that desire all too well. He wrapped the Old Man in blankets and helped Dias and Zarco carry him outside on the cot. There they propped the prince up near the Wind Rose, so that he could gaze down at the crashing waves. Across the bay, a lone caravel was unfurling its sails. As if trying to communicate with the distant ship's captain, the Old Man muttered his last command, one that he had spoken a thousand times.

"Go farther."

That night, the squires and knights carried the Old Man's body in procession to Lagos, where it was kept under perpetual watch in the naval church overlooking the shipyards. When a year had passed, the prince's corpse was moved to its permanent tomb in the monastery of Batalha, the site of Portugal's greatest military victory over Castile. Despite being immured with lime to speed the decomposition, his remains were found incorrupt except for the tip of its nose. Yet that was not the most shocking discovery: When finally made public, the Navigator's last will and testament revealed that he had died a pauper, having spent every last coin of his fortune to finance his sea explorations.

TWENTY-THREE

WASHINGTON, D.C.
FEBRUARY 8, PRESENT DAY

Dawn broke over the rolling Virginia countryside as Jaq's plane landed and taxied to the gate at Dulles International. Blinded by another migraine, she staggered down the exit ramp with her knees swollen and her eyes feeling as if thumbnails were gouging her lids. Unable to sleep on the plane, she was now finding it difficult to focus her thoughts.

Had she caught a bug?

Inside the terminal, she fought the zipper on her carry-on until it finally opened. Damn, she'd forgotten that all her contact information was still on her old Blackberry. She found a phone bank and called directory assistance for Chet Meringer, a CIA attorney who'd had a crush on her in law school. Bracing for the ordeal, she dropped in the coins and dialed the number.

A syrupy Alabaman voice answered. "Well, if it isn't the one that got away."

She was flustered at having been identified without even speaking. "Chet?"

"Jaq of all trades. Long time no hear."

"I'm at a payphone. How'd you know it was me?"

"Have you forgotten where I work?"

"I didn't think—"

"That we Langley lawyers don't have the latest in snoop technology? I'm a senior analyst now. What say you and I have lunch on Uncle Sam today and catch up?"

"I'd love to," she lied. "But I just got back from Europe. Can I take a rain check?"

"I honor those. They have an expiration date, you know."

"Chet, I need a favor."

"So"—his voice drooped—"you didn't call to blow air on an old cinder."

"I'm still a little raw from Paul's death."

"I heard. ... I'm sorry. How can I help?"

"I need some information. Background on—"

"Hold on. Call me back in two minutes on my cell."

Pacing off the time, she dialed the new number he gave her, reminded that the CIA phones were likely monitored by the watchers of the watchers. As she waited, the receiver thrummed against her chin. Her hand was trembling.

What is wrong with me?

Her CIA contact answered from a noisy sidewalk. "Okay, shoot."

"A European national who goes by the name of Elymas."

There was a long pause on the other end. "You're asking me to track down another guy? I guess you're not *that* heartbroken. Who is he? Some Euro-trash playboy you met in Monaco?"

"Just business."

After another skeptical beat, he relented. "Which country?"

"I don't know. He gets around. Just get me whatever you can find. I'll owe you one."

"Damn right you will. When do you need it?"

"End of the day?"

"What am I, FedEx? If I can pull it off, I'll meet you at Chadwick's at seven."

She was about to hang up, but then remembered something else. "Say, Chet. Do you know anybody who specializes in cryptography?"

"You mean like, what, enemy messages?"

"More like word combinations."

"What'd you get yourself mixed up in over there?"

"I'm not sure."

"Send over what you have and I'll make some inquiries."

"I'll text it to you when I get to the office."

Dizzy again, she hung up and braced against the wall. She really could use the rest of the day off, but the gorillas at work were probably thumping their chests about her incompetence. Despite feeling like crap, she decided to take a taxi straight to the Truman Building.

Ochley came storming around the corner when she walked off the elevator. "Where in God's name have you been?"

Several State employees moving down the hall heard his outburst. They stopped to watch the confrontation.

"Bart, we need to talk in private."

"You're damn right we're gonna talk! Darden's been riding my ass for two days! A Rome hotel is threatening a lawsuit over an unpaid bill and a French security official is blabbing to the press about his crime scene being invaded.

And then there's the small matter of those injured tourists in Chartres. The *Post* ran a story this morning about how the American victims were still waiting for help to get home."

"I can explain."

He herded her up the stairs. "Save your breath. You'll explain it to Darden and McCrozier in two minutes."

She was suddenly feeling much worse. "How'd they know I was back?"

"We put an alert out to every customs desk from here to Istanbul. I got the call as soon as you came through the gate."

Ochley perp-walked her into the same office where she had undercut Darden to get approval for the Ethiopia trip. Turning on her like inquisitors were Darden, McCrozier, and a third man who looked vaguely familiar. She heard Ochley lock the door behind her.

Darden's upper lip twisted in a snarl. "Well, if it isn't the Phantom of Foggy Bottom."

"Give it a rest, Fred." McCrozier welcomed her back with a tentative handshake. "Ms. Quartermane, I think you know Deputy Director Mayfield."

Her memory now jostled, she extended a hand to the man she had met at Rev. Merry's prayer breakfast. What was an NSA big cheese doing *here*? Mayfield refused to reciprocate her gesture, keeping his hand in his pocket.

Dispensing quickly with the niceties, McCrozier settled into his leather chair and looked directly at her, as if reading her tell signs. "We've received some troubling calls from the French foreign minister."

"What sort of calls?" Not answered immediately, she turned to the other men, who were lined up on the sofa like parole judges. She was left standing, until McCrozier signaled for her to take the grilling chair in front of his desk.

"The French police say a car you rented was seen parked near the small town of Resson," McCrozier said. "The body of a priest was found in an incinerated chapel there. You could start with that."

Stunned that they had learned of her rogue sleuthing, she took a deep breath to calm her nerves. "I think someone's trying to kill me."

Their cold silence was finally broken by Darden's snort of contempt.

McCrozier formed a steeple under his chin with his index fingers. "What makes you think that?"

"The friend I was traveling with was hit by a car in Rome. The driver refused to stop. Alyssa was wearing my scarf and sweater. Then a taxi driver tried to abduct me. I can't find Alyssa. It's like she's vanished."

Darden relished the role of messenger. "She *has* vanished. ... She's dead."

Jaq stared at each man, praying that one of them would countermand that pronouncement as a sick joke. "The Rome police said—"

"We asked the Italian government to keep the incident under wraps," said McCrozier. "That's why you couldn't get any information over there."

She sat numb with grief, her worst fear confirmed. First Paul and now Alyssa, the two people she had loved most. Everyone close to her seemed to be sucked into danger. Had she become a walking curse? She couldn't understand why Alyssa's murderers weren't being pursued with Interpol alerts.

McCrozier offered her a tissue from the Kleenex box on his table. "What else makes you think you're being targeted?"

Shaking noticeably, she had to hold the box with both hands. "The priest at Resson ... I found him dead. I should have reported it, but I panicked. I didn't know whom to trust. His throat had been slit and his mouth stuffed with a powder. Someone had rigged his basement to release a poisonous gas."

"And you think the gas was meant for you?" Ochley asked.

"I'd visited him the day before. Somebody followed me."

Darden kept tapping his shoe against the carpet in agitation. "What *was* the purpose of this meeting with the priest?"

She took a slow sip of water to buy time, uncertain how much she should reveal. How could she explain keeping company with a professional thief? "The priest was an expert on Gothic cathedrals. I had some questions about what I saw at Chartres."

McCrozier straightened in his chair. "Such as?"

"I don't think the bomb was set off to kill tourists."

Darden fired off a glance of disgust at the other men. "I didn't know a background in explosives was a requirement for a passport lawyer here." He turned his scornful glare back on her. "I'd love to hear more about your theory on why the bomb *was* detonated. I'm sure your skill in forensics detection is far superior to that of the French security experts."

Ignoring his sarcasm, she directed her answer at McCrozier. "I think somebody was searching for something hidden below the Chartres crypt."

"That's a lot of somebodies and somethings." McCrozier sounded dubious. "You can't be more specific?"

She noticed that Mayfield was not reacting like someone who had just been told an admittedly outlandish theory. He sat silent and watched her like a predator. She debated how foolish it would sound if she said what she really suspected. Seeing no alternative, she took the risk. "The Ark of the Covenant."

The four men could have passed for stone statuary.

McCrozier ordered her, "Go on."

"Lalibela, Rome, Chartres, Gisors. In the past month, each of these locations that they've hit has had two things in common. They've all had break-ins into underground vaults."

"And the second?" McCrozier asked.

There were more than just two coincidences, she conceded to herself, but she wasn't sure yet where these tangled strands were leading. "All have legends connecting them to the Ark."

McCrozier sighed like a man who wished he had taken early retirement. He turned to Mayfield. "Are you going to do this, or am I?"

Mayfield spoke up for the first time. "Oh, be my guest, Ben. Then I'll finish by cleaning up the knee-deep shit you jackasses have crapped all over these Augean Stables you call an agency."

McCrozier turned his weary gaze toward the window, which framed the Potomac. "What we're about to tell you, Ms. Quartermane, is classified at the highest level. I don't need to remind you what that means, do I?"

"No, sir."

"Josiah here has been heading up a special covert task force with resources drawn from his shop, CIA, Defense Intel, and us. He runs it under his flagship at the NSA. The President signed an executive order granting it international jurisdiction for a new mission."

"Is that legal?" she asked. "For the NSA to operate overseas?"

"The arrangement is unconventional," McCrozier admitted. "But so is the threat. Because of the extreme danger to domestic security, the congressional committees on intelligence have confirmed the NSA's authority to follow the evidence where it leads, even across borders. The FBI first adopted this approach with its Rapid Deployment Team in its Counter-Terrorism Division. Your little excursions into the underworld stepped on the toes of Josiah's operation."

She snuck a confused glance at Mayfield. "I don't understand."

Mayfield's scowl turned even more acidic; it was obvious he'd rather be water-boarded than give up what he was about to reveal. "Certain sects of Muslim *jihadists* have been expecting the arrival of a messianic savior they call the Mahdi. He's supposed to destroy the current world order and replace it with an Islamic paradise."

Were they trying to pull some kind of sadistic prank on her? Did they really expect her to believe that the U.S. government had been moling around the world trying to foil an Islamic religious myth?

"It sounds like madness because it is," McCrozier said. "Ever since 9/11, that seems to be what we deal in. Insanity wrapped in more insanity. Hell, I thought going after Castro with exploding cigars and recruiting psychics to remote-view into the Kremlin was nuts, too. But we did it. And we did a lot more that hasn't been revealed. Bottom line, this is all too real."

She needed a moment to wrap her mind around it all. "You mean these *jihadists* believe in a kind of Christ?"

"You could look at it that way, I suppose," Mayfield said. "If that helps with your Sunday school grasp on reality."

What the deal was with this NSA prick? He seemed downright poisonous in the way he was talking to her. "Don't tell me this Mahdi character is going to rise from the tomb?"

Mayfield snorted contemptuously. Forced to explain, he made his opinion clear that she was not worthy of this level of briefing by refusing to look at her. "A few years ago, we began quietly recruiting moderate Islamic scholars and reformed *jihadists* to help us understand the Muslim extremists and predict their moves. We modeled it on what the BATFE did by infiltrating the American militia movement to keep tabs on what our own homegrown apocalyptic lunatics were planning."

Apocalyptic lunatics?

Her eyes narrowed. Did he include Rev. Merry and her in that group?

Mayfield twirled an expensive Mont Blanc in his wiry fingers, studying it as if questioning whether the pen really *was* mightier than a sword. He took a deep breath, either trying to determine whether to stop while he had the opportunity or continue divulging more national-security secrets. "About a year ago, we began picking up a lot of chatter about this Mahdi hero of theirs. Our analysts tell us that the *jihadists* watch for certain predicted signs that will confirm the Mahdi's true identity when he arrives."

When he hesitated, she pressed for more. "*What* signs?"

The NSA official was slow on the trigger, so McCrozier answered for him. "According to their prophecies, the authentic Islamic messiah will be revealed only when he finds and displays the Ark of the Covenant."

She leaned in. "Muslims believe in the Ark? Like Christians and Jews?"

Mayfield puffed a wisp of vitriol. "It doesn't seem to matter to these fanatics that there have been as many stakeholders to the title of Mahdi as crackpots claiming to be the returned Christ."

She was at once relieved *and* alarmed. She hadn't been imagining the Ark connection, after all, but someone apparently did want her dead. "Why are you telling me this?"

Mayfield stood to pace the room. "We suspect the mastermind behind this plot is a Pakistani opium kingpin named Tahmeed Hosaam. He runs a sophisticated crime syndicate that extends from Indonesia to the United States. You must have bumped into him or one of his thugs over there."

She thought back to that injured construction foreman's description of the nervous Middle Eastern man in the Chartres crypt. Was he also the taxi driver who had tried to kill her in Rome? What could she possibly have done to cause this Pakistani to target *her*?

McCrozier asked her: "Can you think of anything you did or saw while overseas that could have threatened Hosaam or lead him to believe you know something about his plan?"

She shook her head. "Why not just tell one of our Middle Eastern allies to round him up and give him the usual rendition treatment?"

"Hosaam's too clever to expose himself until the right moment," McCrozier said. "His command structure is patterned on the French Resistance during World War II. He employs a pyramid network and forbids recruits from interacting with more than two fellow members. He also uses coded cryptonyms and acrostics to send assignments over the Web. He's obsessed with keeping his identity a mystery. We've never been able to locate an image of him."

"How do you expect to stop him if you don't know what he looks like?"

Mayfield opened a thin dossier and tossed it on the desk. "We'll search for patterns and idiosyncrasies. He devotes part of his profits to Al Qaeda and the Wahabi schools so that the Arab street is invested in protecting him. He has an IQ of 194 and was educated at Stanford under another name. All known photos from the years he lived in the States were stolen or destroyed. Obviously, he's had this master plan in the works for a while. He speaks English fluently. His consuming passion, aside from decapitating infidels and selling poppy juice, is archaeology. That's about all we have to go on."

"If he stays in the shadows," she asked, "who does his dirty work?"

"The usual religious stooges," Mayfield said. "The man he reportedly patterns himself after was a Moslem warlord who led a sect of assassins against Christian knights during the Crusades."

A synapse in her brain sparked: *Templars?*

Mayfield picked up a Moroccan dagger from McCrozier's curio and admired its workmanship. "This medieval psychopath would drug illiterate boys into a stupor and take them to his harem in the Syrian highlands. After a week of sex parties, he'd knock them out with more hashish and haul them back to the desert. When they awoke, he'd tell them they had just witnessed Paradise. If they cut enough infidel throats, they'd be rewarded with a stay for eternity."

McCrozier sighed. "I guess that's where that forty virgins nonsense comes from, huh. Some things haven't changed much."

"At least we have one thing going for us," Jaq said.

McCrozier looked perplexed. "What's that?"

"This Pakistani doesn't know where the Ark is hidden," she said.

"How can you be so sure?" Ochley asked her.

"He's already tried four locations. He's obviously searching blind."

McCrozier didn't look at all comforted by her hypothesis. "Maybe, but he's moving too fast for my druthers."

"Are you worried he'll use the Ark as a weapon?" she asked.

The men glared at her with gaped mouths.

"Weapon?" Darden snapped. "What in hell are you talking about?"

"It's been awhile since I read my Joshua," she said. "But didn't the Israelites use the powers of the Ark to defeat the Canaanites?"

Darden shook his head at Ochley, as if bewildered how such a naïve woman could have been hired for a government job. "No, we are *not* worried about some goddamn fairy tale!"

"Fred," cautioned Ochley. "Ms. Quartermane has certain religious beliefs."

Darden recoiled as if she were radioactive. "You're not one of *those*?"

Jaq's blood pressure spiked. "Those *what*?"

"Bible-thumping literalists."

She was steamed. What *was* this NSA guy's problem? He claims to be one of the Reverend's supporters, and then ridicules his teachings behind his back? She locked hard onto his disparaging eyes. "I believe that every word of Scripture happened just as it was written."

The men shared uncomfortable glances.

"Our concern here is more mundane, but no less dangerous," McCrozier said. "Should, God forbid, Hosaam somehow come into possession of the real Ark, or at least manage to convince the world that he's found it, he'll unite millions of radical Islamists to his cause."

"He'll also use the discovery to extort Israel's submission," Mayfield warned. "If Tel Aviv backs down under the threat that he'll destroy their hope for salvation as a people, Hosaam will gain control of the Middle East."

"And have us by the ..." McCrozier caught himself before using the salty language.

Jaq's head was spinning. "Even assuming this Pakistani could find the Ark, how would he prove its authenticity?"

Mayfield waved off that perceived difficulty as a non-issue. "Hell, there are Orthodox rabbis in Israel all too willing to perform the identification for him. Jewish tradition requires the Ark be recovered before the Temple of Solomon is restored. Those lunatic West Bank settlers are as hell-bent as the Muslim extremists to summon their messiah. Each faction thinks the other is going to get the cosmological shaft up the ass in the end, so they really don't care who delivers the damn thing. If those rabbis declare a box of plywood from Home Depot to be the real Ark, then it's as good as the real Ark."

"But they'd be signing Israel's death warrant," she insisted.

Mayfield shrugged. "Some of those right-wing nuts believe the Zionist state is a profane presumption against God's prerogative to restore the biblical Israel on His own timetable."

She retraced the incidents of the past week in light of these revelations. Something still didn't add up. If this Pakistani narco-messiah *was* searching for the Ark in Lalibela … she leapt to her feet. "Paul wasn't killed by *qat* smugglers! You lied to me again!"

McCrozier couldn't bring himself to look at her, but Mayfield, sharing none of his colleague's moral ambivalence, revealed with a smug look of satisfaction how little she had really known about the man she was going to marry: "Merion was working for us as an operative. We couldn't have told you if we wanted to. The food project started out as a legitimate enterprise, but it was too convenient a front to pass up. He was gunned down while tailing Hosaam's goons. One of our Ethiopian rabbits probably snitched him out. Hosaam set the ambush and tried to cover his tracks to make it look like a qat deal gone wrong."

"What about the Ethiopian priest?" she demanded.

"He had the misfortune of being a Christian holy man," Mayfield said. "Hosaam chose him to carve up with his demented *Kaa Faa Raa* message. Hosaam wants his fellow Muslims to believe that the message had been left by the false prophet Dajjal, who's supposed to come along just before the Mahdi flies in like Superman to save the day."

McCrozier cautioned: "We share one paramount goal with Hosaam. Neither of us can afford to let this little race to find the Ark become public."

Darden shook his head and waved off that particular concern. "Nobody would believe it anyway."

"I wouldn't be so sure about that," Ochley warned. "The polls say more than half the country is convinced the Rapture is imminent."

Jaq need a moment to catch up. "Does Rev. Merry know about this?"

Mayfield's eyes turned even colder on her. "No. And there's no reason to cause the good pastor more sorrow, now is there?"

She understood that to be a warning, not a question. He probably didn't trust her to maintain confidentiality. Darden was a piece of work, but this NSA asshole *really* gave her the creeps. On top of being a misogynistic troglodyte, he was as much a hypocrite as Darden, glad-handing Rev. Merry at the prayer breakfast while allowing evangelical Christians to be scoffed at in his presence. "How do you intend to stop Hosaam?"

Mayfield twirled the dagger on the arm of his chair. "We'll move on him when we have evidence so convincing that even the dunderheads at the UN won't be able to deny it. Until then, we'll try to forecast his next strike."

"And if he finds the Ark?" she asked.

Mayfield glanced at his watch. "I'm late for a meeting on the Hill."

She arose, taking his impatience as a signal that it was time to leave.

McCrozier motioned her back down. "We still have a bit of housecleaning to take care of. Given these developments, Ms. Quartermane, we feel it's best that you be transferred to Josiah's unit. For a few months at least, until we get a handle on this situation."

Her stomach gripped. These last fifteen minutes had been enough to convince her that she wanted nothing more to do with Mayfield. "I didn't sign on to draft wiretap petitions and eavesdrop on U.S. citizens."

"If one of Hosaam's thugs *is* stalking you, we can't risk your being taken hostage, or worse," Mayfield said in a tone that left no room for debate. "You'll join us over at NSA, where we can keep an eye on you."

"Bart's already started the paperwork," McCrozier said.

"What will I do there?"

"I don't give a damn what you do." Mayfield said as he snapped the buckle on his briefcase. "I'm sure something will turn up, considering your remarkable talent for sticking your nose into everyone else's business."

Chet Meringer sauntered into Chadwick's Pub and slipped into the back booth. He slid a manila envelope across the table to Jaq. "You've been rubbing shoulders with some real upstanding characters, hon."

She craned her neck around the corner post to make certain they were alone. "I suppose it would have been asking too much for you not to read it."

He laughed. "I've never been known for my self-control."

She quickly scanned the document in the envelope:

> *Subject: Moses "Boz" D'Orville*
> *Age: 42 —Alias: Elymas*
> *Summary: An international smuggler who has no valid citizenship and travels on counterfeit passports. He uses Paris as his base. His métier is the recovery of Jewish art and heirlooms stolen by the Nazis. Although descendants of dispossessed Jewish families defend his intentions as heroic, he utilizes unconventional means to inflict retribution on those he considers collaborators in the confiscations. His laissez-faire attitude about legalities has made him persona non grata in several countries, including Israel. His admirers, when they talk about him (and that is rarely), speak with a reverence usually reserved for Simon Weisenthal. He has numerous contacts in the underworld. He finances his stealth recovery missions with less altruistic assignments in the underground antiquities racket.*
> *Legal status: Outstanding arrest warrants in the United States, Israel, and Germany. France refuses to process extradition because of past family contributions to the war.*

Psychological profile: Several members of his extended Jewish family, surnamed Rosen, were killed in the Holocaust. His grandfather, a professor of medieval Sephardic art, and a great uncle, a chemist, escaped Germany as young boys and adopted the surname D'Orville. The great uncle joined the resistance in France and was recruited into a covert operations unit in northern Africa called the Magic Gang, a team of sleight-of-hand performers and con artists led by the famous British magician Jasper Maskelyne. The elder D'Orville's expertise was in the application of invisible and deadly flammables; he worked for the Krupp Steel Works before the war. This team of mischief-makers applied techniques of illusion to confound the Germans. Their most remarkable feat was making the Suez Canal disappear to save it from Nazi Stuka bombers. Boz's great uncle helped raise him and probably passed down many secrets of sabotage. Nothing more is known about his immediate family except that his mother is reported to have died very young.

She reread the line about the uncle who'd had expertise during the war in the application of invisible and deadly flammables.

"You all right?"

She refocused. "Yeah, a little beat is all."

He retrieved the report. "I'd better shred this for you."

"Right."

He studied her. "It's none of my business, but you're not getting over your head in something, are you?"

"I've got it covered."

Looking less than convinced, he got up and kissed her on the cheek. "I haven't forgotten about that lunch." He walked out, but several steps away, spun back. "I almost forgot. Those three lines you texted over. I asked a grad-school buddy over at Georgetown to run them through his linguistics computer program that tracks derivations of lost languages. The software sifts patterns and probabilities. These days, the universities have more capabilities than we do."

"Any luck?"

"He couldn't find even a hint of a pattern. Very strange."

"Why's that?"

"Apparently it's unheard of to come up with no hits at all. Like typing a few words in Google and getting no results. He said the arrangement would almost have to be totally random. You sure you wrote it down correctly?"

She remembered that she was still lugging around the monsignor's writing board. She pulled it from her bag and looked at it again.

"Let me see that. What'd you find over there? Some kind of Rosetta Stone?"

While he examined the board, Jaq saw a reflection of the monsignor's inscription in a Coors Beer advertisement mirror that extended across the top length of the booth.

Turning his nose, he handed the board back to her. "Damn this stinks."

Something caught her interest. "Hold that up again."

Perplexed by the request, Chet lifted it to eye level again while holding his breath to avoid the stench of dried blood.

She gasped—the mirror revealed the carved letters in reverse:

ante dorival 13

NA5551.C5 C42 31

: . /

She slammed a palm to her forehead. Of course! The monsignor had written the lines from right to left, just like he had on the wood palimpsest that day she had first visited him with Elymas. She quickly copied the lines in reverse on a napkin. "What's that look like to you?"

Chet opened his briefcase and brought out a book checked out of the CIA library. He examined the taped ribbon on its spine. "The middle line might be a Dewey decimal number."

She wiggled out of the booth and dashed for the door. "I'll call you!"

The female staffer behind the circular information desk at the Library of Congress produced a slender book that matched the catalog number on the monsignor's reversed carving. "Sorry for the delay. We have our own classification system, so I had to cross-reference it."

Jaq opened it to the title page: Louis Charpentier, *Les Mysteres de la cathedrale de Chartres*, published in 1966. Why would the monsignor have known of an American classification method? She asked the librarian, "Do the French use the Dewey Decimal system?"

"Many French libraries do. The *Bibliothèque nationale* converted when the Mitterand expansion was completed."

She was now even more perplexed. Had the monsignor referenced the Dewey number knowing that someone might be more likely to discover its connection? The imprint of the classification ID, she saw, didn't include the number 31. "Would thirty-one have any significance to the cataloging?"

"No. Perhaps it's a reference to a page number?"

She turned to page 31; the French text on that page was accompanied by strange drawings connecting lines and dots. "Do you read French?"

The librarian nodded. "Would you like me to attempt a translation?"

"Just this paragraph, please."

The librarian typed up her rendition and printed it.

Jaq studied the result:

> *Examination of the situation of Chartres in France as a whole reveals yet another curious thing. There exists in what was Belgian Gaul, in the old provinces of Champagne, Picardy, Il-de-France and Neustrie, a certain number of XIIth and XIIIth century cathedrals, bearing the name of Notre-Dame, which reproduce, taken together, on Earth the constellation of the Virgin as seen in the sky. If one relates the stars with the towns in which these cathedrals stand, l'Epi de la Vierge would be Reims; Gamma, Chartres; Zeta Amiens; Epsilon, Bayeux. Among the smaller stars we find Evreux, Etampes, Laon, all of these having a Notre-Dame of the best period. One even finds, in the place of one of the smaller stars, near l'Epi, a Notre-Dame-de-l'Epine, which was built much later, but its building opens a mystery.*

She was flummoxed. What was the old priest trying to say? Had he just been scribbling research notes? She read the first line again. When the librarian was distracted, she wrote *'ante dorival 13'* on a paper. "I have another note, but for the life of me I can't remember what it refers to."

The librarian turned to examine it. "'*Ante*' in Latin means prior. 'Dorival' is a stumper." She punched a few keys. "The only listing that comes up is for an obscure sixteenth-century French poet. Oh yes, it must be him. Antoine Dorival. You probably wrote 'Ante' as an abbreviation for his first name."

"Of course," Jaq said, dissembling. "Does the encyclopedia include a biographical entry for this Dorival person?"

"A short reference. It says he is best remembered for a poem about an underground chapel in a French town called Gisors."

Jaq froze. "Does the poem still exist?"

The librarian searched on an online French encyclopedia. "You're in luck. A French newspaper printed it in 1898. The late French historian Jean Markale made a reference to it in a book about Gisors." She found a copy of Markale's English translation and printed the poem:

> *Gold, the luminous gleam yet shining*
> *of the altar table, all covered in beaten gold*
> *Shines so clearly that the entire chapel*
> *Resembles daybreak or a beautiful dawn.*
> *Near the well of Jacob, a lover of humanity*
> *Rested in his weariness, when from the Samaritans*
> *A woman arrived, whom God in his glory*

As if in need humbly asked for a drink
Which she refused him, and he received from his bounty
Water drawn from the shoot of his divinity
From the tomb emerged the resurrected Jesus
But dear Uranus, delay a while your course
And, as you have taken the Virgin for your guiding star
At the time you set sail,
Take her Son as your pilot.

She studied the monsignor's notation. What could the number 13 after "Dorival" mean? Did it have some esoteric significance? On a whim, she counted thirteen lines down in the poem:

And, as you have taken the Virgin for your guiding star.

French cathedrals named for the Blessed Virgin? Built to imitate the stars in the Virgo constellation? She was to take the Virgin as her guiding star? Maybe the linchpin clue lay in the last line of the message:

A colon, a period, and a back slant.

Or maybe the monsignor was just ahead of his time, going stark raving mad long before the rest of the world could catch up with him.

While walking to the metro station, Jaq remembered that she had left her apartment key at Alyssa's place before leaving for Italy. Damn. She'd have to talk the doorman into letting her inside.

She flagged down a cab and took it up 16th Street, past the old Masonic House of the Temple. The lights inside were still on. The renovations for the future location of the new End Times theme park looked to be coming along nicely. She'd have to call Rev. Merry tomorrow to tell him that she was back.

An idea struck her. Alyssa's apartment was only a few blocks away. She could walk it from here. The pastor would love a report on the inside work.

She told the cabbie to stop. After paying the fare, she got out, backtracked a block, and climbed the steps of the Temple. Its tall bronze doors were guarded by the giant marble sphinxes and crowned with a frieze that read: *Freemasonry Builds its Temples in the Hearts of Men and Among Nations.* On her first visit, she had failed to notice that one of the sphinxes was wrapped in a coiled serpent and wore a necklace with an insignia. The carved engraving resembled the Tau crosses that she had encountered in France.

She tried the doors. They were unlocked. She cracked them open and called out, but no one answered. The guard was probably making his rounds.

She walked inside and squeaked across a tavernelle floor lit by chandeliers of alabaster bowls. On the walls of the atrium, bronze plaques were engraved with Masonic symbols: a winged globe, Egyptian hieroglyphs, a Teutonic cross, a St. Andrew's cross, and a pelican feeding its brood from the blood of its own breast. This pagan imagery, strangely, unnerved her. She climbed the grand staircase to the second floor and confronted two bronze serpents soaring over a wooden throne. What was the deal with all of these snakes? Was Rev. Merry keeping them for an exhibit about the Devil?

A new sign over the side door said: *This way to the Great Flood Diorama.*

Now she was really intrigued. The pastor hadn't told her about this exhibit. Was he cooking up a new theme ride to mimic Noah's Ark? That would be a real blast for the kids to ride around on paddleboats with dogs and cats, two by two. She just had to sneak a peak at what he was planning.

She passed through the arched portal and descended a spiraling stairwell that led to the basement. A door set with an automatic spring closed gently behind her. She flipped on a light, and gasped. The chamber had been painted to resemble the Paradise of Genesis, with creatures walking through woods and flying in the sky. On the far wall, an arching rainbow lit up after the Flood. There were no windows and only the one door. The confines really created the sense of an enclosed world. All it needed was a big wooden Ark to float and—

Hidden sprinklers on the sky roof opened up.

She ran screaming for cover. Despite being soaked, she laughed and laughed, delighted by the reverend's clever addition to the Ark experience. He was probably planning to issue ponchos to visitors. She must have flipped the rain switch by mistake. She'd have a good chuckle with him about this one. She slogged toward the door and groped for a handle, but it had none.

There was no way to open it.

She thumped it with her shoulder, but it wouldn't budge. She tried to peek through the crevices along the jam, but the door was sealed with rubber edging. The water began pouring down faster.

"Help!" she shouted. "Help me!"

Regressed nozzles in the floor and walls opened up. The water churned to her waist. Surely the exhibit had been designed to level off after a few feet. Yet the water kept rising. She pounded on the door as the surge lifted her off her feet. Backstroking to keep her mouth near the pocket of air, she swallowed a last breath … and went under.

TWENTY-FOUR

SATOR
APERO
TENET
OPERA
ROTAS

VALLADOLID, CASTILE
OCTOBER 1469

In the Archbishop of Toledo's shuttered house, Pero stood surrounded by the grim faces of men who knew their lives hung in the balance. He closely monitored every tic of wavering intent and blink of deceit. Don Gutierre de Cardenas, Isabella's shadowy consul, paced like a felon waiting for the gallows, and Don Fadrique Enriquez, the elderly royal admiral, sat eyeing the door as if contemplating his escape. Castile had become a tinderbox of insurrection, and the spark that would set it aflame was about to be flinted in this austere room whose walls were lined with edgy Aragonese knights.

War between Castile and Portugal was just a marriage vow away.

Isabella's older brother had driven the weakling Henry from the Castilian throne, but when Afonso died weeks later from suspected poisoning, Henry tried to reclaim the crown by marrying off Isabella to the king of Portugal. Yet the headstrong *senhorita* had already set her heart on Ferdinand, the young heir to Aragon. Now, these greedy Castilian grandees, seeing her as a pawn for their designs, were scheming to have her rule jointly with Ferdinand.

And in doing so, they were trampling the rights of Joanna, Henry's heir, whose mother had been Queen Juana of Portugal. Joanna's enemies derisively called her *La Beltraneja* because the Castilian nobleman Beltran de La Cueva was rumored to be her father. That base claim of illegitimacy, Pero knew, was a ruse to deny Portugal its rights. As a result, his mission had become twice as dangerous; with his master, the Duke of Medina-Sidonia, having cast his lot for Isabella, he was now required to fend off the agents of two Spanish factions.

Despite the potential windfall to these grandees, the only man present who appeared eager for the seditious ceremony to proceed was Tomas Torquemada. Earlier that morning, the Dominican prior, his hound's face radiant with spiritual triumph, had preached a sermon in the cathedral proclaiming Isabella's ascension as the first sign of the End Times. There was even whispered talk that he had extracted a vow from the new queen to install the Holy Office of the Inquisition in Castile.

A bell rang, and Isabella entered the makeshift wedding chamber first, an element of stagecraft insisted upon by the Aragon contingent to recognize Ferdinand's superiority of gender. Pero laughed inwardly at that conceit. From what he had observed of Isabella, she was clever enough to surrender such meaningless gestures while preserving real power for those occasions when its application was most useful. Led to the kneeler, the young queen measured the fealty in each face around her with penetrating azure eyes. Pero was struck by the austerity of her unadorned black gown and the modest manner in which she had gathered her wild russet hair. This was a woman who took to heart God's admonition against the vanity of beauty, if not religious pride.

Ferdinand's arrival, minutes later, was as jocular as Isabella's was somber. A year younger than his bride, the dashing prince glad-handed each man and lifted their spirits with jests and stories. He jaunted over to the kneeler and attempted to kiss Isabella, but she demurred, denying him the public intimacy. Yet her blush betrayed an agreeableness to his hot interest.

Pero marveled at her changeling nature. She might be ruthlessly ambitious, but a woman she was, nonetheless. He wondered how smoothly these two mismatched colts, one pious and the other frisky, would yoke.

When the nuptials were finished with haste, Isabella arose from the kneeler and, dispensing with further formalities, turned the proceedings into a council of state. "Last night I witnessed a disturbing sight," she told the grandees. "The *conversos* in this city did not applaud my husband on his arrival."

The abrupt shift from ceremony disarrayed the archbishop. "My lady, you must not concern yourself with such matters on this glorious eve. A bountiful feast awaits your enjoyment."

She waved off such frivolities and issued a warning. "Henry marshals his forces while we stand here idling. Those towns that have offered support will swiftly turn on us if we do not secure their garrisons by morning."

Ferdinand's lusty grin anticipating the marital bed vanished. "My love, do you suspect spies have been infiltrated into our ranks?"

Isabella stole a knowing glance at Torquemada before counseling her husband. "Henry has formed a cabal of relapsed heretics and sodomites to undermine us. These crypto-Jews he coddles are like mites in the foundation of a house. They cannot be seen, but when the storm blows, the walls will collapse."

Medina-Sidonia spoke up to protest. "*Reina*, half the realm is of mixed lineage. There is no good method for determining who is a true believer."

"There *is* a method," Torquemada insisted.

"Pray tell," said the duke, eyeing the Dominican prior with suspicion.

"St. Dominic showed us the way in the Languedoc."

"And laid that region to ruin," Ferdinand reminded the prior.

Torquemada would not be dissuaded from his proposed policy of spiritually purifying Castile and Aragon. "The true believers will exalt Christ by exposing those who do not support the Church."

Wan with alarm, Medina-Sidonia pleaded with the queen to reconsider. "*Reina*, I fear such a sweeping mission would prove too costly."

Isabella came to her former confessor's side in a gesture of support. "The properties of heretics and false oath-givers are subject to forfeiture. The good friar here has assured me that the Holy Office will sustain itself."

A troubled silence overtook the room. Pero sensed that the grandees had little stomach for risking their lands to the same fate suffered by the Occitan nobles during the wars to eradicate the Albigensees.

"Tribunals would have to be installed in every city," the archbishop reminded the queen. "If we are to prevail in this struggle with your brother, we must devote what funds we have to raising an army."

Pero watched with grudging admiration as Isabella deftly deflected every objection to the course of action that she and the Dominican had long ago set upon. She was a natural diplomat, and demonstrated this skill again by playing upon their exalted sense of stature.

"My lords, I am not as wise or worldly as you," she said. "But if the Almighty wills it, I expect to rule to the end of the century. I believe God has inspired you to unite me with my husband for a great purpose. The churchmen promise that the year 1500 will usher in the Last Judgment. Yet God will not return until we first prepare the way. All Iberia must be purified of nonbelievers."

Pero saw from the determination in Isabella's eyes that she would broach no delay in her attempt to ignite the Apocalypse. He had to get a warning to the Old Man with all speed. While the council proceeded, he quietly begged his leave from the duke with the excuse that he needed to purchase his master's provisions for their return journey south. Making his way quickly outside and past the archbishop's grounds, he found the streets full of crazed pilgrims pouring forth from the churches. They were ranting and bawling about Dominican sermons that morning promising the imminent approach of Our Lord's fiery return. He took a side alley to avoid being followed.

A mob armed with clubs turned the corner, and a half-naked flagellant leading the feverish horde aimed a towering crucifix like a spear at him. "You there! Recite us the Creed!"

Pero tried to retreat, until a rock caromed off his scalp and crumpled him. Dazed, he revived on his knees, tasting his own blood. He searched his vest for the duke's safe-passage document, but he had left it in his quarters. Outnumbered, he signed his breast. "I am a Christian!"

"Any liar can cut the air with his hand!" The gang's leader challenged him with a test. "Where is the True Cross guarded?"

Pero was at a loss to answer that question, for every town from here to Italy claimed to have a piece of the worthless lumber. "That depends."

"On what?"

"The village you were born in."

His tormentor was the one now confused. "What's your name?"

Pero dared not give them his real name. "I am in the service of Medina-Sidonia. You would do well to let me pass, or you will answer to the Duke."

The thug wasn't convinced. "You have a Jew face."

Pero saw the rabble-rousers grip their clubs tighter at hearing that indictment. He searched the scum, praying for forgiveness from both God and his father for what he was about to do. This profession assigned to him by the Old Man did not allow the luxury of a philosopher's ethics. Choosing a cross-eyed brute that seemed the daftest of the lot, he pointed a finger at him in accusation and shouted: "I saw you spit out the host in San Pablo!"

The mob turned on the man, who backed away, too stunned and frightened to utter a protest in his defense.

Pero seized the moment by drawing his dagger. "False *converso*!"

"Run him through!" shouted a jury of voices.

The mob's bloodlust was now blistering, and Pero knew that someone had to die. He confronted this wolf leading the pack with false bluster. "You still think I'm a *converso*?"

"Prove me wrong! Or prove it to God and—"

Pero slashed the accused man's throat. "There is God's proof!"

Gushing blood, the scapegoat fell to his knees, trying to gurgle a claim of innocence. Unable to make another sound, he fell lifeless to the cobblestones.

Impressed by the Holy Ghost's alacrity in lifting Pero's hand to render divine judgment, the leader of the mob led his savages on down the street to find more sinners and send them to Hell on the Lord's Day.

Left alone with his bleeding victim, Pero stood trembling from the horror of his first killing.

TWENTY-FIVE

Waking up, Jaq reached a hand up to scratch her nose and felt an air tube in her nostrils. "Where am I?"

Rev. Merry's worried face, girded with those familiar jowls that hung like a creel under his chin, slowly came into focus. Sitting aside the bed, he grasped her hand in relief. "Georgetown Medical Center. I flew back as soon as I heard. I don't know what I would have done if we had lost you."

"Lost me?"

"My security guard found you unconscious in the Great Flood exhibit. Another thirty seconds and …" He shook his head. "I fired him on the spot."

It all suddenly came back to her, and she remembered being trapped in the water tank below the converted Masonic Temple. "It was my fault. I went in wandering on my own. I wanted to see what you had done with the museum."

He kissed her forehead. "You're safe now. That's all that matters."

"Did I flip the wrong switch?"

"I had the reservoir installed with automatic sensors. When it's fully operational, the water will imitate a flood when human warmth is detected. Of course, visitors will be in boats with lifeguards and tour guides."

She sighed heavily, upset at having made yet another bone-headed mistake. "Mayfield will have a field day when he finds out."

"Josh Mayfield? Over at the NSA?"

She nodded. "I've been transferred from State." She found him waiting to hear the reason for the move. "I'm not supposed to talk about it."

The pastor seemed a little hurt. "I understand."

She debated telling him of her doubts about the two officials who claimed to be his supporters. "How well do you know Mayfield and Fred Darden?"

"We cross paths at political fundraisers and events. Why do you ask?"

"I don't know if I should bring this up. But I've heard them say some pretty unflattering things about evangelicals."

The pastor smiled. "Politics is a rough business. These are good men at heart. They make great sacrifices to serve Christ and country. They've supported our cause on several congressional bills. If they don't agree with us on every theological nuance, we must forbear them their faults."

"It's more than that. Sometimes they seem so two-faced to be Christians."

He gently chided her with a patting hand. "In the fourth century, when Christians suffered horrible persecutions at the hands of the Romans, some of our brothers and sisters lost courage at the last moment and surrendered their copies of Scripture rather than endure the tortures. The descendants of those who accepted martyrdom argued that these apostates should not be recognized as true Christians. This schism threatened the very survival of the Church. We must never presume to know what is in another's heart."

She was humbled by his capacity to forgive. "I've got a lot to learn about faith, I guess. How can one ever be sure who truly believes in Christ?"

"I always try to apply two of His most important commands: Judge not lest ye be judged, and by their fruits ye shall know them."

She was about to tell him about some of the questionable fruit she had seen produced at State when a doctor walked into the room. He nodded to her and checked the chart. "I'm Charlie Mossel." He listened to her heart with a stethoscope. "You've been out for a while. How are you feeling?"

She coughed painfully. "My chest is sore."

"That's from the water we pumped from your stomach. We're going to keep you another day just to be safe. Were you experiencing any unusual symptoms before this accident?"

"Such as?"

"Inflammation of the joints. Headaches. Blurred vision."

"I guess I have been feeling a little off center lately. I just chalked it up to a few hectic days overseas."

"We ran some standard blood tests." The doctor glanced at Rev. Merry, concerned about patient confidentiality. "I'll discuss them with you later."

"He's my pastor. You can tell him anything."

The doctor tested the range of motion in her elbow. "What do you know about your family's genetic history?"

"Nothing, really. I'm no longer in contact with my mother. And my father took off when I was a kid."

"Any grandparents still alive?"

Thirsty, she reached for a glass of water. "My grandmother on my mother's side lives in a nursing home in Kentucky. I haven't seen her for several years."

Are you Jewish?"

Nearly spewing the sip, she turned on the reverend, wondering if this was one of his pranks to lift her spirits. Finding him equally surprised by the question, she told the doctor, "No. Why would you ask *that?*"

"The tests show a possible indication for Behcet's syndrome. It's an autoimmune disease that affects the blood vessels and body tissues. Very rare, particularly here in the United States. It can be triggered and aggravated by high levels of stress."

"Is it inherited?" she asked.

"Behcet's seems to have a genetic component. But it isn't passed on like other diseases. There's probably a predisposition to it that, frankly, we don't fully understand. Sometimes we find it in those with Sephardic Jewish ancestry."

"Sephardic?"

"Jews from Iberia and North Africa," Rev. Merry explained. He turned to the doctor. "Is this condition life-threatening?"

The doctor waved off that worry. "Just chronic. But it can worsen as one ages. Behcet's is controllable with corticosteroids, if started early. We like to get blood work from as many family members as possible before ruling out other possibilities." He told Jaq, "I'll pass the results along to your primary-care physician. If the inflammation becomes more painful, you might want to ask your grandmother if she remembers anyone in your family who suffered similar symptoms."

She held it together until the doctor left the room. When the door closed, she burst into tears. Ever since learning of Alyssa's death, she had been attacked more and more by these crying spells.

Rev. Merry squeezed her hand. "It doesn't sound so bad."

"No, it's not that ... I don't know what's happening to me. I feel like I'm having a nervous breakdown."

"You've been through a rough patch with Paul's death, and now this scare at the museum."

"Would you pull the curtain?"

The pastor gave them privacy by shielding the bed from view of the nurses and doctors passing in the hallway. "Have you been praying every day, Jaqueline?"

She nodded through the tears. "But I don't know whom to trust anymore."

"Trust in the Lord, and all will be revealed."

In the past, she had accepted such counsel without questioning it. But now, she wasn't so sure. Hadn't she been trusting in the Lord all along? She had trusted Him when she fell in love, and Paul turned out to be a sinner who repeatedly lied to her. The Lord had also led her to the job at State, only to transfer her to the NSA to work for a man who seemed a hypocrite in his Christian virtues. There was only one person she knew she could really trust, and she thanked God that he was now at her side. She drew a deep breath for the courage to endure his judgment. "I think … I may be in danger. I feel as if I'm falling apart. Like something's lurking around every corner."

The pastor caressed her bangs to calm her. "The water was an accident, darling. No one was trying to hurt you."

She shook her head, overcome by another surge of raw emotion. "My friend Alyssa was killed in Rome by a hit-and-run driver and …" She wanted to tell him more of what she knew about Alyssa's killer, but she remembered her vow of confidentially on the classified NSA mission. She tried to be careful. "In France, I met a priest who practiced alchemy."

The reverend lost his paternal smile. "Alchemy?"

She hadn't felt so ashamed since going to confession as a child. "I found him in his residence with his throat cut. Somebody tried to asphyxiate me while I was there. And in Italy, someone ran down Alyssa thinking it was me. I've been finding pagan messages and signs. I don't know what they mean."

The pastor reached into his breast pocket and pulled out a small bible that he had apparently purchased to replace the one he had given to her as a gift. "Hold this, my love, and be completely truthful with me. Have you exposed yourself to demonic influences?"

She couldn't look at him directly, fearing the disappointment in his eyes. "I keep being led to places connected to a Roman god called Mithras."

"Mithras? What's this all about?"

"There's this magical square that I discovered in Ethiopia. It begins with the word SATOR. It's Latin for Saturn, another name for the Mithras god."

He regarded her with even more alarm. "Child, you must renounce these evil forces from foreign lands. They have attached themselves to your soul. Satan is tempting you, just as he tempted Our Lord in the desert. Your forty days of fighting the seductions of the occult have commenced. Demonic attacks often manifest as physical assaults. We must protect you as best we can."

"How?"

He studied her, as if debating the best strategy to combat Satan's wily tactics. "Have I not always had your best interests at heart?"

"Of course."

"I want to check you into a mental-health facility. There's a fine one in Rhode Island that's operated by an affiliate church of ours. They deprogram cult victims there. You'll get round-the-clock counseling and power prayer."

"You really think that's necessary?"

He pressed her hand firmly to indicate his resolve. "I couldn't live with myself knowing that I'd not done everything possible to see you protected."

"What about my work? If Mayfield finds out I needed treatment—"

"Let me take care of Josh Mayfield. And don't worry about the cost. You'll have a whole month there to fortify yourself with prayer."

She sank into the pillow. "I guess I *could* use a rest. If you think it's best."

"I do."

Tears streamed down her cheeks. "How can I ever repay you?"

He smiled lovingly at her. "It is the giver who truly receives the reward. You have been my gift from the first day I met you."

She felt safer just being in his presence. "I've so missed your sermons. Have you given the one about the Rapture recently?"

"Two Sundays ago. I feel the time is ripening."

"Tell me again," she begged. "What will that glorious day be like?"

The reverend took the bible from her hand. He opened it and read a passage from Matthew: "'No one knows the day or hour, not even the angels in heaven, nor the Son, but only the Father. As it was in the days of Noah, so it will be at the coming of the Son of Man. For in the days before the flood, people were eating and drinking, marrying and giving in marriage, up to the day Noah entered the ark; and they knew nothing about what would happen until the flood came and took them all away. That is how it will be at the coming of the Son of Man. Two men will be in the field; one will be taken and the other left. Two women will be grinding with a hand mill; one will be taken and the other left.'"

"Do you believe the Antichrist is now among us?"

"I am certain of it," he said. "I also believe that our government knows who it is. The forces of Good and Evil are mustering this very hour."

"If we ever become separated … what should I do?"

He glanced at the door. "Keep daily watch on the international news. When the Jewish temple in Jerusalem is rebuilt, events will move rapidly."

She couldn't fathom how such a miracle could happen in a modern Israeli city where half the inhabitants were Muslim Palestinians. "But for Our Lord to come, won't the Temple have to be restored in the same place where it was built during the time of the Old Testament?"

"Stone by stone. Even the floor will be swept with the dust walked upon by the prophets." The reverend held a distant gaze, as if envisioning the setting. "All thirteen treasures of the Holies of Holies will be returned to their former places of honor. My father used to have me stand up in church as a boy and describe them for our congregation. My presentation became somewhat of a crowd pleaser. I suppose I hammed it up a bit."

She laughed through the tears. "I want to hear it."

Inspired, he found a notepad on the table and wrote down the list for her:

1) Golden Jar of Manna
2) Aaron's Rod
3) Tablets of the Covenant
4) Mercy Seat with Cherubim
5) Golden Altar of Incense
6) Stone of Destiny (base)
7) Menorah
8) Ark (acacia wood overlaid with gold)
9) Ark Handles (staves)
10) Golden Table of Shewbreads
11) Ashes of the Red Heifer
12) Urim and Thummim (breastplate of the High Priest)
13) Torah

After he had described each treasure in detail, she applauded his performance. "You must have been such a hit! How did you manage to remember them all in front of the entire church?"

"I made replicas," he explained with a sheepish grin. "The ashes of the red heifer caused quite a row. I charred a perfectly good steak and powdered it with a bottle of cayenne from our cupboard. My mother nearly had a fit."

"Your father must have been so proud of you."

He sagged in his chair. "Papa had a difficult life."

She pressed his hand into hers, encouraging him to tell her more.

"You know he created the Millennial Broadcasting Network."

"Yes, I heard. People at church said he was a great man."

"He was … until they turned him into a broken man."

"What happened?"

The reverend looked inward. "One night, he awoke from a dream of Ezekiel's wheels within wheels."

"From Revelation?"

He nodded, his eyes hooding with evident pain from the memory. "Scripture promises that one of the first signs announcing the Divine Throne will be the appearance of four smaller wheels turning within a larger wheel."

"Like a machine of some sort?"

"No one knows. But we must remain on alert for anything that appears to operate like wheels within wheels."

"What did your father do?"

The pastor hesitated, nearly overcome. "He cancelled the network's broadcasting and began distributing mimeographed handbills telling everyone how they should prepare for the End in two weeks. Many sold their farms and houses. On the night the Lord was supposed to arrive, hundreds of us gathered on a hill just outside Milledgeville. When morning came …" He turned aside to hide the shame.

"That must have been so hard on you."

He pulled himself from the grip of the memory. "I grew stronger in my faith, but Papa was never the same. People would cross to the other side of the street when he passed. That's why I always begin my sermon on the Rapture with that passage from St. Matthew about no one knowing the hour. I so yearn for that day when Papa and I are reunited. I *will* see him vindicated."

"You feel it's coming soon, don't you?"

His clenched face was fearsome with the Lord's mighty power. "Very soon."

She pressed a kiss to his flaming cheek. In these few moments, her heart had been cleansed anew and her faith restored. The Almighty, it seemed, always married a burden with a compensating gift of grace. Growing up, she had been denied a loving father, but this man had been brought to her in fulfillment of the Biblical promise that the meek shall inherit the Earth. Whenever she suffered such doubts, he was the one bedrock of certainty to which she could cling.

London
February 10, Present Day

Jamaal limped down a narrow alley in the downtrodden Muslim section of the East End. Finding the address that he had been sent by encoded email, he slipped into a small *shisha* café through its delivery entrance. A cook in the kitchen motioned him down a shadowy hall, and he felt his way along a wall filmed with grease grime until he came to a door. With a deep breath of anticipation, he slid open the lacquered panel.

Inside, the small room was dark, but he made out the silhouette of a man sitting cross-legged on a rug; he wore a business suit, and wrap-around sunglasses and a taut *keffiyah* headdress obscured his lean face. White smoke, fragrant with the sweet aroma of charcoal and rose water, hazed around the waiting stranger like a saintly aura. Motioning for the door to be closed, the seated host pointed for Jamaal to take the seat opposite him. He offered his nervous guest one of the mouthpieces of a hookah pipe branched with two hoses.

Jamaal's heart was racing. Was this truly Yahya in the flesh? As directed, he sat down opposite his master and brought the pipe to his mouth. He closed his eyes as the apple-mango concoction soothed his nostrils like the delicate caress of a beautiful virgin. After several deep puffs, his gaze softened and his lids drooped.

Yahya's posture remained firm, his occulted face expressionless. Finally, he removed the pipe from his bloodless lips. "Were my orders not clear?"

Jamaal took another hit from the pipe to calm his nerves. From the harsh brevity of that question, he sensed that his repeated complaints and demands to meet in person again had angered his superior. His hand trembled as he reached into his jacket and produced a page torn from *The London Times*. He showed Yahya a headline:

WITH IRAQ WAR NOW A MEMORY, BAGHDAD NOT ONLY SURVIVES, BUT THRIVES.

As Yahya read the article, his mouth twitched slightly.

Rattled by his master's lengthy silence, Jamaal sucked furiously on the pipe, desperate for the narcotic to melt his anxieties.

"You have placed our lives in danger to bring me a news story?"

With an unsteady hand, Jamaal pointed to the headline. He spoke English, as he had been commanded to do from the start of his mission, to avoid suspicion. "I do not understand how this can be."

Yahya set his pipe hose aside. "What is not to understand?"

"The hadith of the Risalat al-Khuruj says Baghdad must first be destroyed by fire before the Mahdi will appear. You promised the time of triumph was near."

Yahya held a corner of the clipping against the pile of charcoal heating the pipe; the paper quickly took a flame and curled into black ashes. "The Great Deceiver schemes to thwart us by planting such lies in the Western media to sow disillusion."

"But why has the Awaited One not sent the fire to destroy Baghdad?"

"He has not yet loosed all of His arrows."

Jamaal puffed harder on the pipe, trying to reconcile this explanation with the conditions of preparation required by the apocalyptic hadiths. "Yesterday I attended a sermon. The imam said an eclipse of the sun and the moon during the same month of Ramadan must occur before the Mahdi comes."

Yahya took a moment to adjust his sunglasses higher up the bridge of his nose. "So it is written, so it shall be."

"After prayers, I asked the imam when the blessed celestial event would occur. He said that another ten years must pass before a month sees both the sun and the moon blotted from the sky."

Yahya stared through him, as if reading his soul. "Do you miss your home, my son?"

Tears came to Jamaal's eyes. He nodded, shamed by his weakness.

Yahya pulled a small packet from his breast pocket and gave Jamaal a sprig of shrubby leaves. "*Your* home is not of this world. The Awaited One asked me to bless you with these Leaves of Paradise from Yemen. He wants you to have a taste of what is soon to come."

Jamaal stared at the sprigs in his shaking palm. He had not chewed his beloved *qat* since being initiated into the Mahdi's army. He accepted the offering with gratitude and placed the leaves under his tongue. Soon his head filled with that old familiar feeling of divine ecstasy.

Praise be unto to Allah.

Yahya leaned to his ear. "Listen carefully, my son, to what I am about to tell you. The Evil One has seduced you into his dungeon of despond. Every soldier of *jihad* confronts such a crisis of faith. You must not allow the doubts of the Great Satan to infect your mind. The Awaited One has told me that He will appear to you very soon. At that time, He will reveal the proof you seek."

Jamaal chewed the *qat* harder, squeezing every ounce of comfort from its heavenly juices. His eyes began to flutter more rapidly, and he felt as if he might be lifted up to Paradise that very hour. Everything around him dazzled with pulsing light. Slowly, the walls melted like molten gold.

His head fell forward.

Two men in black suits carried Jamaal, unconscious, through the back door to the alley. They lifted him into an unmarked van equipped inside as an ambulance. A waiting physician strapped him to a gurney and covered his nose and mouth with an anesthesia mask to keep him knocked out.

After checking the alley to insure no witnesses were lurking, Yahya climbed into the van and closed the back doors. He nodded for the physician to proceed with the operation.

The physician put on surgical gloves and tore open a sterilized package with a label: *Voice-to-Skull satellite microwave*. He cut an incision, barely perceptible, behind Jamaal's ear and implanted a tiny chip near the cochlea bone with a magnetized instrument. He closed the incision with a clear suture, daubed the slender seep of blood, and sculpted the obtrusion to resemble a mole. After examining his work, the physician gave Yahya the thumbs-up sign.

Yahya opened the van's doors and signaled for his two men in black to carry Jamaal back into the café. They placed him, still unconscious, on the same spot where—drugged by the *qat* laced with ketamine—he had fallen slumped near the hooka pipe.

TWENTY-SIX

As Pero waited in the gardens of the *Recolhimento da Encarnacao*, memories of that morning when he had first stepped foot into this convent came flooding back to him. Now, eighteen years later, he would gladly have returned to the bloody battlefield of Toro to avoid the task at hand.

Would Catrina accept his request to see her?

Pacing anxiously, he prayed for the chance to finally explain his disappearance. His bandaged wrist, wounded on the desperate retreat from Castile, began to ache again. Was its throb the portent of yet another defeat, this one of the heart? Even now, he had trouble believing what he had witnessed during these past months. After Isabella launched her brutal war of succession by refusing to recognize Portugal's rights, King Alfonso had recalled him from his spy mission to serve on the military campaigns in the royal guard, with disastrous results. He had not heard from Zarco and Dias since returning. They were likely serving on the high seas. If this miserable land fighting ever stopped, he too intended to take up his old dream of—

A quivering hand touched his injured arm. He spun to find a veiled woman in robes, and his spirit sank—Catrina had sent one of the older novices to turn him away. He nodded, accepting her decision. What woman worthy of love would have kept her feelings alive after being abandoned for so long? Ashamed at having come to beg, he bowed and took his leave.

The novice caught up with him at the gate. She turned his palm and traced a finger down one of its lines. "The Isle of Neptune remains unexplored."

That voice buckled his legs. The woman retracted her veil, and he stared into Catrina's lovely face, altered only by the worry lines of age. Her smoldering eyes still held that same clairvoyant power. The abrasiveness of her starched habit rubbed his skin, causing his heart to miss a beat. Had she taken the vows?

Catrina studied his palm, just as she had done when they first met. "You have not yet sailed."

He was desperate to kiss her, but he feared such an act of intimacy now would be too bold. "Can you ever forgive me?"

"I knew you would leave me." She pointed to a ridge on his palm. "The marriage line is broken. I saw it when we first met."

"Why then did you continue to accept my visits?"

She stroked his hand. "The line resumes here."

He dropped to a knee. "Will you marry me?"

"Your hand has many broken lines."

"Come with me to the cathedral this hour." When he saw her shake her head, unable to utter the rejection, he dropped his eyes in resignation and confirmed what he had feared. "You have given yourself to God."

She smiled sadly. "God owns my soul, but not my heart."

He looked up, confused. "Then you no longer love me?"

"I love you dearly." She glanced at a high window where another veiled novice was watching them from behind a curtain. "But for now, I must remain here with Filipa."

He searched the window again, but the lurking novice had disappeared. "I thought Filipa had married Zarco while I was away."

Catrina paled. "You have not heard?"

"Heard what?"

She drew him deeper into the garden for more privacy. Bracing his arm, she whispered, "Salvador is to be executed."

"Salvador Zarco?"

She glanced at the archway to insure that the abbess was not around. "The sentence was handed down last week. Filipa is beside herself with terror. The Tomar knights will not allow her to see him."

He could easily imagine the temperamental Zarco taking umbrage at some slight involving his honor. "What is he accused of? A crime of passion?"

"Salvador sold portolans to the Venetians."

He refused to believe the report. Was Catrina making this story up to take her revenge on the Order? After all, the knights had cost her the best years of her life. He grasped her shoulders. "Where is he being held?"

"At Sagres. They intend to hang him after the Sabbath. I tried to get word to Dias, but he is at sea."

He studied her. Did she still think him the naïve boy who had left Portugal? While spying in Castile, he had learned many things about human nature that caused him to question the ulterior designs of everyone he encountered. Zarco was the grandson of a Lusiad hero. The friend he once knew would have died first before shaming his family. He was certain that someone, perhaps a former enemy of the Old Man, must be trying to get rid of Zarco in some sinister plot. "I have to stop this!"

Catrina tried to restrain him. "You will only bring suspicion on yourself."

"Zarco would do the same for me."

Seeing his determination could not be bent, Catrina pulled him to a corner of the chapel and kissed him passionately. Finally, she broke from his embrace and whispered, "Do you truly love me?"

He stared at her in astonishment. *She kisses me until my legs go weak and then asks such a question?* "You know I do."

"But you still place the welfare of your Order ahead of mine."

That indictment burned him like a hot stoker. And yet, he understood her reluctance to commit her heart fully again after having it broken. "How can I prove the sincerity of my feelings for you?"

Smiling provocatively, she whispered: "If truly you love me ..."

"*Sim?*"

"Sneak a letter from Filipa to Salvador for me. But you must not open it."

His sleuthing instincts sparked. Why was she trying to send him on such a dangerous enterprise? What if Filipa was trying to implicate him by extortion in an attempt to save Zarco? He searched the eyes of this woman he loved, trying to assay her motives. Was this the same Catrina he had fallen for so long ago? He owed her a demonstration of his good faith, *that* he could not deny. After a hesitation, he nodded his agreement to her perilous request.

Pero reached Sagres a few hours before dawn and found the fortress heavily garrisoned and a gallows constructed near the Wind Rose. He searched the grounds for a familiar face, but most of these knights now stationed here had been recruited into the Order after he was sent to Castile.

Alerted to his arrival, the new seneschal marched through the commandery doors. "You're just in time for the hanging."

Pero dismounted. "I have to speak to Zarco."

The officer folded his arms in defiance. "The grand master has ordered no one sees the traitor."

Pero produced a royal decree for the meeting. "A king trumps a grand master."

Confirming the order's seal, the seneschal sneered at the preemption of his authority and waved Pero toward the dungeon. "You have fifteen minutes."

Two guards unlocked the iron door, and Pero entered the darkened chamber with only a tallow candle for light. Along the dank wall, he came to a man who was curled on his haunches with his head bowed between his knees. Pero jostled his old friend by the shoulders to rouse him. "Tell me it's not true!"

"It's not true," the shadowed prisoner said with no emotion.

Pero took a tentative step closer. "Who set you up for this false charge?" When the prisoner merely stared blankly at him, he tried to shake some lucidity into him. "Don't you recognize me? It's Pero, your comrade from Covilha."

The man shrugged. "I don't know anyone from Covilha."

Pero lifted him to his feet. "Have they racked all memory from your head?"

A voice in the dark behind him shouted, "I remember that *ratao* stench!"

Pero spun and searched the far corner for the source of that jest. There Zarco sat across the dungeon, bound in leg manacles. Confused, Pero turned back to reexamine the prisoner whose identity he had mistaken. This red-haired man before him could have been Zarco's brother, so similar were their features. He rushed across the strewn hay to bring Zarco to his feet and embrace him.

Seeing the bandage on Pero's wrist, Zarco lifted his old friend's arm to his eyes. "We heard you slew a hundred Castilians at Toro."

Pero dismissed the report of his valor. "For naught. Isabella has bigger balls than her eunuch half-brother."

Overhearing them, the redheaded stranger from across the cell shouted, "That bitch intends to rid the world of Jews! That is what I hear!"

Pero glared at the loudmouth through the dim light. "Who is that foul man?"

"My new friend from Genoa." Zarco waved his cellmate over for an introduction. "Cristobal, say *olá* to Pero da Covilha. He'll look after you when I'm in the ground."

Pero blenched. "Look after?"

Zarco brought Cristobal's hand to Pero's, forcing them to grasp palms. "His galley was attacked by French corsairs off Lagos a few days ago. For a weaver, he's a *bom* swimmer. He had to cover six miles to reach shore."

The grinning Genoese weaver wouldn't let go. "God has a destiny for me."

Pero pulled away, repulsed by the Italian vagabond and Zarco's unnerving banter with him. He wondered if the knights had drugged his old classmate, but he smelled no narcotics on his breath. "What is he doing in here with you?"

"The Grand Master doesn't know what to make of his story," Zarco said. "I've been teaching him Portuguese and instructing him about the sea. You must take him under your wings when I'm gone. Perhaps God will have mercy on me in return for the kindness."

"Bless you, Master Zarco!" Cristobal cried.

Pero took Zarco aside so that this queer cellmate could not overhear their conversation. "What has happened to you?" When Zarco would not look at him directly in a silent admission of guilt, Pero grasped his chin to demand his eyes. "I don't believe it."

"Dias was given the new commission for the African coast," Zarco said. "Filipa is in debt to the convent. I needed money to purchase her freedom. The Venetians made an offer, and I accepted."

Pero slugged him. "You betrayed us because you didn't get the caravel you wanted? I spent eighteen years going to sleep each night not knowing if my throat would be slit! I hope the Old Man is waiting to escort you to Hell!" He threw Filipa's letter to the ground.

Zarco recovered to his feet, rubbing his jaw. He rebuffed Pero's attempt to force the letter upon him.

"Aren't you going to read what the woman you love wrote as her last words to you?"

Shrugging with indifference, Zarco took the letter and slid it under his shirt. "Perhaps I will peruse it on the gallows."

Pero itched to hit him again. "Cold-hearted knave!"

Zarco laughed and waved to the Genoan, who was mumbling to himself. "Cristobal, tell us more of your adventures on the seas! Where did we leave off?"

Cristobal leapt up to deliver the requested performance. "Before this boorish oaf interrupted us, I was regaling you about my voyage to Iceland."

Zarco applauded as if egging on a jester. "In the service of King Rene of Anjou, as I recall. Tell us your tale again, and don't leave out any details."

Pero watched gape-jawed while these two men carried on as if they hadn't a care in the world. He could have found more sanity in an asylum for half-wits. He pulled Zarco closer by the collar and tried to talk some sense of his predicament into him. "You are about to meet the Almighty in judgment! And all you wish to do is——"

The doors swung open. Four guards entered and unchained Zarco.

Cristobal shouted at his condemned cellmate, "*Adeus, meu bom amigo!*"

"Your Portuguese is improving." Zarco saluted the Genoan as he departed. "Godspeed, Cristobal. All that I have, and that is very little, is now yours."

At the dungeon's door, Zarco turned and pinned Pero with a sharp glance, displaying his first moment of seriousness. "You must take care of my new friend here. Promise me this, Pero, as I am about to die."

Now even more dumbfounded, Pero could only nod his agreement to the surreal request. He followed the execution procession as Zarco was marched out of the dungeon to his death. Looking back over his shoulder, Pero saw that two of the guards remained in the cell to watch over the Genoese prisoner.

In the bailey, the knights of the Order of Christ had formed ranks around the gallows. Framed by the rising sun, the beams cast growing shadows across the Wind Rose as sentries walked the allures along the walls, prepared to repulse any attempt to breach the defenses and stop the execution. Below them, Zarco's mother and three sisters, clad in mourning black and weeping inconsolably, stood next to a spare coffin. On the seneschal's signal, the knights formed a gauntlet and shouted curses as Zarco was shoved past them toward the scaffold, where a masked executioner stood waiting. Before Zarco ascended the steps, one of the knights stopped him and roughly slid a black hood over his head.

Disgusted by this last act of humiliation, Pero asked the executioner, "Is that necessary?"

The executioner yanked the hood tighter over Zarco's head. "Orders from Tomar. He is not to lay eyes upon the sea ever again."

Overhead, gulls cawed sharply, and Pero turned toward the cliffs. In the bay below, he saw a ship carrying the Castilian flag circling the point. He was alarmed that the waters had not been swept free of the foreign spies. In the old days, the Navigator would never have allowed such a dangerous breach of security. He whispered sternly to the seneschal, "That galley is within sight of us. Should you not—"

An explosion rocked the sky.

The ground under the naval compound shook and thundered. Concussed, Pero looked up from his knees and saw the ranks falling out. Had the Castilian ship fired on them? The Portuguese knights rushed to the walls to defend against an attack, and a signalman transmitted the seneschal's command for the caravels to drive off the intruder. Within minutes, order was restored, and the Castilian ship had been chased.

Zarco, still hooded, had been held below the gallows, uninformed of the cause for the commotion. Pero felt sorry for his old friend despite his treachery; to wait in confusion so long for one's death had to be excruciating. At last, the executioner dragged Zarco up the steps and fitted the noose around his neck. As a traitor, he had forfeited the privilege of addressing his fellow knights of the Order. His legs were shaking, and he was struggling under the hood in an attempt to speak. His façade of indifference, Pero saw, had given way to the terror of death's approach.

The executioner pulled the handle on the latch, and Pero lowered his head when the trap door dropped.

TWENTY-SEVEN

NEWPORT, RHODE ISLAND
FEBRUARY 11, PRESENT DAY

Iaq had arrived only that morning at the Godspring Retreat Center, but already she was feeling better. She had wanted to attend Alyssa's funeral in Washington before coming, but Rev. Merry had insisted that she check into the facility immediately. And thanks to his intercession, she didn't even have to explain her absence from work to Josh Mayfield. With some free time until her first counseling session, she decided to take a walk through the expansive Gilded Age mansion that housed this spiritual oasis operated by evangelical Baptists.

Overlooking the white chops of Narragansett Bay, its thirty rooms on two floors were clustered around a central stair hall. She entered the activities wing, where the residents gathered to play cards and ping-pong. As she surveyed her fellow patients for the first time, she casually thumbed through a few books on the shelves. A Scrabble game with a pile of squares sat on the coffee table. Bored, she fiddled with the letters. The last person to play had been arranging them in one-line poems. On two racks set end-to-end, a sentence sat spelled out: *Mary sat or stood, depending on her mood.* But that didn't really rhyme, did it?

She zeroed in on one segment of the sentence: *sat or.*

Exasperated, she shook her head. The demons were still tempting her with combinations from that damn magical square. Wait … wasn't she supposed to be spiritually guarded here? Maybe this was an angelic message. She gathered up several of the wooden letters and recreated the Templar square:

```
S   A   T   O   R
A   R   E   P   O
T   E   N   E   T
O   P   E   R   A
R   O   T   A   S
```

She segregated the letters in their order of frequency: AAAA—EEEE—OOOO—RRRR—TTTT—SS—PP—N. Three vowels. Five consonants. Nothing clicked. She reset the letters in the square and stared at them.

"Altar."

A spindly bald man wearing Coke-bottle glasses stood leaning over her shoulder. Afflicted with a nervous tic that caused his head to jerk, he pointed to the second line in her square of letters. "Altar heroic."

"I don't understand," she told him.

The adorable little man separated the letters AREPO to form two words: AR EPO. "*Ara Epos*. Altar heroic."

She hadn't considered the possibility that the square contained abbreviated combinations. "My name is Jaq. What's yours?"

His head bobbed faster; he seemed too shy to answer.

"Arthur!" shouted a male counselor from across the room. "You're not bothering the nice lady, are you?"

As the counselor came toward them, she quickly jumbled the letters.

"You must be Jaqueline. I'm William Bratton, the director here. I'll be handling your first session. We'll get started in a few minutes."

"Okay." She shook his hand while standing in front of the Scrabble board to hide what she had been doing.

Bratton gently led the bashful male resident away. "Arthur, why don't you go to your room and start your afternoon Bible reading. We left off at Deuteronomy, didn't we?"

Head still bobbing, Arthur finally managed to slow his chin long enough for a nod. He obediently shuffled off, mumbling what sounded like Latin.

Jaq waved at him. "Goodbye, Arthur. Thanks for the help."

Bratton frowned, as if wondering by what assistance his mentally challenged patient could possibly have provided her. "He's very vulnerable spiritually."

"Is he some kind of, you know, idiot savant?" she asked.

"That's what the secularists call it," Bratton said. "Most of these so-called disabilities are Satanic in origin. Arthur has a photographic memory and sees patterns where most people don't. He also understands Latin. It's not so much a fluency in speech. More like he reads the words in his head."

"Did he study Latin in school?"

Bratton shook his head. "His parents passed to the Lord before he reached grade school."

"And he learned Latin on his own? How is that possible?"

"Such cases are rare, but we've had reports of similar possessions. Latin is Satan's favorite language of attack."

"Why is that?"

"The *Malleus Maleficarum*, the Roman Church's handbook on Satanism and witchery, was written in Latin," the counselor said. "The armies of Darkness and Light have used Latin to do battle through the ages."

"You think the Devil is speaking through him?"

Bratton whispered the name of Christ to banish any lingering effects from the invocation of the Evil One. "I've seen the marks on his body. The medical doctors have given up on him. We're his last hope. But enough about Arthur. We'll go over all the rules here during our session. We do have a strict policy of segregating residents who may be under demonic assault. We find that Satan often works by bringing together souls whose spiritual immune systems are compromised. I'll have to ask you not to socialize with Arthur, at least until he gets better."

The odd injunction caught Jaq by surprise. "Of course."

That afternoon, after finishing her therapy hour, she decided to take a stroll outside. Her door pass required her to remain on the grounds, so she walked down the grassy slope and along a high wrought-iron fence that protected residents from the traffic on Bellevue Avenue.

In a park across the street, a father and his two young boys were playing hide-and-seek around a strange circular tower built with stones of varying shapes and sizes. Rising nearly thirty feet on eight cylindrical columns, the structure resembled a giant cooking kiln with space left underneath for a fire. She watched with an unsettling mixture of amusement and sadness as the father hugged his kids and wrestled them playfully to the grass, rubbing his day-old stubble into their cheeks to make them giggle and scream for surrender. The scene made her think of Paul, and how they had talked about starting a family a year after the wedding. She lifted her face to the sun to dry a tear.

Looking over, the father saw her and smiled. She guessed him to be no older than thirty. He must have started his family quite young, she figured. He had curly black hair and dark skin, and his eyes sparked with a Latin intensity. He grasped the hands of his two boys and helped them wave to her. She laughed and called out, "Hello! What is that? Some kind of sculpture?"

The father lifted a boy to each shoulder and, bouncing them as if on a pony, walked across the street to talk with her. "This is the *Touro*. Our most famous landmark."

She peered at it through the fence. "What was it used for?"

The man's sexy smile could have melted an iceberg. "That depends on who you ask. Some say it was part of a mill built by Benedict Arnold during the Revolutionary War."

"It doesn't look like a mill."

"You remind me of my mother, may she rest in peace." He lowered his sons to the ground and made the sign of the cross. "You have her same eyes and chin. *Muito bonita*, she was." He asked his boys, "Doesn't the pretty lady look like the pictures of *Avó Dores*?"

Although the boys were too shy to speak to her, she took the comparison to their grandmother as a compliment, even though the woman would have had to be triple her age.

Their father patted their heads. "I am Aleixo. This is Gabriel and Nico."

She made bug eyes at the youngsters, drawing giggles. "I'm Jaqueline. Your wife must count her blessings, having a husband who takes the kids to the park in the afternoon." When the merriment in his face sank, she knew at once that she had made a very wrong assumption.

The man lowered the boys to the ground and patted their heads. "Go play on the *Touro*. I'll be there in a minute." When the kids had scampered off, he turned back to explain his reaction. "I've been divorced for nearly a year. It's not been easy for them. Or for my father."

"I can see they love you dearly," she said.

He looked beyond her shoulder, losing his smile as he glared at the mansion behind her. "Are you one of their prisoners?"

She was flabbergasted by the question. "This is not a prison. It's a health resort. I'm here for some rest."

"I know what that place is. I mean, are you allowed to leave?"

"Of course. If I get permission."

"So, you *are* a prisoner. Too bad."

She was determined to set him straight. "I assure you, I can leave anytime I want."

His judgmental frown reversed into a disarming grin. "Then there's no reason you can't have dinner with me and my family tonight."

She laughed, realizing that she had stepped right into his trap. "I don't even know you."

"My father is cooking *bacalhau à minhota*. Cod is God's fish. When it is prepared properly, eating it is better than making love."

Her eyes rounded at his brashness; he was really putting on the full-court press. "Thank you for the invitation, but I'm going to have to pass."

"I understand. The religious man in the big house up there snaps his fingers, and the beautiful woman obeys. It is the way of the world."

This guy was starting to remind her of someone else she knew. No wonder he was divorced. He kept taunting her with that devilish smirk. She could hear

Alyssa prodding her on, complaining that she never took chances in her social life. She really did need to move past Paul. Even Rev. Merry had told her so. And Elymas, well, that was another story altogether.

The two boys began fighting under the *Touro*. Torn between going to break them up and waiting for her answer, their father finally became resigned to her refusal, and turned to leave.

She glanced over her shoulder at the mansion's columned entrance. One of Pastor Bratton's firm rules was no departures from the center without a twenty-four-hour notice. The counselor was already beginning to remind her of Josh Mayfield, a bit of a control freak. What harm would it cause if she enjoyed a night out? She was a fully functional adult, after all, not some Alzheimer's patient, and she was already feeling a little claustrophobic. It would be nice to spend an evening with a real family for once. She called to the departing father, "Can you have me back by midnight?"

He turned, grinning. "We'll have to pick my papa up at his work."

She meandered nonchalantly toward a corner of the estate, as if admiring the landscaping along the fence. Near the far end of the iron enclosure, she found a gate and tried the latch. The gate swung open.

She enjoyed the passing New England landscape as Aleixo drove her and his two boys twenty-five miles north. Soon after crossing the Massachusetts border, he turned into the entrance for Dighton Rock State Park, a bucolic preserve along the Taunton River. He parked in front of a small museum that was no larger than a shed. "Papa is the gardener here. I'll go inside and tell him we've arrived. Would you like to see the museum?"

She looked around and saw no other cars in the lot. "Museum of *what?* This building couldn't hold a decent-sized restroom."

Climbing out of the car, Aleixo chuckled as he opened the back door of the museum with a key and chased his two boys inside to find their grandfather.

She followed them into the small octagonal building. Suddenly it occurred to her that the museum's architectural design mimicked the shape of that old tower in Newport. "Does this place have anything to do with your *Touro* back in town?"

Before Aleixo could answer her, his elfish father, clad in a mangled fedora and a muddy overcoat, rounded the corner and smothered his grandsons with kisses and blessings in a foreign language. When the old man saw her, his weathered face whitened with the shock of recognition.

Aleixo nodded knowingly, as if having expected such a reaction. "She could be the ghost of mama, eh *Pai?* Her name is Jaqueline. She has agreed to join us for dinner."

The diminutive patriarch dove in on her for kisses on both cheeks. "*Boa tarde! Boa tarde!*" He shot a wicked wink at his son in approval. "*Mulher muito bonita. Mulher muito.*"

Blushing, she asked Aleixo, "What is he speaking?"

"Portuguese."

She was delighted to be treated to an example of the famously sensual language. "How long have you lived in Newport?"

"Our family came here from Portugal in the 1600s to escape the Inquisition," Aleixo said. "There is a legend that they landed on the coast of America after a *melungo.*"

"*Melungo?*"

"A shipwreck," Aleixo explained. "I have a bad habit of slipping into the mother tongue when I'm around *Pai*. He insists on speaking it even though he has lived in America all his life."

Aleixo's father understood enough English to detect Jaq's interest in their family's heritage. He insisted on showing her a large boulder that was kept under glass in the center of the museum:

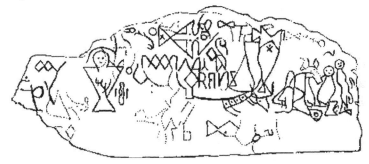

Jaq leaned over the case to better see the rock. Petroglyphs covered its nearest side, and one of the etched figures resembled a knight in chain mail. The entire tableau looked as if someone had tried to memorialize a story starting with several individuals on the right and progressing to a lone survivor on the left. Nearby, a poster displayed a tracing of the petroglyphs created in 1830 by the Rhode Island Historical Society.

"This is Dighton Rock," Aleixo told her. "It sat hidden for centuries under mud and ice on the banks of that river out there."

While the two boys ran laps around the museum, Aleixo and his father led her to another exhibit that reconstructed the surviving portion of a cross carved into the stone. Aleixo asked her, "You see how the tip of that cross is drawn at a forty-five-degree angle?" He nodded a signal to his father.

The old man reached into his long overcoat and pulled out a wad of paper— an old receipt, perhaps—and licked the stubby pencil that he kept stashed in his shirt pocket. Hovering over the paper until his nose nearly touched it, he drew the cross for Jaq, filling out the outlines of the traverses that were faintly visible on the rock. He had apparently performed this ritual for visitors many times, deeming it a sacred duty.

Aleixo explained the symbol's significance. "This was the cross sewn on the sails of the Order of Christ."

She couldn't say just why, but the insignia looked vaguely familiar. She asked the old man, "Who belonged to this Order?"

Aleixo translated his father's answer. "Portuguese explorers led by a visionary named Henry the Navigator. Some were descendants of an earlier monastic order called the Knights Templar."

Suddenly she was *very* interested. The old man brought her to yet another exhibit, this one of a rock that had been found at second New England location. Its side was carved with the image of a medieval knight dressed in chain mail and holding a sword and shield.

"This is called the Westford Knight," Aleixo explained. "Some think it's the effigy of a fourteenth-century Scottish knight connected to the Knights Templar."

"Are you saying the explorers who made these drawings also built that tower in Newport before they went back home?"

"Some of them didn't go home." Aleixo pointed to one corner of the Dighton Rock. "Do you see those letters carved near the V-shaped marking? They spell a Portuguese name. Next to them is a coat of arms. Some believe it to be the emblem of the Corte-Reals, a family of explorers that served the Navigator."

"Why did these men come to New England?" she asked.

Aleixo shrugged. "Perhaps they were looking for lost comrades."

"And you think that old tower in Newport was their signal station?"

Aleixo asked his father her question, and translated the response. "He says it was too fancy for a signal station."

"Then what *was* it used for?" she asked.

Aleixo reported his father's theory. "A church, or perhaps a place where knights could be initiated into the mysteries of a religious brotherhood?"

"When was the tower built?" she asked.

Aleixo translated, "He says some of the *Touro's* stones have been carbon-dated to the fourteenth century."

She turned on the old man in disbelief. "Is he saying that the Portuguese were in North America *before* Columbus?"

Aleixo relayed her question, and chuckled at his father's grinning reply. "He wants me to remind you that *he* is not saying it. Rather, the beautiful woman is saying it."

That night, after lights were out for curfew, Jaq tiptoed back into the Godspring mansion and quietly climbed the stairs to the men's floor like a truant coed. She slithered along the shadows to Room 417. Knocking gently, she whispered, "Arthur?" She heard a rustling inside. The door was unlocked, so she cracked it open. "Would you like to play letters with me?"

Arthur sat up in his bed and nodded eagerly.

She emptied her pockets filled with the Scrabble squares and arranged them on the bed into the SATOR square. "Let's try a game called 'say their meaning.'" She started with the two words he had recognized earlier that afternoon: AR EPO.

Arthur's eyes rolled up in his head, as if he were reading pages between his brows. "*Ara.* An altar of stone. The seat or resting place of a victim. A constellation in the Southern Sky."

She was amazed. This man-child who usually uttered barely a word had transformed his voice with such authority that he could have been reading for *Books On Tape.* Bizarre as it was, it seemed that, somehow, he was consulting a Latin-English dictionary in his head. She wondered if he had ever seen one. She quickly scribbled down the definitions into her notebook. "Good job!"

Arthur grinned, pleased with the praise.

"Now, EPO."

"*Epos* ... a heroic poem or epic."

She spelled the third word with the wood chips. "How about TENET?"

He was talking faster now. "An inflected form of *teneo.* To hold, to keep, to possess, to maintain, to persevere, to grasp, to understand, to protect, to gain mastery of, to hold fast and defend. Also, a noun derived from *tenere.* A principle, belief, or doctrine held in common by members of an organization, abiding throughout time."

She was writing so fast that her hand threatened to cramp. "Let's try another one, okay?" She spelled out O-P-E-R-A.

Arthur didn't even hesitate. "Work. Pains. Labor. A desire to serve of one's own free will. Servants for a cause."

She pulled a candy bar from her pocket and dangled it in front of him. "Here's the Final Jeopardy question for the big prize. Are you ready?"

Arthur rocked with excitement while she formed the next word: ROTAS.

He frowned, delaying his answer, as if confused by multiple entries on the screen of his mind's eye.

Come on, Arthur. Don't spit the bit.

At last, he recited, "Wheel. Disk, like the sun. Globe."

She quickly scribbled a chart of the possible combinations, including the alternatives that she had stumbled on in Europe:

SATOR	AREPO	TENET	OPERA	ROTAS
SATURN	ALTAR	PROTECT GRASP	LABOR	WHEELS
GOD	HEROIC SEAT	PERSEVERE	WORK	DISCS
THE SOWER	EPIC	POSSESS	FREE WILL	GLOBE
MITHRAS	HERO CONSTELLATION	PRINCIPLE OF AN ORGANIZATION	DESIRE TO SERVE OR SERVANTS	ROSE WINDOWS

Arthur suddenly became agitated. "Oh mistake! Mistake! Mistake!"

She tried to calm him. "That's okay. Which one?"

"Arepo! *A Repo*! 'A' is a preposition meaning to move toward something. *Repo*. To crawl or creep slowly. Slow travelers. Slang for *reporto*. To bear, carry or bring back. To repossess or save."

She tried a couple of combinations with the Scrabble letters:

GOD'S ALTAR HEROIC PROTECTED BY SERVANTS WHEELS
GOD'S ALTAR HEROIC REPOSSESSED BY HIS SERVANTS GLOBE
GOD'S ALTAR HEROIC IS SAVED BY HIS SERVANTS GLOBE

After gobbling down his prize, Arthur returned to the game and inserted more letters into her creation, forming the defined words into a giant circle. He ran to his desk, pulled out a box of large plastic letters used for his speech therapy, and substituted the larger letters for the 'N' in the center and the 'T's on each quadrant. He added a final touch by rotating the 'T's to form:

Jaq flipped to a blank page in her notebook and copied what Arthur had just created. Something on the diagram caught her eye. She traced lines around the 'T's and connected them.

Her mouth dropped. It was the cross that had been carved into the Dighton Rock. The 'T's were obviously meant to form the traverses, but what did the 'N' in the center—

The door flew open.

In his office, Pastor Bratton dismissed his two burly orderlies. Alone with Jaq, he stared at her for several moments. Finally, he said, "You have placed Arthur's recovery in great jeopardy."

"We were just playing a word game," she insisted.

He examined her notebook. "What are these drawings?"

She silently asked the Lord to forgive a white lie. "A kind of Sudoku. It's all the rage these days. Now, if you don't mind, I'd like my property back."

Looking unconvinced, Bratton returned her confiscated notebook and shook his head in disappointment. "Two infractions on your first day."

"Two?"

"I know about your unauthorized departure this afternoon."

How had he found out? Surely that Portuguese family didn't rat her out. She tried to remember anything that might have held a hidden camera on the fence around the grounds.

The minister seemed to take perverse enjoyment in her surprise. "We are well-versed here in the many machinations employed by Satan. This is a pattern we often see with new arrivals. I had hoped that, given your recommendations and level of intelligence, things might start out better with you."

She was getting the creepy chills. "I've been having second thoughts about my stay here."

"Of course you have," Bratton said smoothly. "Demonic possession is a fever that must boil before it breaks. We'll have to intensify your resistance with a new regimen. Double sessions. And I think it best that we have you set apart from the others for a while."

"You mean solitary confinement?"

Bratton waved off the accusation. "That's a penal term. More like a spiritual quarantine, until we can get the upper hand on these malefic influences."

She felt the hair rising on her arms. "I'd like to leave today."

Bratton stood from his chair and came round the desk to tower over her. "I'm afraid that's not possible."

Outraged, she leapt to her feet to confront him. "I came here voluntarily! I can stop treatment whenever I want!"

Bratton buzzed in the orderlies. "We take our work here very seriously, Miss Quartermane. To release an afflicted resident before her treatment is complete would be as negligent as allowing a patient with the Ebola virus to leave a hospital."

She dashed for the door, but the orderlies entered and blocked her path. She glared daggers at Bratton, silently vowing he'd be toast once Rev. Merry found out about these shenanigans. "Are you running some kind of cult?"

Bratton opened a file and produced a legal document. "Your church made quite a sacrifice to help you get well. Reverend Merry and the good people in Knoxville must love you dearly."

She grabbed the document from him and read it. "*What* sacrifice?"

"The church council executed this guaranty to insure the fee for your stay. The contract also includes a liquidated damages clause should you fail to see through the entire thirty days."

"This is unenforceable!"

"The contract been upheld in our state courts. We have a reputation to protect. That is why we accept only those who contract to stay the course. The church council in Knoxville put its buildings up as collateral for the fee. It would be a shame for Reverend Merry's name to be dragged into a public lawsuit."

She made another break for the door, but the orderlies restrained her.

"You've become overwrought," Bratton said, signaling for the orderlies to take her away. "That's to be expected with such a nasty spiritual assault. We'll get you feeling better with a hundred milligrams of Phenobarbital."

Forced to remain in her room for two days and nights, Jaq had been allowed to see only Pastor Bratton during the therapy sessions, the attendants delivering her meals, and the male nurse who came three times a day to administer her meds and shots. The migraines were worse, and she was feeling increasingly listless. She was sure these drugs they were giving her by injections were aggravating her Behcet's symptoms. Was that asshole trying to turn her into a zombie? She couldn't even get to a phone to call Rev. Merry for help. She had to find a way to avoid those meds before it was too—she heard footsteps.

The male nurse was coming with her midnight sedative.

She grabbed the lamp stand and hid in the corner, until the door creaked open. She tried to hit the white-coated orderly with the lamp, but he saw her shadow and ducked in time. She fell to the carpet, then recovered to her feet and leapt at him. "You son of a bitch!"

He grasped her shoulders and drove her against the wall. *He's trying to rape me!* She was about to kick him in the groin when he flipped the light switch.

She froze, convinced the drugs were causing her to hallucinate.

"I see you haven't lost your sweet innocence." Elymas examined the rip in the white smock he was using for a disguise. "This was a rental."

She fought from his grasp. "How did you find me here?"

"Some of the ladies in the Knoxville charity bake-off spilled the beans."

She glared at him, wondering if he was serious. She knew there'd be no finding out how he really learned she was here, not from him. "So much for confidentiality. Who let you in?"

"The pharmacist is sleeping off a nasty head thump."

"You flew all the way from Europe to grope me again?"

Elymas searched the room. "Don't flatter yourself. I want to know what you saw the night the monsignor was murdered."

"Who told you—" Her eyes narrowed as he reached into his pocket and pulled out a small plastic bag with the charred pages of the travel journal that she had dropped at Resson.

"The French cops missed it," he said. "Why did you go back to see him?"

She folded her arms in defiance. "That's none of your business."

"The monsignor was my friend. I introduce you to him and two days later he's murdered. Do you know who did it?"

She hesitated. "I have an idea."

"I'm waiting."

She was getting pretty damn tired of his overbearing attitude. "How do I know *you* didn't kill him? Your great uncle—"

"What about him?"

She led with her chin in a challenge. "He was an expert in flammables."

"I see you and your fellow spooks have been doing your research."

"How does it feel to be on the other end of it … Boz?"

Hearing that, he flinched slightly. "So, you know my real name. Bloody good for you."

She was on his heels. "Moses Rosen, aka Boz D'Orville, aka Elymas the Thief. Or should I say hired assassin? But tell me something. How do you get Boz from Moses? Is that some kind of code name?"

He didn't seem too eager to come clean. "My grammar-school teacher had a fondness for Dickens. He apparently wrote under the pseudonym 'Boz.' It was short for 'Bozes.' She gave me the nickname."

She thought that sounded like a crock of bullshit. "And why Bozes?"

"Dickens had a brother named Moses. The kid suffered from a speech impediment. He pronounced his name 'Bozes.'"

Even a clever thief, she conceded, wouldn't make up such a stupid and far-fetched tale. After all, what self-respecting Jewish atheist would take on a transmogrification of a famous biblical name? "Do you have a favorite alias? Or do you just like to rotate the names to amuse yourself?"

"Most women call me Boz. It's easier to scream in the throes of passion. But then, that's something you wouldn't know about."

"How charming." She continued gripping the lamp. "Getting chased and nearly killed by a man named Boz doesn't make it any more pleasant."

"If I wanted you dead, believe me, it would have been a done deal by now. And if you want to get out of this Waco North, you'll tell me what you know about the monsignor's death."

Reminded of her current predicament, she debated giving him another chance. With no good option, she finally revealed, "A Pakistani opium dealer who calls himself the Mahdi is trying to find the Ark of the Covenant."

"Yeah, right. Now tell me the real reason."

"This Muslim messiah wannabe killed Paul and that Ethiopian priest. He killed my friend Alyssa. He killed the monsignor. And he's trying to kill me."

"Why does he want to kill *you*?"

"I don't know. This Pakistani and his thugs must have been tracking me when we went to Resson. I think they tried to force the monsignor to reveal what we told him." She opened her notebook and wrote the three lines that the priest had inscribed on the bloodied palimpsest. "This was the last thing he carved on his board before I found him."

Boz studied the message. "What does it mean?"

"I think it has something to do with a poem. The number may refer to the thirteenth verse."

"Saying what?"

She braced for a wisecrack. "That I'm to take the Virgin as my guiding star."

"You've done that to the nines. And what about this second line?"

"It's a library catalog number for a French book about Chartres. Page thirty-one says the Notre Dame cathedrals in northern France were built to recreate the constellation of Virgo."

Boz paced the room, trying to make sense of what he had just been told. "Do the Moonies who run this place have a library around here?"

"A small one in the rec room. One floor up and—" Before she had even finished, the guy had left her alone. As the door closed and locked behind him, she muttered, "Damn him."

Several minutes passed, and she began to wonder if Elymas—or Boz or whatever his name was—had left her in the lurch yet again. She was about to go looking for him when he slipped back into her room armed with an atlas, an encyclopedia on astronomy, and a French travel guide. What in God's name was he doing? Had he turned the entire library upside down?

Boz opened the astronomy book to an entry on the Virgo constellation and placed it next to the travel guide's map of northern France. He circled every Gothic cathedral with the name *Notre Dame* and overlaid it with the tracing of the Virgo stars:

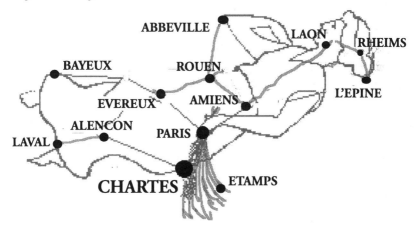

She could hardly believe her eyes. "They line up!"

He studied the connections between the stars. "Maybe it's just a coincidence. Why would those cathedral masons go to all the trouble of recreating an image of the Virgin Mary's constellation?"

"They had to build the cathedrals in existing cities," she said. "The Virgo grid probably wouldn't have matched the locations exactly."

Boz shrugged. "Looks close enough for government work. Let's start from the beginning. Who built the cathedrals?"

"The guilds?" she suggested.

"And who financed the guilds?"

She nodded in mutual discovery. "The Templars."

Boz's eyes filled with his familiar lust for the hunt. "Always follow the money. If the Templars put up the funds, they also chose the locations. For some reason, they went to extraordinary lengths to preserve a message for future generations by arranging the cathedrals in the Virgin's image. What do all of these Notre Dame cathedrals have in common besides being dedicated to Mary?"

"They all have crypts."

Boz shook his head. "So do nearly all cathedrals. It has to be something else." A vase of red roses on the windowsill caught his eye. "That's it!"

"Roses?"

"Rose windows … Rose windows *dedicated to the Virgin*."

She opened her notebook and found the notation she remembered. The dead monsignor's mentor, the alchemist Fulcanelli, had called the rose window a ROTA in his book on the cathedrals. She wrote another modified translation of the SATOR square:

GOD'S HEROIC ALTAR IS PROTECTED AND REPOSSESSED
BY HIS SERVANTS AT THE ROSE WINDOWS.

They stared at each other in amazement.

She cracked the door and, seeing no one around, gathered her belongings and threw them into her bag. She ordered Boz, "Bring the books."

They slithered down the hallway to Arthur's room. He was asleep, so Jaq tiptoed to his bed and whispered to his ear. "I wanted to say goodbye."

Arthur awoke and rubbed his eyes. "Going?"

"My friend here has come to take me home. But don't say anything about this to Pastor Bratton, okay? He is very sad about my leaving."

Arthur nodded, promising to keep her secret.

"Will you play one last word game with me?" When he smiled, Jaq pulled some Scrabble letters from her pocket and formed two words: ARA and ARK. "Does anything come to you?"

Arthur's eyes rolled up into his head as if he were reading a passage across his mind's eye. Then, he rattled off: "According to the *Etymologies* of Isidore of Seville, the word for chest is '*arca*,' because in one's chest resides hidden wisdom, the '*arcanus*.' A secret thing from which other seekers are denied is '*arcere*.' From this also comes the word for a treasure box, '*arca*,' or 'ark, and an altar, '*ara*.' Both derive from the word meaning 'secret things.'"

Hearing that, she shot a flustered glance at Boz. "That Pakistani narco-messiah must have been searching for the Ark of the Covenant at Chartres. There's an inscription on a column there that could be read to indicate that something called an *arca* was moved out of Ethiopia."

"You're saying the Ark is hidden below one of those Notre Dame cathedrals?"

She examined the drawing of the Virgo stars again. "Maybe, maybe not. Hosaam hit Gisors, Scotland, and Rome, too. That means he hasn't found it yet. I think the monsignor was trying to tell us that Templars built those cathedrals as a giant treasure map for finding the Ark *somewhere else*. What's the brightest star in the Virgo constellation?"

Boz ran a finger across the constellation schematic. "*Spica*."

She positioned the tracing of the Virgin constellation so that Chartres matched up with the star *Spica*. "Chartres was the most important cathedral for the Templars. We have to assume they wanted Chartres to represent the most important star in Virgo." Using those two points as a fulcrum, she rotated the tracing and searched for a pattern. "I don't see anything, do you?"

"That's because we're using a modern map," Boz said. "Medieval maps would have looked much different than this."

She tossed back her head in defeat. "Then this Virgo code is useless without the medieval map that goes with it."

"Hosaam must have the map." Boz turned to her with a worried look and added, "For some reason, he thinks you have the key to unlocking the map's secret. That's why he's been chasing you."

She suddenly felt a lot more vulnerable. "Unless we find his map or he finds the Virgo code, it's a race to every possible hiding spot for the Ark." She slowly recovered from the discovery, and kissed Arthur's forehead. "I'm going to miss playing our games."

Tears flooded Arthur's eyes. "Bye."

She turned to leave when she was doubled over by a sudden bolt of pain across her temples.

Boz steadied her. "You okay?"

She sat down and rubbed her head. "I'm a little woozy."

Boz poured her a glass of water. He wouldn't let her get up until she drank it. "I know a map dealer here in the States who might help us."

She tried standing again, and nodded to indicate that she felt a little better. "You do realize there's a warrant outstanding for your arrest?"

"I'm not too worried," Boz said. "I carry a little black book with names that some people on high would rather not have exposed."

After hugging Arthur goodbye, Jaq slipped out into the hall and led Boz through the back door. As they ran across the lawn toward the gate, she whispered to him: "Have you got your plane nearby?"

"Yeah, why?"

"There's something I need to do first before we go Ark hunting."

Navan, Ireland
February 12, Present Day

Unable to sleep, Jamaal limped down the steps of the shabby tenement where he and the other highway construction workers were being lodged. His headaches and the ringing in his ears were getting worse. He had been sick for two days, ever since that night in London when he had shamefully fallen asleep from chewing the *qat*. Yahya, no doubt disgusted with his lack of discipline, had left him where he had collapsed, to wake up alone. Now, his throat was swollen and he couldn't hold down food. Was he dying? He had no money to consult a Western doctor. He didn't trust them, anyway.

At least the rain had passed. This was the first clear sky he had seen in weeks. Allah willing, tomorrow the sun would restore his health. He coughed and wheezed as he staggered down the desolate road into the rolling countryside, hoping the fresh night air would clear his lungs.

"*Ana mabsout beshughlak.*"

He stopped. That voice sounded so very near. He searched the pastures for the source of that Arabic praise for his service, but he saw no one around, not even a cow.

"Is it not written that my face shall shine upon the surface of *Qamar*?"

Hearing the same discarnate voice again, he gazed up at the sky.

A full moon looked down on him.

He fell to his knees. There, on that bloodless circle, was the mouth that just spoken to him. And above it, the broad forehead and prominent nose ending in a sharp point and the eyes flickering like hot coals. This was the sign of the approaching End Days, just as the hadiths had prophesied.

The Mahdi had come to him at last!

"Do you doubt me now, *ghazi*?"

He gasped—the Messiah's voice sounded right behind his ear. He bowed repeatedly, banging his forehead against the ground in contrition. "Forgive me, Awaited One! Forgive me!"

"You suffer for me."

He remained on his knees, bent in submission. "It is nothing!"

"I command these pains from Satan to leave your body. In return for this intercession, my son, you must have faith in me."

He heaved for breath. "Forever! My life is yours!"

"Obey Yahya," the Mahdi's voice commanded. "He is my messenger and your commander. His orders are mine."

"*Na'am*, Master!"

"I will not come to you again before the last *Jihad* commences. Be unbending in your courage, dear soldier. *Ma salaama*, until our standards are raised upon the corpses of the *mufsiduun*."

After a long silence, Jamaal risked looking up at the moon again. The face of the Awaited One had vanished. Miraculously, he no longer felt the headaches and the ringing. Tears poured down his cheeks.

The Mahdi had healed him.

TWENTY-EIGHT

TOMAR, PORTUGAL
MAY, 1478

Pero stood atop the castle's observation tower and gazed southwest toward Lisbon. He longed for Catrina, but his service to the crown had taken him away from her so many months that he feared she no longer held the same feelings about him. "Salvador, what did she say about me?"

Cristobal Colon glared at him. "How many times must I tell you? My name is *not* Salvador."

Dias hissed a command for Pero to pull his frazzled thoughts together. "Are you going soft in the head? Zarco has been dead for two years."

Pero raised his palms in contrition for the lapse. Speaking the traitor's name was no longer permitted in the Order, but he had spent so many years in training with Zarco that he still found it difficult to accept Colon as the new member of their threesome. The Genoan was pushy and intrusive, just as Zarco had been, and he pestered returning mariners about wind patterns and coastlines, insisting that everyone call him 'Admiral.' Too soon after the execution for propriety, Colon had also begun courting the widow Filipa, employing all the subtlety of a siege engine. He had even proposed marriage to her with a life on Madeira, where her family held properties.

"I did not speak with Catrina," Colon told Pero with a smirk of mischief. "But Filipa said she saw her walking the gardens with Vasco da Gama after Mass last week."

Pero turned livid. "That sniveling school boy from Evora?"

Dias struggled to suppress a grin as he stoked Pero's temper. "I hear da Gama has petitioned the King for a caravel to command."

Pero steamed and huffed. "He barely has hairs on his *cajones!*"

Dias winked at Colon. "Maybe she prefers a promising young man over an old *ratao.*"

Pero could not decide which of his two tormentors to thump first. "I will use that *bastardo* da Gama for shark bait after I fillet the both of you!"

A new voice, speaking behind them, suggested, "Why not conjure a golem to guard your lady?"

The squires turned to discover that a gnomish old Jew in a ratty turban had been listening to their banter. Stoop-shouldered and lousy with unkempt hair, the man had the round, sunken face of a withered apricot.

Pero demanded of the intruder, "What is a golem?"

"A creature formed from clay by magic," the Jew said. "A golem cannot speak, only obey."

Pero didn't know what to make of this odd manikin. "Who are you?"

"Joseph Vizcaino."

Impressed, Dias whistled his surprise. "The King's cabalist?"

The Jew jingled his coin purse at them in a taunt. "The Old Man left an endowment for your instruction."

Pero waved him off. "Mariners have no need to learn philosophy."

But the scholar did not move. "The skill of navigating the outer world is useless if you cannot find the hidden routes to the inner cosmos."

"Most seamen can't even write their own names," Pero reminded him.

"If I prove the worth of my teaching," the Jew asked, "will you cease your carping?" Gaining Pero's skeptical assent, the cabalist unrolled a scroll and ran his finger down the Old Testament while counting. When he reached Numbers 21, he ordered Pero to read the passage aloud.

Pero smoothed out the scroll and read from it: "And the Lord said unto Moses, Make thee a fiery serpent, and set it upon a pole. And it shall come to pass, that every one that is bitten, when he looketh upon it, shall live."

The cabalist waited for a reaction. Receiving none, he asked, "What do *you* half-formed golems make of *that* divine command?" Still without a response, he gave them a hint. "What does 'pole' mean?"

"A stick in the ground," Colon said.

The Jew circled them like a hairy planet in orbit. "No, what does a pole mean for a *navigator?*"

The squires struggled for an answer.

Finally, Dias risked a guess. "The Pole Star?"

"Why would God tell Moses to put a serpent on a pole, do you think?"

"Perhaps he wanted to impale the Devil?" Pero said.

The cabalist sighed with disgust. "Look up at the sky, you addled brains!" When the squires turned their eyes toward the stars, the old Jew asked them: "What do you see near the Pole Star?"

"The constellation *Draco*!" Pero yelped in discovery.

"The serpent on the pole!" Dias cried, now seeing the same formation.

The cabalist clapped his hands in mock applause. "The Scriptures abound with such secrets of the cosmos. Moses was a master navigator of the stars. He studied with the Egyptian priests. How did you think he managed to lead the Israelites through the desert?"

The squires took seats, eager to hear more of these strange teachings.

"Who can recite from Revelation?" the cabalist asked.

Colon volunteered a passage: "And a great sign appeared in Heaven. A woman clothed with the sun and the moon under her feet, and on her head a crown of twelve stars."

"Why twelve stars?" Drawing no guesses, the cabalist answered his own question: "Twelve plus the Woman of the Apocalypse equal thirteen. Thirteen is the sacred number of the highest power. The Virgin and the Twelve Apostles. What did the Woman do?"

"She cast the Serpent down to earth," Dias said.

The cabalist made a poofing sound, which seemed to be his method for confirming the validity of an answer. "Therein lays a great secret about the constellations."

Trading doubtful glances with Dias and Zarco, Pero asked the cabalist: "Are you saying the Word of God is not to be interpreted literally?"

"The arcana contains many levels of meaning," the old Jew said. "Only those with the keys to the gnosis will gain the profound understanding."

"What are these keys?" Dias asked.

"Letters."

Colon leaned forward. "Of the alphabet?"

The cabalist pulled a rope from his bag and laid it out in an undulating coil. He began forming Hebrew letters with its length. "What was the Serpent?"

"Lucifer in disguise?" Pero suggested.

"And what does the name 'Lucifer' mean?" When the squires, stumped, shook their heads, the cabalist answered his own question. "Light Giver."

Dias looked at Pero and Colon, as if convinced he had not heard the old Jew correctly. "Satan brought Light to the world?"

"The Light of Wisdom," the cabalist affirmed.

Colon kneaded his brows in suspicion. "Why then did God banish him?"

Receiving no answer, at least none spoken, the squires watched, perplexed, as the cabalist cut the rope into sections and formed smaller Hebrew letters from the strands.

Pero slapped his hands to his head in an epiphany. "The full power of the Light was too much for man to bear. God must have killed the Serpent and cut it up in pieces to give us the letters."

Colon suddenly understood what the cabalist was doing. "Letters that formed interconnecting pieces of the Wisdom."

The cabalist smiled at how his demonstration had borne fruit. "Each letter carved from the dismemberment of the Serpent carries its own unique power. And each letter combination evokes even greater powers. To know how to manipulate these letters is to serve God as His co-creator."

Dias stood from his stool to protest. "You make Creation sound like a giant cryptogram. To understand God's intent for us, we would first have to know all the rules of this divine cipher."

"Letters carry the power of sound in addition to the powers of denotation and connotation," the cabalist said. "Every word"—he shaped his own name—"possesses meaning just from the sound of the letters in combination."

"So," Colon asked, "even *our* names wield their own force?"

"Let us use the Latin alphabet as an example," the cabalist said, nodding. "What does the letter 'S' sound like?"

"A hiss," Dias suggested.

The cabalist posed, "What does the letter *look* like?"

"A serpent rearing to strike," Pero offered.

"What power would it therefore carry?"

"Preparation," Dias said. "Defense. Anger. Tautness."

"And if the serpent returns to its repose?" The cabalist manipulated the rope to mimic a sleeping snake. "What letter captures *that* power?"

"The letter 'N'," Colon said. "The Serpent's head angles back to the ground. And the sound is more muffled."

The cabalist clapped his hands in approval. "When you study sacred texts, you must always apply such technique of analysis. Every permutation carries its own revelation."

Pero let out a puff of exasperation. "You expect us to remember them *all?*"

"There are devices to assist the memory," the cabalist insisted. "You must learn the art of concentration. There are no libraries on the seas." He brought out a contraption with multiple wheels that rotated separately. "The sage Raymond Lull invented this *rota* to find the endless combination of virtues and powers."

"If we use this magic of yours to create new worlds," Dias asked, "are we not usurping God's role?"

"God requires our help," the cabalist said.

Pero was mortified. "That is blasphemy!"

The cabalist beckoned the squires closer to examine his magical square. "You must never forget what I am about to tell you. At Creation, God withdrew part of His Being to allow freedom to exist. He poured His Light into the Sephirot that formed the Tree of Life, but the vessels could not hold His power. They shattered and sent the divine sparks falling into this world. Here the sparks of God have remained trapped. Only mankind can release them. And only then will the heavens be at peace."

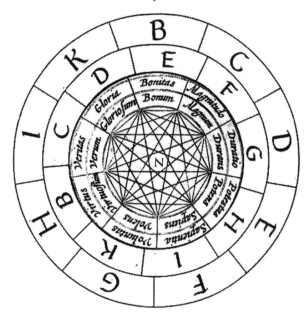

After staring at the circle for several moments, Pero looked up to ask another question of the old Jew. "Are you saying that *we* must save God?"

"I am."

"But the Church teaches that God must come to save us," Pero said. "The End of Days will arrive only with the return of the Messiah."

The cabalist gathered up his scrolls and loaded them into his knapsack, indicating that their lesson was finished for the night. "Thousands have predicted the hour of the Apocalypse. And all have been exposed as fools. Unlike these wolves who lead the sheep astray, the true brotherhoods have passed the Ancient Tradition down from mouth to mouth, as I have now done with you. The New Jerusalem must first be established before the lost Light can return to its Divine Source." He fixed on them with an unsettling look of compassion. "A burden is about to be placed on your shoulders. Soon you will awaken the sleeping Serpent. God Himself awaits the mercy of your efforts."

Pero glanced worriedly at Dias and Zarco, shaken by the cabalist's claim that God required *their* mercy. Had the Old Man secretly embraced such a dangerous heresy, too? If so, then perhaps this reversal of all they had ever been taught about the Almighty and His Creation had some connection to the unrevealed mission for which they were being trained.

TWENTY-NINE

SATOR
APERO
TENET
OPERA
ROTAS

"Grandma, it's me. ... Jaqie."

Slumped in a wheelchair at the Cave Hill Nursing Center, Maggie Goins raised her head and tried to place the face looking down at her. "I had a granddaughter by that name."

Jaq winced at how feeble her grandmother had become. Determined to find an answer to her worsening Behcet's symptoms, she had convinced Boz to fly her here to southeastern Kentucky to speak with the only family member who might offer a clue to her condition. She motioned him closer for an introduction. "Grandma, this is Boz."

Maggie peered past him and through the window, toward the Appalachian Mountains in the distance. "You'd best shoo those chickens back in the coop, Daniel. The rains are coming over that holler."

Jaq tried to jump-start her grandmother's memory by wrapping her mottled hands around a box of Stuckey's chocolate pralines, which had always been her favorite sweets. "Has Ma or Pa been to visit you?"

That question did the trick. Thrust back into the lucid present, Maggie shouted, "To Hell with them! Worthless brood!"

When several residents in the lobby looked over, Jaq wheeled her to an alcove for more privacy. "Grandma, I need to ask you something. Did anyone in our family have a rare disease?"

Maggie's eyes flashed recognition, followed by suspicion. "Disease? What kind of disease?"

"Inflammation in the joints. Headaches. Anything unusual?"

Maggie's thinning brows narrowed. "How old are you now?"

"Twenty-seven."

"Been feeling like your head's about to explode?" Receiving a nod, Maggie hesitated, as if she wished to be doing anything else. With a huff of resignation, she kicked at Jaq's foot. "Take your shoe off."

Entertained by Maggie's homespun ways, Boz made an arch expression to insist that Jaq obey the order. Pouting, Jaq plopped down on the couch and yanked off her running shoe. She was relieved to see that her ankle sock didn't have a hole in it.

Maggie pointed to her own lap. "Put it up here" She leaned over Jaq's foot to aid her sight and caressed a bump on the right side of the pinky toe.

"That's nothing," Jaq said. "It's been there all my life."

Maggie slung her foot to the floor. "Gal, you don't need to tell me what's been there all your life. I was there when Doc … what was his name?"

"Doc Hopkins?"

"Coulda been. Anyways, another toe used to be on that bump. He removed one from each foot when you were born."

Jaq jackknifed her leg onto the opposite knee to inspect it more closely. "I was a freak?"

Maggie struggled to lift her own foot off the wheelchair's support flange. She kicked for Jaq to remove the orthopedic shoe and sock. Jaq stared down in horror at the six toes on her grandmother's foot.

"That no-count father of yours didn't give a damn," Maggie said. "But I made Doc cut yours off to save you the embarrassment I suffered."

Boz barely hid his amusement. "What causes this?"

Maggie examined him, as if seeing his face for the first time. "You look right familiar."

Jaq scowled at Boz for not helping her keep her grandmother focused. She tapped on her grandmother's hand to regain her attention. "What did the doctor say about these extra toes?"

Maggie motioned her closer to prevent the other residents from overhearing. "We come from a different race of people. Melungeons is what they called us. Our folk brought the afflictions with them when they settled in these mountains. Most of us had the curse."

Melungeons.

Jaq's gaze turned inward. Where had she heard that word before? Wait, didn't that guy in Newport say that '*melungo*' was Portuguese for shipwreck? "Where did these Melungeons come from?"

Maggie shrugged. "Great-grandma Mendoca always told those hifalutins from Lexington that we was Lusiads. I never understood what she meant."

"Why didn't you or Ma ever tell me about this?"

Maggie's glassy eyes shadowed from the memory. "We was shunned like colored folk. Nobody would believe we was just dropped down into these mountains like some lost tribe. I didn't want you to go through what I did. When your mama hauled you off to Kentucky, I told everyone up there that you were part Cherokee. Hell of a country when you have to claim redskin blood to get any respect."

Jaq wasn't sure she could believe this tale, given that it sounded like so many of the whopping mountain yarns she'd heard growing up. "You sure grandpa wasn't pulling your leg?"

Maggie rebutted that possibility with a shuddering glare from her famous evil eye. "You ever been to our family plot?"

"The one in Tennessee? No, why?"

Maggie wheeled herself into her room and lifted a spray of dandelions from a vase. "Put these on mama's stone for me. Tell her I'll be with her soon. Doc still lives down there. He's too old for the practice now, but he can tell you more about what's been happening to you."

Jaq kissed her goodbye. "You take care, Grandma."

"Wait, there's something else I want to give you." Maggie opened the bottom drawer of a chest and brought out a frayed tome bound in leather. "Our family Bible. You're all I got left now."

Jaq thumbed through the tattered King James edition and found the title page. The margins held a scribbled family tree going back to the 1700s.

While her granddaughter studied the family record, Maggie set her sights on Boz again. "You look right familiar. You one of our cousins?"

"No, ma'am. Just a friend of your granddaughter's here."

Maggie wasn't about to take his sass. "You're one of us."

"I don't think that's possible—"

"Open your mouth."

Jaq grinned and, getting revenge, nodded for him to obey.

Maggie squinted into Boz's gaping mouth. "Shovel teeth in front. And you ain't never had wisdom molars, have you?" She left him with the dazed look of a man who had just consulted the Delphic Oracle. "You're one of us, all right. Now you all scat before I miss dinner."

Flustered by what she had learned, Jaq hugged her grandmother goodbye, and closed the door behind them. As she and Boz walked toward the exit, a nurse attendant came running up.

"A man named Mayfield called here yesterday." The nurse handed Jaq a pink message slip. "He was asking Miss Maggie if she knew where her granddaughter could be contacted."

Jaq looked at the message and crumpled it in her fist. That bastard Bratton must have ratted her out for going on the lam from his Rhode Island brainwashing mill.

That afternoon, after a three-hour drive to Strawner's Gap, Jaq and Boz got out of their rented jeep and walked through the old graveyard that overlooked a tree-lined mountain valley just across the border in northeastern Tennessee. Most of the slanting stones were engraved with names like Brogan, Mullins, and Collins, but on the oldest markers, the spellings were different: Braganza, Magoens, and Colinso. The epitaphs included symbols such as the Star of David and a compass with a contractor's square. Some of the headstones had also been decorated with miniature A-framed houses to protect bowls filled with milk and bread.

Shielding his eyes from the low sun, Boz pulled a compass from his pocket and took a measurement.

Jaq saw the puzzlement on his face. "What's wrong?"

"These graves are all laid east to west. That practice was developed with the Talmudic tradition. These people had rabbinic guidance."

She knew *that* couldn't be right. This was pure Christian country. She knelt to place the flowers on the grave of her great-grandmother. The stone said that Mahala Mendoca had lived in Strawner's Gap from 1858 to 1904. She noticed that one of the nearby markers in her family's section was inscribed with a strange cross:

Before she could investigate the unusual epitaph, she heard the faint strum of a dulcimer wafting up from a white-board church in the ravine below. Worshippers walked through the church doors and headed in a column and toward a creek. The women wore bonnets and ankle-length calico dresses, and the men, many bearded, were attired in black suits and brimmed hats. She had to blink to make sure she wasn't imagining it all.

Had this valley somehow been sealed off from the march of time?

At the creek, a bent old man with the scored face of a heavy smoker headed the procession. He led a young girl in a white smock into the water, dunked her, and then raised her drenched and spewing. He pawed the water until he captured a copperhead, then raised the writhing snake to the sky and shouted: "The Holy Ghost sends us messages in the water and the wind!"

The congregants hovering around the snake-brandishing pastor chanted: "Water and wind! Water and wind!"

They continued fluttering ejaculations while the baptized girl was given the copperhead to hold. The girl trembled and fell backwards, as if overcome by some spiritual force. One of the men rescued the snake while the others fished the girl from the water before she drowned. They carried her unconscious in their arms as the pastor led his singing flock back into the church.

Alarmed, Jaq jumped to her feet. Had the poor child been bitten?

"All religions are crazy," Boz muttered, shaking his head. "But yours takes the prize."

She turned a sneer on him. "*That* down there isn't my religion. And, by the way, don't Jews fling live chickens around their heads to transfer their sins to the poultry? How is that any different?"

"Hey, at least chickens don't kill you with venomous bites."

She rushed down the hill to the church opened the door slowly, fearful of finding the girl dead. She led Boz inside. To her amazement, the worshippers were filling paper plates with fried chicken, collared greens, and sweet potatoes. The baptized girl who only minutes before had appeared comatose was now laughing and unwrapping gifts. The scene was typical of any small-town Sunday gathering, except for the corral in the corner that held perhaps a dozen snakes. Whenever the Holy Ghost gave inspiration, one of the celebrants would pick up a copperhead with no more concern than if petting a puppy.

The pastor saw them the standing at the door. "Come in, please. All are welcome. Are you new to the area?"

"Just visiting." Jaq kept her distance, unnerved by the proximity of the snakes. "My mother's family grew up here."

"What was the name?" the pastor asked.

"Mendoca."

"Any relation to Mahala?"

"She was my great-grandmother."

"My daddy put ol' Mahly in the ground," the pastor said. "The gal was a prosperous moonshiner, but that ain't what got her the real notoriety. She weighed over four hundred pounds. When she died, they couldn't lift her out of the house, so they had to use her bed as the coffin and cut a hole through the chimney to take her to her Maker. Have something to eat, won't you?"

Jaq glared a silent warning at Boz to avoid making a snide comment about her family's affinity for eating. "Thanks, but we're on a tight schedule. I was wondering if you could tell me where I'd find Dr. Hopkins?"

The pastor pointed the way. "Two miles down the road toward Kyles Ford. He usually throws horseshoes in the front yard on Sundays."

Retreating back-first to the door, Boz mentioned to the pastor, "One of those stones on the hill is carved with a snake on a cross."

"That's Pec Niccan's grave. He was a snake charmer like me. We've been marking the headstones like that for as long as I can remember."

Boz thanked the pastor and, with eyes fixed on the copperheads, backed out of the church. He muttered to Jaq under his breath, "The snake was probably too afraid to bite the old coot."

She retaliated for his crack by taking a greasy leg of chicken from the potluck table and stuffing it into his shirt pocket. "Eat up. I'm sure it's kosher."

Boz drove up a gypsum lane and parked in front of a rickety clapboard house with a log foundation that looked as if Daniel Boone might have built it. An elderly gentleman, in suspenders and with sleeves rolled to the elbows, sat rocking in a chair under a large oak tree.

Jaq leaned out the passenger window. "Doc Hopkins?"

"Yep. What can I do for you, missy?"

She suppressed a grin, marveling at how he would have been right at home in a sepia-toned daguerreotype of an old Confederate veteran. Feigning umbrage, she said, "You took something that belonged to me."

The doctor stood from his chair and squinted, trying to make out the features of his accuser. "I reckon you better come out here and say that again straight away, young lady."

She jumped out of the car barefoot and aimed her flexed ankle at him. "You cut off a couple of my toes about twenty-seven years ago."

The doctor broke a wide grin. "Well, I'll be. Li'l Jaqie. You seem perfectly capable of walking, so I don't think you've got much of a malpractice case."

She hugged him and then brought Boz closer. "This is my ..." She tried to think of the best way to describe him. "My colleague, Boz."

"Pleasure." The doctor shook Boz's hand. "What brings you back into the wilderness, Jaqie? I heard you went to law school to escape these suffocating old mountains."

"I've been experiencing some strange symptoms lately. A physician up in Washington said he thinks I may have something called Behcet's disease."

The doctor felt for the bump at the base of her skull. He turned her hands over and examined several bluish-gray spots near her wrists. "You still got those splotches on your back?"

Her jaw dropped. "You knew about those?"

"I tried to convince your mother to tell you what they were," the doctor said. "She wouldn't hear of it. But don't worry. You're one of the lucky ones."

"Lucky?"

"It's not enough that the good folks here have to endure discrimination. Sometimes they're born with peculiar infirmities."

Stunned that her mother had known about this and didn't warn her, Jaq hardly heard what the doctor was saying.

But he kept explaining the disease in that professional dry tone that she remembered as a child. "Yeah, you've got Behcet's, all right, but it won't slow you down much. Plenty of others here in Hancock County got it worse."

She turned a triumphant glare on Boz, and found him pasted with the look of a man who had just walked into a leper colony.

Boz asked the doctor, "What do you mean when you say others are worse?"

The physician raised his hand to demonstrate the tremor symptoms from the disease. "Some around these parts suffer disorders of the central nervous system. Others have painful kidney inflammations."

Jaq needed a moment to take it all in. It wasn't all about her, the good doctor was obviously trying to tell her. Easy for him to say, though. He didn't seem to be any worse for the wear. But of course, he was right. She had seen others in this poverty-stricken backwoods in pretty bad shape. She asked him politely, "Why do these diseases afflict people here?"

"A few years ago, a lab down in Houston did a DNA study on some of the folks in this county. Seems we have the same genetic makeup as Jews from Spain and Portugal. Most people here are as Christian as you can get. They'll deny it to God Himself, but there's Jewish blood in our ancestry."

"That explains the Stars of David on those older stones," Boz said. "And the burial direction."

Jaq still couldn't quite believe that Jews had settled here. "I never saw a synagogue in these parts. This used to be dyed-in-the-wool Baptist country."

The doctor laughed. "Still is, mostly. But that doesn't mean it's always been that way. You always were a questioner, Jaqie." He glanced at their rental vehicle. "If you got room for a third in that jeep, there's something I'd like to show you."

With Doc Hopkins in the back seat, they sped across the county and came to Sneedville, population 1257. A sign proudly announced they were entering the home of Jimmy Martin, the King of Bluegrass music.

"Notice anything different?"

She shrugged, vaguely recalling some of the passing buildings. "The price for a root-beer float at the A&W has gone up about a dollar."

The doctor pointed out a corniced brick edifice on the main street through town. "Remember that one?"

"The old Masonic lodge."

"Every county seat around here has one."

Suddenly, she made the connection. "Those were Masonic compasses on the gravestones. Did the Masons here have anything to do with the Melungeons?"

"There's my old office," he said, apparently not hearing her question.

Boz pulled in, and after they parked and got out, he and Jaq followed the doctor to an entrance that stood next door to the office that she had visited years ago with sore throats and the whooping cough. The doctor pulled out a ring of keys and unlocked the door to the Masonic headquarters.

Jaq thought he had chosen the wrong entrance because of his nearsightedness. But then the door opened, and he motioned her to take the lead. She turned on him in disbelief. "You're a Mason?"

He winked, enjoying her surprise. "Not just any old Mason. I'm the Master Mason of the Sneedville Lodge. I also happen to be the local historian. I've piled up a little collection of books in my sixty years of reading while waiting for the next patient to show up."

He led them into a small meeting hall that could have passed for any small-town social club, except for the dozens of photos lining the walls. The families shown in the frames had dark complexions and dour, joyless expressions, as if they had been rounded up for a criminal lineup.

"Who are these people?" Jaq asked.

"Melungeons who lived hereabouts."

Remembering what her grandmother had said about her Melungeon roots, she examined the photos, looking for familiar features. "They all look so sad."

"Gee, I wonder why?" Boz quipped.

Doc Hopkins scanned the shelves of the lodge's small library and pulled down a volume titled *Melungeons: The Last Lost Tribe in America* by Elizabeth Hirschman. He opened it to a page with a photograph of a tall bearded man with a drawn, forlorn face like those in the wall photographs.

Jaq did a double take at the page. "Abraham Lincoln was a Melungeon?"

The doctor grinned at her shock. "His mother, Nancy Hanks, was born up the road in Mineral County, West Virginia. People were always making fun of the way Old Abe looked. He probably suffered from some of our diseases."

"So Lincoln would have had Jewish blood," Boz said.

"Probably," Doc Hopkins said. "I guess calling him Father Abraham wasn't such a stretch."

Jaq walked along the decorated walls and stopped to read a plaque that held a Templar Cross circumscribed by an octagon. Eight corners, just like the number of columns on that old *Touro* in Newport. Verses from a Masonic ritual accompanied the insignia:

MASTER: What inducement have you to leave the East and go to the West?

JUNIOR WARDEN: To seek for that which was lost, which, by your instruction and our own industry, we hope to find.

MASTER: What is that which was lost?

SENIOR WARDEN: The genuine secrets of a Master Mason.

MASTER: How came they lost?

JUNIOR WARDEN: The untimely dead of our Master, Hiram Abiff.

MASTER: Where do you hope to find them?

SENIOR WARDEN: With the Centre.

MASTER: What is a Centre?

JUNIOR WARDEN: A point within a circle, from which every part of the circumference is equidistant.

MASTER: Why with the Centre?

SENIOR WARDEN: That being a point from which a Master Mason cannot err.

MASTER: We will assist you to repair that loss and may Heaven aid our united endeavours.

Several intriguing books sat on a shelf below the plaque: *The Secret Jews of the Southwest, The Forgotten Portuguese,* and *Tennessee Templars.* She thumbed through one of the volumes titled *Mackey's Encyclopedia of Freemasonry.* An entry in it caught her eye:

> *Serpent and Cross: A symbol used in the degrees of Knights Templar and Knights of the Brazen Serpent. The cross is a tau cross T, and the serpent is twined around. Its origin is found in Numbers xxi 9, where it is said, "Moses made a serpent of brass, and put it upon a pole." The word Nes, here translated "a pole," literally means a standard, or something elevated on high as a signal, and may be represented by a cross as well as by a pole. Indeed, Justin Martyr calls it a cross."*

She read that last line again. The reference to the serpent caused her to think of the girl baptized in the river that afternoon. "We saw people down at the Strawner's Gap church handling snakes. How'd that get started?"

"I'm not rightly sure, to be honest," Doc Hopkins said. "Snake handling has always been pretty common in these parts. I was always told it was part of the Gospel of Mark." He quoted the passage from memory: "'They shall speak with new tongues and they shall take up serpents.'"

"But that's from the New Testament," she said. "If the first Melungeons here were Jews, why would they follow a Christian gospel?"

"Well, you know ..." The doctor wiped the moist inner band of his hat with his kerchief. "In the past, being a Jew in the South wouldn't have been a joy ride. There was a Jewish boy named Leo Frank who was lynched by a Georgia mob in 1915. The first Jews to settle here probably hid some of their rituals. Heck, they may have been doing that before they came to America. Before long, their kinfolk that came after them would have forgotten their Jewish identity altogether. Maybe the first settlers in these parts took up snake-handling to make people think they were Christians."

Jaq scanned the photos again, now looking at them in a new light. She kept being drawn back to the Masonic plaque that had fascinated her. "This Templar cross is similar to crosses I saw in Ethiopia and France. Why would Jews who came here to America adopt a Christian cross?"

Stumped by the oddity, Doc Hopkins searched through one of his books on medieval Jewry for a possible explanation. "It says here that in 1307, many Jews in France were rounded up and exiled at the same time the Templars were imprisoned. Who knows? Maybe the Portuguese Jews had something in common with those persecuted monks."

Jaq snuck a sheepish glance at Boz and found him studying her face as if seeing it for the first time. She had dismissed as ludicrous that hospital doctor's suggestion about her lineage, but now she wasn't so sure. If her ancestors here *were* in fact Melungeons descended from shipwrecked Portuguese Jews, then her blood carried the sin of those who had first turned away from Christ. How could she ever explain this to Rev. Merry? Yet one thing still didn't ring true: Why, of all the New Testament rituals and passages to choose from, would these secret Appalachian Jews adopt the bizarre and dangerous practice of snake-handling to make others think they were Christian? There had to be another reason. She asked the doctor, "Isn't the serpent supposed to be a sign of healing?"

"Ah, you're talking about the caduceus. They told us in medical school that the symbol came from Egypt. The two serpents represented the sun and the moon balancing along the spine."

Boz was lost in his own thoughts. Rousing, he asked the doctor, "Just out of curiosity, do you have any idea which Egyptian hieroglyph was used to represent a serpent?"

Stoked for a good scavenger hunt, Doc Hopkins consulted his dictionary of ancient languages. "Says here the zigzag line represented water. The Latin letter 'N' came from the hieroglyph for serpent. I reckon the letter does fancy a coiling snake."

"The letter 'nun' is the Hebrew equivalent to the letter 'N'," Boz remembered. "'Nun' also represents a snake."

"Now you've really tweaked my old gray matter," Doc Hopkins said. "I think I once read something about the importance of the serpent for the Templars." He pulled down a book titled *Gnosis* by Philip Gardiner and searched the index. He turned to page 133 and showed them the passage he had found:

> *Another symbol seen in various forms from Sumeria to France is the abraxus. A figure with snakes for legs is a symbol used for gods such as Oannes (the father of Baal), which later became the symbol of the Grand Master of the Templar Order. What could this mean? That the head of the Order of the Templars saw himself as the chief of the serpents?*
>
> *The Templars also used the serpent symbol of eternity and immortality; the snake eating its own tail. Thus we have a serpent secret being held by the very highest of Christian organizations. The abraxus reveals a man/deity who is empowered by his balancing of the twin serpents. These are symbols of mystical knowledge. The Templars are revealing, through symbolism, just what ancient wisdom they uncovered at the Temple of Solomon.*

Jaq reread those last words: *ancient wisdom they uncovered at the Temple of Solomon.* Could all of this serpent imagery have something to do with the Ark of the Covenant?

"Most people don't know that the Friday the Thirteenth superstition got started when the French king ordered the Templars arrested on that day," Doc Hopkins explained. "The king and the Church probably chose the thirteenth to buck up their case that the Templars were in cahoots with the Devil."

"Why was the thirteenth considered demonic?" Jaq asked the doctor.

"The number thirteen in Masonic and Kabbalistic lore has always been symbolic of the serpent. Odd thing is, it's also considered the number of the Virgin Mary." The doctor showed them another book; published in 1887, it was titled *The Gnostics and their Remains* and had been authored by Charles William King. He pointed to the page in question and observed, "The sun god Apollo is another name for Aesculapius, the healer. Both were represented in ancient times by the image of a serpent."

Looking over his shoulder, Jaq saw the next sentence of the paragraph he was reading. Her eyes widened:

> *It has been already stated how, in the Mithraic worship, the image, surrounded from foot to head by the spiral convolutions of the serpent, had become the established emblem of the deity himself.*

The doctor noticed her vexed reaction. "Constantine adopted Christianity as the official religion of the Roman Empire after he saw a cross in the sky that resembled the Mithraic symbol for the sun. Some historians believe that the white mantles and insignia of the Templars were patterned after the robes worn by the initiates of Mithras."

Boz grasped her elbow in discovery. "Look, the center letter in the SATOR square is an 'N'"—he emphasized his point—"an 'N' on a *cross*."

She knew at once what he was thinking. "The serpent on that gravestone at Strawner's Gap … it wasn't engraved there to remember a snake charmer."

Boz studied the wall photos of the Melungeon families again. "Yeah, and those Portuguese Jews who came to these mountains didn't take up snake-handling as a test for demonstrating their faith in Christ. The ritual must have been a forgotten vestige from another belief that required their ancestors to honor the serpent. These people who live here now don't have a clue as to the real reason their forefathers were taught to take up snakes."

They waited for Doc Hopkins to confirm their new theory, but he shelved the book without commenting.

Jaq's head swam with the implications of what she had just learned. Had a covert brotherhood steeped in some kind of esoteric serpent wisdom survived since ancient Egypt? If so, had it passed its mission down to the Israelite priests who guarded Solomon's Temple, to the Roman soldiers who worshipped Mithras, to the Knights Templar of the Crusades, to the Portuguese Order of Christ and their American descendants, the Melungeons and Freemasons? The grand masters of these esoteric fraternities had all adopted the serpent on a cross as their emblem. Whatever this serpent mystery was that they guarded, she was now convinced that it had something to do with the Ark of the Covenant.

She looked at Boz and wondered if he was thinking the same thing: Was Hosaam closing in on the decoding key to the Virgo map and the SATOR-Templar square—she swallowed hard—by following the trail of these Serpent Knights?

THIRTY

SAGRES, PORTUGAL
SEPTEMBER, 1485

As the sun died to the cold autumn night, Pero was led from the dungeon and forced to stand shivering in a white burial smock at the epicenter of the Wind Rose. The knights of Tomar, in full regalia, marched out from their barracks and formed up around the perimeter of the giant circle. Above them, the stars of the Virgin shimmered at their highest point in the constellation's annual journey across the ecliptic.

The seneschal strode before his ranks and repeated the Order of Christ's motto from the Gospel of John: "No one may enter the Kingdom of God unless he is first born of water and wind."

"Water and wind," a hundred voices affirmed.

Pero searched their stony faces for an explanation of why he had been arrested that morning in Lisbon and escorted south with such haste. Had the grand master finally decided to cleanse the Order of its secret Jews? He looked for a gallows, but saw none. The collar of his death shroud remained untied, exposing his neck. Was he to be decapitated?

The seneschal came before him. "Name the prevailing wind."

He could not fathom the purpose of such a strange question. Were these knights bent on humiliating him before the death stroke?

"Answer!"

He looked down at the stone *rota* where he had spent hours being drilled by the Old Man on the many winds with their qualities and effects. A slight pressure built on his right cheek, and he was drawn to one of the thirty-six pie sections on the far side of the circle. The wind, he estimated, now came from the northeast. That was the direction the sun rose during the summer solstice. The hint of a morning storm in the offing firmed his suspicion. It had to be the Caecias, a volatile, traitorous huffing that often doubled back and spawned ill weather and heavy cumulus. The maxim had been burned into his memory long ago: *Bringing it on himself, as Caecias does the clouds.*

The seneschal's glare made clear that he would not ask a third time.

Pero remained loyal to his first instinct. "Caecias."

"Which dominion?"

Was this some perverse game? Identifying the dominion was much more difficult, for each of the twelve winds had its own section on the Wind Rose, which in turn was divided into three slices of dominions. Failing to locate the dominion direction on the high seas could result in a navigational error of several hundred miles. His eyes dropped to his feet, where the intermittent stones marked off the quadrant lines. A puff of dust swirled over a section to his far left. He steadied against the freshening breeze and gave his answer: "The sinistral."

The seneschal blindfolded him. Spun until he was disoriented, he heard the officer order: "Thirty degrees north by northeast. That dominion leads to land. When given the signal to proceed, you will walk in that direction and not stop until commanded."

He felt a blade come to his throat.

"If you hesitate, you will be executed. Make your peace with God."

His shivering intensified, for he now understood what was happening. The Order placed the lives of a crew in the hands of only those men who had demonstrated the ability to read the winds during great danger. This was September, the holy month dedicated to the Merciful Virgin of the Stars, and the final initiation of a Tomar knight always took place under the full gaze of the Stella Maris. If he erred, he would plummet to his death on the rocks below. He conjured up the image of the Wind Rose in his memory and prayed to the Virgin for guidance:

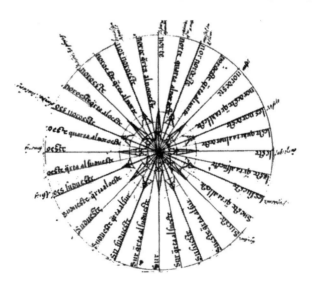

The seneschal set the deadly initiation into motion. "Godspeed!"

"Godspeed!" the knights chanted, watching in the round.

Pero had to will his knocking legs to move. Several steps into the ordeal, doubt began creeping into his mind like bilge water. Was it truly the Caecias wind that he had felt moments ago? He would have concentrated harder minutes ago had he known his life was to hang in the balance. Now, denied his sight, it was too late. He took slow but steady steps, trying to buy time to think. A shiver of panic rushed down his spine. The Caecias, he remembered, gave way at the approach of dawn to its opposite wind, the Lips Anemos, named after the Greek god of the southwest tempests.

The sea's breath became warmer and drier. Could this be one of those deadly nocturnal moments when the winds changed their guard? Had the seneschal chosen this hour to trick him? Winds, like mortals, suffered birth and death, he knew. They were living entities, spawned by the sacred marriage of the sun and the moon. When rising, the sun set some winds in motion and halted others. The moon, like a mother, gave emotion to the winds and articulated their personalities. The Aajej wind from Morocco was so cutting and vicious that the Moors attack it with daggers, and the red Harmattan wind was said to leave the stain of blood across the Sahara. Another cyclone, the Simoom, was so poisonous that it once destroyed an entire Persian army commanded by King Cambyses.

Caecias or Lips?

The cabalist Vizcaino had taught him that the Holy Spirit sent messages through the winds. If a navigator did not trust such communications, the angels would soon tire of delivering them. Here, more than a millennium ago, Roman legions had worshipped the four wind gods of Mithras by throwing sailors to the rocks below. Was he doomed to become just another bloody sacrifice?

He felt the pressure on his face shifting, so he recalculated his course by turning to place the wind on his left cheek. Every step was excruciating, each touch of ground ecstatic. How long had he been walking? If he were destined to die, he might as well make it quick. The knights were no doubt laughing at his halting steps. He had set his course using all the knowledge he had learned. His life now rested in God's hands.

Be damned with it all!

He began taking longer strides, and the crash of the waves on the shore became louder. The bitter irony hit him like a squall. He had never been allowed to go to sea, yet his grave would be—

"Halt!"

He stopped abruptly and nearly fell. His legs threatened to collapse. Was he hovering at the precipice?

His blindfold was removed. He stood facing the small church dedicated to the Stella Maris, where the mariners always kept their vigil before launching into the Sea of Darkness. The knights came up to him in a column, two by two, preparing to enter the sanctuary behind him. Several nodded their admiration for his courage. The seneschal opened the oaken door and bade him step into the smoke-charred sanctuary.

Thirteen flickering candles lit the dim chapel. *Why thirteen?*

He blinked, trying to adjust to the hazy light. Then, he saw a frisson of movement, and his heart leapt. Dias and Colon, attired in white smocks, turned from their kneelers and rushed to embrace him. They too had survived Wind Rose initiation that night. Heartened to see his comrades, he took his place aside them on the kneelers in front of the altar, and the knights behind him formed up in a semi-circle along the interior walls.

Latching the door, the seneschal commenced a ritual composed of questions. "What inducement have you to leave the East and go to the West?"

The knights, tightening their cordon around the three squires, answered: "To seek for that which was lost."

"Where do you hope to find that which was lost?"

Maintaining their half-circle formation, the knights came shadowing over the initiates. "Within the center."

"What is a center?"

The knights chanted; "A point within a circle from which every part of the circumference is equidistant."

The seneschal turned to the altar and lifted the ceremonial sword that had been handed down from Gualdim Pais, the founder of the Portuguese Temple. He approached the initiates and tapped their shoulders with the blade. "Do you, Pero Covilha, Bartholomeu Dias, and Cristobal Colon, swear to faithfully serve the Virgin of the Wind Rose, even unto death?"

The three squires affirmed the vow.

"All that has come before was in preparation for this night." The seneschal unlocked a tabernacle recessed into the wall. From the small vault, he withdrew a parchment that was pressed with the Old Man's seal. He unrolled it across the altar. "The time has come to reveal your mission."

Pero held his breath as he listened to the message that the Old Man had dictated just hours before his death. When the reading was finished, he glanced at Dias and Colon and saw that they too were shaken by what the future now held for them. The last words of the Old Man's instructions still echoed through the church:

Gain God's Mercy for me.

THIRTY-ONE

The stumpish proprietor of the Georgetown Rare Maps and Prints shop stopped pushing a large magnifying glass on rollers across a drafting table. Peering down his long nose, he fixed one beady eye on Boz, then the other on Jaq. "You're looking for *what?*"

Boz remained in the dusky shadows, keeping his face obscured. "Information about a map used by the Knights Templar."

The antiquarian dealer, who appeared more Hobbit than human, waved them off as just a couple more of the many New Age kooks who often stumbled in asking for the latest books on Atlantis or the Pyramids. "You want the Third Eye Emporium. Three blocks down."

Boz quipped to Jaq, "I told you this was the wrong place. Malachy Caverio supplied Edmund Hillary with his first map of Everest. This blind troll couldn't tell us where to find the Potomac."

Clambering down from his high stool, the annoyed shopkeeper traded his magnifying loupe for a pair of pince-nez. His nearsighted eyes dilated in sudden recognition. "I thought they locked you away in an Israeli jail years ago."

Boz grinned as he reached for his old friend's hand and locked him in an arm-wrestling contest. "That Sinai map you sold me was so riddled with errors that I ended up in Syria."

Still sparring with Boz, Malachy turned to assess Jaq's topography. "What's a fine *belladonna* like you doing hanging around this two-bit tomb robber?"

"Long story," she said.

"No doubt. And I'd wager it's about to get longer."

She conceded that prediction with a beleaguered smile. "Boz tells me you could find a map to Shangri-La."

"Only if the fee was right." He slapped Boz's grappling hand away. "So, you want a map used by the Poor Knights of Christ. You know what Umberto Eco said in *Foucault's Pendulum*?"

"I skipped that chapter," Boz said.

"The lunatic is easily recognized. Sooner or later, he brings up the Templars."

Given her experience so far, Jaq was ready to admit that Eco might have had a point. "I take it you receive lots of inquiries about the Crusader monks?"

Malachy huffed. "Not a week goes by that I don't get somebody in here expecting me to provide them with a treasure map to a bar of Templar gold buried up George Washington's ass."

Jaq was hoping Boz would explain their predicament, but he left it up to her. "We're searching for a needle in a haystack, but the haystack is more like a silo. We need to check out all the maps of the world that existed around 1300."

"You mean of Europe and the Mediterranean?" Malachy asked.

"North America and the Atlantic, too," she said.

Malachy glared at Boz, as if suspecting his old friend was playing a practical joke to impress his latest female conquest. He turned back to Jaq. "You do know that America wasn't discovered until 1492?"

"I'm not so sure about that."

As Malachy climbed a ladder to reach his highest shelf, he grumbled something about what passed for public education these days. He brought down a large folio and dusted it off. "The first Christian maps of the world depicted the Mediterranean as a 'T' inside a giant circle. Jerusalem was placed at the center. As you can see, the medieval understanding of the world was more symbolic than realistic."

Taking its plastic sheath off, Jaq gently unrolled the scroll and saw that the 'T' of the ancient Mediterranean looked just like the Tau Cross of Mithras. Hopeful, she opened her notebook to the tracing of the Virgo constellation and placed the transparent sheet over a map identified as the Hereford Mappa Mundi. She sighed in disappointment, seeing no correlation to the stars. "I don't think the map we're looking for would have been of this type."

With a grumpy mutter, Malachy rolled up the map and returned it to the shelf. "The next step up the cartography evolution was the portolan."

"Porto what?" she asked.

Malachy searched his drawer trays. He pulled out an example, a modern copy of a brittle parchment that showed lines radiating across the page like the spokes on a wheel. "Portolans were navigation charts that gave directions for sailing from port to port. They were drawn on sheepskin to memorialize coastlines. These crisscrossing strands represented the thirty-two directions on the mariner's compass. The circles were called wind roses. Most portolans didn't attempt to portray a realistic depiction of the shores. They were sufficient for dead reckoning navigation, but not much use for crossing an ocean."

Boz studied the portolan. "What's the oldest one in existence?"

"The Carte Pisane dates from 1296," Malachy said. "The Catalan Atlas came later, around 1375. A Jewish cartographer named Abraham Cresques created it. His sons worked for Henry the Navigator."

Jaq remembered the old gardener in Newport having mentioned that name. "The Portuguese prince, right?"

Malachy nodded. "In the 15th century, the Navigator ran a nautical school in Portugal on a desolate finger of land called Sagres. His collection of maps was probably the most extensive and advanced of the time."

"Why do you say probably?" she asked.

"The Portuguese were paranoid about keeping their charts secret, so we really don't know what they possessed. Their archives have never been found."

Jaq laid the Virgo tracing on the Catalan map, but nothing matched up.

The dealer brought out more copies for her to try: the Zeno Map of 1380, the Piri Reis Map of 1513, the Cantino Planisphere of 1502, and the Reinel Map of 1535. On all of these maps, most of the Virgo stars landed deep into the Atlantic Ocean, where no land existed.

Something about the shape of the Virgo constellation caught Boz's interest. "Do you have a map of Lalibela in Ethiopia?"

"I can print one out from an online database." The dealer waddled into his office and returned minutes later with the Lalibela plat. He rolled it across the table, smoothing its curling corners.

Eyeing the print, Boz asked Jaq, "How many holy sites did Lalibela have?"

She did a quick tally from memory. "Thirteen, I think. ... Eleven underground churches and the tombs of Adam and Lalibela."

Boz looked up at the ceiling while doing the math. "And how many Gothic cathedrals with the name *Notre Dame* were built in northern France?"

Trying to divine what was sprouting in his head, she hesitated. "Thirteen."

Boz brushed a hand through his hair, scratching his scalp in puzzlement. "Didn't your doctor friend tell us that thirteen was the number of the Serpent and the Virgin Mary?" He laid sketch paper over the map and drew two shaded boxes over the Lalibela sites, one each around the Virgin's upper and lower torsos, and rotated the image upside down to correlate with the directions.

"What are you getting at?" she asked.

Boz kept staring at the Lalibela map, trying to find a pattern.

She tapped her watch. "Uh, you can take a nap tonight."

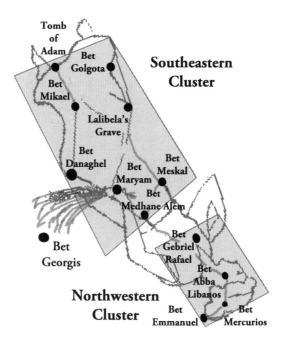

He traced his finger from dot to dot. "Bet Georgis was set apart from the other churches. The constellation has one star outside the Virgin. That could explain why Bet Georgis was excavated in a remote location. Both the Lalibela plan and the Virgo constellation have two clusters of holy sites. One group could represent the womb of the Virgin."

She saw what he meant. "Yeah, and the other could be her heart and head. The occult centers of love and wisdom." She pondered this possible solution. "The northwestern cluster in Lalibela has four churches. The head of the Virgin has four major stars represented by four French cathedrals."

He tested the theory. "The southwestern cluster has eight. That's the same number of stars in the torso section of Virgo. The church locations aren't an exact match with the stars, though."

She threw his favorite phrase back at him. "Close enough for government work. The Templars probably would have had to dig around existing tunnels."

He didn't look convinced. "It all sounds pretty far-fetched. Most archaeologists dismiss the idea that medieval Europeans built those Ethiopian churches."

"What if they're wrong? What if the Templars designed the churches and tombs in Lalibela as a miniature map of the Notre Dame cathedrals?"

"Why would they do that?" he asked.

"Maybe as a backup map. In case the cathedrals were ever destroyed."

Malachy had been listening with a quizzical smile to their debate. "Several churches in France did suffer close calls during the French Revolution."

"Even if Lalibela and Virgo are connected," Jaq cautioned, "that still doesn't solve our problem. None of these medieval maps matches up with the constellation or the Lalibela plat."

Boz gazed up at the ceiling again, recalling the Virgo constellation from memory. "The monsignor once told me that cabalists consider the true nature of the world to be the exact reverse of perceived reality. The French Resistance used mirrors to read coded messages in reverse."

"I'm not following," she said.

Boz was talking to himself. "Maybe the Templars set the Lalibela churches as a mirror image of the Virgo stars. Like a reverse schematic on the ground."

She turned the Virgo tracing upside down and positioned the star Spica at the top of the medieval maps, but there was still no correlation. Frustrated, she shook her head and apologized to Malachy. "Looks like we've hit a blind alley. Sorry we wasted your time."

As she walked down Wisconsin Avenue with Boz, the sun began setting over the twin gothic towers of the National Cathedral. Sad to see the last day of her semi-enforced vacation almost over, she stole a glance at him, wondering what he was thinking. "You wanna grab a bite?"

He checked his watch. "It's getting late. I need to file clearance at the Manassas airport before they close flights for the night."

She felt a twinge of regret at the thought of him leaving. She knew that tomorrow she'd have to confront Mayfield. She couldn't keep putting off the inevitable blowback from the treatment-center fiasco. "Back to Europe already?"

"My clients are threatening to fire me."

"I've got a couch. And I cook a mean chicken Marsala."

"I thought men weren't allowed inside the temple of Xenia the Virgin Warrior Princess."

In a show of defiance at his dig to her sexual innocence, she clasped his hand and wouldn't let go. "They say Xenia had a hundred male slaves who always kept her company. ... Will you stay over tonight? I don't mean, you know ..."

Impressed by her bold move, Boz brought up her clasped hand and kissed it. "I guess it'd be okay, now that you're one of the Chosen Ones. But you have to promise to respect me. I'm thinking about trying this virginity thing."

She felt his lips—and then a quick touch of his tongue—before he let her hand drop. She playfully pushed him away. "Hey, just because some distant ancestor of mine ate kosher doesn't mean I'm Jewish. And I'm going to check to see if you've got six toes."

He found her hand again, this time drawing her arm behind her back in an embrace.

As they walked, she began to feel uneasy. She shouldn't be doing this, flirting with a guy who didn't believe in the threat of Hell's punishment. What would Rev. Merry say if he knew she had asked an atheist back to her place? After studying him for several steps, she snuggled closer. "Can I ask you something?"

"I prefer my Marsala with brown rice."

She kicked playfully at his ankle. "When did you stop believing in God?"

He slowed their pace. "Nietzsche said there were two types of people. Those who want to know and those who want to believe. You and I are just different in that way, I guess."

"Everybody believes in God when they're kids. What caused you to change?" She saw that he didn't surrender such intimacies easily, so she squeezed his hand to push him to continue.

Finally, he admitted, "My father died when I was seven. He was only forty-two years old, but the world gave him enough troubles for two lifetimes. He spent his last painful words telling me what happened to my grandfather."

"The one who was in World War II?"

He nodded. "Grandpapa Elie served as the rabbi for a small synagogue in Schwedt, near the Polish border. When the Nazis came to round up his congregation, he gathered them into the synagogue and held to his breast the Torah that had survived in the village for six hundred years. The S.S. officer in charge of the operation decided to create some amusement for his storm troopers. He ordered my father to the front of the congregation. Papa was ten years old at the time. The officer told him he had a choice. Papa could burn the Torah or send his father to his death."

"What did he choose?"

"He burned the Torah."

She wondered what *she* would have done, had this been her dilemma and the book was her family Bible. She tried to brace him with an uplifting thought: "He chose life for your grandpa. God would have approved."

He couldn't look at her. "Grandpa died of a heart attack while watching the Torah destroyed by his own flesh and blood. The night my father told me that story, I vowed never again to pray."

"But you've devoted your life to recovering Jewish relics," she said. "Why do that if you don't believe that they carry divine power?"

He shrugged. "Maybe I haven't been honest with myself."

"How so?"

"Maybe I *do* believe that there's an all-powerful god, and He's just an evil bastard." He tightened his grip on her hand, not realizing that the anger was coursing through his muscles. "If God wanted those artifacts stolen, the only way I can take revenge on Him is by restoring them to their rightful owners.

I wish I could be like you. Makes life a lot easier always believing that a god is looking out for you."

"It's not that easy."

"I've never understood faith," he said.

"I don't think it's supposed to be understood."

"You're too young to remember Jonestown."

"Where those people in Guyana committed suicide?"

"You think they had faith?" he asked.

"Not the right kind."

"And how do you decide which is the right kind?"

She thought for a moment. "Jesus said that by their fruits we shall know them. Suicide is not a fruit of faith."

"Somebody should have told that to those martyrs who chose to face the lions in Rome. What makes you so sure this minister of yours knows more about God than a rabbi or a sheikh?"

"We Christians have an advantage," she said. "We have a book that tells us everything we need to know."

"And which book would that be? The Greek version? The Latin? The Aramaic? The German? The English? They're all different."

"Don't be silly. God's word is God's word."

"So, we're having a nice Cabernet Sauvignon tonight?"

She slapped his shoulder playfully. "You know I don't drink."

"Why not? The Bible says wine is okay. Jesus turned water into wine at the wedding feast in Cana."

"That was unfermented grape juice," she insisted.

"Genesis says that Noah planted a vineyard and drank so much wine that he became drunk. The word used in Hebrew for wine is *yah-yin*, which means fermented."

"Old Testament. Jesus changed all that."

"So when St. Paul told the Ephesians they shouldn't become drunk with wine, he was worried they'd swill too much grape juice and start belching?"

She was stumped. "I'm sure Rev. Merry could explain it."

"No doubt. The godly man who knows it all. ... What about you? I've told you what made me give up my belief. What made you find yours?"

She didn't want to tell him, figuring he'd just scoff at her innocence again. She tried to change the subject by coaxing him to a jewelry store window. "That necklace would make a nice going-away present."

"Answer me, or I'll go back to Knoxville and tell those ladies at the bake sale that you're more Jewish than Moses."

"Extortionist!"

"Come on. Round about's fair play."

She played for time. A kiss would divert him. Then maybe he'd stop asking her so many of these uncomfortable questions. She could just lean over and ... but instead, she gave him what he wanted: an answer. "I never knew who I was growing up. When we moved to Kentucky, the other white kids teased me for being different. And the black kids wouldn't have anything to do with me, either. I didn't have any boyfriends. More of a loner, I guess. Then I met Rev. Merry in law school. For the first time, he made me feel like one of God's children. I started reading the Bible. Every page seemed written for me and my problems."

"How do you feel now? After learning about your ancestry?"

She felt a seep of tears. "Now I *really* don't know who I am."

He hugged her. "Tonight, you're my chef, that's who you are. Let's buy some expensive grape juice and get drunk as Noah."

Jaq awoke with the morning sun in her eyes. Damn, she had overslept on her first day back to work. Mayfield would have her drawn and quartered. She threw on her robe and cracked open the door to the living room. The couch was empty. She found a note on the coffee table:

> *Off to leap the pond. Thanks for dinner. There's still some fermented grape juice in the fridge if you get thirsty. Love, Boz.*

Was that *Love, Boz*, as in you are the love of my life? Or *Love, Boz*, let's pal around again sometime?

And again, he didn't leave a phone number.

She stood in the middle of the living room, the note clutched in her hand. But then she reminded herself that she had no time this morning to ponder the mystery of Boz d'Orville right now. She jumped in the shower, threw on a suit, and grabbed a taxi to Fort Meade.

Forty-five minutes later, she made it through the NSA security checkpoints and walked into the mid-morning meeting.

A staff of twenty fell silent on seeing her at the door.

Mayfield, sitting at the head of a conference table, turned redder than South Carolina on election night. "Ladies and gentlemen, allow me to introduce Jaqueline Quartermane, our new addition to the team. She specializes in taking medical absences and disappearing for days at a time. I hope we didn't interrupt your beauty sleep."

She grabbed an open seat. "Sorry I'm late."

"Not at all," Mayfield snarked. "We were just discussing a few of the inconsequential matters that come across our desks from time to time. Such as how the hell we're going to stop this Pakistani hashish head who's trying to convince half the Muslim world he's the new Superman! I don't suppose you have any great insights to offer on that?"

"As a matter of fact, I do."

Necks straightened in surprise. She knew what they were thinking: This newcomer walks in an hour late and answers in the affirmative what was clearly meant as a rhetorical put-down.

"This ought to be good," Mayfield said. "Let's hear it."

"He hasn't found the Ark yet," she said. "But I think I've narrowed it down to thirteen possible targets where it may be buried. The Mahdi imposter has already hit five of them. Lalibela, Rome, Chartres, Scotland, and Gisors. That leaves eight still untried."

"Why thirteen?" asked a skeptical team member.

"The Knights Templar built thirteen cathedrals."

"Templars?" hooted Mayfield, rolling his eyes.

She didn't back down. "I think the Templars situated the cathedrals in a kind of map code to indicate where the Ark was hidden."

Amused glances and smirks ricocheted across the room.

Mayfield barked, "What kind of drugs did they give you in that asylum?"

"Please, just hear me out. All five locations that Hosaam has hit have Templar connections."

Mayfield's glare tightened. "Where are the next eight?"

She hesitated. "I don't know."

Muted laughter in the room rippled into snorts and guffaws.

"The Templars didn't want them found for some reason," she said. "But if we stake out all the possible Templar sites, we may come up with something."

Mayfield stood and walked around the table to loom over her. "I do things a little differently here than McCrozier does over at that banana republic he runs at State. I know it's a little old-fashioned, but we like to use proven cryptographic techniques, not witch hunches or mystical visions. Let me give you an example of how we approach a problem." He turned and ordered a male security analyst sitting three chairs down: "Burnett, brief her on our target."

The analyst opened his file and flashed the contents of a red-covered binder. "We've combed all of the telephonic communications, online websites and blogs, as well every page of Islamic material ever written on the Mahdi. There's an old tradition in the hadiths of the Koran that says the Mahdi will remove the Ark from Lake Tiberias."

"In Israel?" she asked.

The analyst nodded. "We're zeroing in on the Sea of Galilee area. We have all the Palestinian political factions there under surveillance."

"Do the Israelis know about this?"

Mayfield shook his head sternly. "There's no need to get their hackles up."

She pointed out a flaw in the NSA official's strategy. "If Hosaam thinks the Ark is in Galilee, why is he hitting all of these other locations?"

Mayfield shaded darker. "I don't give a damn where the Ark *is*. Hosaam won't be accepted as the Mahdi unless he convinces the Arab street that he found the relic in Lake Tiberias. Wherever he finds it, he'll hide it in Galilee. And we'll be waiting to take him down before he goes public."

"Seems like that's putting all our eggs in one basket. "If you're wrong—"

"I'm *not* wrong!" Mayfield snapped.

She tried to act unfazed by the verbal assault, but inside she was shaking. "Then you don't need me on this Israel operation. Let me see what I can dig up on the other locations."

He was honed in on her like a red-dot laser. "No."

"Why not?"

Mayfield gestured for his staff to leave the room. When alone with Jaq, he tossed a manila file across the table toward her.

She opened the file and found photos of her with Boz in Tennessee and Washington. "You had me followed?"

"You were given clearance to handle highly-classified information. Then you abscond from that Rhode Island nut house and go traipsing across the country with an unidentified accomplice. A federal judge found probable cause for the surveillance. ... Now, tell me. Who is this man?"

"Or what?"

"You'll be suspended."

She erupted to her feet. "My private life is none of your business!"

Mayfield buzzed in two security officers. "Check her bag. Then escort her off the premises."

She flailed away their pawing hands. "Bastard!"

Mayfield sent her out of the room with a warning. "I'm setting an administrative hearing for Monday morning at nine to review possible violations of the Classified Information Act. This time, I suggest you not be late."

Exhausted and depressed, Jaq sat alone on her bed in her apartment that Friday night. She didn't have the money to hire a lawyer to fight Mayfield, and she wasn't about to impose upon Rev. Merry again, not after wasting his donations on the Godspring fiasco. Afraid of hearing the disappointment in his voice, she hadn't called him after leaving Rhode Island.

At least one thing had gone right that day: she had forgotten to take her travel notebook to work. If Mayfield's goons had found it in her bag, he would have had a field day with it on Monday. *Lord,* she prayed, *if there was ever a perfect time for the Rapture, this weekend would be it.* How wonderful it would feel to be taken up to Heaven and leave these problems behind—except that she would never see Boz again.

That realization gave her a pain in her heart. He wouldn't be taken up with her, that was for sure. He was, after all, an atheist Jewish thief. She had to find a way to bring him to the Lord before it was too late. She imagined the profanities he'd spew if he knew she was going to subtly proselytize him. She grinned, certain she could have him in the arms of the Lord before he knew it, like a live chicken being slowly boiled in a pot without being aware that the temperature was creeping up the entire time.

She reached over her head to the bed shelf and brought down the Mendoca family bible. She opened it to Revelation to remind herself what that blessed day of Heaven would be like. As she read, she started to frown. She remembered that passage differently from her classes. She compared this King James translation with the one in the bible that Rev. Merry had given her. Included in that edition were a commentary and a notation the pastor had made in the margin:

> *We know from the close reading of our Scofield Bible—the only true revelation—that the last of the seven judgments will be for the wicked dead, when the history of the present earth will finally end.*

Boz was right, she realized. There *were* different accounts of God's words. She made a mental note to ask Rev. Merry about the discrepancy when she next saw him. Another of his handwritten comments in the margin read: *How will the End of Time appear to us? Refer to Ezekiel's Wheels within Wheels.* Intrigued, she turned to Ezekiel and read the passage in question:

> *The appearance of the wheels and their work was like unto the colour of a beryl: and they four had one likeness: and their appearance and their work was as it were a wheel in the middle of a wheel.*

Four wheels set within a larger wheel? This Ezekiel contraption sounded like some kind of device with gears that rotated inside a master cylinder, like the chains of a bicycle or the workings of a watch, or even … the combination on a padlock.

She scrambled for her notebook and opened it to the page with the Templar-SATOR square. She drew rings of various sizes around the letters and tried different arrangements. Could the word square have been designed to recreate Ezekiel's wheels within wheels? Maybe the Knights of the Brazen Serpent were passing down the combination codes to manipulate the wheels like a lock:

In her mind, she tried rotating the outer wheel clockwise:

One	Two	Three	Four	Five	Six	Seven
Letter	Letter	Letter	Letter	Letter	Letter	Letter
Turn	Turns	Turns	Turns	Turns	Turns	Turns

ASATO	TASAT	OTASA	ROTAS	OROTA	TOROT	ATORO
TREPR	OREPO	RREPT	OREPA	TREPS	AREPA	SREPT
OENEO	RENER	OENEO	TENET	AENEA	SENES	AENEA
RPERT	OPERO	TPERR	APERO	SPERT	APERA	TPERS
OTASA	TASAT	ASATO	SATOR	ATORO	TOROT	OROTA

Writing down her results, she powered up her laptop and ran an online search for these new combinations. After the tenth word gave her no intelligible results, she figured it was just another blind alley. Halfheartedly, she typed OROTA and got the following entry:

> *Orota is a mountainous region in Eritrea adjacent to Ethiopia. During the 3rd and 4th centuries AD, Eritrea and Orota were part of the Ethiopian kingdom of Axum, which spread from Sudan across the Red Sea to Yemen.*

Lalibela, she remembered, was located in northern Ethiopia, near the Eritrean border. According to this description, that area would have once been known as Orota. The word possibilities from other inner and outer turns in both directions seemed endless. The four wheels of Ezekiel could also have been set around the letters in each quadrant. She drew smaller circles within a larger circle. The graphic formed the Templar Cross:

She played with the wheel in the upper left quadrant. If she kept spinning it, the letters spelled SARAS. Wasn't that the city the monsignor had connected to Chartres? She Googled it and read the search result:

> *SARRAS, sometimes spelled SARAS, was the mystical isle that protected the Holy Grail in the Arthurian legends. In the Lancelot cycle, SARRAS is located somewhere "across the sea," perhaps in Egypt. The word is believed to have given the name "Saracens" for the Muslim fighters in the Crusades. The Grail legends and the knights of the Holy Grail have generated speculation about their possible connection to the Knights Templar.*

She dropped down to the lower left quadrant of her encircled word square: OPOR. If she rotated that wheel two letters to the left, it spelled PORTA from bottom to top, and connected with SARAS.

PORTA SARAS … Port of the Grail?

She typed "Port of the Grail" in the online search box and came up with:

"*'Portugal' may have derived from "Port of the Graal."*

Intrigued, she checked her address book for Lanny Brendan, an intern in the State Department's research division who was a whiz at calculus. She punched in his number on her phone. "Hi, Lanny? It's Jaqie Quartermane. Sorry to call you so late, but I've been struggling with a thorny math problem. First person I thought of was you."

The intern sounded hesitant. "We were told you'd been transferred."

"Just for a few weeks. Nobody over at the NSA can do math. Could you help me out?"

"I guess so."

"Here's the problem. I've got twenty-five letters, four each of A, E, O, T and R. Two 'P's, two 'S's, and one 'N.' I need to know how many different combinations of four letters and five letters can be formed from that group."

"Do they have to spell out actual words?" he asked.

"No, just any combination in fours and fives."

"That's a simple equation of combinatronics," he said. "Let me spit it out on my calculator." After nearly a minute went by, he reported to her, "There are over seven thousand possible combinations of five-letter words."

She fell back into the pillow. "That many?"

"There'd be a few less for the four-letter combinations," the intern said. I'll send over my calculations."

Ten minutes later, her fax machine churned out the intern's formula:

She pulled at her hair in frustration. Now she understood why that Vatican priest had warned her that the square drove investigators mad. It seemed designed to thwart anyone who did not have its cipher codes. She only had two days left to solve its message before Mayfield ruined her career and Hosaam found the Ark. To soothe her nerves, she thumbed through her grandmother's Bible.

A folded parchment fell out.

She picked it up. Unfolding it, she saw that the fragile, yellowed sheet of parchment held a drawing of a woman and a knight surrounded by animals, and a serpent crawling from the man's chest. Meridians of longitude and latitude checkered the page. On the bottom, the word *Canistris* was written in an ancient script. What was such a strange map doing in her family's Bible?

She wondered if that map dealer was still in his shop. She found his card and dialed the number. "Mr. Caverio? Jaqie Quartermane. We met yesterday. Does the name Canistris mean anything to you?"

The dealer didn't answer immediately, evidently surprised by the question. "The Opicinus de Canistris was a Venetian map created in the medieval animistic style. The earliest known version was created in 1335 A.D."

"What are these images on the map?"

"What are you looking at?" he asked.

She was forced into a little white lie. "Just a copy."

"Medieval cartographers adapted geography to human and animal forms. They believed that certain lands carried the essence of living creatures. Give me a moment and I'll pull it up on my screen. ... Ah yes, here it is. Iberia is shown as a woman. The English Channel as a lion."

"And the snake?"

"The serpent emerges from the heart of Egypt. I've heard stories from other dealers ..." He paused on the line, as if debating whether he should reveal what he had nearly uttered.

"Stories about what?"

"That Columbus may have carried a map based on the Canistris. I've never seen a hard copy. Did you find a reproduction in another store?"

"Not exactly. Thanks for your help."

She hung up before he could get wise to her. She placed the page with the Virgo constellation over the Canistris map and turned the tracing upside to mimic a mirror image of the sky, just as Boz had earlier suggested:

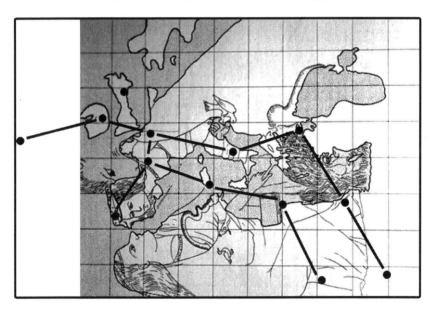

She bounded off the bed with a surge of excitement.

The constellation lined up with Chartres and Rome! Portugal was at the head of the Virgin. Gisors might be the star just north of Chartres. Another star fell on Scotland, and one on Ireland.

But just as quickly, her spirits sank. She couldn't possibly investigate all of these locations in two days. Ireland was the closest to Scotland. Maybe Hosaam would hit there next.

She called the intern at State again. "Lanny, those letter combinations I asked you about. Is there a program that can churn them into a database?"

"I could probably manage it with Oracle SQL or Navicat."

"How long would it take?"

"I've already got it booting up."

While waiting for Lanny's program to power on, she asked him, "You guys in research have all the place names of every town and burgh in every country stored digitally, right?"

"Yeah, we call it the Webcat Gazetteer."

"I need you to pull out every Irish place name with four or five letters. Cross-check the names with the database of the letter combinations you just ran."

Twenty minutes later, she received Lanny's text message with the list of places in Ireland that contained letters in the SATOR-Templar square:

Four-letter names: Tarn Reen Aran Arra Raps Roes Rapa Near Tooa Nora Rapa Nora Nare Tara Nart Roan Nore Raps Aran Toon Tooa

Five-letter names: Tents Posae Porta Rooan Tates Anner Rappa Arena Soran Toran Roran Naran Eaton Soarn Sonna.

She called him back. "Are the daily embassy reports digitized?"

"Yes, ma'am. We started doing that in May."

"I need you to run these thirty-two place names through the archives for the last month. See if anything comes up. Travel warnings, crime incidents, anything at all."

"Back at you soon," he said, signing off.

She hung up and studied the Canistris map again. One of the stars on the Virgo tracing fell over the Mediterranean. The map dealer had told her that medieval cartographers weren't known for their spatial accuracy. She checked the atlas. Could be Mallorca, Rhodes, Sardinia, Malta, or Cyprus. Another star fell on the image of a book along the coast of Africa. That was likely Alexandria. The star to the north might be Istanbul. She traced the constellation eastward and found another star near Jerusalem. And farther south … was that Ethiopia?

Only two stars remained unidentified: The ones farthest east and farthest west, which went off the map. Was she seeing patterns where none existed? She couldn't even be certain if this was a copy of the entire original map.

The phone rang.

It was Lanny getting back to her. "Just one name came up. … Tara."

"Tara? Wasn't that the plantation in *Gone With The Wind?*" She realized from his confused silence that he was probably too young to have ever seen the movie. "Did you find anything else about it?"

"According to this," Lanny said, "Tara is a complex of hills and caverns near the River Boyne. Lots of mysterious stuff about the place."

"Such as?"

"Says here that it was the most sacred site in Ireland. Apparently, a famous relic with mythical powers was once guarded there. They called it the Stone of Destiny."

Her memory flashed back to the conversation she'd had with that Scottish businessman on the flight home from Europe. "I thought the Stone of Destiny was moved to Scotland?"

There was a pause while Lanny read down the agency's aggregate of newspaper stories. "Yeah, eventually it was. But it seems like other relics may still be buried there. And here's something else interesting. It was a capital offense to light a fire within sight of Tara."

"Why would that be?"

"I'm not sure, ma'am. Maybe the Druids used it as an astrological observatory and didn't want artificial light to blind their measurements."

"What's caused Tara to come up on your check?"

"The Irish government is building a new motorway through the Skryne Valley. There was a big protest there last week about contractors destroying old underground vaults. Probably didn't help that some of the hired workers were from Dubai and Yemen."

She slammed the mattress with her fist. *Laborers from the Middle East!*

That conniving Mahdi imposter must have targeted Tara. After all, this Irish construction job had all the same fingerprints that he had left at Lalibela, Rome, Chartres, Gisors, and Macbeth's Hill.

She crossed another place name off her list. Six down. Seven to go. But which location would Hosaam hit next?

She studied the Canistris map again. Ireland lay beyond Scotland. Maybe he was working his way west. She didn't have any other clues to go on, so she might as well try that possibility. But to follow through on that lead, she'd have to identify the star that extended off the map into the Atlantic. One of the latitude lines ran through the star representing Tara. The most westerly star of the Virgo tracing looked to be about eight degrees below that line.

She searched the web for the latitude of Tara and came up with 53.3267 degrees. She found the 53rd parallel in an atlas and subtracted eight degrees. She traced her finger along the 45th latitude line until she hit land.

Nova Scotia … *New Scotland.*

She dived into her pillow, defeated. She didn't have the money to buy a ticket to Canada on such short notice, and the train would take too long. There was no way she could get up there before Hosaam, unless …

She scrambled for her phone and called the control tower at the Manassas Airport. "This is Jaqueline Quartermane with the National Security Agency. I need to know if a Moses D'Orville has filed a manifest."

"Let me check."

Moments later, the flight controller came back on the line. "Sorry, no pilot by that name."

"Have you had a white Cessna take off for Europe today?"

"We've got one on the runway right now."

She pressed the phone to her forehead, debating the wisdom of doing what she was thinking. *What are you getting yourself into, Jaq? The guy romances you with sweet embraces and tender kisses and then skedaddles off the next morning without even waking you to say goodbye. You're out of your league with his type. He's probably playing you. Just let it go.*

"Hello?" the controller asked, wondering if she was still on the line.

She threw her legs over the bed and kicked the rails under the mattress with her heels several times in frustration. Calming down, she brought the phone to her ear again. "Tell the pilot to cut his engine. He has a passenger on the way."

The controller reported back. "He's not being real cooperative on that."

She glanced over at the refrigerator, and grinned. Returning the receiver to her ear, she told the controller: "The pilot in that Cessna out there has been drinking alcohol to excess. Pull him off the plane and give him a Breathalyzer test. And while you're at it, make him walk a straight line ten times. I should be there by the time you have the results."

THIRTY-TWO

"Colon … Colon. …The name does not sound Genoan."

Cristobal Colon set his teeth in anger, but he did not take Isabella's bait, remembering Pero's warning that the clever Castilian queen rarely abided the usual niceties of court. He had yet to offer his credentials, and already she was boring in on his *bona fides*.

Torquemada sat smirking at Colon's scruffy doublet and salt-chewed shoes. Arrayed with other members of the queen's council, which included Cardinal Mendoza and the Dominican Talavera, the haughty inquisitor leaned to Isabella's ear and said, "You should not waste your time on such penurious importuners."

Colon's blood began to boil. Did these Castilians expect him to stand mute while they carried on as if he were not present?

"I agreed to give him hearing as a favor to Medina-Celi," the queen told the inquisitor. "I am told he has a naval enterprise to propose."

Talavera scoffed. "He looks more like a cobbler than a seaman."

Agreeing with his Dominican brother, Torquemada offered a reminder to the woman for whom he had served as confessor since her childhood: "The king has counseled us not to become distracted from Our Lord's important work. We must remain steadfast in our endeavors to drive the infidels—"

"Colombo!" shouted Colon.

The court turned on the pushy supplicant, stunned by his outburst.

"My name is Colombo in Genoa. In Iberia, I am called Colon. And in the Indies, they will call me Don Colon."

The royal councilors stewed in dangerous silence.

Then, like an explosion, Isabella let out a laugh of astonishment. "I know not which is more remarkable. That you, *Seignior*, expect to be called by *any* name in the Indies, or that you feel entitled to a nobleman's rank."

Colon bowed slightly, remembering his assigned part. He suspected that more than mere intellectual interest had played a role in Isabella's grant of this audience. He and the queen were, after all, the same age, and rumors were rampant that her husband stayed away on campaigns much too long for her pleasure. He locked on her eyes, and when she trumped him with a girlish smile, he surrendered in their private joust. "My dream is indeed to hear my name spoken in the Indies, but only as a servant of the star-crowned Woman of Revelation."

Isabella stared at him quizzically, as if wondering how he had become privy to her most intimate prayers. "You are a student of theology?"

He pressed a hand to his heart. "A mariner must learn all there is to know about the cosmos. To do that, one must seek the Holy Spirit's guidance."

"And how do you find such guidance?"

"The art of sailing is favorable for studying the world's secrets. The Holy Dove reveals the future with nautical signs."

The queen held a mystified glare on him, looking uncertain what to make of his claims. "Why have you come to Castile?"

He resolved to give her no time to take counsel of her qualms. "The prophet Joachim of Fiore foresaw that a Spaniard would rebuild the Temple of Solomon. I believe Your *Reina* to be that presaged benefactor."

The Dominicans bristled with indignation; a layman's claim of direct communication with the Holy Spirit whiffed of heresy.

Yet to her councilors evident dismay, Isabella reacted as if she had found a kindred soul. Drawing closer to the Genoan, she inquired: "And have your visions told you how the Temple will be resurrected?"

Colon risked meeting her halfway, closing the traditional royal space of deference. "By your armies. Financed with gold from the Indies."

Isabella halted his advance with an upturned palm. She walked to a window and watched the galleys being loaded on the Guadalquivir River. "The Venetian Polo said it would take ten thousand nautical miles to sail to the Indies. Even with favorable winds, you would require a hundred days. Such a feat of endurance has never been approached."

"Polo spent too many months on a camel," he insisted. "There are three-hundred-and-sixty degrees of circumference around the Earth. The Egyptian cosmographers have measured each degree to fifty-six-and-two-thirds Arab miles, which equals only forty-five nautical miles. By sailing on twenty-eight degrees latitude to decrease the distance, I am certain India can be reached within twenty-four hundred nautical miles. A mere twenty days."

She turned and bored in on him with her hard sapphire eyes. "Ptolemy said the degree measured fifty nautical miles."

"The Greek astronomer was a pagan," he reminded her. This queen, he knew, had made no secret of her conviction that the recent victory over the Moors at Ronda was the first of many prophesied events that heralded the End Times. As instructed by Pero, he now played on her vanity by quoting Psalms. "'They that go down to the sea in ships, they that do business in great waters, the Lord bringeth them unto their desired haven.'"

Isabella remained frozen in meditation at the window.

He allowed the verse to work its full effect, then suggested softly: "If God wishes the Temple rebuilt, who can doubt that He will send His stewards to the far ends of the earth to accomplish the task?"

Without turning, Isabella asked: "What would you require?"

His heartbeat quickened. She had swallowed the hook, and now he had to draw her in. "Three caravels. Manned with crews of my choosing and provisioned for a year. I will sail under the title of Don with all rights accruing an admiral of Castile. I will also be paid a tenth of all revenues and metals discovered, along with an eighth of all revenues gained by trade."

Isabella ignored the murmuring about his audacious demands. Instead, she circled him like a tigress feeling out the strength of her prey. "The crown has never awarded such generous terms to a private enterpriser."

"God lifts all who carry His Cross," he said.

While Colon and the queen sparred, Talavera read some papers handed to him by a functionary. The friar cleared his throat to gain their attention and waved the documents. "It seems, *Seignior*, that you are a better poet than navigator. I have been advised that you presented this same proposal to King John in Portugal. And he rejected it as unfeasible."

Blindsided, Colon struggled to check his temper. "I hope My Grace is not equating the perspicacity of the queen to that of a Portuguese monarch?"

Talavera met that insolent parry with a haughty sneer. "I also see from these reports that you have many Jews among your supporters."

Show no fear. The duel is now on in full tilt.

He had indeed received assistance from several notable Castilian Jews, including Isabella's own tax collector, to promote this Indies expedition. And yet only now did he realize that these Dominicans had sent their agents into the darkest corners of the juderias in Toledo and Seville to gather surveillance on him. Recovering from this dangerous exposure, he confirmed the report with an affectation of nonchalance. "The Jews are adept at making maps and astrolabes. Our Lord said they are to be used to bring forth the Kingdom."

Isabella tested him with a jarring silence. Then, she announced: "I am aggrieved, *Seignior* Colon."

He braced for an arrest—until her glare melted into a flirtatious pout.

"You went to the Portuguese first?"

He bowed again, this time releasing a slow breath of relief. "My brother lives in Lisbon. I spent a few years there learning mapmaking. I am a wandering mariner with a passion for Our Lord's mission. I came to see the error of my judgment. God has always meant you to be the sponsor of this endeavor."

Isabella dissembled a lack of interest in his proposal by rifling through a pile of correspondence. After allowing him to suffer in hope for nearly a minute, she looked up again, acting surprised to find him still present. "You navigate a council chamber well enough, *Seignior*. You are clearly devoted to God. Unfortunately, my husband and I are hard-pressed to fund our war in Granada. I cannot offer a surety for your voyage."

Colon tried to mask his desperation with another bow, but this one he snapped off in a curt manner to convey his dismay at her shortsightedness. "I am nevertheless grateful for your consideration. I will take my petition to England and France and impose upon you no further."

Isabella repulsed that veiled threat with a glower of challenge. "Genoan, if in those kingdoms you find your Star-Crowned Queen of Revelation, I suggest you take up their offer." The corners of her mouth turned up slightly, forming the first hint of a taunting smile. "Until then, you are welcome to remain in Castile and benefit from the wisdom of our sages."

The Southern Seas
August, 1486

Dias kept staring at his compass on the aftcastle of his flagship, not knowing what to make of the needle's gyrations. He had sailed the *Sao Cristovao* over two hundred miles south of Cape Cross, where a year earlier the mariner Cao had erected a *padrao* pillar to mark the farthest reach of the expeditions. But now the lodestone was acting strangely. Had the magnetic poles reversed in these virgin waters below the equator? He searched the sky for gulls. Land had last been sighted land thirteen days ago, when a gale blew his two caravels and small provisions ship off the coast of Africa. He had confided the truth to no one, not even his brother, Diogo.

He was lost.

His crew glared up at him with hysteria rising in their red-rimmed eyes. Veteran seamen could smell approaching death before even carrion crows gained the scent. Had the Sea of Darkness sucked them into its whirling pull? Was the angle of descent too steep to allow a return home? Their barrels of potable water were nearly dry, and even if they stumbled upon land in the next day or two, there was no assurance that a well guarded by friendly natives could be located in time.

"We should turn back," whispered his pilot, Pero d'Alenquer.

Dias smiled grimly; when King Joäo had insisted that only lateen-rigged caravels could reach African Guinea, the cocksure d'Alenquer had boasted he could accomplish the feat with a square-sailed *navio redondo*. Now, cuffed by the rough seas here, Dias could only hope that they survived to endure the king's chastisement for placing too much trust in the square sails.

"The headwinds here are diabolical," the pilot insisted. "If we continue south, we'll only keep bloodying our heads against this invisible wall."

Go farther.

Dias heard that raspy voice as clearly as if the Old Man were standing next to him. He had not told his crew of the true nature of their mission; if they knew what awaited them, none would have signed on. He prayed the Greek Ptolemy was wrong about the existence of a landmass connecting Africa to Asia. The Order's cosmographers dismissed the possibility of a water route to the Indies, but the Old Man had insisted to his last breath that the sea curled below Africa.

You cannot find a peril so great that the hope of reward will not be greater.

Only now did Dias fully appreciate the terrors that Eannes had suffered at Cape Bojador. He remembered what Eannes had told him and the other squires years ago: *A mariner has one great voyage in him.* This plunge into the unknown might be his last chance to prove his worthiness of the Old Man's confidence.

With a heavy sigh of trepidation, he ordered the pilot: "Turn east."

Alexandria, Egypt
July, 1488

A Jew hiding as a Christian hiding as a Mohammedan.

That riddle of existence kept looping through Pero's fevered mind. Panicked, he writhed on his cot and cried out, "Catrina! Am I dying?"

He felt a hand press against his mouth.

"You must be quiet, Master Pero! Else the infidels will discover us."

Pero ... that name rattled his memory. *Sim*, it was coming back to him now. He was Pero da Covilha, a spy on a mission for the Order of Christ. But who was this man hovering over him? Recoiling into the corner, he drew his dagger. "Away from me, assassin!"

"I am your companion, Afonso Paiva. The illness has dangerously loosened your tongue. You must be still or we will be found out."

"Illness?"

"You have been delirious with the Nile Death for three days. The Egyptians now suspect us, for only Christians and Jews suffer the plague here."

A shrill sound hurt Pero's ears. "What is that noise?"

"The infidels are calling their brethren to prayer."

Disoriented, he gazed down at his strange garb. "What am I wearing?"

"The robes of a Moslem merchant," Afonso whispered to his ear. "They are our disguises."

Pero fought to his elbows and peered out through the archer slit. The streets teemed with infidels hurrying toward their mosques. Slowly, the sights and smells of the bustling harbor revived his memory. Two years ago, he had left Portugal on foot, setting out first for Barcelona. Paiva, assigned to accompany him because Jewish merchants never traveled alone, had been told only that they were heading overland to find spices.

"My lord," Paiva said, rousing him from his straying thoughts. "The Sultan has confiscated the cargo of honey we purchased in Rhodes."

Rhodes.

His febrile thoughts were slowly becoming more lucid. Before crossing to Egypt, he and Paiva had met on the isle of Rhodes with two friars from the Knights Hospitallers, the rival order that had confiscated the properties of the Templars. Those friars had led them to the vault where—

"I have no means to employ a physician!" Paiva cried.

Pero struggled to maintain a clear mind, fearful that he might inadvertently speak Portuguese in his deliriums and divulge the true purpose of his journey to the Arabs.

Paiva inched closer to his ear. "There is a Levantine waiting outside. When I thought all was hopeless, he appeared to me in the market. He claims to be a healer."

A flash of movement flickered in the corner of Pero's eye. He turned and squinted at the door. Lurking there was a swarthy man with irises like those of wild Gizan cats. Was he hallucinating again? The intruder's black robe appeared cinched by a brooch with a snake coiled around the Star of David. He rubbed the fever mucous from his swollen eyes. Where had he seen that insignia before? Of course, when he had translated Prester John's communication for the Old Man. He remembered the emissary who wore it that day had been a member of an Egyptian hermitage called the Theban Brotherhood.

The Egyptian healer came forward. Placing a palm on Pero's burning forehead, he turned to Paiva and said: "I must minister to your master alone."

Paiva hesitated, reluctant to leave his comrade, but Pero waved him out.

Alone now with his patient, the healer stoked the fire until it was brought to a rage. He drew from under his robes a small sack containing pungent herbs. He boiled a medicinal tea and offered it to Pero. "The hyssop and thyme will ease the *febris*."

Within minutes, Pero began sweating profusely. Wiping the beads from his brow, he asked the healer: "Who are you?"

"I have been sent by the Qadosh Fathers."

"You practice the Mohammedan faith?" When the healer frowned to negate that suggestion, Pero, alarmed, tried again. "Then you are a Christian."

The healer shook his head as he brought the cup of tea to Pero's lips for another sip. "Those faiths are but streams from the first river."

Pero swallowed the warm concoction, keeping his eyes fixed on the coiled serpent engraved on the healer's brooch. "Are you an adherent of Satan?"

"Why do you ask such a question?"

Pero pointed to the serpentine insignia on the healer's brooch. "You walk behind the Tempter of the Garden of Eden."

The healer smiled at his confusion. "You disembarked first in Rhodes."

Pero nodded uncertainly, wondering how the man had learned of this.

"You do know how that isle came by its name?"

Pero shook his head.

"The Ophites were wisdom teachers of the Great Serpent. They settled on the isle because it teemed with serpents. They named it Rhodus from Rhad, their word for Serpent Island."

Pero pressed his shaking palms to his eyes, trying to sharpen his thinking. Could he trust this mysterious stranger? The infidels had spies behind every corner in this part of the world, and this Qadosh holy man's reference to Rhodes seemed more than coincidental, for he and Paiva had been ordered to stop on that island to search the vaults of the old Templar castle.

"I come from the Tribe of the Serpent. We have been waiting for the Knights of the Temple."

Pero wasn't sure he had heard correctly. Why would this healer expect to find the ghosts of the Templars in Egypt? "Waiting for them to do what?"

The healer checked the door to confirm that no one was listening. "Before leaving Palestine, the Christian knights vowed to return and finish what they had left undone. For centuries, my brethren have preserved the gnosis."

"What is this gnosis you speak of?"

"There was a sign agreed upon to be used by our envoys."

Remembering his instructions, Pero drew a series of Latin letters on the dirt floor and quickly erased them with the hem of his robe.

Satisfied with the confirmation of trustworthiness, the Egyptian revealed: "We protect the rituals and dimensions of King Solomon's Temple. My brothers, the Therapeutae, transmitted the secrets to Moses. His Israelites maintained the Serpent on the cross in the Jerusalem sanctum and passed on its mysteries to the Dionysian Artificers of the Greeks, the Mithraists of the Romans, and the Essenes of the Judean wilderness. When the French holy man Clairvaux sent his knights here during the wars of the faiths, they too received the initiation."

Pero was dumbfounded. Could it truly be that this desert healer and his followers had never been advised of the French calamity nearly two centuries ago? There was no way to prepare him for the disappointment, so he told the Egyptian straightly: "The Templars no longer walk this earth under that name. Most were murdered by their enemies, the French king and the pope."

Shaken, the healer turned inward, praying for the souls of his lost spiritual allies from the north. "Why then do *you* come to Egypt?"

"My brothers, the Order of Christ, have taken up the duty of fulfilling the Templar plan."

The Egyptian seemed comforted by that news. He removed his brooch and offered it as a talisman of protection. "When you regain your strength, follow the Nile and turn east into Arabia. Go to the monastery atop Mt. Sinai where Moses taught the Serpent Wisdom. Show the archivist this signet and tell him that Brother Climacus bids you examine the codex titled *The Ladder of Divine Ascent*. On the leaf marked XXXIII, you will find a map to your destination."

"And after the Sinai?"

The Egyptian chose not to answer him directly. "Learn the ways of the Bedouins. You will enter lands where no Christian has ever stepped foot. If challenged, say only that you are on pilgrimage to Mecca. The Mohammedans deem it a holy duty to assist all pilgrims."

Pero reached to clasp the healer's hand in gratitude.

THIRTY-THREE

Dead tired from the overnight flight, Boz sped their rented Range Rover out of the Halifax airport lot and headed south along the coast. He glanced over at Jaq and caught her playing with her Blackberry again. "You're going to drive us both crazy with that thing."

She kept her eyes glued to her newest obsession, a 3-D software app that let her rotate the wheels of the SATOR-Templar square with a swish of her index finger, as if she were manipulating a digital Rubik's Cube. "Maybe the center 'N' is a wild-card letter. Look, I formed RONE. That could mean Rome. And another turn spells NOTRE. That would be Chartres. ROSS could be Rosslyn in Scotland."

He tried to steal the phone, mumbling about tossing it out the window, but she blocked his reach with her shoulder. Spinning a few more gyrations on the screen, she came up with another word: TERES. She consulted her Latin-English dictionary: *Rounded or well-turned, as if on a lathe or wheel.* She waved the screen at him. "See? They're telling me I'm getting closer!"

He rubbed his sleepy eyes, trying to wake up. "Are we just going to drive around until we see a sign that says 'Ark of the Covenant Buried Here'?"

"Don't be such a moping smart ass. You know you would have missed me too much if you'd gone back to Paris."

"Aren't you supposed to be at work on Monday?"

"Just a little hearing on the future of my career, is all. If I don't come up with something fast, I'll be handling traffic tickets for the public defender's office."

"You do know that Nova Scotia is larger than Massachusetts?"

"Let's stop at a library. We'll get some maps and travel guides."

He saw a tavern and pulled into its empty lot. "I've got a better idea."

"It's ten in the morning!"

"You've driven me to drink."

When he made good on his threat to leave her in the Rover, Jaq huffed out and followed him into a dark pub that reeked of beer and cigarettes. He had already sidled up to the bar. Motioned over, she wiped the dust from a stool covered with torn red vinyl before sitting on it.

A burly bartender in a logger's checkered shirt two sizes too small finally sauntered out from the kitchen. "We don't serve breakfast."

"I'll bet you serve *my* breakfast," Boz said, affecting a passable Canadian accent. "I'd give my left one for a Willie's Highland."

The bartender suddenly lost his surly attitude. "You've had a Willie's, eh?"

"I told those lads in Dublin that they'd start using Guinness for motor oil once they tried Canada's finest. The ol' lady here will have cranberry juice."

"Preacher's daughter?"

"Never touches the sin sauce. She's a hellcat in the sack, though."

Astounded at how smoothly Boz had shape-shifted into a believable redneck, Jaq was determined to put the record straight. "We're not a couple."

Winking at Boz in some male code, the bartender opened the bottle with a flick of national pride. "What brings you folks to our neck of the woods?"

Boz brushed his teeth with his first gulp. "We're jonesin' for moose season."

The bartender kept leering at Jaq's breasts. "Not real talkative, is she?"

Before she could explode in a tirade, Boz silenced her with a beer-sloppy kiss and surfaced licking his lips. "That's just the way I like my womenfolk. Still waters run deep, ya know. Besides, she performs her best oratory with the boom end of a Four-fitty-four Casull."

She slapped Boz's pawing hand away. "I've had just about enough of—"

"You got that flamethrower out in the truck?" The bartender tried to see through a smoke-smeared window. "I'd love to fire off a couple clips."

"Left it in the Airstream down at the trailer park." Boz downed another swig of Willie's finest and extended his hand. "I'm Jack McGann."

"Sol Guthrie."

Boz practiced taking a one-eyed aim down an imaginary gun sight. "Yeah, I let the little lady come along to search for Bigfoot while I track game. Ever since we got that Discovery Channel on the telly, she's been obsessed with finding the damn creature. I'm starting to think she's got a thing for hairy dudes."

Jaq glowered at his ribs, trying to decide which one to crack. "Can we get out of here now?"

"Bigfoot, eh?" Sol seemed oblivious to both Boz's sarcasm and Jaq's disgust. "The last sighting of the old boy up here was over on Oak Island."

Boz stirred the ghosts with a belch while elbowing her. "What'd I tell you, hon? I ain't never left a bar stool without being more educated."

She leapt grumbling off her stool and headed for the Range Rover.

"Course, there's been a lot of strange stuff reported on that island," Sol added. "The whole damned place is haunted, if you ask me. Strange lights at night. Lots of Masonic connections."

She stopped at the door, and turned. "Did you say Masons?"

Still on his stool, Boz took another slurp and mumbled as if he half-cared: "Aren't those the guys who drive the miniature cars in parades?"

"Nah, them's the Shriners," Sol said. "The Masons are part of the Illuminati. Lots of famous Masons have tried to find a treasure that's supposed to be buried in a shaft on the island. "

Intrigued, Jaq returned to her perch at the bar. "Really?"

Sol leaned in for a better view of her cleavage. "Oh, yeah. FDR, for one."

"President Roosevelt?"

"He was still just a young fella at the time. Spent an entire summer digging around that island with other members of the Trifecta Commission. But if you're thinking about meetin' up with Bigfoot on Oak Island, you can forget about it. Some wealthy foreigners purchased the island a couple of months ago. They won't let anybody near it."

"What was the name of—"

Boz kicked her ankle under the bar. Draining his bottle, he crooned: "By golly, could it be that this Willie's brew has gotten even tastier? Fill me up again, will you, Solomon?" He slapped down a fifty-dollar bill to portend a generous gratuity. "So, what's down that ol' rabbit hole, anyway?"

"Everybody's got their theories. Blackbeard's gold. Captain Kidd's booty. Viking loot. Francis Bacon's secret manuscripts."

Boz pointed an admiring finger at his new source for local gossip. "Yeah, but what's the best damn barkeep on Mahone Bay think?"

Try as he might, Sol couldn't hold out. "The treasure of the Templars."

Boz fiddled with a stray matchbox. "Templars? Never heard of them."

Sol grimaced as if insulted. "You don't read much, do you, pal?"

"Always been a little slow on the school stuff."

An antique coat of arms on the wall distracted Jaq. "Is that your family?"

"Damn right it is, lassie." Sol barreled his chest in a ridiculous Celtic swagger. "The Guthries came here with the Sinclairs from Angus. An old clan legend says that some of the Templars sailed with them here to Arcadia."

Hearing that, she nearly slid off her stool. "Arcadia?"

"That's what they used to call this region," Sol said.

A chain of words cascaded through Jaq's brain: ARCADIA … ARCA … ARA … ARA REPO. Now that she thought about it, she remembered coming across some research about Francis Bacon wanting to form a New Jerusalem in a paradise of free conscience called Arcadia. Hadn't there also been something about Bacon and a *Rota Mundi?* "Would that name have come from—"

"Hell, hon!" Boz slammed his bottle to the bar. "Those bucks'll be halfway to Manitoba if we don't get a move on!"

Interrupted again, Jaq glared at him, wondering if he was ever going to let her finish a sentence.

But he just pulled out a thumbtack stuck in the wall and, taking two quarters from his pocket, placed the tack on top and wrapped another fifty-dollar bill around the makeshift dart. He sent the donation airborne with a flick of his finger, and the money stayed pinned to the ceiling. Escorting Jaq out with a hand to her elbow, he saluted the bartender goodbye. "If Bigfoot ever comes in, buy him a couple of Willie's compliments of the old lady here, will you, Sol?"

Sol's grin could have been the model for a warning poster in a dental office.

Holding hands like newlyweds, Jaq and Boz walked into a local real estate office.

A female agent greeted them. "May I help you?"

Jaq snuggled closer to her fake husband. "We're looking for our first house. We just moved to the area. To be honest, we don't know the neighborhoods."

The realtor shot forward and went into action before her colleagues could steal the walk-ins. "I'd be happy to help. What's your price range?"

"All we need is a little cabin," Boz said.

The realtor's enthusiasm deflated. "I'll have one of my junior associates—"

"Two million tops," he added.

The realtor hit the cancel button on the call to her flunky.

"He likes to fish," Jaq said. "We're hoping for something around water."

The realtor ushered them into a conference room and turned on a laptop computer. "You've come to the right place. We have more beach-front properties on inventory than any agency in Halifax." She punched in her password into the keyboard. With a remote, she operated a graphics program from the computer that flashed photographs of houses onto a large flat-screen television mounted on the wall. "This one has twelve bedrooms and three Jacuzzis."

"Actually, some friends told us about an area that sounded perfect." Jaq turned to Boz and purred, "What was that name again, hon? Oakville?"

Boz imitated a monkey scratching his scalp. "No, I think it was two words, sweetie."

"Oak Island?" the realtor asked.

"Yes, that's it!" Jaq gushed.

"I'm afraid your friends were mistaken. There are no housing developments on Oak Island. It's never been zoned for habitation."

Jaq put on her best pouty face. "There aren't even any lots for sale there?"

The realtor shook her head. "No one can get on the island."

Jaq sagged her shoulders. "How disappointing."

"Not to worry." The realtor began scrolling through her computer database. "We'll find your dream house for you."

Jaq stumbled and flung the back of her hand to her forehead.

The realtor caught her before she collapsed. "Are you okay?"

"Sweetie pie," Boz scolded. "Did you eat that granola bar I gave you?"

Jaq shook her head as she sank into the chair, too weak to speak.

"She's diabetic," Boz explained. "You wouldn't happen to have a vending machine in the building, would you?"

"No, I'm sorry. But I may have something in my desk in the back."

Boz hurried the realtor from the room. "And I'll check in the car."

When they were gone, Jaq shut the door and rolled up to the laptop. The program was still logged into the shared database of properties accessible only by licensed agencies. She typed in "Oak Island." A page opened with statistics on the most recent sale. She found the buyer: *Bilqis Development, LLC.*

The door opened.

The realtor walked in a step ahead of Boz. She unwrapped a candy bar and handed it to Jaq. "Here you are, dear."

Jaq quickly hit the "Off" key on the laptop as she stumbled to her feet.

"Are you feeling better, peaches?" Boz asked her in baby talk.

"Much better." Jaq took a bite of the bar. "I just needed a moment."

Boz pawed at her shoulders, giving her a groping massage. "I'd better get you back to the hotel, hon. We can't be too careful with your condition."

The realtor blinked with concern. "Condition?"

"We're pregnant with triplets." Boz ignored Jaq's glare warning him that he was pouring it on too thick now.

The realtor sized Jaq up and down, perplexed by her slender figure. "There are still several houses I'd like to show you."

Boz hurried Jaq from the conference room. "The doctor says she's such a delicate flower that I need to keep her barefoot and in the kitchen." Slapping her bottom to prod her outside, he waved to the realtor. "We'll contact you after the babies arrive."

Jaq groaned as she loaded another roll onto the microfilm scanner in the research room of the Halifax *Chronicle-Herald* newspaper. "Haven't they heard of digital archives in Canada? This could take us a month."

Hovering over her, Boz gave up on watching the articles scroll down. "You're not going to find anything about Bilqis in the papers here. Hosaam probably paid off the editors to keep the sale quiet. That bartender said FDR moled around on

Oak Island before he became president. The Roosevelts were a famous family. There had to be an article in the local rag about when he came here."

"What year did he vacation in Nova Scotia?"

"The encyclopedia said 1909."

She opened the metal file drawer and pulled out the roll for June through August of that year. She spun it from week to week until she was nearly blind from staring at the poor resolution. She was about to give up when a headline in the society section caught here eye: *Teddy Roosevelt's Cousin Spends Summer Searching for Oak Island Treasure.* "Here we go."

Boz honed in on the screen. "Was the island ever excavated?"

She skipped down to the paragraphs that gave a short history of Oak Island. "Look at this! The shaft is booby-trapped. Five men have lost their lives trying to reach the bottom of the hole."

"When was it discovered?"

She kept reading. "Just after the Revolutionary War. Three boys found a depression under a large tree. They dug into a layer of flagstones two feet down. Then they went another ten feet lower and found a layer of oak logs. Same thing at twenty and thirty feet."

"Sounds like somebody went to a lot of trouble to hide something there."

She leaned closer to the screen. "Here's something else interesting. A stone with mysterious writing on it was discovered ninety feet down."

"What'd it reveal? The Willie's brew recipe?"

She rolled to the next page. "Apparently, the stone disappeared several years ago. But one of the men who found it made a drawing of the markings on it. They've got a picture of here in a sidebar with the story. It says most people think they're directions of some kind. But nobody's been able to get below the level where the stone was discovered."

Boz was wearing out the carpet pacing back and forth behind her. "Did that realtor's database include a corporate address for legal service of process on Bilqis Development?"

"Given my delicate condition, I only had time to waddle over to the laptop for a quick glance." She shot him a feisty look while racking her memory. "I think it was listed at an industrial park in Halifax. Something like ... Burnside?"

Boz took another look at the glyphs in the microfilmed article. "Print us a copy of this."

Dressed in a white jumpsuit, Boz walked up to the security guard at the Burnside Commercial Complex, a series of industrial park offices in Dartmough, across the harbor from Halifax. "I've got a furniture delivery for Bilqis Development. Where's the loading dock?"

The guard checked his roster. "You're a little late."

"Yeah? How come?"

"Bilqis closed up shop this morning. The moving truck left two hours ago."

Boz had to think fast. Asking for a description of the fleeing tenants might draw suspicion, so he tried another approach. "My boss'll can my ass if I don't leave a delivery notice on the door. Legal stuff. What was that office number?"

The guard stared at him for a dangerous moment. "Hell, I'll just have to take the damn thing down. But you gotta do what you gotta do, I guess. Forty-five eighty-one. Don't tape it. That sticky stuff is hell to scrape off."

Giving him a thumbs up, Boz released a held breath as he walked out of the kiosk. He turned the corner, where Jaq was waiting out of sight in the Range Rover, and signaled for her to pick him up. Jumping into the passenger seat, he whispered, "Hosaam scampered off this morning. He must know we're here nosing around. Drive down that street over there."

When they came aside the office in question, Boz got out and tried the door. It was locked, and the windows were coated dark to prevent peering in. He walked to the rear of the building and saw two haulers loading trash bags into a garbage truck in the alley. He ambled over, acting as if he just wanted to shoot the bull. "Hot day for that kind of work." Receiving an unfriendly grunt in response, he followed up: "You cleaning out 4581?"

"What's it to you?" one of the haulers grumbled.

He slipped the surly yahoo a hundred bucks. "My wife is sleeping with the asshole who's been renting that office. I'd be grateful if you could tell me what they left inside."

The cash worked like truth serum. "The place is as empty as my fridge," the garbage man said. "Didn't look like much was going on in there. A desk. Lots of old newspapers on the floor. The bastards were too damn lazy to put their litter in the cans. Looks like they left in a hurry. So, you think the tenant was using this office to screw your old lady on the sly, huh."

"I'm gonna ask him that very question when I find him." Boz glanced at the two trash bags that the hauler was about to toss into his truck. "How about you let me take those off your hands."

The hauler looked around. "I could get fired for that."

Boz slipped another wad of cash into the man's front pocket. "Just in case, this oughta keep you fed and watered for a few months."

Boz pulled the Range Rover into an isolated picnic spot in Point Pleasant Park, a forested municipal oasis on the southern tip of the Halifax peninsula. He and Jaq jumped out and dumped the contents of the garbage bags on the ground to search for anything that might offer a lead.

"Why would Hosaam leave his research files behind?" she asked.

Boz shrugged. "Maybe he's too cheap to buy a shredder. Or maybe he and his goons didn't have time to get rid of them." He smelled the inside of a wrapper. "Chickpeas and hummus. Still fresh."

Jaq found the torn corner of a document that contained some kind of sketch. She poked through the debris for the other parts of the drawing, and pieced the puzzle together:

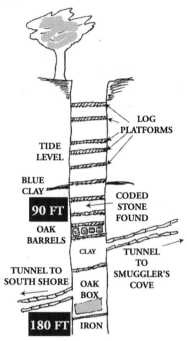

She read what appeared to be an engineer's summary of an inspection. "This must be a cross-section of the shaft. It says here that it was built with two horizontal tunnels."

Boz came over and examined what she had found. "One tunnel runs to a place called Smuggler's Cove. The other one goes to South Shore. These horizontal tunnels must have been designed to flood with the tidewater if anyone tries to go lower in the vertical shaft."

She showed him an addendum that had once been stapled to the sketch. "Looks like somebody was drilling core samples around the shaft. "

"They must have been poking around for another way in."

She rifled through the pile and dug out another newspaper article, dated 1976. A paragraph circled in red ink stating that some diggers had hit metal links and spruce planks about a hundred feet down. According to the article, every time someone tried to damn the water tunnels, the shaft threatened to collapse. She read a paragraph aloud for Boz's benefit. "Before the cave-in, the exploration team drove a steel tube into the ground a few yards northeast of the original pit and lowered a camera into the hole. Images caught by the camera included a severed hand and a wooden crate."

Holding his nose, Boz pulled a yellowed document from the mess. He turned the paper over and found a map of the island on it. "I wonder what this stone triangle on it means?"

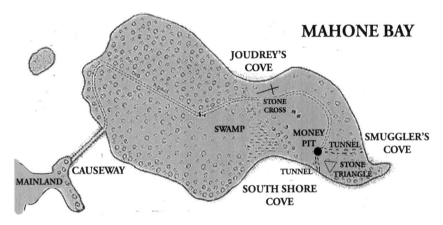

"Maybe it's some kind of ancient monument," she said. "See, there's a stone cross, too."

Boz turned the map sideways. "Let me see the copy of those stone markings from that FDR newspaper story."

She pulled the Xerox copy from her bag and laid it next to the map:

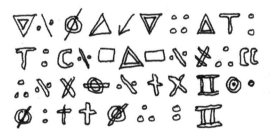

He pointed to the top row of glyphs. "There's only one arrow. All the other symbols have at least one duplicate."

"Always look for the variance," she recited, remembering what the monsignor had instructed her. "An arrow usually means direction."

"You see what surrounds that arrow?"

"Three triangles. So?"

"And what does the arrow point to?"

Her jaw dropped. "The two crosses in the last line."

He nodded, sharing her discovery. "I think whoever carved this was indicating the direction to look for a hidden entrance."

"From the triangle to the cross," she said to herself.

Boz stood and gazed toward the coast. "Let's say, for argument's sake, that the Templars did build this shaft to hide something. They had to leave a way to get back into the vault."

"You think the real entrance is not through the top of the shaft?"

"Those flooding tunnels were built to extend toward Smuggler's Cove and South Shore," he said. "Pretty fancy workmanship for medieval stone hacks."

She took his hint. "Yeah, engineered by someone skilled enough to build a cathedral, maybe."

Boz traced his forefinger across the map. "There's only one direction that the true tunnel could run and open into a vault at the very bottom."

"Joudrey's Cove," she said, finishing his thought. "Where the stone triangle points toward the stone cross. But these newspaper articles say that every inch of the island has been searched."

"That's because everyone has been searching *on land.*"

"Where else could the entrance be?"

"Below the water."

"But the entrance would flood as soon as it was opened."

Finding a blank paper in the pile, Boz pulled a pen from his pocket and sketched another drawing. "Not if the entrance sits in an air pocket under the shoreline table. The Templars would have known the timing of high and low tides. Even in medieval times, experienced divers could have swum under the crest and into the tunnel, then be back out before the air pocket flooded again."

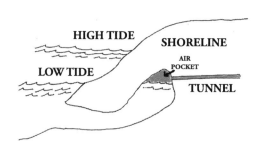

Boz waited for her to acknowledge his brilliance, but she was reading another news clipping dragged from the pile. He asked her, "What's wrong?"

"This says that some stones were unearthed on the island in the 1930s."

"More stones. Big deal."

She looked up at him. "These were carved with Portuguese words."

As they approached Joudrey's Cove late that night, Boz cut the engine on their small fishing boat. In the distance, headlights of a patrol jeep flickered through the trees on the island. He zipped up Jaq's wetsuit. "You sure you can handle this?"

"I dived in Puerto Rico last summer."

He loaded his belt with the six underwater flare sticks he had purchased at the Halifax diving shop where they rented the boat and gear. "This isn't snorkeling for coral. We'll be going down a hundred feet. Take it slow."

"When's low tide?"

"Just after midnight. We'll have an hour before it starts coming back in."

She strapped on her tank. "What's in these?"

"A new mix called Hydrox. Better than nitro for deeper dives. Just be careful around these flares. The oxygen and hydrogen combo is pretty flammable."

Flipping over the side, she followed him into the water and checked her compass for the direction to the cove. Fifty feet down, they found the under-belly of the coastal shelf. Just as they had hoped, the crust was pocked with holes. The problem was choosing which depression to explore. A school of spring fish emerged from a large burrow, and Boz motioned her into that one. The water was murky, so they had to grope the limestone above them. After several hundred feet of swimming laterally, they felt the crevice's ceiling rise.

Boz broke the water's surface.

She popped up next to him and slid up her mask. They were in an air pocket. She smiled and nodded a concession, impressed that he had guessed right.

He lit a flare and swung open a grate above them. The entry appeared to lead to a dry tunnel, just wide enough to crawl through.

She pointed to her watch. They had forty minutes until high tide.

They crawled for another fifteen minutes. This tunnel, she realized, could go for hundreds of yards without even reaching the shaft. She was about to tell him to head back when she heard a creaking. She looked up. The low ceiling had given way to a dark ascending hole. Twenty feet above their heads hovered a platform of logs tethered together with rawhide twine. They were in one of the shaft's lower vaults—and it looked just like the cross-section on Hosaam's map.

Boz ripped open another flare for more light. Around their feet lay slats of iron panels that had fallen from their bracings below the ceiling of logs.

She inched closer to the far wall. On the floor lay a narrow chest that she estimated to be fifteen feet long, two feet wide, and a foot in depth. The chest had rings on each end and had once been surrounded by the iron panels and suspended from chains to avoid the high tide. She carefully opened its lid. The interior, lined with cedar wood, was empty. Each third of its length had been set with brackets, apparently designed to hold long poles in place.

Boz fingered some shreds of a blue geosynthetic liner with a modern label that lay nearby. "Rip cords for waterproof bags." He crouched to examine footprints in the mud near the liner. "Somebody got here before we did."

She ran a hand down the cedar panels. "This chest isn't wide enough to hold the Ark."

"How would you know?"

"The Book of Exodus gave the Ark's measurements in cubits," she said. "We were taught in Bible study to convert the cubits to feet and memorize the dimensions. Two-and-a-quarter feet wide. Three-and-three-quarters feet long. And that's without the crown and four rings."

"Maybe the chest was used to carry spears or weapons."

She stared at the long box. An image from Rev. Merry's Rapture Theme Park suddenly came to her mind: The Ark of the Covenant being carried by the Israelites into battle. Awestruck, she whispered, "The staves ... this must have held the handles that the Israelites used to carry the Ark during their battles against the Canaanites."

"Why would the Templars go to all the trouble of hiding—"

She slammed her fist against the chest. "Why didn't I see this before?"

Boz looked at her as if she had lost her mind. "What?"

"Rev. Merry told me that once, when he was a boy, he made replicas of the furnishings in the Holy of Holies."

"Bloody good for him. But what does that—"

"*Thirteen* replicas." She counted them off on her fingers. "The Templars didn't hide the Ark in one spot. They broke it down with the other Temple furnishings and hid them in thirteen different places around the world. That's why they built the Notre Dame cathedrals and the Lalibela holy sites to imitate the Virgo constellation. Each Virgo star, each French cathedral, each Lalibela holy site represents one of the Temple treasures listed in the Old Testament. The Templars were too clever to put all of their eggs in one basket."

Boz pondered her theory. "If you're right, then Hosaam hasn't been searching blind, after all. He's been finding relics at every location." He checked his watch. "We've got twenty minutes before that air pocket disappears."

"We'd better get going." Starting back toward the tunnel, she stepped on something loose. She stopped short, grabbing at Boz.

She heard a click followed by a scratching sound, like a door swinging on rusty hinges. She looked at her feet. One of the iron plates on the floor had a rope tied to it. How had she not seen this? The plate had apparently slipped and triggered a latch somewhere in the darkness. The creaking above them became louder. She watched as Boz stalked the source of the rope by pulling on it.

The log platform above them came crashing down.

She and Boz curled into balls.

Surrounded by dust, she climbed out from under the debris. Her vision slowly cleared. She felt Boz's hand checking her head for cuts.

"You okay?"

She needed a moment to steady from the wooziness. She felt a drop on her head, and then another. "Is there a leak in here?"

Boz stared at his own hands—they were streaked red.

He turned back to her with alarm and wiped blood from her hair. "You sure you aren't hurt?"

"I told you. I feel …" A drop of blood hit her nose.

They looked up at the dark hole, fearful that another depth charge of logs might come hurling down at any moment.

Boz searched for his pack and found the flares. He lit one and aimed it into the shaft.

A bloodied face stared down at them.

Jaq screamed and retreated into Boz's arms.

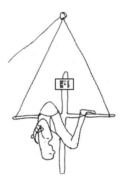

Above them hung a crucified man.

The beams of the cross, formed with two logs from the ceiling platform, had dropped down through the shaft. The horizontal traverse hung suspended on chains that had been threaded through a pulley. Jaq traced the chains and discovered that they led to a rope attached to the iron panel that she had just stepped on.

Boz pulled the staves chest directly under the crucified victim. He stepped atop it to examine the grisly sight. "That Pakistani asshole is taunting us! Look at that! He twisted that poor sap's torso to form the letter 'N.' It's the Serpent on the Cross. He's telling us he knows we're onto the Templar Square."

Jaq risked another glance at the victim. Had he been flogged like Christ? The muscles on his right leg looked atrophied, and his biceps were tattooed with Middle Eastern calligraphy. She gasped and stepped back. "That's the taxi driver who tried to kill me in Rome!"

Boz lifted the victim's arms to inspect the inked hadith.

She held her stomach. "Why would Hosaam execute one of his own men?"

"The sonofabitch must be getting close to finding all of the Temple relics. This is the typical modus operandi for these warlord scumbags. They kill off their rabbits when they're no longer needed. He's covering his tracks for the day he proclaims himself the Mahdi."

She craned her neck to better see the plank that had been nailed above the man's head on the cross. "What's on that board?"

"I can't read it." Boz linked his hands into a stirrup. "You get closer."

"Oh, no," she protested. "I'm scared of heights."

"I'm not that tall. Come on. Take a chance. I won't drop you. I think."

Grousing, she reluctantly climbed atop his shoulders for a closer view:

NW SW NE SE	1 CC
INNER	1 CC
NW SW NE SE	2 C
NW SE	1 C
INNER	1 CC
NW SE	1 CC
SE	1 CC
INNER	3 CC
OUTER	1 CC
SW NE	2 CC
OUTER	3 C

She squinted. "Are those Roman numerals? I think he's mocking the board that Pontius Pilate hung over Jesus." She slid back down Boz's body and detached herself from him, reluctantly. "What does 'C' stand for in Latin?"

"A hundred years," Boz said. "But those other words are in English. If Hosaam intended for the 'C's to refer to centuries, he would have used 'X's and 'I's, too."

She kept staring at the board. That left column looked like quadrant directions. Corners. Inner. Outer. "The 'C's could mean clockwise and counterclockwise. He's giving us directions for turning the letter wheels on the SATOR square. The quadrants must be the corner wheels." She removed her Blackberry from its waterproof pouch and powered it up. She popped open the 3-D graphics program and turned the wheels in the order Hosaam had directed:

OUTER WHEEL	INNER WHEEL	QUADRANT WHEELS
SATOR	SATOR	SATOR
AREPO	AREPO	AREPO
TENET	TENET	TENET
OPERA	OPERA	OPERA
ROTAS	ROTAS	ROTAS

NW SW NE SE 1 CC	INNER 1 CC	NW SW NE SE 2 C	NW SE 1 C	SATPE 1 CC	INNER 1 CC	NW SE 1 C
ARTRO	ARTRO	ESTPE	SATPE	SATPE	ESTPE
SAEOP	SEOEP	RAOOR	EROOR	EOOAR	OAOAR
TENET	TANAT	TANAT	TANAT	TRNRT	TRNRT
POEAS	PEOES	ROOAR	ROORE	RAOOE	RAOAO
ORTRA	ORTRA	EPTSE	EPTAS	EPTAS	EPTSE

OUTER 3 C	SW NE 2 CC	OUTER 1 CC	INNER 3 C	SE 1 CC
EOEST	STPRR	STPER	ESTPE	ESTPE
ROAEP	EOAET	EOART	OOARR	OAOAR
TONAR	OONAE	OONAE	TONAT	TRNRT
PRAOR	ERAOS	TRAOS	RRAOE	RAOOE
TASET	RTPTA	REPTA	EPTAS	EPTAS

None of the resulting words made any sense to her. "He's just toying with us." She was about to give up when she heard more creaking above her. She flinched, but nothing fell. She cautiously looked up.

The crucifix had flipped, rotating like a gyroscope.

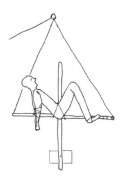

"Bloody hell," Boz said. "You see what *that* forms?"

Jaq couldn't believe her eyes. "An 'M.'"

"You were right," he whispered. "He's telling us that the 'N's and 'M's in the Templar Square are interchangeable."

"RONE *is* Rome. But why go to all that trouble just to change letters?"

"He's enjoying this little chase. Cocky bastard."

She substituted 'M' for 'N' in the square and read the resulting words. "You ever heard of anything called TOMAR?"

Boz shook his head. Then, an idea struck him. "Which of the Virgo star locations not yet hit by Hosaam is closest to Nova Scotia?"

She traced the stars in the constellation from memory. "Portugal, I think."

"Portugal? Hell, there's nothing in Portugal but cork and—" Boz saw that she was distracted. "Am I talking to myself here?"

She looked down at her wet feet ... why was water seeping in?

"My God!" She grabbed Boz's hand and ran for the entrance.

The mouth of the tunnel was blocked. When the logs had fallen, one of the iron panels had slammed across the gap. They realized that Hosaam had rigged a trap door with the chains drawn taut from the weight of the crucified man. There was just enough space under the panel to allow the water to enter but prevent them from crawling out.

Boz hammered at the panel, but it wouldn't budge. The water gushed in and surged to their waists. In minutes, they'd be pressed against next level of logs and suffocated. Lifted by the incoming tide, he threw off his air tank and kept leaping for the cross. Finally grasping the beam, he climbed atop it and stood astride the crucified body. "Give me the tanks!"

"What are you doing?"

"The tanks, damn it!"

Jaq dragged the heavy tanks across the water. With a desperate heave, she rolled them up the wall of the tunnel to him.

Boz hung the tanks on the beam by their straps. Balancing precariously, he cut loose the corpse and sent it splashing to the water. He pulled the rope through the iron eye and threw one end at her. "Thread it through the hole on that panel!"

When Jaq finally managed to tether the iron slat to the rope, Boz levered the panel up and set it vertically on the beam.

The water reached her neck. She paddled furiously for the far wall.

Boz opened the tank valves. He ignited the last flare. "Dive!"

She heaved for one last breath and kicked to the bottom. The ignited gas exploded the water up the shaft like a geyser and the iron panel knifed through the oak platform above them. A recoiling wall of water slammed her. Submerged and disoriented, she thrashed and groped. She couldn't find Boz.

Everything went black.

Moments later, her head broke the surface. Gasping for air, she climbed to her knees atop the oak platform. The blast had propelled her through the hole in the ceiling.

In the settling water, a body floated toward her.

THIRTY-FOUR

SEA OF DARKNESS
FEBRUARY, 1488

D ias tried to hide his growing alarm from the crew as he signaled for his
three caravels to continue tacking east in search of the African coast.
He had not seen land for five days, and the men now held that same look
of incipient mutiny that he had witnessed years ago on Corte-Real's ill-fated
voyage. Preparing for the worst, he took inventory in his mind of the arma-
ments stored below deck: three small cannons, two matchlock-firing pieces, five
arbalests, and a dozen pikes. His only chance for survival was continuing to fool
these men into believing that he knew where he was going.

His fretful pilot, d'Alenquer, leaned over the gangway again to inspect the
churning froth. "The water is red. I tell you, there are flames below us!"

Dias warned him with a glare to avoid making such incendiary observations
within earshot of the others. "It is only the reflection of the setting sun."

Overhearing their exchange, a jittery first mate on the lower deck could no
longer hold back his certainty that they were doomed. "Dragons lurk in these
fire seas! The Africans said they saw beasts off the coast of Gambia!"

Dias felt his hold on the command slipping away. The men were falling into
a collective delusion; many now scanned the sky for predators that might sweep
down on them, while others began sliding toward the bow, convinced that the
caravel was being tipped into the abyss. Above him, a new panoply of constellations dazzled the night sky. Had the Old Man been wrong about the shape of
the world? If the earth *was* flat, as the cosmographers at Sagres insisted, he and
his crew might indeed be on the underside of the disc. There could be only one
other explanation for such a prolonged absence of land.

Had they sailed south of Africa?

There was but one way to find out. Drawing a bracing breath, he ordered
d'Alenquer, "Turn north."

The pilot, exchanging glances of disbelief with the swain, refused to convey the command for yet another change of direction. "You send us west, then east, then south. And now north?"

Rattled by the order to alter course, the men on the lower deck abandoned their duties and massed with threat near the armory.

Dias leapt down from the aftcastle to repulse their mutinous surge. Cornered, he saw that he could no longer keep them in the dark about the mission. Bracing for another onrush of outrage, he admitted in a near whisper: "We have been sent south to find the passage around Africa to the Indies."

A groan of panic rumbled down the deck, and one of the crew shouted, "No ship can sail back from the far side of Africa!"

"Prince Henry said it could be done," Dias insisted.

"I won't burn in the sea fires because of a dead man's fantasies!"

Dias gripped the railing to steady his stance. "Follow me north! And I will prove his vision was sent by God!"

The pilot pointed to the volatile compass. "The lodestone cannot be trusted in these waters."

When the near-hysterical crew clamored for the portolans to be surrendered, Dias resorted to desperate negotiation. "Two more days! If we do not find land, I will relinquish the command!"

The men fell to arguing among themselves, but finally they accepted the compromise and returned to their stations. Knowing he had purchased only a few hours at most, Dias retired to his cabin to pray and write his last will and testament. If forced to give up the caravels, he could never return to Portugal. The crew would put him ashore at São Jorge da Mina on the Guinea coast, where he would remain in exile for the rest of his life. Exhausted, he lay on his cot and wondered if Pero had made it into the lands of the infidels. The poor *Ratao* was denied the comfort of speaking his native tongue. And Colon had drawn the worst lot of them all. ...

The cabin door pounded.

Dias sprang to his feet, disoriented. How long had he been asleep? Had the scum not given him even the full night before launching their mutiny?

"Captain! To the deck!"

He cocked his handgonne and raced up the stairwell, prepared to fight to his death. The men were jammed against the starboard rails, shielding their eyes from the first morning light.

Rising in the distance stood a purple mountain range.

He took in the view from several angles on the deck, questioning if he had become trapped in some cruel hallucination. As his lead caravel sailed closer to land, green pastures dotted with skinny cattle came into sharp relief. The crew gave up a throaty yelp of joyful celebration, spooking the cattle into a stampede. The naked aboriginals tending the bovine turned and, seeing the caravels for the first time, retreated inland chasing their herds.

With his good fortune confirmed, he ordered ten men, chosen by lots, to row with him to the shore to search for drinking water. Taking care to keep the ignition fuses on their firing pieces dry, they jumped from the sanded rowboat and clambered up the dunes. The natives retreated inland and disappeared into the scrub brush. He sent out a search party of three men to find a stream.

An hour later, the scouts returned with a report of a fresh tributary deep in the jungle. Ecstatic, he and his men scrambled for the bluffs, desperate to fill their canteens. They hacked through the dense foliage while watching for giant snakes and monsters, and at last the gurgling of a waterfall was heard. They shouted prayers of gratitude as they ran for this blessed miracle granted by God. Yet before they could fall to their knees and slake their thirst, a shower of arrows pattered the ground around them.

Surrounded by curdling screams, Dias looked up from the water. Two of his men were impaled, and hundreds of angry savages surrounded him and his scouting party. He fired a crossbow in warning at the attackers in the trees, but the Africans became bolder and leapt to the ground in the hundreds. Denied even a drop of water on his cracked tongue, he was forced to order a retreat to the boat.

He and his survivors backtracked through the jungle path they had just cut while dragging their wounded. Reaching the clearing, they staggered down to the beach and pushed off in their small rowboat only moments before the aboriginal hordes came hurdling down the bluffs, screaming curses and flinging arrows. A cannon shot from one of the caravels exploded on the beach, maiming several of the natives. Frightened by this roar from the gods, the Africans gave up their chase and looked to the sky as if questioning the anger of the heavens. Hoisted up to his flagship, he ordered his caravels to set sail at once.

After several hours of hugging land, he sensed that the shore was turning northeast. The men, already spooked by the bloody attack, became even more frightened. Had they stumbled into a narrow isthmus and become trapped on the far side of Africa?

"We turn back here," d'Alenquer insisted, speaking for all of the crew.

Dias looked longingly toward the east, across the Indian Ocean. How many more days it would take to sail to the kingdom of the Prester John? A week? Maybe less. Pero might be there now, waiting to be taken back to Portugal with the precious treasure of their quest. He turned to d'Alenquer and pleaded, "India is within our grasp."

The pilot would not hear of it. "We have barely enough water to make Lisbon on half rations. If you go to the East, you will go without us."

Dias fought back tears. During his apprenticeship at Lagos, he had heard horrid tales of captains resisting the demands of a frightened crew, only to be cast aside, sometimes even thrown overboard. He had pushed these men as far as their primitive notion of the world would allow. Resigned to failure, he ordered a stone cross be set ashore to mark the southernmost point that any Christian had stepped foot. He named the river the Rio de Infante, after the Old Man.

As dusk fell, his caravels caught the winds that would carry them back to Portugal, and the *padrão* monument on the cliffs slowly disappeared from sight. He was struck by how similar these desolate African headlands appeared to the cliffs of Sagres. The angry waves here crashed with such vehemence that they seemed determined to conquer the very idea of land itself. Exotic animals grazed on its sloping scrubland; wild ostriches the size of mules, lurching baboons, white deer, and black-striped horses. On the sea's horizon, he spied a strange sight: Three storms, sent by different worlds and currents, were converging to do battle near the cape's tip. This was the place that kings and mariners had only dreamed of attaining, and he had discovered it. But were those approaching tempests an omen of his future?

"You should christen this spot," d'Alenquer advised.

He shook his head ruefully, convinced that the distant finger of land hazing from his sight was the same tip of Africa that the Old Man had seen in his dreams. "Tormentoso," he muttered. "The Cape of Storms."

"Not a very hopeful name," the pilot said.

He turned aside to hide his despair. What came next to his mind was the old mariner Eannes's warning that every admiral had but one great voyage in him. Was this to be his only opportunity for the Indies? He offered up a prayer for a return, and with bitter regret whispered: "If hope brings me back to this cape, *then* I will rename it Hope."

Arabia
November, 1488

As the dust-caked caravan of pilgrims and traders descended from the mountains, Pero began to fear that he had been tricked into paying a fare to some Egyptian backwater instead of the jewel of the Arabian Peninsula. He had expected to find a thriving metropolis rivaling Constantinople or Rome, but this birthplace of the Moslem Prophet was little more than a ring of squat houses surrounded by desert. Waffled with circular warrens of narrow streets, the dusty oasis offered not a tree or shoot of vegetation for shade. At the hub of this caravansary, surrounded by a wide expanse of sand pounded by centuries of worshippers' sandals, sat the mysterious box that he was now risking his life to see.

No Christian had ever stepped foot inside Mecca—at least none who had survived to tell of the venture.

He lashed his camel toward the Kaaba shrine that had been built by the biblical Abraham with alternating layers of red stone and wood. The ancient monument stood twelve feet in height and was covered by a blue and black woolen cloth with broad chevron stripes. The lone door to the giant cube had been raised from the ground to thwart trespassers from entering its sacred confines, which reportedly held a magical black stone that had fallen from the heavens. Hundreds of worshippers circled the shrine on foot, kissing and embracing it in prayer. Others rushed back and forth between two small hills, reenacting the anguished search for water by Hagar, one of Abraham's wives. This mass circumambulation of thousands gave the entire vale a strange whirling aura.

The Bedouin guide who led this train of camels chanted a *muezzin's* call to prayer, and the fifty or so riders behind him, their faces wrapped against the cutting wind, climbed down from their saddle blankets and fell to the ground walked by Mohammed eight hundred years ago.

Pero followed their example, having learned the ways of the infidels as a boy. He now counted it a fortuitous blessing that his Iberian Arabic sounded no stranger than the dozens of other dialects heard along this pilgrimage route. He felt a twinge of regret for having sent Paiva on to Africa. He had not trusted his nervous companion to pull off the subterfuge required, for one slip of the tongue and he would be torn to pieces.

"Have you gone on *Hajj* before, my friend?" asked a slender Persian who, until now, had uttered not one word to him during the journey.

Pero had encountered this same gregarious behavior from Christian pilgrims returning to Portugal, who felt compelled to tell their life stories to strangers upon reaching Compostela and Jerusalem. He answered tersely, hoping to avoid further conversation. "My first."

"You have the quiet aspect of a Tunisian."

"Granada."

"It is too late this night to perform our absolutions. Have you prepared a place to lodge?"

"I will sleep under the stars."

"My name is Shamsi."

Cornered, Pero lied by offering his alias, "Ibn Baj."

"Come with me, Ibn," the Persian insisted. "The days here are unbearably hot and the nights freezing. I have made arrangements at a lodge run by my brethren. We will share the space."

To decline the infidel's offer of hospitality might bring on suspicion, so Pero saw no choice but to follow the Persian down a maze of narrow streets and come to the lodge. Inside, he encountered a spectacle most queer. Dozens of men in flowing white robes whirled on like spinning tops across an arena of lacquered boards while musicians played mystical notes with flutes.

Had he been seduced into a demonic ritual?

These spinners seemed lost in a trance with their eyelids half-open, as if on the verge of death. Rotating deftly across the floor, they whispered prayers while holding their outstretched arms limp in the air for counterbalance. In the center of this swirling madness stood an elderly man, in a turban and black frock, who directed the gyrations like a carnival trainer. Their movements resembled planets orbiting around a black earth.

"Have you ever performed the *Sema*?" the Persian asked.

Pero shook his head, fearing his ignorance of the Mohammedan religion would be exposed, a revelation that would result in his swift execution.

The Persian intertwined an arm with Pero's elbow in a confiding gesture. "It is a tragedy that the Wisdom of the Sufi has not reached Granada. This is our dance of Heart Love, the evocation of the Serpent of God handed down to us by the Greek Pythagoras."

Pero angled his ear. "Serpent, you say?"

The Persian nodded. "We spin to release the chains of the senses and coax the rise of the Baraka. God's Love climbs up the Lataif centers of our spiritual bodies. We are called dervishes."

Pero had picked up enough of the regional Arabic in this land to know that 'dervish' meant one who stands at the door to enlightenment. "How long does it take to attain this serpent power?"

"For some, a lifetime," the Persian said. "For others, God offers His Grace in the flash of a lightning bolt."

Pero felt a heat rising from the base of his spine. He became dizzy from watching the strangely hypnotic whirl of the dancers.

"The initiate is raw when he first seeks the Serpent," the Persian said. "He is cooked by the fire of the Turn and finally he is burnt by the Holy Light for the greater Glory of God."

Pero watched, perplexed, as the dervishes passed around a gourd and breathed on it as they spun. After several revolutions, they offered the water to sickly men who lay on cots on the periphery of the dance floor.

Detecting his unease, the Persian explained the strange ritual by leading his new friend to a square board that held a wooden peg driven into its center. "They are transmitting the healing radiance of the Serpent's breath. This is called our learning box. An initiate who wishes to enter our brotherhood must spend a year cooking and cleaning for his elders. If he is deemed worthy, the dance master requires him to practice twirling on this board."

Such training of sacrifice and abnegation, Pero saw, was not so different in principle from the discipline he had undergone to learn the nautical gnosis. Removing his sandals, he placed the peg between his toes and tried to spin, but he stumbled awkwardly. The Persian assisted him until he became accustomed to the motion. Soon the area around his heart felt aglow, and he sensed a growing affection for this stranger. How could these infidels worship a false god and yet radiate such love and kindness?

"Appear as you are," the Persian counseled. "Be as you appear."

Jolted from his reverie, Pero fell in a clump, his heartbeat quickening. The last thing he wanted on this mission of espionage was to appear stripped of his disguises.

The Persian helped him to his feet. "An admonition written by the great Rumi. Our whirling cuts all pretenses of the soul."

"Who is this Rumi you speak of?"

"The master of the Mysteries. The great Rumi could trace a man's past and read his future by merely being in his presence."

Pero shuddered. "Can *you* read my past and future?"

The Persian softened his penetrating gaze. "I see the mosques of India in your eyes. Have you been to that far land?"

Pero shook his head, amazed by such spiritual powers. He feared what more the Persian might discern clairvoyantly about his covert mission.

"I feel you have a strong pull there."

"You have traveled to India?"

"Two years ago, I went to pray at the feet of Shaikh Salim Chisti, one of our most venerated mystics."

Pero drew the man aside. "Did you see any Africans in India?"

The Persian reacted with astonishment. "Africans? Of course! They dock their ships at Cochin to trade metals for spices."

"Tell me ... did any speak of a sea route below their land?"

"Have you been living in a hermit's cave, my friend?"

Pero moved quickly to allay his suspicion. "I am not a learned man, forgive me. I have long held a curiosity about the geography of the cosmos."

The Persian laughed gently. "The esteemed navigator Ibn Mahid of Arabia wrote long ago of the channel connecting the Atlantic and Indian oceans."

"Praise be to Allah," Pero muttered, struggling to hide his excitement. "His miracles know no bounds."

"But you must sail to India only between the months of *Jumada* and *Dhu al-Qi'dah*. The monsoons will cast you adrift during the other seasons."

"I am blessed to have made your acquaintance," Pero said. "If you will now allow me to take my leave, I wish to stand before God this night and offer prayers of gratitude."

The Persian grasped Pero's hands in comradeship. "We shall meet in the morning and together perform our sacred duties at the Kaaba."

After bowing to the infidel, Pero departed the *sema* lodge and hurried down the nearly deserted streets. He spied a shopkeeper on a corner preparing his wares for the market that would open in a few hours. He asked the trader when the next caravan was scheduled to leave for the Red Sea port of Aydhab. Informed that one would be forming that morning, he purchased a fragment of papyrus and borrowed the shopkeeper's quill. He wrote five Latin words, each with five letters, and blotted the ink. He folded the papyrus and paid for its delivery to Cairo, where two Portuguese Jews would be waiting to serve as his couriers to Lisbon.

Al Andalus, Spain
August, 1492

As the *Santa Maria* floated down the Tinto River toward the Atlantic, Cristobal Colon could only watch in helpless despair while hundreds of his fellow Jews staggered half-naked aside him down the banks. He coughed back the anger in his throat and hung his head in shame.

I am too late.

Many of these Jews had spent their last night in Iberia digging up the remains of their ancestors before the graves could be plundered. All along this march of misery, the local Christians blew horns at them in taunts and inserted their fingers down the mouths of the exiles to make them vomit the gold they had swallowed. Those not mutilated by the Moors in the hills would confront pirates who would simply unload their pitiful passengers on some desolate isle to starve.

He had tried to save as many of them as possible without drawing suspicion, having even hired a Hebrew interpreter and surgeon for the voyage. Yet these few were only drops salvaged from an ocean of suffering. Was it mere coincidence that he was leaving on the same day that these last remnants were being sent away on their pitiful exodus? Six years he had spent wooing the mercurial Isabella, and all the while her Dominican flatterers had been boiling their cauldron of terror. Those bloodthirsty friars had finally found their spiritual *casus belli* a year ago in the village of La Guardia, where a *converso* returning home from a pilgrimage to Compostela had been accused of dropping a Eucharistic wafer from his baggage. Submitted to the rack, the poor wretch could stop his agony only by confessing that he had helped Jews nail a Christian boy to a cross and cut out his heart for magical potions.

Torquemada—now so hated that he now had to travel with armed guards and carry a unicorn's horn for protection against poisoning—had seized on this falsified crime to convince the queen that a violent Hebrew uprising was imminent. Four months ago, filled with apocalyptic fervor, Isabella and Ferdinand had ordered all Jews to accept baptism or leave the realm. This day, the ninth of *Av*, the holy day commemorating the second destruction of the Temple, would see the last of the Sephardim in Spain. Isabella's rabid Christian militia, the *Santa Hermandad*, lurked in the nearby towns, lusting to kill those Jews caught violating the expulsion order.

He could feel his pulse rising with his rage.

He had prosecuted this westward voyage with that rabid queen's council of sycophants during too many sessions to count, only to be rejected each time. When, finally, he had given up despondent and had left Castile for France, Isabella's *caballeros* had intercepted him at the border. Returned under guard to her private pavilion at Sante Fe, he had found her dressed in armor like an Amazon and spending the nights alone. Her husband Ferdinand, preoccupied with the siege of Granada, had vowed to avoid the marital bed to hone his concentration for battle. At least, that was his excuse.

Isabella's greeting to him that fateful night below walls of Granada still lingered in his memory ...

"I am deeply aggrieved," the queen said. "You chose to leave me?"

"*You* are aggrieved?" Colon cried in exasperation, giving vent to the many years of frustration. "You spurn me and lead me about by the nose like some bull refused the ring!"

"Are you?"

"Am I what?"

Isabella loosened the straps on her breastplate. "A bull?"

He stole a glance at the tent's flap. "*Reina*, there are a thousand men out there who would run me through if we were to be discovered together."

She brought his hands to her breasts, still firm despite having birthed five children. "And yet not one of them will run *me* through."

He stared into her provocative eyes, trying to determine who was being played in this exchange. Perhaps because of her strong belief in destiny, she had always been a reckless risk-taker. Weeks earlier, she had narrowly escaped assassination by a Mohammedan in this very tent. Now, he kissed her passionately and whispered, "I can give you so much more. I can make you a saint and—"

She placed a long-nailed finger to his lips. "You will have your voyage, Don Colon. I have convinced my husband of its merits."

He froze with his tongue inside her begging lips. *Did she call me Don?*

Isabella surfaced from their kiss and led him to her bed. "Why do you bargain so obstinately? Most men would have compromised in the negotiations long ago. Torquemada believes you to be a lunatic."

"God's servants do not compromise."

She nuzzled his neck and breathed hotly into his ear. "Santangel has offered to put up seventeen thousand ducats from his personal funds as collateral for your enterprise. You have many admirers in my court. I wonder why?" Her eyes locked on his as she asked, "Are you the Antichrist?"

Santangel the Jew? Is this a trap set by the Dominicans?

He forced himself to flatter her, punctuating the lie with another throaty kiss. "Your councilors are visionaries. They were chosen by an even greater visionary."

Isabella unbuttoned his shirt. "After you pass through the Pillars of Hercules, what route will you take to the Indies?"

He was aroused, not by her bold touch, but from the anticipation of finally setting sail. "I will provision my caravels in the Canaries."

Her nails brushed across his abdomen. "And from there?"

"The easterlies will take me across the twenty-eighth parallel. I intend to make a new chart of navigation."

"*New* chart? You mean the first chart."

He had nearly given up the secret. "Of course."

Her fingers crossed the equator of his waist. "Tell me again. How many days will it take you?"

His breathing deepened. "Cardinal d'Ailly confirmed in the *Imago Mundo* that the greater part of the globe is land. The Book of Esdras says seven parts land and one part water. The Atlantic is quite short in breadth. The voyage will require no more than three weeks."

"You always quote from the Old Testament," she observed. "Why is that?"

"Our Lord quoted only from the Old Testament."

"You are a strange man, Don Colon." She stared at him intently. "And so, the last crusade begins. Soon we shall cleanse the world of unbelievers."

His ears rang with a biblical warning: *Ezekiel saith that the Redeemer will come when the demonic ruler of Gog erects a mighty kingdom in the land of Magog.* Was he now wrapped in the arms of that Dragonness Gog? Remembering her craving for prophecies, he brought his lips below the arch of her neck and whispered: "Jupiter and Saturn will conjoin this month. This voyage—*your* triumph—will soon open the Seals of Revelation."

She captured the jewels in his lush tropics, fondling them with threat. "It had best be as you say, my dear Genoan. Or I will have these hung from the clerestory of Sevilla's cathedral. ..."

A shudder of foreboding wrenched him back to the agonizing present.

Shuffling uncomfortably in the stiff sailing doublet that Isabella had gifted him for the crossing, he looked over his shoulder to confirm that the *Nina* and *Pinta* were staying in close formation. Finding ninety crewmen for these ships had proven nearly impossible, for most Spaniards considered this to be a voyage of the damned. He had no illusions about their loyalty. After all, what mariner in his right mind would take to the Sea of Darkness in an old Galician merchant *nao* of a paltry hundred tonnage? Only when Isabella issued her penal decree against the port of Palos for harboring smugglers had the mayor grudgingly supplied him with the ships and men to pay the fine.

As the vessel cleared the Saltes sandbars and slid past the pearl curve of coastline, his thoughts turned to Filipa, who lay cold in her grave in Lisbon. He so wished she could witness this bittersweet triumph. Would she hold him in harsh judgment for having taken a Castilian mistress? Beatriz was a simple peasant woman of secret Jewish blood who had given him a second son, Fernando. He had left both Beatriz and Fernando in Cordoba, thinking that he had traveled to France.

Would he ever see them again?

Those half-naked Jews on the beachhead were weeping and waving at him. They could not know that he carried their fate on these three ships. Black irony! This enterprise of his was being financed on the backs of these pitiful exiles whose families had lived on this land since the time of Christ. *There but for the grace of God,* he cursed silently as the Gulf of Cadiz came into view. *A God who is either cruel or impotent.*

THIRTY-FIVE

PORTUGAL
FEBRUARY 17, PRESENT DAY

As Boz sped north along the Nabão River, Jaq reached over to adjust his head bandage, concerned he might have suffered a concussion during the Oak Island shaft explosion. "You sure you feel okay to drive?"

He let go of the wheel and turned a blank stare on her. "Do I know you?"

"Hold on to that!" She was about to slap his shoulder for the goofing act when her watch alarm buzzed. It was now Monday morning in Washington. At that very moment, Mayfield was likely asking a hearing judge for a default order confirming her dismissal. If her theory about the Templar plan to hide the treasures of King Solomon's Holy of Holies turned out to be wrong, she'd probably be back in Kentucky waiting tables within the week.

"We've always been at least a day behind Hosaam," Boz reminded her. "Just out of curiosity, what makes you think this time will be different?"

"He has to slip up at some point. He's turning on his foot soldiers now. Maybe one of them will do us a favor and turn on him."

Racing the disappearing sun, Boz spun the Alfa Romeo around another sharp bend through the olive and fig fields of the Ribatejo. "We're not dealing with the Sopranos here. In the real world, cartel kingpins don't reach the top of the criminal career ladder by making careless mistakes—"

"There it is!" she shouted.

Up ahead, rising high on a distant promontory above the city of Tomar, stood the medieval monastery of the Portuguese Order of Christ. Surrounded by a circle of vast fortifications, its bell-shaped tower fanned with ribbed buttresses was reputed to be the best preserved of the surviving Templar commanderies in Europe. The guidebooks said that if any secrets about the Templars in Portugal were to be discovered, then Tomar—the name that Hosaam had hinted at in the revolved SATOR-Templar square—was the place to search.

Boz weaved the sports car up the hill to an entrance called the Blood Port, but the sign on the gate said the castle was closed. Yawning with fatigue, he searched the modern town below. "Time to find a hotel and call it a night."

Jaq unlocked her door. Before he could stop her, she got out of the car and walked along the battlements toward an old olive tree whose limbs hung over the ramparts. Seeing no guards around, she climbed its trunk, scuffing her new Skechers. She laughed at Boz, knowing that this was the one skill from her Appalachia tomboy days that would put him to shame.

"It hasn't been that long since Portugal was a dictatorship," he warned. "I'd just as soon not take a tour of the penal system here."

She stood atop the allures and taunted him with a beckoning grin. Finally, he stepped out, grumbling, and levered atop the wall. On the far side, hundreds of medieval stones lay scattered across a shadowed bailey. Obscured by the falling darkness, she and Boz hurried down stone stairs and ran for the monastery's jewel, a church said to have been modeled on the Church of the Holy Sepulcher in Jerusalem. One of its arched entrances had been sealed off using a slab carved with an undulating monster. They looked at each other, wondering if this had been an esoteric remembrance of the Brazen Serpent.

With no time to ponder the mystery, they threaded through a couple of interior courtyards lined in blue tiles and colonnades with nautical motifs. One cloister, the *Claustro do Cemitério,* held the tombs of members of the Order who had spent their last days in this medieval version of an old sailors' home. Milling around, Jaq found a discarded tourist brochure whose cover was blazoned with the seal of Afonso Henriques, the first king of Portugal and a grand master of the Templars. The crest held a Chi Rho Cross superimposed with Greek letters "P" and "X" that divided the name "Portugal" into four quadrants. A small "O" bejeweled the center of the Mithraic sun cross, and the "R" in the country's name was affixed to its foundation:

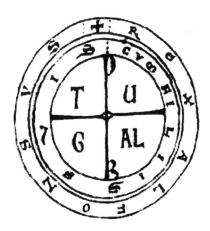

Boz motioned her over and led her into an adjoining church whose vaulted ceiling was glazed in scarlet and gold. An impressive, eight-columned drum turret rose from the epicenter of the octagonal sanctuary.

Jaq consulted the brochure again. A short description in English of the elevated platform said the Portuguese called it a 'charola.' She was struck by its resemblance to the stone tower she had seen in Rhode Island. Had these high arches been built to allow the crusader monks to worship here on horse-back? Slipping the brochure into her back pocket, she led Boz down a narrow stairwell into the crypt. They found a circle of raised stones that guarded a well. She tossed a pebble down the well and heard it bounce. "Dry as a Baptist."

Boz retreated to the nave and returned with an armful of drapes that he had confiscated from the windows. He tied the drapes end-to-end and fastened them to an iron bar near the shaft. After testing the makeshift rope, When Jaq slid over the lip. Boz snapped on his Maglite and, putting it between his teeth, followed her down, hand-over-hand.

Jaq stole the flashlight from him and searched the darkness. This bottom led to another chamber with two opposing rows of seats carved along its walls. Was this a Mithraeum? A large stone—perhaps an altar or throne—sat under a round seal that depicted two horsed knights carrying Templar crosses. Three words were inscribed on the seal: *Sigillum Xpisti Militum.* She had encountered so many Latin epigraphs during the past week that guessing their meaning was almost becoming second nature to her. She remembered seeing these words on the Templar seal in Gisors. *Militum* probably meant 'soldiers' or 'army'. Was the 'Xp' in 'Xpisti' some form of the Chi Rho cross? At the far end of the narrow cavern, she saw that packed rock shards had been shoveled to block a small opening. She clawed away the debris blocking the hole and found it led to a tunnel.

Boz pointed to the Maglite flickering in her hand. "If those batteries go dead, we'll just be a couple of skeletons."

She ignored his warning and kept crawling through the tunnel. After several minutes, she stopped to let him catch up. "The passage splits."

Boz ran a finger along the elbow between the diverging forks. Grabbing her hand, he helped her trace the six-pointed carving on the left passageway.

"The Star of David?" she asked in a whisper.

He nodded as he brought her hand to the other side of the tunnel. "The right fork is marked with the Seal of Solomon. I've seen this engraving on Israelite coins. It's a variation of the five-pointed star."

"Why would the Templars use ancient Hebrew signs?"

He shrugged. "Didn't that doctor of yours tell us that medieval Judaism might have had a connection with the Templars?"

"Yeah. ... So, which one should we take?"

"The Star of David is supposed to bring good luck."

"Wasn't that the star the Nazis forced Jews to wear?"

That reminder caused Boz to reconsider. "This could have been an underground route for refugees from Franco's Spain."

She headed left, making the decision for him.

After twenty minutes of crawling, they came to another dry well, this one with rusted iron rungs driven into its ascending walls. They climbed the ladder and lifted themselves over the stone neck. They stood in a courtyard adjacent to a small, whitewashed building. Five hundred yards to the west, the old Templar castle loomed over them.

In the corner of a garden, a bespectacled rabbi wrapped in a yarmulke was on his knees tending a bed of hyacinths. Looking up at Boz, the elderly man turned white, as if convinced the earth had just disgorged a ghost. "Hiram?" He climbed to his feet clutching his chest. "Have you come to take me?"

Boz figured the poor fellow must be senile. "We got lost in the castle. Sorry to bother you."

Relieved to hear him speak, the rabbi muttered something about demons rarely forming audible words. He grasped Boz's arm to delay his departure. Reassured that his visitor was indeed in the flesh, the rabbi came closer to examine Boz's features. "My God ... his *doppelganger*?"

Boz fended off his clutches and tried to escape through the garden's gate. "We'll be on our way now."

"You could be the twin of a man I fought with in France."

Boz turned back. "What was his name?"

"Hiram Rosen."

"Hiram was my great uncle."

The rabbi joyfully embraced him. "Elymas!"

Boz nearly fell backwards from the force of the hug. "Do I know you?"

"You don't remember? I am Baruch Acuta. Five years ago, you recovered stolen heirlooms for my cousin's family in Toulouse. Not a morning has passed that I have not prayed for the honor of offering you my thanks in person. God has blessed me by bringing you to my Synagogue of the Arch. Is it not a miracle?"

Jaq silent challenged her atheist sidekick to come up with a logical explanation for *that* act of divine grace, but he just winced with embarrassment at the profuse praise.

The rabbi captured Jaq's hand and insisted on leading both of them on a tour of the small synagogue. "No services have been performed here since King

Manuel exiled our ancestors in 1496," he explained. "This sector of Tomar used to be the Juderia ghetto. God forgive us, but the building has been abused as a church, a jail, even a barn. Now it is the Abraham Zacuto Museum."

"Zacuto," Jaq repeated. "Where have I heard that name?"

"He was only the greatest astronomer of the fifteenth century," the rabbi said. "Master Zacuto perfected the astrolabe for the Portuguese kings and navigators. Jews from all over the world now come to see my museum, but none have arrived as you just did. Come, I must show you the interior."

The odd little man was adorable, but Jaq had more important things on her mind. She signaled with a dart of her eyes for Boz to get them away.

But the rabbi wouldn't be denied. He nearly dragged her into a square prayer room with white walls and groin-vaulted ceiling supported by four cylindrical piers. A table draped in a maroon cloth blazoned with a golden Star of David sat in front of a high cabinet. On its shelves were a menorah and the scrolls of the Torah. Several grave headstones sat against the wall.

Boz ran his palm across a patch of masonry that had been set to block off the original arched entrance. "This archway ... Was this the reason they called it the Synagogue of the Arch?"

"Most visitors make that assumption. But the synagogue was named for the Arcos, a distinguished Jewish family from Tomar. A 'z' was often added to the beginning of those Portuguese names that were preceded by a middle name ending in 's.' Eventually 'Arco' became 'Zarco.'"

Familiar alarm bells went off in Jaq's head: *Arco ... Ara ... Ark.* "I saw the name Zarco on one of the gravestones in the castle."

The rabbi nodded. "Goncalves Zarco was a high-ranking member of the Order of Christ. His son, João Goncalves Zarco, discovered the Madeira Islands for Henry the Navigator."

Jaq was confused. "These Zarcos were Jewish? But I thought Jews were persecuted in Portugal at that time."

The rabbi flitted around the room pointing out its features. "The Inquisition came here later than it did in Spain. For centuries, the Portuguese kings welcomed our people. Some continued to practice Judaism. Others, like the Zarcos, preserved it in secret. Such tolerance was abandoned by King Manuel."

Jaq whispered to Boz, "If this Zarco family was affiliated with the Order of Christ, then those knights must have—

"Dug that tunnel out there," Boz said, finishing her thought. "To connect this synagogue with the fortress."

The rabbi led them into a room lined with parchments preserved under pressing boards. "I have a copy of the Zarco family tree in the archives." He spread the contents of one folio onto the table. "Ah yes, here it is."

Jaq had difficulty following the intricate web of lineages in the folio. "What does it mean when a star is placed inside parentheses?"

"The person was born illegitimate," the rabbi said.

Boz grinned with a shake of his head at one asterisk-dazzled page. "Looks like a lot of bastards were running around medieval Portugal."

The rabbi pointed to the next indication of illegitimacy in the folio. "I'm afraid the nobility in the fifteenth century was quite incestuous."

Jaq recited the name that he had pointed out. "Salvador Fernandes Zarco."

The rabbi explained the family connection. "Salvador's father was Prince Fernando, the nephew of Henry the Navigator. Fernando married his own cousin, Beatriz de Braganca. But he also had a mistress, Isabel Goncalves Zarco, daughter of João Goncalves Zarco, the discoverer of Madeira. Isabel gave birth to the bastard Salvador. She was forced to give him up to another family."

Jaq rubbed her temple to chase a headache. "Sounds complicated."

"Unfortunately, it becomes even more so," the rabbi said. "Prince Fernando's eldest legitimate son, Diogo, married Isabel Zarco."

"His own father's mistress?" Boz asked.

The rabbi nodded. "To hide the shame, Salvador was placed in the care of Diogo's brother, João Afonso Aguiar. He was raised as a foster brother of his real father's grandchildren."

"But he took the last name of his mother?" Jaq noted.

"Such was the custom," the rabbi said.

"What does the cross next to Prince Fernando's name signify?" she asked.

"After Henry the Navigator died, Fernando became the grand master of the Order of Christ."

Boz tried to make some sense of the crisscrossing genealogical lines. "What happened to Fernando's illegitimate son?"

The rabbi adjusted his spectacles to read the minuscule script. "It says here that Salvador was betrothed to a woman named Filipa Moniz de Perestrelo. The Perestrelos were another renowned family connected to the Order of Christ."

Jaq whistled, impressed. "Quite a pedigree. Did young Salvador go on to perform great deeds on the seas?"

As the rabbi read further, a look of perplexity darkened his face. "There is no record of him after 1476. This is very strange, for he must have been groomed to be a mariner like da Gama and Magellan. Perhaps the circumstances of his birth limited his ascent in the Order."

Jaq examined a series of crests that had been drawn along the borders of the folio. One coat-of-arms had three 'S's that resembled serpents and were similar to the toppled 'S' on her family's gravestone in Strawner's Gap. She asked the rabbi, "Whose was this one?"

"The Mendocas. A family of crusader knights related to the Zarcos."

Mendoca, she remembered, had been her great-grandmother's last name.

As the rabbi reshelved the folio, a loose page fell from its crease. She picked the sheet up and saw handwritten quotations in Latin on it.

Detecting her interest, the rabbi brought the document closer to his failing eyes. "I have never seen this."

"There's something written on the other side." Boz flipped the parchment over to show them:

Jeremias 18-3
Ecce ipse faciebat opus super rotam.

Below that caption, three columns had been written in a different hand and ink. The first column, on the left, had only one line: *Orsa.* The second and third columns had an extensive table of lines, perhaps thirty each, in the form of: *Infernus oriens dexter duo: Supernus occasus laevus una: Externus duo: Supernus oriens/Supernus occasus laevus ter: Penitus dexter una*, and so forth. Written below them was *Deus tem Misericórdia de mim. Padre João Gomes.*

In the lower right-hand corner, a cluster of letters formed what appeared to be a letterhead or monogram:

"Is that some sort of signature?" Jaq asked.

"I'm not certain," the rabbi admitted. "But whoever wrote this was an expert cabalist. Do you see how that 'S' in the last line is shaped?"

Boz angled the sheet for light. "The one with the flourish going up?"

The rabbi nodded. "It's not really an 'S'."

Only when it was pointed out did Boz detect the subtle change in the letter's shape. "You're right. It's an inverted Lamed."

"The Lamed is the twelfth letter of the Hebrew alphabet," the rabbi explained to Jaq. "When a letter is turned upside down, it carries an instruction to introduce the opposite meaning."

"As if saying it's not as it should appear to be," Boz said. "I had that rule drilled into me in Hebrew class as a boy."

Jaq wondered if Rev. Merry knew about this upside-down rule. The Old Testament, after all, would have originally been written in Hebrew. The last line in the signature intrigued her. "XPO are the letters of the Chi Rho cross. I saw them on the seal of the first king of Portugal. But why is this line started with a colon and ended with a period and a slant?"

"This would have been used by a Portuguese Jew, and a very clever one at that," the rabbi said. "Years ago, I read about this quirk of Portuguese grammar in a scholarly article by Professor Saul Ferreira. He found that two signs were used for a colon in medieval Portuguese. The one we use today, with two dots. And a second variation, with a dot followed by a slant."

"Why two?" Boz asked.

"Both colons once served as dividers of members in a sentence. The word 'colon' now means the intestines, but during the Middle Ages, 'colon' was also slang for a man's member."

"Like *cajones?*" Boz shot a jabbing grin at Jaq. "Those are testicles, in case you've never came across the term."

She ignored his little dig at her virginity, just to spite him.

"*Cajones* is a derivation," the rabbi confirmed. "The slang came to refer to a member of any group. Hence the grammatical colon is used to introduce a series of members comprising an ordered sentence."

Members of an order.

Jaq glanced at Boz, wondering if he also saw the possible connection to the Order of Christ. "But why would the Portuguese need two colons?"

"The pure or perfect colon alerted the reader that a series of members was approaching," the rabbi explained. "The impure or imperfect colon warned that the series was finished. Eventually, the imperfect colon fell out of use."

"And both were called *colons?*" she asked.

"Yes, but this Lamed alteration is even more mystifying," the rabbi said. "The 'S' shape stood on its side is the sign for the Hebrew equivalent of the tilde. It is applied in chanting to signal a change in the cantillation."

"The pointed diacritical arch," Boz said, reminded of his Sabbath-school grammar. "What's the tilde's equivalent in Hebrew?"

The rabbi looked stunned. "It's called the *Zarqa*, or ... "

"Or what?" she asked.

"*Zarqo.*"

She turned to Boz, not sure if she should be excited or apprehensive about this revelation. "You remember the last line the monsignor wrote on his board the night he died?"

Boz paled a shade. "A colon, a period, and a slant."

She asked the rabbi, "What about these letters above the colons? The three 'S's have dots on each side, but the other letters don't."

The rabbi adjusted his glasses to see what she was asking about.

Boz set the page in question next to the folio that contained the Mendoca coat of arms. "The 'S's are set in a triangle. Just like on the crest. But what do these dots mean?"

The rabbi traced his finger down the center of the inscription. "I have seen these three letters written together many times: *S.A.M.* The seamen and fishmongers sign their receipts with the anagram. Their gravestones are also carved with it. It is the abbreviation for the *Stella Ave Maris.*"

"Of course," Boz said, now understanding the reference. "Every sailor knows the *Ave* hymn by heart. I've heard it sung on the docks in Canada."

"That is not surprising," the rabbi said. "The *Ave* is the national anthem of the Acadians."

Jaq perked up at hearing of the connection to Nova Scotia. "What is this *Stella Ave Maris?*"

"A hymn to the Virgin Mary. Composed by St. Bernard of Clairvaux."

That name tweaked Boz's memory of his research about Chartres Cathedral. "Bernard ... wasn't he the spiritual father of the Templars?"

The rabbi nodded. "Mariners here have always believed the Blessed Mother protects them at sea. For years, they prayed to the Virgin's star and navigated by Her fixed presence."

"Which star was it?" Jaq asked.

"*Spica* is its modern name," the rabbi said.

Her jaw dropped. "The brightest star in Virgo."

"And the star representing Chartres," Boz confirmed, divining what she was thinking.

Jaq pulled out her Blackberry and snapped photos of the front and back of the parchment with her camera. She asked the little rabbi: "Can you draw me a picture of this *Stella Maris?*"

He broke a toothless smile. "I don't need to draw it. I can show you one."

On the far side of the river from the Tomar castle, Jaq and Boz stood with the rabbi under a towering rose window that crowned the 12th-century church of Santa Maria do Olival. Above its archivolt portal, which descended several steps into the ground, hovered a stone carving of a five-pointed star, the *Stella Maris.* Jaq stole a worried glance at Boz, wondering if he saw that this was the same star they had found in the tunnel leading to the synagogue.

"The Templars interred their grand masters here," the rabbi explained. "There is a legend that an underground passage ran to the castle for an escape route during Muslim attacks. Infrared tests on the ground have proven inconclusive."

"Why weren't the masters buried in the castle?" Boz asked him.

"This church is much older than the *conventio*. Santa Maria has always been revered as the spiritual home of the Templars in Portugal."

Jaq walked the grounds and came upon a well that had been dug near an old bell tower in the front courtyard. She wondered if it had been set there to serve as the ventilation shaft for the tunnel.

The rabbi opened the church door with a key. "As a museum curator in the town, I have certain privileges. If the Vatican knew that a Jew had access to one of its most famous churches, the dead popes would rise from the grave."

With the men following her, Jaq walked in and descended a row of steps. Another *Stella Maris* hovered backlit over the high altar. She looked down at her feet and saw that she was standing on a large flagstone set aslant from the others in the floor, just like the sun stone at Chartres. Did it cover the entrance to the tunnel? Nearby, a stele on the wall contained a Latin inscription.

The rabbi noticed her interest. "This is the tomb of Gualdim Pais, the most famous grand master of the Portuguese Templars. He built the castle here."

She examined the edges of the stele. "The mortar feels fresh."

Boz ran his finger down its creases. "It's been reset recently. I'd say within the last two days."

"What's behind this?" she asked the rabbi.

"A small recess. It holds the grand master's ashes and bones."

She turned back to the wall above the altar, to look up at the eyes of the *Stella Maris*, half hoping for guidance. "Has there been construction here?"

"None that I know of," the rabbi said.

She insisted to Boz, "We need to get into this reliquary."

The rabbi was aghast. "That is not possible!"

She pleaded her case to him. "The tomb has already been desecrated. By a Pakistani warlord who is trying to steal the sacred artifacts that accompanied the Ark of the Covenant. If he's gotten his hands on them, the survival of Israel could be in jeopardy."

The rabbi, incredulous, looked to Boz for confirmation of this wild claim. "Does the great Elymas believe that the Holy Ark was hidden in this tomb?"

"I don't know. But we have to find out."

Distraught over what he had just been told, the rabbi locked the door to prevent anyone else from entering. After a hesitation, he turned, face paling, and nodded his permission for the excavation, unable to utter the words. Boz searched a janitor's storeroom. He found a hammer and a chisel under a canvas. Bringing the tools into the nave, he chipped at the mortar around the stele while Jaq and the rabbi held the stone in place.

When the plate was finally loosened, they carefully removed it. Jaq motioned for Boz to hand over his Maglite. She peered into the depths of the narrow slot and saw shards of broken jars scattered amid ashes and bone fragments. She shook her head, indicating that they had come up empty again. This time, at least, Hosaam had found nothing, too. She took some comfort knowing that without all of the Temple relics, the Mahdi imposter could not yet launch his grand *coup.*

Long on odds as it was, they still had a chance to stop him.

First thing the next morning, Jaq and Boz stopped at a camera shop to purchase two prints of the digital photographs they had taken of the loose folio page. The nearest library, they were told, was a few kilometers away at the University of Coimbra. To save time, they decided to split up. He agreed to take one of the copies to the Romance Languages department to get a translation while she searched the library for more information about the Zarco family.

Dropped off in the middle of the campus. Jaq hurried to the library and asked at the reference desk for someone who spoke English. When a graduate student working part-time as a librarian offered help, Jaq showed her the photocopy of the Tomar folio page. She pointed out the strange monogram at the bottom. "Is there a way to research what these four lines might be?"

The student smiled. "No research is necessary. It is a sigil."

"What is a sigil?"

"A kind of signature with a secret message. Sigils were believed to contain magical powers."

"You wouldn't, by any chance, happen to know who used this one?"

"Of course. Cristobal Colon."

Jaq was perplexed by the student's smirk. "Who was he?"

The grad student became even more amused. "I think you Americans call him Christopher Columbus."

With jaw dropping, Jaq took another look at the copy. "*This* is the signature of Christopher Columbus?"

"Yes, of course. Everyone who studies history in our country knows of this sigil."

"Can you tell me what it means?"

The grad student chuckled. "If I could do that, I would not be writing my doctoral thesis on such a boring subject as Manueline architecture. No one has ever deciphered the sigil's meaning."

"Is there a professor here who specializes in Columbus studies?"

The student checked the university directory. "Most of our instructors are away on holiday. But you may be in luck. A conference on the Age of Discovery is being held here this weekend. Dr. Benedict Masterson from Yale University is one of the panel participants. It says here that he is an expert on fifteenth-century Iberia. Perhaps he can help you. Would you like me to try to arrange a meeting?"

"That would be great."

The student librarian connected the call. After explaining the purpose of her inquiry and receiving a response, she thanked the person on the other line and hung up. "That was Dr. Masterson's assistant. I'm afraid the professor has no time available. He is preparing remarks for a reception tonight in his honor. His flight leaves early in the morning. I'm sorry."

"I understand." Jaq scanned the volumes on the shelf behind the information desk. "I wonder if I might consult your Gales Directory there?"

"Of course." The student turned to retrieve the reference book.

Jaq leaned over the desk and glanced at the message screen on the phone. She memorized the number for the call just placed on her behalf. When the librarian turned back to deliver the volume, Jaq asked her, "Can you recommend a good clothing store in town?"

"There are several boutique shops on the Rue Quebra Costas."

Jaq picked up a brochure with map directions written in Portuguese for the multi-storied building. "Does the library have a section for English-language books on Columbus?"

"Yes, a rather extensive one. On the second floor."

She thanked the student. On her way up the stairs, she dialed the number she had just memorized from the reference computer screen. A man answering in sexy Portuguese welcomed her to the Hotel Quinta Das Lagimas. Praying that he understood English, she asked: "I've misplaced my invitation. What time is the reception for Dr. Masterson?" She pumped her fist when she got her answer. "Eight tonight? *Obrigado.*"

Dressed in the strapless red cocktail dress that she had charged to Boz's credit card that afternoon, Jaq ordered a glass of wine for show and sat down at a table in a corner of the Hotel Quinta's plush lounge. The place was packed with well-heeled people who looked to be the cream of the country's academia. She positioned herself close enough to the reception room to hear Professor Masterson finish his boring speech on the symbolism of St. Elmo's fire in Portuguese epic poetry. The reedy American scholar, mid-fifties with a goatee and a lugubrious face that made her think of a modern Don Quixote in tweed, finally finished his tedious presentation and walked into the lounge. Followed by a gaggle of tongue-wagging admirers, he commanded a seat at the bar and toasted his own performance with a double Scotch.

From the corner of her eye, she monitored this group of over-degreed toadies, waiting for the right moment to pounce. When a furry little man clinging to the professor's side finally excused himself to use the restroom, she shot up with her wine glass in hand and stole his spot at the bar. She rubbed a bare shoulder against the professor's back.

He turned—and she spilled wine on her chest.

"I'm so very sorry." The professor, seeing her for the first time, sized her up and liked what he saw.

She took the napkin he offered and slowly daubed the trickle running to the valley of her breasts, making certain he had a clear view. "That's what I get for taking a night off from my studies. I should be back in my room reading Morison and working on my thesis."

"Samuel Eliot Morison?"

She nodded, fluttering her lashes. "I find him so much more reliable than these modern revisionists." She smiled at him flirtatiously and cooed: "The newest is not always the best in many things, don't you agree?"

The professor ran a hand through his graying hair and sucked in his stomach. "Admiral Morison was my graduate advisor at Harvard."

She looked sadly into her glass. "I'm doing my graduate work here at Coimbra on Columbus. To be honest, I've hit a dead end. I thought maybe a night out would help clear my mind."

Mesmerized by how well she filled out the skimpy dress, the professor turned caring. "What's the subject of your thesis? Maybe I can help."

"Columbus's contacts with Portugal during his American voyages."

Only then did the professor break off his fixation on her cleavage. "That's a pretty thin topic."

She dipped her forefinger into her drink and tasted it. "Too bad I don't have you as an advisor."

He glanced around the lounge, as if making a quick risk-reward analysis. "It's awfully loud in here. Let's talk in my room, shall we?"

She let one of her straps drop over her shoulder. "Wow, you're so helpful. Most scholars wouldn't be this generous with their time."

"We'll, if the torch of wisdom had never been passed, we'd all still be hovering around fires in caves, wouldn't we?"

He paid for the drinks and escorted her into the lobby, resting his hand on the small of her back. They took the elevator to the fifth floor. He walked her down the hall, opened his door with a magnetic card, and offered her the path into the room. With one step into the bathroom, he grabbed a satin robe from a shelf and winked at her. "Give me a moment?"

As soon as he disappeared, Jaq sat at the foot of the bed and pulled out the photocopy of the folio parchment from her purse. She set it next to her cosmetic compact.

Seconds later, the professor reappeared in his robe. "Now, where were we?"

She gave him a come-hither look. "Do you always advise students in such formal attire?"

"Only the very bright ones." The professor sat next to her and brushed her hair across her forehead. He was about to go in for a kiss when his eyes landed on the paper that she had strategically positioned next to her hip. He picked it up and examined it. "Where did you obtain this?"

She acted surprised. "Oh, that? It must have fallen out of my purse. Nothing important. Just some research."

The professor's eyes were now more dilated than when he had first looked down her neckline. "You saw the original of this?"

"I think this one was in the archives of an old synagogue in Tomar. I've been through so many files, I can't remember. Is it something important?"

The horny scholar's frontal lobe had apparently short-circuited the reptilian stem of his brain. "If authentic, it's one of the most important Columbus discoveries in decades. Were there more pages like this?"

She played innocent. "I don't think so. It was in a collection of genealogy records for Jewish families who lived in medieval Portugal."

The professor placed the document on a table and studied it while stuffing a wad of tobacco from a half-filled package into his pipe. He lit up and quickly poisoned the room with smoke. "During the two years between his third and fourth voyages to America, Columbus wrote a rather dismal work called *The Book of Prophecies*. It was mostly a compilation of Scriptural quotations taken from theological works to support his belief that the Apocalypse was imminent. The book remained unpublished, stored in the cathedral at Seville until 1892. It wasn't even considered worthy of being translated into English until 1991."

She crossed her legs, trying to reclaim his attention. "You mean Columbus believed in the End Times?"

The professor puffed like a coal plant as he devoured the contents of the document. "A rather unfortunate aspect of his personality. I suspect this obsession of his was one of the reasons he got on so well with Queen Isabella. She considered herself to be the reincarnation of the Virgin Mary. She also believed herself to be the woman prophesied by the Book of Revelation who would usher in the Apocalypse. Columbus left on his first voyage only a few weeks after she issued her edict expelling the Jews. It was part of her grand plan to spur Christ's return to defeat the Antichrist. He seems to have become caught up in her bizarre visions. Some have even called him America's first Millennialist. The prevailing view is that he became a bit unhinged toward the end of his life."

"So, you think Columbus wrote this during his, you know ..." She twirled her index finger aside her temple.

He glowered at her, disgusted by her flippant attitude about the explorer's mental decline. "No doubt it was a case of too much stress and time on his hands while waiting for his next voyage. Fourteen leaves from *The Book of Prophecies* have been lost. This appears to be one of them."

"Is that his signature on the reverse side?"

The professor turned the document over, and huffed. "Ah, the blasted sigil. This damn thing has been the source of endless grist for the conspiracy crackpots. Adding fuel to the fire is a notation that someone, perhaps his son, wrote on a margin of one of the surviving pages that the missing leaves contained the best prophecies in the collection."

While he was reading, Jaq opened her purse a bit wider to sneak a look at the notes she had made on index cards during her hurried research in the library that afternoon. "You know, Bernard—may I call you Bernard?—some things about Columbus don't make sense to me."

The professor began pacing back and forth across the room, trying to understand this new discovery. "Such as?"

"Columbus said he was Genoese. But he married into a Portuguese noble family of high rank in the Order of Christ."

He waved off the anomaly. "A man brave enough to sail the unknown seas would have had little qualms about courting a lady of superior station."

"Maybe so, but from what I've been able to pick up, this Order of Christ was very protective of its maps and secret knowledge of the seas. Why would such a paranoid organization allow a foreigner so much access?"

He stopped his agitated shuffle to stare at her. "What are you're driving at?"

"Columbus first arrives in Portugal by miraculously swimming six miles to the southern coast after his ship is sunk in a battle with pirates. Then, almost immediately, he's accepted into the confidences of the royal court in Lisbon. That doesn't seem odd to you?"

The professor seemed distraught about something that he had just seen in the document. "His brother was already working in Lisbon as a mapmaker. Columbus likely obtained introductions through this family connection."

"But even after he went to work for Spain," she reminded him, "he always stopped first in Portugal on his return voyages."

"The southwestern coast of Portugal offered the nearest ports for Atlantic-bound ships. A mariner with depleted stores and a starving crew could not afford to be particular about where he obtained provisions."

"I thought Portugal and Spain were enemies," she said.

"Of course they were enemies! Columbus was chased by Portuguese caravels during one of his returns from America."

"Couldn't that have been just for show?"

The professor gave up a condescending chortle. "I think not."

"The Portuguese allowed him to leave Lisbon heavily in debt to the crown and go to Spain. Even after being commissioned by Isabella, he received royal audiences here. The Portuguese king referred to him as 'our special friend.'"

"Diplomatic niceties."

"Columbus told Isabella that he was not the only admiral in his family. What did he mean by that?"

"A mariner was a fifteenth-century version of a fast-talking wildcatter. He was probably stretching the truth a bit by referring to his wife's forefathers."

She zeroed in on the pompous ass. "But he was allowed to be present in the Portuguese court when a knight named Bartholomeu Dias gave a report of his voyage down the coast of Africa. This Dias fellow was also the first man to board the *Nina* and greet Columbus on his return from America. Surely Columbus's crew would have reported such a meeting to the Castilian court. What could he and this Dias have been discussing in private?"

The professor, turning redder by the second, was now comparing the document with footnotes in a book that he had taken from his briefcase. "Dias was probably inspecting the ship's log to make certain Columbus hadn't violated Portuguese territorial waters."

"Come on. You really think the Portuguese would send one of their most renowned explorers to perform such menial patrol duty?"

Shaken, he puffed furiously on his pipe. "I'm afraid we'll have to wrap this up. I have an early flight tomorrow."

She lay back on the bed in a coy play for more time. "You know, Wikipedia says that during his last voyage, Columbus diverted course to rescue a besieged Portuguese garrison in Morocco."

He twisted his face into an expression of horror. "Wikipedia? Couldn't you have consulted a more dependable source like, say, a comic book?"

"Wouldn't helping the Portuguese have been considered treasonous?"

He began shoveling piles of papers from his desk into his briefcase. "You could take any historical character and cherry-pick anomalies like this. George Washington was Benedict Arnold's friend. That doesn't mean Washington was a secret supporter of England. Now, if you don't mind—"

"To be fair, Washington never used a mysterious signature." She pulled the index cards from her purse to better see her notes. "Here's something else strange. Columbus's own son wrote that the Admiral, although endowed with all the qualities that his great task required, chose to leave in obscurity all that related to his birthplace and family."

The professor's pipe nearly fell from his mouth when he saw the index cards. "You planned this little ambush?"

She finished reading the quote, "'Just as most of his affairs were directed by a secret Providence, so the variety of his name and surname was not without its mystery.'"

"Fernando barely knew his father," the professor snapped, realizing now that he had been the one seduced. "Of course Columbus was a mystery to him. As are most famous fathers to their adoring sons."

"Why would he leave orders for his heirs to sign all legal documents with this sigil? It's as if he desperately wanted to preserve a hidden message."

He angrily tightened his robe strap around his waist. "I would never have invited you up here had I known you were promoting wild speculations."

She sat up on the bed, repeating with emphasis, "*Secret* Providence! Why would his son use the word 'secret?' If 'Providence' meant God, there was nothing to be kept secret by God, was there? Did Columbus possess a secret Portuguese map? Was that why he kept a second log?"

Flustered, the scholar began grabbing clothes from the closet and throwing them into his suitcase. "Ah, the *Siglio* theory rears its ugly head!"

"I'm sorry? Sig what?"

"There is a discredited school of thought, nurtured mostly in *this* seawash-addled country, which holds that the Portuguese knew of America long before Columbus. According to this claim, the Portuguese kept their discoveries secret to prevent the Vatican and the Spanish from learning of them. So now everything that can't be explained is attributed to this Portuguese mania for secrecy. Such arrant nonsense could have been avoided if only Henry the Navigator's archives had survived."

"What happened to them?"

"No one knows. They were probably lost in a fire or earthquake."

"Where do you think the Navigator's records would have been kept?"

"My guess is somewhere in the Algarve. Perhaps Sagres."

"Where is that?"

"The southwest tip. For centuries, Sagres was considered the end of the world. The Romans built a temple there to worship the god of the setting sun."

"Which god was that?"

"Saturn," he said. "Now, are you going to leave, or must I call security?"

The word 'SATOR' rang in her ear. "Henry the Navigator had a connection to Saturn?"

The professor regarded her as if she were daft. "I said nothing of the sort. Why would a devout Christian monarch possess a modicum of interest in a pagan god? He chose Sagres for his naval complex because of its secure location. The extent of his activities there are still in dispute, but he may have maintained what we might call an academy of nautical science. The closest modern equivalent is perhaps NASA or a black-ops unit."

"And the Templars?"

He rolled his eyes. "Oh, lord. Please don't bring *them* into this discussion."

"The Order of Christ took in Templar refugees," she reminded him. "Isn't it possible that the Templars discovered America and the Portuguese learned of its existence from Templar maps? Columbus wrote of seeing the wreckage of a ship in the Americas. In Rhode Island—"

"Morrison debunked that absurd contention years ago. By signing the Treaty of Tordesillas with the Vatican and Spain, the Portuguese gave up all rights to what would become known as North America. Why would they do that if they already knew about the continent?"

"What did Portugal receive as compensation in the treaty?"

"All lands yet to be discovered east of a meridian that ran near the Cape Verde islands."

"And that included Africa and India?"

"No one in Europe knew where precisely India was located."

"Maybe the Portuguese knew more than we give them credit for," she suggested. "Maybe they were searching for something they considered far more valuable than America."

He nearly bit off the end of his pipe in utter dismay at her naiveté. "What could possibly have been more valuable than a new continent rich with gold and silver?"

"The Vatican used the Portuguese spelling of Colon's name," she reminded him. "He wrote notations in Portuguese and christened many of his discoveries with Portuguese names. He also kept two logs."

Irritated beyond all forbearance, the professor glared at her as if chastising an unruly undergraduate. "You are treading on dangerous ground, young lady. Important people have a vested interest in preserving the truth about Columbus. You need to drop this *now*."

She bolted up from the bed to confront him. "Is that a threat?"

"A statement of fact, which is what historians like me deal in." He closed in on her with menace in his steely eyes. "I didn't spend forty years building a sterling academic reputation to have it undercut by some upstart. If you mention a word of what I am about to propose to you, I'll deny ever saying it. No one would believe you, anyway. I'll pay you twenty thousand dollars for the original of that page, accompanied by a nondisclosure clause to remain in force for the duration of your life."

She grabbed her purse. "I know someone at the National Security Agency who would find you quite charming."

"I can make sure you never get a job at a university."

She pulled out her phone from the purse and snapped a photo of him in his bathrobe. "And I can make sure you lose yours! I wonder if your wife would appreciate a little memento from the conference?"

He herded her toward the door. "Get the hell out of here!"

Outside, she remembered a critical question. She stuck her foot on the jam before he could close the door. "Columbus owned a book called the *Imago Mundi*. He wrote two words in its margin. 'Presbytr Johannis.' What did that mean?"

"Prester John!" the professor barked. "There's another myth you can waste your time chasing." He kicked her foot away and slammed the door.

Still steamed, Jaq flagged Boz down in front of the hotel and jumped into the car. They headed west for the motorway that ran along the coast.

Boz ogled her in the new cocktail dress. "That's what you used my Am Ex card for? Whatever you were doing in it, I hope you got paid by the hour."

She was in no mood for wisecracks. "I was just thrown out of a hotel room by an asshole from Yale who makes Josh Mayfield look like Francis of Assisi!"

Boz checked his watch. "We can get flight clearance out of Lisbon if we hurry. What'd you find out about that monogram?"

"Whatever's on that parchment was written by Columbus."

Boz's head spun faster than a mariner's gyroscope in a hurricane. A horn blared, warning that he had crossed the centerline. He swerved to avoid the oncoming car. "*Christopher* Columbus?"

"They call him Colon here. Did you find a translator?"

Back in his own lane, he handed her the English rendition of the Latin verses. "Fifty euros wasted for a bunch of useless Bible quotes."

She read the results:

Mark 4:22

For there is nothing hidden, except that it should be made known; neither was anything made secret, but that it should come to light.

Apocrypha

… revealing the steps of hidden things…

Numbers 21:8

Yahweh said to Moses, "Make a fiery serpent, and set it on a standard: and it shall happen, that everyone who is bitten, when he sees it, shall live."

Isaiah 65: 1-5

I reveal myself to those who did not ask for me; I am found by those who did not seek me. To a nation that does not call on my name, I say, "Here I am, here am I."

Isaiah 57:13

The wind will carry all of them off, a mere breath will blow them away.

She turned the copy over for the translation of the reverse side. The top caption was rendered:

Jeremiah 13-8

… Behold, he wrought a work on the wheels.

She scanned down to the translation of the left column, which read: *The first words as presented.* The lines down the second and third columns were: *Southeast right two; Northwest left one; Northeast and Northwest right three; Inner right one,* and so on. The line below all three columns had been translated as: *God's Mercy is with me. Father John Gomes.*

"Any of that make sense to you?" Boz asked.

"'God's Mercy is with me,'" she repeated. "What does *that* mean?"

"Probably just a generic closing. Like 'Yours truly' or 'God be with you.'"

"These look like some kind of directions." She kept coming back to the Jeremiah quote about the wheels. Powering up the shape-rendering program on her Blackberry, she rotated the wheels on the Templar square according to directions from the translation for the second and third columns. She came up with the following permutations:

THE	PEROP	ROTAS
FIRST	RATAO	APERO
WORDS	EANOS	PENET
AS	SATET	OSTRO
PRESENTED	TERRA	REATA

Boz leaned over for a peek. "More gobbledygook?"

She tossed the translation aside. "Looks like it. Another dead end."

He shrugged. "That student I hired did say one interesting thing. When I showed him the signature, he told me that *'Ferens'* means 'messenger' or 'servant' in Latin. It's also a nickname for Fernandes."

She studied the sigil again. "These three 'S's with the dots. If you take away the other letters, do you see what they form?"

"Looks like an arch."

She straightened, her interest suddenly rekindled. "An arch," she corrected him, "with stars."

"Hey, maybe it's the dome of the sky with the Virgo stars. The 'S's could be the Serpent of the brotherhoods. And S.A.M. would be the *Stella Ave Maris.*"

"You remember that coat of arms in the folio at the Tomar synagogue?"

"The one with the three 'S's?"

"The 'S' on the left was reversed." She opened her journal and drew the sigil with the left 'S' reversed. Did this arched arrangement crowned by the three 'S's represent the Temple of Solomon? Did the 'A' refer to the Ark inside in the arch?

"The 'X' could mean rebirth or renewal," he said. "I've seen 'X's used for the Resurrection on First Century stelae."

"What about the 'Y'?"

"I don't know about Latin, but the Greek alphabet didn't have the letter 'J'. The early Christian writers who wrote in Greek substituted 'Y' for 'J'."

"Jesus? John the Baptist?"

"If the Temple and the Ark are on top," he said, "then the 'Y' could stand for Jerusalem."

"The *New* Jerusalem."

"The 'M' might mean Millennium."

Jaq heard the monsignor's admonishing voice in her ear: *Think like an occultist.* All esoteric codes carried multiple levels of meaning. These sigil letters and their combinations could be layered with multiple messages. "That professor back there said Columbus was obsessed with the Millennium."

"Secret societies used the New Jerusalem prophecy as a covert reference for a future paradise or utopia," Boz said. "The Templar seal had '*Militum Xpisit*' for its motto. The *Chi Rho* cross would mean Christ. What about the 'O'?"

"Order?"

Boz combined the possibilities and revealed the result aloud, "This Member of the Order of Christ is a Messenger-Servant."

Jaq drew an arch under the three 'S's in her journal. "If the left-side 'S' is reversed like on the Mendoca coat of arms and ARCO is substituted for the arch, it spells ZARCOS."

"Zarco appears twice," he observed.

"Where's the second instance?"

"The Lamed inverted for the Hebrew tilde is called a *Zarqo*."

Jaq watched the countryside go by as she tried to clear her mind. "That still leaves the colons. Why are the colons in there?"

"Speaking of colons, those scrambled eggs we had this morning aren't going down so well. Mine's a little less than optimal right now. I may have to stop and—"

Jaq slammed her hands against the dashboard. "That's it!"

Boz hit the brakes so hard he almost skidded off the road. "What?"

She was nearly bouncing off the seat. "The two colons! Columbus was called Colon in Spain and Portugal. In medieval times, one colon was called the perfect colon. The other was called the imperfect colon. Whoever wrote this with the inverted Lamed was telling future generations that the Colon who appears to be Colon was not really a Colon."

"You're saying that Columbus was somebody else?"

"He did everything he could to hide his true identity."

"If he wasn't Columbus, then who *was* he?"

"It's written right here in front of us." She put the finishing touches on her revised drawing of the decoded sigil and showed him her artwork. "In 1476, a Portuguese knight from a famous family of explorers suddenly disappears from history. That same year, another man with an equally mysterious past swims ashore near Lagos."

"You mean—"

"Christopher Columbus," she said, "is Salvador Fernandes Zarco."

S
★ ALVADOR ★

A R C O
S ★ ★ S

X   M   Y
NEW   MARY   JERU
XPISTI MILITUM SALEM

MEMBER   P O FERENS
          X ORDER SERVANT ZARQO
             OF   MESSENGER
          CHRIST   FERNANDES

COLON ————————→ IS NOT A
                 PERFECT COLON

Boz spoke his next words slowly. "If you're right ... that means Columbus was a secret Jew. But why would a Portuguese knight from a noble family in the Order of Christ want to pose as a foreigner?"

"There's only one way to find out." She located the phone number for the library at Coimbra, and dialed. "Ms. Arenga? Jaqueline Quartermane. You helped me with the Columbus research this afternoon. I had one more question. Can you tell me where Prince Fernando, the nephew of Henry the Navigator, is buried?"

While waiting for her to get the answer over the phone, Boz scoffed, "I'm sure it's all explained on the tomb. Here lies the man who fathered the bastard who claimed to be Christopher Columbus."

Hearing the librarian's voice again, Jaq repeated the response for Boz's benefit. "The Religiosas da Conceição monastery in Beja? Thank you."

He waited to be told how that bit of trivia solved their problem. "So?"

She smiled wickedly at him. "Didn't I read something a while back about the Spanish government conducting a DNA test on Columbus's remains?"

"Yeah, I think it was in Valladolid. There was a dispute about whether it was actually him who had been buried there. So what?"

"So some bureaucrat has Columbus's genetic history in his desk," she said. "How long does it take to get a DNA test done?"

Boz looked at her as if she had flipped out. "Four to six weeks, if you're lucky and have ten thousand dollars to blow."

"We need it in forty-eight hours. You're always bragging about the dirt you have on people in high places. It's time to pull some strings."

"First of all, you have to find a sample that's not been degraded," he said. "For remains that old, it's a crapshoot. Then we'd have to get our hands on the Columbus exhumation report from the Spanish government for comparison. And if that isn't enough of a challenge, just how do you expect to obtain access to the tomb of a five-hundred-year-old Portuguese prince?"

"I remember studying a case in law school about a UN treaty that requires exhumations when needed to prove Jewish ancestry for Israeli citizenship."

"In some countries. But the petition has to be submitted by a rabbi and—"

She grabbed the wheel to prevent him from taking the exit toward Lisbon and the airport.

"Are you trying to get *us* exhumed?"

"Let's go check out the end of the world."

"We almost did!"

"Now I know what we've been doing wrong. We haven't made an offering to Saturn." She handed him her Blackberry. "Give your rabbi admirer in Tomar a call. He owes you a favor. Tell him the female friend of the Jewish Robin Hood is thinking about moving to Israel."

"You want me to submit a fraudulent legal claim?"

"That should be right up your alley. Just tell the rabbi I need to know if I'm related to the Mendocas."

Hearing herself speak those words gave Jaq pause. She sucked in a breath, wondering how far she had come since losing Paul. What else had she lost? Her own identity? After pondering that depressing thought, she recovered and found Boz staring at her as if thinking she really did belong in that Rhode Island nut house. At that moment, an idea suddenly occurred to her. "And while he's at it, have him send a sample of those ashes in the Grand Master's church tomb to the lab, too. Maybe our famous Portuguese Templar has some connection to all of this."

"Is that all?" Boz asked. "You sure you don't want to test Mary Magdalene's bones, just for laughs? Maybe both you and this Columbus imposter were the long-lost descendants of Christ."

"Don't be ridiculous. Salvador Fernandes Zarco was Jewish. Everyone knows that Jesus was Christian."

After driving south all night to the Algarve, Boz spun the car into the small coastal village of Sagres and stopped at a point whose headland cliffs dropped sharply to the roiling sea. All that remained from the site's days of glory were a white-walled fortress and a small chapel.

Jaq had expected to find hordes of tourists at the famous spot, but there wasn't a soul around except for a leathery-faced fisherman who carried a bucket of bait and sang what sounded like a sad song as he walked. "Excuse me!" she shouted at him. "Do you speak English?"

The fisherman ambled over to the car. "*Um pouco.*"

"Is this where Henry the Navigator had his naval academy?"

"*The Navigades? Sim!*"

"This all that's left of it?" she asked.

"Not even this. The cannons of the Englishman Drake destroyed the *fortazela* of the Navigades. These walls were rebuilt many years later. All that remain of the *Navigades* are the foundations of the *capela* and the *Rosa Rota dos Ventos*."

"*Rota?*" she repeated.

The fisherman nodded. "The Wind Rose."

Trading stunned glances, Jaq and Boz hurried from the car and followed the fisherman into a fortress that guarded the boot-shaped peninsula like a shackle on an ankle. To their left sat a giant stone circle, approximately 150 feet in diameter, with lines radiating from its center like spokes.

"The *Rota* was discovered only last century," the fisherman explained. "It sat outside the walls of the old fortress. Everything is now closed for the off-season. I take care of the buildings and give tours on weekends in the summer. My English is just okay, no? But it will improve as we practice."

Boz stared at the stone circle. "What was this wheel used for?"

The fisherman smiled cryptically. "No one knows ... but me."

Jaq pressed him. "How do *you* know?"

The fisherman cupped a hand to his ear. "I am a man of the sea. Certain knowledge is passed down by the wind. The wind has told me what once happened here."

She leaned in. "And?"

The man began walking off. "You would not understand."

"What if I hear the wind, too?"

He turned back on her with a scoffing glare. "Prove this claim."

She drew the letters of the SATOR-Templar square in the sand.

The fisherman's eyes narrowed with suspicion. "Anyone can form letters. But can you tell me what they mean?"

She offered what she had managed to decipher so far. "This peninsula was once dedicated to Saturn, the SATOR god of the sun. The ROTAS must be this wheel, the Wind Rose. TENET means to gain, hold, to comprehend, or to reach an object striven for. AREPO means to repossess an altar."

"And OPERA?" the fisherman asked, still testing her.

She shook her head, conceding that she was stymied on that one.

The fisherman reached into his bucket and pulled out a mackerel. He lifted one of its gills. "Do you know what the Romans called this part of the *peixe?*"

Jaq and Boz shrugged, clueless.

"*Opercula,*" the fisherman said. "Little lid."

Jaq dug the Latin dictionary from her bag and looked up the word. She was amazed to discover that this fisherman knew what he was talking about. '*Opercula*' came from the Latin '*operire,*' which means 'to open, uncover, or disclose.' How had she missed this?

Lid ... lid.

She pulled out her copy of the Tomar parchment and read the translation of the last line on the reverse side again. *God's Mercy is with me. Father John Gomes.* She asked the fisherman, "Have you heard of a priest named João Gomes?"

"*Sim*, Padre Gomes. He was sent to Ethiopia in the sixteenth century."

"Did he return to Portugal?"

Their impromptu guide turned guarded. "Maybe. Maybe not."

Boz was perplexed by her questions. "You think that priest had something to do with this wheel?"

"This Father Gomes brought back a message about God's Mercy."

"I'm not following."

She drew a picture of the Ark and its covering in her journal. "The *opercula* lid is the Mercy Seat that covered the Ark. Zarco must have used the blank side of the letter from the priest as parchment for writing his *Book of Prophecies.*"

"So the Portuguese priest found the relic?" Boz asked.

She studied her drawing again. "I think he was bringing back this message from *someone else* who found it."

Boz noticed that the fisherman was listening intently to their debate. He turned back to Jaq. "*Who* exactly?"

She reread the translation of the Latin directions that the priest had sent to Zarco. The left column said: THE FIRST WORDS AS PRESENTED. She figured that meant she should start without turning the wheels. She added in her new definitions and wrote: SATURN'S WIND ROSE HOLDS THE COMPREHENSION FOR REPOSSESSING THE ALTAR LID. She moved next to the translation of the middle column of directions, then wrote the letters in the sand with a stick:

$$
\begin{array}{ccccc}
P & E & R & O & P \\
R & A & T & A & O \\
E & A & N & O & S \\
S & A & T & E & T \\
T & E & R & R & A \\
\end{array}
$$

"TERRA could be land," Boz said.

Agreeing with him, she played with the remaining words. Only one combination made sense. "NOS means 'we.' EA is an adverb for 'there.'"

THERE WE ARE.

The fisherman had been observing their stumbling decoding efforts with a bemused smile. He pointed to the line RATAO. "That word is a humorous insult in my country. A rat, but a special kind. More like a land rat. Any boy who hasn't gone to sea is called a *ratao*."

Jaq tried that definition, but failed to come up with anything relevant:

HERE WE ARE IN THE LAND OF LAND RAT.

She was about to give up when the fisherman saw something in her scribbled Templar square that hooked his interest. He led Boz and her into the chapel of *Nossa Senhora da Graca*, whose only accessories were a Baroque retable behind the altar and a few gravestones.

"Was there a cemetery here?" she asked.

"*Sim.* For bodies washed ashore from shipwrecks."

Walking in the sanctuary, she felt a sudden chill. Was this place haunted?

The fisherman reached under the altar and pulled out an ossified sliver of wood. "The *Nossa Senhora da Graca* was built in 1579," he said. "It sits on the foundations of an older chapel. Here mariners spent their last nights before sailing into the Sea of Darkness. Years ago, I found this beam in the charnel house. It contains carved names and dates. The seamen had a tradition of preserving their memory should they become lost at sea. There is one name on it that may interest you."

Jaq followed his finger down the beam, until he stopped it on:

Pero da Covilha, 1487.

The word PERO, she realized, was formed by the first four letters of the top line in the second column of the translated SATOR-Templar square. "Who was this Pero da Covilha?"

"King João sent him to Ethiopia to find Prester John."

Wasn't that the name Columbus wrote in the margin of the *Imago Mundi?* The same Prester John that professor had dismissed as a myth? She asked the fisherman, "Who was Prester John?"

"A legendary Christian king in the East."

She curled a vengeful grin. Nothing would give her more pleasure than to throw this discovery back into that asshole professor's puffing face. She opened her journal and reexamined the middle column of the square translations. The left vertical row spelled PRESTER down and across the bottom. The opposite outer row down spelled POSTA. She consulted the Latin dictionary: Posta was an abbreviation for *Post Annis*, or AFTER MANY YEARS. She asked the fisherman, "When did Pero da Covilha sail for Ethiopia?"

"He did not sail," the fisherman said. "He walked."

She pounded a fist into her palm in triumph. Now, finally, she understood the RATAO reference. Yet one word still eluded her: SATET. There was nothing about it in her dictionary. She waited for Boz and the fisherman to speak up, but when they had no suggestions to offer, she dialed the librarian at Coimbra and asked for a search. Hearing the result, she required a moment to take it all in. "Satet was an Egyptian goddess of water and serpents. Her domain was the source of the Blue Nile."

"That's Lake Tana," Boz said. "In Ethiopia."

She stitched together the possible new decoding of the message that Covilha had sent back to Portugal with Father Gomes:

AFTER MANY YEARS, THERE WE ARE, PERO THE LAND RAT
IN THE LAND OF THE SERPENT GODDESS SATET,
THE SOURCE OF THE NILE, ETHIOPIA.

"But why 'We Are There?'" Boz asked. "Who is with him?"

"Prester John," she said. "Or maybe the Mercy Seat for the Ark."

He looked puzzled. "Why would this priest give the message to Zarco?"

She searched the names carved on the beam. Salvador Zarco wasn't among them, but another name on the list intrigued her. "Bartholomeu Dias is written next to Pero da Covilha. This guy Dias always seemed to be around when Columbus returned from America."

The fisherman explained, "Dias was sent to find a passage around Africa."

She checked the date next to his carved name. "At about the same time Covilha was sent to Ethiopia." She studied her translation of the third column of the Zarco parchment:

R O T A S
A P E R O
P E N E T
O S T R O
R E A T A

The first word was easy: the Wind Rose, again. The dictionary said APERO was a variation of *aperio*, derived from the root *apere*, to "reveal" or "lay bare." PENET was the root for *penetrare*, to "enter, go deep, pass through, or penetrate."

The fisherman pointed to REATA. "This word is *Espanhol*." He spat as if to cleanse his mouth. "I have heard *caballeros* in Andalusia use it. It means a rope tightened around something."

"Like a lasso?" she asked.

"Or a noose. But the word also has two other meanings. To reopen something that has been closed."

"And the third?" Boz asked.

The fisherman hesitated. "Not for the ears of a *senhora*."

"You can tell me," Jaq assured him.

The fisherman struggled to avoid being too graphic. "In *Espanha*, the bobos use it to refer to a man's privates, like a long rope."

"A man's member ... a colon." Jaq gathered the meanings in the third column together in a sentence: PENETRATE THE WIND ROSE TO REVEAL COLON. After a hesitation, she looked up from her notebook. "I think something's buried under that wheel out there."

Boz stared at her in disbelief. "Even if you're right, where would we dig? That circle is huge."

The fisherman grinned knowingly. "You have not completed the square."

Jaq suddenly remembered that they had not solved the word OSTRO. Before she could ask the fisherman if he knew what it meant, he took her hand and led her from the chapel. The setting sun had now cast the Wind Rose on the headland in a golden tint. She tightened her jacket, chilled.

Followed by Boz, the fisherman brought her to the center of the giant wheel. Pulling a bandana from his back pocket, he tied it around her eyes and spun her around several times. "Do you feel the wind?"

She nodded, uncertain where this bizarre experiment was leading.

"There are thirty-six different winds on the sea," the fisherman said. "Which one are you now facing?"

Disoriented and dizzy, Jaq struggled to maintain her balance. "I don't know anything about winds."

"Here the final initiation for the knights of the Order of Christ was held. No mariner could take to the seas until he identified every wind while being blinded at night."

"How could anyone do that?" she protested.

"When deprived of one's bearings, a mariner must resort to his instincts. You are lost in a thick fog, *senhora*. No land for hundreds of miles. Your crew fears the approach of death. The men are panicked. You alone, their admiral, can save them. If you are truly a descendant of mariners, the gift has been passed down to you in your blood. Which wind do you feel?"

She realized that she was experiencing just a taste of the terror that her ancestors must have felt before they sailed for the Sea of Darkness.

"There is an old saying in my country," the fisherman said. "If you want to learn to pray, *truly pray*, go to sea."

She tried to focus on the wind at her cheeks. It was not a stinging blast like others she had encountered along the coast. No, it had a warmth, and a wetness too, a humid zephyr. She remembered such winds on late spring days in Kentucky, when the rains were coming over the mountains. Was that a taste of spice it carried? Maybe a hint of cumin or clove? A vision of red sands flashed across her mind's eye. She couldn't explain why, but she felt the pull of Africa.

"The wind," the fisherman ordered her again. "Name it."

"South," she guessed, not knowing its official navigational designation.

"Tack into it."

She began walking with bated steps, keeping the rib of the Wind Rose at the sides of her feet.

"Stop *aqui*." He removed the bandana from around her eyes. "You have shown me, *senhora*, that you have the heart of a Lusiad. You have just boxed the compass."

She looked down at her feet. She stood at the far edge of a pie section that formed the Wind Rose.

"This is the compass point for the southern wind," the fisherman explained. "A wind my ancestors called the *Ostro*."

OSTRO ... the last unsolved word in the message.

She compiled in her mind the meanings of the square when the Templar wheels were turned as directed by the third column of the Zarco parchment:

PENETRATE THE WIND ROSE AT
THE OSTRO TO REVEAL COLON

The fisherman opened a shed near the chapel and brought out three shovels, a rope, and a lantern. "There is an old saying in my country. God gave us a small nation for a cradle, but the entire world for our grave. Let us see if a new world can be found in a grave *here*."

The three of them began digging at the Ostro wind point. Four feet down, Boz's shovel hit metal. They lifted a coffin from the pit. The fisherman pried it open. A man's skeleton lay inside. A rotted rope was wrapped around his broken neck. His teeth still clenched a wooden rod.

"There is your *Reata*," the fisherman said. "The noose."

Boz examined the frayed rope. "Looks like he was executed by hanging."

Jaq stole a questioning glance at the Portuguese man who had just initiated her on the Wind Rose. Sure, he probably had to learn some of this stuff to qualify as a tour guide, but he seemed unusually informed about these old navigators and their secrets. Could there be more to him than met the eye? If so, why was he helping her? She reached down and pulled a ring from the victim's finger. Its facing held a red cross on a white background.

"I've seen this at soccer games," Boz said. "It's the Cross of St. George. Fans of the Sampdoria football club wear it."

"Where is Sampdoria?" she asked.

"Genoa."

Suddenly, it came to her. "This is the *real* Columbus!"

Astounded, Boz took a step back. "The Portuguese must have executed him after he swam ashore from the shipwreck. Zarco stole his identity. They were just waiting for the right moment."

Jaq realized that the Order of Christ had used the Spanish slang for noose in the message as a private joke, a sort of flip of the finger at the Castilians. "How could those Portuguese knights fool so many people?"

Boz carefully picked up the decaying hood that was hooked around the buried victim's skull. "They used the Distraction and the Switch. The world's oldest trick of illusion. Zarco, with head bare, would have been marched to the gallows. The Portuguese were counting on the Spanish spies to be watching with their telescoping glasses from the hills or their ships in the bay."

"But why would the Spanish believe Zarco was a criminal?" she asked.

Boz looked up to the sky, as if imagining a gallows above him. "The Order probably handed him a death sentence on some trumped-up charge. That's why his records are silent after 1476. His wife and brother would have been sworn to uphold a vow of silence and take the Colon name. That also explains why Fernando Colon was so confused by his father's origins. He was likely never even told of the switch in identity."

Jaq was still perplexed by one missing key. "How did the Portuguese convince Columbus to go along with the scam and give up his life?"

"Those knights weren't the persuasive type," Boz said. "My guess is the real Columbus would have been hooded and gagged and kept out of sight near the gallows. Something distracted the Spanish spies who were lurking in the hills or on the sea. A mother's shriek. Or maybe a brother's shout promising revenge. In the blink of an eye, Zarco would have been spirited off to safety while Columbus, in identical sackcloth and hood, was substituted for him. When Columbus was marched up the steps, he would have been weak from fear and soporifics. This noose was tightened around his neck. The door under his feet dropped. It all would have happened in minutes."

The fisherman made the sign of the cross over the rotting coffin. "Poor weaver from Italy. He signed on with a galley to avoid starving. And he died not knowing why."

Shivering, and not from the breeze, Jaq stared down at the skeleton. "But why would the Order want Zarco to become Italian?"

"Marco Polo was Italian," Boz reminded her.

She circled the excavated grave, thinking. "Something that Yale professor told me didn't make sense. If the Portuguese knew about America, why would they give it up in a treaty? And why would the Order of Christ send Zarco to Spain to petition Isabella to send him west toward a land it didn't want and couldn't hold anyway?"

The fisherman hissed with contempt. "The *Espanhols* are fools. They thought India could be reached by sailing west."

Jaq gasped—the dots suddenly connected for her. "That's because Zarco convinced them of it!"

Now understanding what had happened, Boz grinned with admiration at the cleverness of his medieval comrades in illusion. "They pulled off this fake execution and sent Zarco to Spain as Columbus to serve as a decoy. Those Portuguese knights *wanted* the Spanish to sail to America."

Jaq drove the theory to its logical conclusion. "The Templars hid the thirteen Temple artifacts around the world and left directions for their discovery by using the SATOR square. The Navigator must have revived the aborted Templar mission."

Boz was fast on her heels, matching conclusion with conclusion. "And the Portuguese would have known from the Templar archives that the Mercy Seat was in Ethiopia. Covilha was sent by land and Dias by sea to find Prester John. To give them time and cover, Zarco-Colon kept the Spanish distracted with his scheme to sail west to reach India."

Jaq ran a hand through her wild, thick hair, slowly coming to a shocking realization. "Isabella must have been as desperate as the Portuguese to find the Ark and the Temple treasures." She looked at Boz and saw that he was equally shaken. "The Queen of Revelation had to find the thirteen treasures to rebuild the Temple before igniting the Apocalypse."

"Our race with Hosaam …" Boz's words trailed off.

She finished his thought for him. "It all happened once before. Refugees persecuted by the Church formed a secret alliance. Blacklisted Templars. Cathar heretics. Jews and cabalists driven out of Spain."

"All guardians of the original mission. The Knights of the Brazen Serpent must have passed the duty down to the Mithraic initiates to the Templars, the Masons …

She examined the dark skin on her arms. "And to the Portuguese knights whose descendants became … my Melungeon ancestors."

Boz began pacing faster around the grave. "The Order of Christ claimed to be a supporter of Rome."

She nearly had to run to keep up with him. "But the Tomar knights were scheming all along to thwart the Inquisition."

Boz shook his head in amazement at the similarities. "Torquemada and his Dominicans were the medieval versions of Hosaam and his Islamic thugs."

She nodded. "The Navigator wanted to build the Templar New Jerusalem before Isabella and her inquisitors could ignite the Apocalypse."

"Maybe," Boz cautioned. "But one piece of the puzzle still doesn't fit. The Columbus imposter also believed in the Apocalypse."

"No, he didn't," she countered. "Zarco wrote his *Book of Prophecies* to convince Isabella that he shared a belief in her destiny."

Impressed with that insight, Boz turned toward the Wind Rose and asked the fisherman, "Did Pero da Covilha ever find Prester John?"

The Portuguese man shrugged. "Our history is silent on this."

Boz's eyes filled with that old look of treasure lust. "That means the Mercy Seat is still in Ethiopia."

"Unless," Jaq said, "Hosaam's men found it the night Paul was murdered."

"They didn't find it."

"How can you be sure?"

"Those *jihadists* tortured that Ethiopian priest. If they had already found the Mercy Seat, they would have killed him quickly and high-tailed it off. They were trying to force him to reveal where it was hidden."

"So if the Mercy Seat is no longer in Lalibela …"

"The Portuguese must have sent a caravel to Ethiopia to retrieve it," Boz said. "That's why the priest brought back the message from Covilha. The spy was telling his fellow members of the Order of Christ to come for it."

Jaq rushed back into the chapel for another look at the beam inscribed with the mariners' names and dates. When the two men followed her inside, she pointed to one of the carvings. "Padre Gomes delivered Covilha's message to Zarco in 1506. It says here that a mariner named Afonso de Albuquerque set sail that same year with five caravels bound for the East." She asked the fisherman: "Who was this Albuquerque?"

"A famous admiral. He was called our Portuguese Mars."

"Would he have been a comrade of Pero Covilha's?" she asked.

A twinkle flashed in the fisherman's eye. "Albuquerque was of the next generation. They certainly would have known each other."

She thanked him for his help and then hurried with Boz to the nearby Pousada Infante, a popular lodge that overlooked the cliffs of Sagres. After washing up, she found a book on Portuguese history in the gift shop that showed the route Albuquerque took to the East Indies. The admiral, it said, had sailed around the Cape of Good Hope to the Red Sea and the coast of present-day Eritrea. A footnote caught her eye: His treasure ship, the *Frol do Mar*, had been lost off Malabar. The wreckage and its contents had never been recovered.

Boz looked over her shoulder. "What'd you find?"

She slammed the book closed. "Get your plane fueled."

"For what?"

"A very long flight."

Before Boz could demand an explanation, Jaq's Blackberry rang, and she answered it. As she listened to the voice on the other end, her eyes widened.

"Who is it?" Boz asked.

She hung up, needing a moment to recover. "The lab."

"No results. I told you the sample would be too degraded to—"

"The DNA markers are positive for Prince Fernando. The man buried in Columbus's tomb is Salvador Zarco."

Boz was amazed that her wild hunch had paid off. "That confirms it, then. The real Columbus is out there in that grave under the Wind Rose."

"There's more. Those ashes we had the rabbi scrape out of the Santa Maria tomb also came back positive."

"Positive for what?"

"Bovine."

He blinked hard. "You mean ... like a cow?"

"I mean *exactly* a cow. And a rare one. They've never seen this pattern of bovine genome before."

"What were *cow* ashes doing in a Templar tomb?"

She stared up at the full moon and wondered if the SATOR god was laughing at them from above. "Rev. Merry told me that one of the artifacts from Solomon's Temple was a jar of ashes from a red heifer. Hosaam must have found the ashes in Tomar. That means we've got one chance left to stop him now."

"Which is?"

"Let's just hope that Mercy Seat lid was on Albuquerque's treasure ship when it went down."

┼HiR┼Y-Six

┼HE WES┼ERՈ A┼LAՈ┼ic
OC┼OBER, 1492

Wasted from thirty-three days at sea, Zarco slid the slat through the
rings of his cabin door and collapsed behind his cramped writing
desk. He rubbed his swollen eyes, trying to stay awake, for this was
the only time of the night when he could steal a few moments alone. He lifted
his secret journal from under the loose board and opened it to his last entry:

> *11ᵗʰ of October: Made fifteen leagues despite indifferent easter-
> lies. Told the men we made nine, and showed them the second log to
> deny their claim that we have sailed too far. Pinzon and the pilots
> are becoming suspicious. They begged me to turn southwest and
> follow the birds, but I maintained course due west.*

He had contracted the three ships and their crews for 750 leagues only, the
distance at which he had assured Isabella they would reach Cipangu. These
Spaniards on board were loyal to Pinzon, not to him, and if they discovered
that the ships had covered 1,200 leagues, they might throw him overboard. He
had suspended sailing after dusk, affecting a bold confidence of nearing land.
When that ruse produced no results, he had won three more days by shaming
the crew with the prospects of confronting their monarchs in failure.

But he needed another miracle, and soon.

He had to keep faith. Had he not been blessed with divine intervention
from the very inception of this enterprise? How else could Isabella's sudden
conversion to the mission be explained? Winds sent from Heaven had saved
him from the dead calms. And the crews were blind to his navigational falsifi-
cations only because the Dove of Light had clouded their eyes.

Isabella had extorted a promise from him that, after provisioning on the
Canaries, he would not sail south of the 28ᵗʰ parallel, the line demarking

Spanish and Portuguese waters set by the Treaty of Alcáçovas. But to catch the trade winds essential for making good time, he had been required to drop to the 20th parallel near the Cape Verde Islands. He had told no one of this deviation and, by altering the astrolabe, had convinced Pinzon that his apocryphal calculations were accurate. The trap had been sprung when, in a prearranged ploy, three Portuguese caravels began tailing him. His Spanish crews, certain that the Portuguese would attack if the boundary were to be violated, had simply assumed that he was maintaining the *Santa Maria* on a northern course.

A distant caw attacked his ears. Day and night these gulls now taunted him. The riggings clanged, an indication that the wind was freshening. This strengthening of the westerlies always caused the men to fear that the caravels could not beat back to Spain. He unfolded the sheepskin map from Sagres and checked his figures against the secret measurements used by the Order. They were very close now to the continent that the Templars had discovered.

Sim, he could feel it in his bones.

But how much longer could he maintain this artifice? The game had nearly been given up five days ago when the compass had begun acting strangely. Checked against the Polestar, the needle had dropped a full point to the west. That discovery had set off a panic on deck, but he had purchased a few more hours by ordering the pilots to retest the compass at dawn. The next morning, to his relief, the needle had pointed true north. He had told them, falsely, that the circular movement of the Polestar had caused the anomaly.

A Lombard cannon boomed in the distance.

That tinny crack came from the *Pinta*. Overhead, he heard a rush of feet pound to starboard. Isabella's promise of an annuity to the first man who spotted land had caused the crews to become so obsessed with searching the horizon that they now shirked their duties. As a result, there were now so many false sightings that he no longer gave them credence.

Instead, his thoughts turned to his comrades. Would the *Ratao* have reached the East this month? Or would Dias have beaten him to those distant shores? Pero was headstrong and determined, but he was traveling on foot through infidel lands. Dias had always been the quiet one, still waters running deep, and caravels were faster. Still, he would put his wagering coin on Pero. After all, on the night of their initiation, in the tunnel at Tomar, Pero was the one who—

A fist pounded on the door. With a heavy sigh, he slid back the bar.

His pilot stood at the threshold with the look of joy that only another seaman could understand. "Captain Pinzon has just signaled a confirmation. The *Pinta* has found land!"

He braced for his next false performance, for he would now have to convince these Spaniards that the primitives they encountered, with their curly hair and gaudy feathers, were citizens of ancient and wise India. How would he explain the absence of ports like Calicut? And how long would he be able to keep them trolling the coast for nonexistent gold and spices?

No, the Old Man had not left him instructions for *this* challenge.

Lalibela, Ethiopia
June, 1493

Covering his face with his white shama, Pero fell in with a procession of priests walking toward the maze of underground churches. Thin and blackened by the harsh Eastern sun, he had little trouble passing himself off as one of the holy hermits who lived in the caves here, and he had quickly picked up their language, finding many similarities in it to Hebrew. As he came over a barren hill, tears of discovery bathed his weary eyes.

The old Kingdom of Prester John lay before him.

The eighth wonder of the world had somehow been cut whole into the red earth, just as the Templars had described it. He carefully descended into the subterranean sanctuary of Bet Georgis and lingered at the rear of the holy procession. When the priests were not looking, he split off and hid in one of the many crannies. There he would wait until early morning. Then, after all became quiet and desolate, he would at long last retrieve the precious object of his quest.

In the darkness, he slid to his haunches and whispered a prayer of thanksgiving that tomorrow he would finally begin his journey home. His thoughts turned to the many marvels he had witnessed on his seven-year journey. He had cooled himself in the shadows of the Pyramids of Giza and had stared down the inscrutable face of the Sphinx. After escaping from Mecca, he had gone to Yemen, only to learn that Paiva had died in Africa of a mysterious illness. The loss of his traveling companion had cast him into a black melancholy for months. Yet he had kept his vow to the Old Man, making his way to Calicut to inspect the ports of India, where he had found Hindus wearing gold and Moslems spreading their faith to the painted worshippers in the pagan temples. Even more remarkable, he had discovered of a long-lost sect of Christians who called themselves Nestorians and claimed to be descendants of Thomas, the apostle sent by Christ to India to convert the East.

After Calicut, he had wandered along the Indian coast and had eventually returned to cross the Red Sea. The king of these Ethiops, Eskender, had welcomed him warmly, but to his keen disappointment, the monarch proved not to be Prester John, only a descendant. He had been informed that the Prester died many years ago, exactly when no one here could remember, and nothing remained of his once-thriving kingdom except a few empty churches and these ruins of his palace. Yet these impoverished Ethiops had fulfilled their vow to protect the treasure until the Knights of the Red Cross returned for it. Eskender had revealed to him the location of its hiding and promised to provide an armed entourage to help him take it to the port on the Red Sea.

Now, only one obstacle remained.

Even King Eskender could not order the priests to give up the relic, for they had taken oaths to protect it. He would have to retrieve it by his own devises. *Egzer yst'iny*, the king had said to him in a blessing. *May God provide.*

He peered around the corner to make certain the holy men who guarded these underground churches had departed for the night. Reassured, he climbed to his knees and crawled toward the Tomb of Adam, having memorized its location from the Templar map. He found the stone sarcophagus and slid away its slab. Denied a light, he reached into its depths and felt two sharp points.

Sim. His life's mission was only seconds away from being accomplished.

Distant voices echoed from the antechamber. With no time to retrieve the trove and carry it out, he pushed the stone back over the tomb and ran toward the far end of the church.

A cadre of priests armed with clubs confronted him at the portal.

The head priest shouted, "*Badalyana!*"

Surrounded, Pero spoke *Ge'ez* and insisted that he had been granted permission by King Eskender to worship in this church.

"The king is dead," the head priest said.

Pero retreated a step. Had Eskender been murdered by a rival? He tried to put up a front of authority despite having lost the only person who could explain and defend his presence here. "I must see the king's body!"

"You are to be held prisoner."

"By whose command?"

"The king's brother, Naod."

"For what crime?"

The priest signaled for his men to arrest him. "No foreigner enters the land of the Lion of Judah and leaves to tell of its mysteries."

Pero closed his eyes in despair as his hands were clasped into manacles.

Lisbon
June, 1497

With the royal summons in hand, Dias fought a path through the palace crowds. After returning from the southern African cape, he had been assigned to Lagos to oversee the construction of the new armada that would make the attempt for the Indies. So much time had passed that he had all but given up hope of ever seeing his life's mission accomplished.

But, at last … had a message from Pero truly arrived?

A host of sycophants, spawned by the realm's lucrative new trading business, surrounded the twenty-six-year old monarch, Manuel. Dias's stomach turned at this sight of the Old Man's legacy being trampled under such a rush for riches and titles. The deceased King João had made the Old Man's secret quest a priority by putting down the conspiracies incited by these recalcitrant nobles, including the relatives of Manuel's wife. But this inexperienced royal cousin had gained the throne after King João perished under mysterious circumstances in a horse fall, and now Manuel was consumed with lust for revenge and wealth.

"Shipwright!" The youthful king shouted on seeing Dias limp into the court. "You move slower these days than you did below the ass of Africa!"

The scornful laughter of the courtiers burned Dias. Had he risked his life only to be branded a coward for failing to convince his rebellious crew to continue on to India? These fools knew nothing about the demands of the sea. On his return from that voyage, he had suffered even more humiliation when Manuel insisted on changing the name he had given to his discovery. To promote trade, this callow king now called Tormentoso the Cape of Good Hope, as if the maiden voyage through those treacherous waters had been nothing more than a pleasure jaunt. Yet all of that ignominy meant nothing now, for Pero was confirmed alive. He begged to know more. "Sire, what does Covilha say?"

Manuel waved a fragment of papyrus at him. "The message is indecipherable! The man has fallen stark raving mad. The couriers from Cairo swear it is in his hand, but none of us can fathom it. We were hoping you might understand his demented mode of communication."

Dias's heart quickened when he saw the five-worded message:

$$
\begin{array}{ccccc}
A & P & O & S & \underline{O} \\
T & E & R & R & E \\
N & E & P & T & S \\
E' & R & O & T & A \\
R & A & T & A & O
\end{array}
$$

The last line of the word square confirmed that Pero had written it. Dias rubbed his temples while trying to recall the rules of translation taught to him so long ago. APOS meant "past", he suspected, but why was the "O" underscored with a half-circle? TERRE could mean "land". Why would Pero not use the more conventional *"pais"*? TERRE could also refer to "terrible" or "feared." They had, after all, been drilled as squires to adopt code words in the square that could perform double work. Terrible land? Feared land?

The monarch tapped his foot impatiently. "You take longer to read than you do to reach the ends of Africa. If you tarry much longer ..."

That was the last word Dias heard of the king's petulant complaint. Of course! TERRE meant the land of fear—Africa. NEPTS, however, made no sense to him. E'ROTA, with the diacritic, would be read 'is the route.' What could the underlined 'O' at the end of APOS mean?

Study the image of the letter, the old cabalist had instructed them as boys.

What does an underlined 'O' resemble? A cannon's barrel? A mouth with a chin? The opening to a tunnel?

No, the *globe*... and the half circle meant *go under*.

He released a breath of discovery. Why had he not seen this from the start? NEPTS means *Neptune's domain*... the sea. He put them together: PAST THE LAND OF FEAR. GO UNDER. THE SEA IS THE ROUTE.

That was it, he said to himself. Pero was confirming that the way to reach Prester John was by sailing below Africa.

"Do you understand this correspondence, or not?" the king demanded.

His breast swelled with pride. "By God's grace, my comrade says that a sea route exists to attain the object of our desire."

Manuel broke a wide grin and clapped loudly. "At last, we will wrest the spice trade from the Levantines and Venetians!"

Not certain he had heard correctly, Dias came closer to the youthful king's ear and whispered, "My lord ... the Prester."

When Manuel reacted blankly to that hint, it slowly dawned on Dias that the elders of the Order had not revealed to this untrustworthy monarch the true purpose of Pero's overland journey. All had been set in place for this hour of victory, but it was to have been King João who would drive the stake into the heart of their enemies. The sea passage to Prester John was now in Portugal's exclusive control. Yet Manuel had commandeered the grand mastership of the Order for his own enrichment, and now he was stocking the monastery at Tomar with his allies and cronies, using their hallowed headquarters as a staging base for his political purgings.

Dias was desperate. How could he prevent Manuel from abandoning all that the Old Man had worked so hard to attain? If the guardians of the Order had deemed it best not to advise Manuel of Pero's mission, they no doubt also withheld Zarco's secret assignment from him, too. Reluctantly, he held his silence, hoping fervently that the superiors in Tomar who had been assigned to keep the Old Man's quest alive now possessed a backup plan to rescue Pero.

The king pranced about like a child with the promise of a new bauble. "We must exploit this passage at once before the Spanish learn of its existence!"

Dias straightened on hearing the call of duty. "The caravels at Lagos are being given their final coats of tar as we speak, Excellency. I can be launched and on my way to India within the week. I suggest we rig the masts with square sails and—"

The king shook his head. "I have another assignment in mind for you. I am in need of a competent governor for São Jorge da Mina."

His spirit plummeted. "On the Guinea coast? Excellency, I am the only man who knows the dangerous reefs around the Cape."

"D'Alenquer was on that voyage, no?"

"*Sim*, but ..."

"He will serve as the pilot," the king ordered.

Dias felt the smirks of the younger mariners who had spent weeks vying for this task rightly his: The brash lad Ferdinand Magellan, once a page to Manuel's wife; Pedro Alvares Cabral, son of the governor of Beiras; and the most ruthlessly ambitious of them all, Vasco da Gama, whose father had been a knight in the house of the Duke of Viseu. All three men hailed from families that had supported Manuel in the bitter rift with João. Only now did he decipher the diabolical scheme that Manuel was setting into motion. The monarch was bent on erasing from history all the glorious deeds of his predecessors by culling the archives and rewriting the chronicles to make it appear that he alone had been the father of Portugal's emerging sea empire. In the process, Manuel had altered the Order's mission from its original spiritual quest to crass commercial colonization designed to maximize royal profits.

He lowered his chin in defeat. As a boy, he had made jest of the old mariners and had bragged how he would accomplish the feats they had left undone. Now God was punishing him for that youthful hubris.

The king snapped his fingers to regain his attention. "Old mariner, whom would you recommend as captain for this enterprise?"

That question stung Dias like an asp's bite. If an inferior navigator were to be sent, Pero might be left stranded in the East. So, he swallowed his pride and resolved to propose the most promising of the untested pups. Magellan, the youngest, hadn't even served as a squire. Cabral was a firebrand who took too many dangerous risks. Da Gama, on the other hand, had at least studied astronomy at Evora and had managed to seize a few French ships off Setubal; a cold-blooded cutthroat who would toss his own mother overboard to improve the ballast, the upstart from Sines was the only snake in the brood who might stand a chance of finishing the journey. With little enthusiasm, he told the king: "I would assign da Gama."

Manuel debated the recommendation. Finally, the young king turned to da Gama and confirmed the appointment. "Four caravels will be provided. You will launch for India with all possible speed."

Amid murmurs of envy and disappointment, da Gama bowed, hiding a preening smile of conquest.

As the other mariners and courtiers, dejected and conniving revenge, took their leave from the court, Dias hung back. With trepidation, he approached the king and whispered: "I beg a word in private with you, Majesty."

Annoyed, Manuel motioned him up with a petulant flick of the hand.

"My lord, I recently witnessed an incident in Lagos that I feel duty-bound to report," Dias said. "Hundreds of Africans were unloaded from a *naos* and sold at auction. They had been hauled for weeks under miserable conditions in the hold. A third of their number died en route from heat and lack of water. They are being treated no better than animals."

"Mohammedans and pagans," the king reminded him sharply. "They *are* no better than animals."

"But Prince Henry insisted in his last testament that the Africans should be offered the opportunity to convert to Christ."

Manuel erupted from his seat. "That senile old fool nearly bankrupted the kingdom! I will not indulge his lunacies! The slave trade will provide cheap labor and the treasury required to defend the newly discovered lands. If I grant these Africans too many rights, they will become as troublesome as the damnable Jews."

The damnable Jews?

Dias was stunned. Did this new king intend to follow Isabella's example and bring the Inquisition to Portugal? Shaken, he held an obedient bow as he turned to leave, trying to shadow his Sephardic features.

Ten days later, Dias was forced to wait outside the small church at Restelo, which had been built on the banks of the Tagus centuries ago to offer mariners a last chance for spiritual solace before they entered the Atlantic. Denied the privilege of attending Mass with the crew, he had been ordered to escort da Gama to the African coast to insure that the youthful admiral was set upon the correct course.

When they reached Mina, he dropped anchor in the harbor and watched as da Gama disappeared over the southern horizon with a fleet under the Cross of the Order of Christ—an insignia that no longer represented the self-less brotherhood that had once served the Old Man.

THIRTY-SEVEN

aq dived off the leased fishing trawler and followed Boz into the watery depths below Karang Timau, a rocky finger of jungle below the volcanoes of the lush Barisan Mountains. Silted by runoff, the choppy Straits of Malay were as murky and deceptive as the many legends told here about the *Frol do Mar*, the richest shipwreck in history. Flippering down into the slate darkness, she wondered if the Portuguese mariner Albuquerque had been lured to this island because of its Sanskrit name: the Land of Gold.

After dropping below fifteen feet, Boz turned and signaled for her to stay closer. She didn't need to be told twice, for the Sumatrans had warned them of invisible currents here that picked up force near the northeastern tip of the island and swept all in their wake to the Indian Ocean. She kicked harder to escape the drift and finally caught up with him.

As they approached the site where Albuquerque's treasure caravel had foundered, she imagined the terror that the crew must have felt that horrible day in 1507. Loaded with gold, diamonds and ornate porcelain, the *Frol do Mar* had been returning from the sack of Malacca, the richest seaport in Asia, when a storm drove the flagship against these hidden reefs. More than a hundred Portuguese sailors and slaves had been trapped below its deck when the caravel went down. Albuquerque, who barely avoided drowning, had saved a young Indonesian girl on board by dragging her to another caravel.

But that begged a question more to the point: Did the admiral also save the Mercy Seat?

Wielding a metal detector, Boz honed in on the coordinates that had been reported as promising by the last salvage crew to search here. By some estimates, a billion dollars in bounty lay only twenty-five feet below the surface causing many drawn by the legend to ignore the probability that the strong currents would likely have swept off all but the heaviest items, such as the cannons—or, God willing, the Ark of the Covenant's lid.

After they circled the littered seabed for an hour, Jaq signaled that they would have to change their air tanks soon. When Boz didn't reply, she motioned more forcefully for him to abandon his inspection of a coral-crusted mound. But he just ignored her and kept searching the mounds of coral. This was a fool's errand, she now realized. If experienced teams had spent months combing these straits, how could she and Boz expect to find the ship in one day? She grabbed his arm to insist that he ascend without delay.

He shunted off her grasp and made one more thrust with his knife. He broke through a large clod of coral and exposed the interior cell below an aftcastle.

Exasperated, she tugged on his dive gauge to warn that he had dropped below 1,000 p.s.i. of air. He raised a couple of fingers to beg two more minutes. She reluctantly agreed, knowing they'd never be able to find this spot again. He widened a breach in the mass of coral, and she followed him into the hole. Finding an alcove, she gasped into her regulator, sending bubbles upward. Boz had found what appeared to be an officer's quarters strewn with barnacle-clotted tables and chairs.

Was this Albuquerque's private cabin?

She shivered with the awful feeling of invading a grave. Rusted eating utensils floated near her head, and a broken sandglass lay wedged in a shelf designed to hold personal belongings in place on the rough seas. Had anyone been trapped inside? She looked around the corners but saw no signs of human remains. If the Mercy Seat *had* been part of the cargo, she figured it would have been kept locked in this room.

Boz motioned her over to a wooden compartment protected by a rusted lock. He kicked at the panel, but it wouldn't budge.

She checked her gauge and signaled with a beckoning motion for him to get out with her at once. They were running out of air. He flashed two fingers and formed a circle, begging twenty more seconds, then motioned for her to leave through the hole and get as far away as possible.

Her eyes bulged in protest as he pulled a cartridge of gel explosive from his belt pouch and set it in the crease of the compartment's door. Was he nuts? He was preparing to pull the ignition lanyard. If they didn't get away, and fast, they'd suffer a concussion from the shock wave. Just before he yanked the switch, she swam back through the coral breach as fast as she could. She looked over her shoulder and saw he was still struggling to get his tank through the hole. She hurried back and slid it off.

An invisible explosion hammered her.

She regained consciousness swallowing water. Her regulator had been blown from her mouth. She searched behind her back for the dangling tube and saw her tank floating away. She tried to go after it, but Boz grabbed her wrist and gave her his spare regulator. He waited until she took another breath, and then he swam back into the aftcastle.

He's going to drown us!

Seconds later, Boz reemerged from the hole carrying a small strongbox. Eyes now distended with panic, she gripped his shoulders as they ascended together. After what seemed an eternity, they finally broke the surface. She kicked him away from her in flailing anger. Before she could throw a fist, the Sumatrans pulled her into the trawler.

As Boz climbed over the side behind her, she ripped off her mask and found him on his knees, examining the lock box. Coughing and gagging, she finally regained her breath and shouted at him. "You nearly killed us for *that?*"

Boz displayed the top of his find to indicate what had caught his eye: The five *fleurs-de-lis* of the Albuquerque coat-of-arms.

She crawled over to get a better look. Was that the admiral's correspondence cache? She watched Boz lever open its rusted lock with his knife. Inside lay a glob of water-ruined parchments that looked to contain nothing intelligible. In the bottom of the box, he found a bronze plate the size of a bank check. Letters and symbols had been engraved into its facing:

```
:U      :]      :S~S     ::]     :CD
:S~S   :S~:C   ::CD     :C      ::]
:S:C   :S~S    :S      :CD      :C
::]     :C      ::]      :T      ::]
:C     :S~S     :U      :CD      ::]
```

"Looks like some kind of Morse Code," he said. "Those alternating rows of dots might have a binary function."

She rubbed her finger over its indentions. "Why would the Portuguese go to the trouble of inscribing a bunch of letters and dots on metal?"

"The salt in the sea air corrodes parchment," he said. "Whatever is written on this plate must have been important enough to preserve for a long voyage."

She searched for a pattern. "Five rows. Five columns."

"Just like the Templar square," he said. "But these letters are all different."

She angled the plate into the sunlight to get a better view. Where had she seen such dots before? Of course! Leaving the plate behind with Boz, she hurried below deck and found the page in her notebook with the drawing she had made of the round seal of King Afonso they'd found in the Templar castle at Tomar.

The seal's outer ring had two lines of dots on each side of its cross. The second inner ring had one line of dots that lined up above the 'P' in the *Chi Rho* cross at the center. Did this seal have a connection to the Templar Square? She played with the combinations, but none made sense.

Exhausted, she dropped the notebook over her face to cover her eyes against the harsh sunlight from the porthole. She opened her eyes again with a start. On the cover of the notebook, the official emblem of the National Security Agency stared down at her. She jumped up and screamed, "I've got it!"

Boz came running into the cabin. "What's wrong?"

She held up the Afonso seal aside the NSA emblem. "It's a cipher wheel."

Boz looked at the two circular emblems and shook his head in amazement. "Damn, you're right. Both were designed to operate as wheels within a wheel."

"Just like Ezekiel's wheels in the Book of Revelations," she said. "And just like the SATOR-Templar Square."

Boz wiped the message plate from the wreckage with an oil rag. "These dots next to the letters must indicate which of the two wheels on the Alfonso seal to consult. See those two columns of dots on the outer wheel?"

"Yeah, but which wheel is the cipher and which wheel gives the solution?"

He rotated the seal. "The 'U' on the second wheel lines up with an 'S.' "The 'I' in the same wheel is closest to the 'A'."

"Maybe the letters with the dots next to them are the cipher indicators," she said. "They point to the corresponding letters on the other rings to be used to solve the message."

"That would mean the 'S–S' with the one row of dots refers to the space between the two adjacent 'S's on the second wheel. That space lines up with the 'O' on the outer wheel."

"What about 'S–C'?" she asked. "Each letter in that combination has its own row of one dots."

"'S–dash–C' must be the space between the 'S' and the 'C' on the second wheel," he said. "That would line up with the large P on the innermost wheel."

She tried those translations and compiled a list of the possible cipher solutions. The resulting eight letters were identical to the eight letters used in the Templar square:

$$
\begin{aligned}
::1 &\simeq \text{A} \\
:\text{ↄ} &\simeq \text{E} \\
:\text{S~S} &\simeq \text{O} \\
:\text{C} &\simeq \text{R} \\
:1 &\simeq \text{T} \\
.\text{u} &\simeq \text{S} \\
:\text{S~:C} &\simeq \text{P} \\
:\text{S} &\simeq \text{N}
\end{aligned}
$$

Boz nodded, still stunned. "Someone sent this plate to Albuquerque as a second blind for the SATOR code. Maybe the Portuguese were worried the Spanish were getting wise to their plan."

She substituted the cipher for the letters as instructed on the bronze plate from the wreckage and came up with:

$$
\begin{array}{ccccc}
\text{S} & \text{T} & \text{O} & \text{A} & \text{E} \\
\text{O} & \text{P} & \text{E} & \text{R} & \text{A} \\
\text{P} & \text{O} & \text{N} & \text{E} & \text{R} \\
\text{T} & \text{R} & \text{A} & \text{T} & \text{A} \\
\text{R} & \text{O} & \text{S} & \text{E} & \text{T}
\end{array}
$$

"There's OPERA again," she said. "The Mercy Seat."

Boz scanned down to the bottom line. "ROSET would be red."

She consulted her Latin dictionary. "STOAE is the plural of '*stoa*.' A covered platform or walkway where people stop to converse. Comes from the root '*Sto*,' which means to 'stop.'" Another entry caught her eye. "Wait a minute. '*Stoa*' also has a nautical meaning: To drop anchor or cease one's current course."

"They were telling Albuquerque to stop and change his mission."

"Change it to do what?"

"What's TRATA?" he asked.

She checked the dictionary, and her mouth dropped as she read the definition. "It's a Portuguese version of '*trada*.' To negotiate, to trade in commerce."

Boz studied the square. "Were they ordering Albuquerque to trade the Mercy Seat for something else?"

She stared with even more disbelief at the definition she found for PONER. The word came from the Latin '*ponere*,' meaning to discard, to lay aside, to leave buried, as if in the grave … to abandon.

"What's wrong?" Boz asked.

"Where did Albuquerque go after he passed the Cape of Good Hope?"

Boz checked their map of the admiral's routes. "The Red Sea."

"The *roset* sea," she said, correcting him with the code word. "Albuquerque must have received this order while he was in route to Ethiopia. He would have memorized the Afonso seal by heart before leaving Portugal so that no one could decipher the messages if they were lost or captured."

When she fell silent, shaken by the implication, Boz spoke what she was thinking. "Only one thing could be important enough to cause the Portuguese to go to all the trouble of sending a message like this to Albuquerque. King Manuel was ordering the admiral to give up the search for Prester John and the Mercy Seat."

"But why?"

"He wanted him to find trading partners around the Red Sea instead."

She stared at the code plate, trying to fathom the motive for such an order. "That means Albuquerque stranded Pero da Covilha in Ethiopia. But why would the Portuguese king do such a thing?"

Boz gazed out at the watery horizon. "Maybe Manuel didn't care about the Templar dream of creating a New Jerusalem. Maybe he wanted the riches from trade with the kingdoms around the Red Sea and the Indies instead."

She traced back the series of events that would have led to such an abrupt change in Portuguese policy. "Before Albuquerque left Portugal, some of his superiors in the Order of Christ must have commanded him to retrieve the Mercy Seat without King Manuel's knowledge. The king probably got wind of the Tomar subterfuge and sent this message to countermand it."

Boz nodded. "Infighting between the old and new guards."

"That's probably why Albuquerque continued on to Indonesia. Ignoring a royal command like this would have been treason."

Boz frowned, puzzled. "Then if Hosaam didn't find the Mercy Seat ..."

"It's still in the place that Pero da Covilha hid it. But where?"

Boz ran up the stairs and shouted over his shoulder, "Covilha told us!"

"Told us how?"

"In that message the priest delivered to Zarco!"

Lake Tana, Ethiopia
March 16, Present Day

Jaq stood staring at the harbor of Bahir Dar, which overlooked a glittering expanse of 1,400 square miles of water, a body larger than Lake Erie. Thirty-seven islands alone sat within Tana's boundaries, each with its own ferry. Disheartened by its size, she shook her head. "How are we ever going to find it here? It would take us months to cover every possible hiding place."

On the beach, an Ethiopian boy pulling in a net overheard her cry of dismay. He shouted up to her: "What is it you seek?"

"Nothing," she said, wanting to be left alone.

"I can help you find anything you need. Ten *birr*."

She rolled her eyes. Figuring the quickest way to get rid of the pest was to suggest an outlandish task, she told the boy: "You can find anything, huh?"

"Yes, yes."

"Fifty *birr* if you can take us to the Ark of the Covenant."

"No problem."

Boz tossed a pebble at the beggaring boy to chase him off. "She wasn't serious. *Heda!* Go away!"

But the boy remained adamant. "The Ark is kept on an island in the lake."

"Which island?" Boz asked, suddenly interested.

The boy grinned, having hooked his two fish. "Twenty *birr* more, and I will show you."

Jaq looked at Boz, trading helpless glances with him. They didn't have any better leads, so she nodded their agreement to the deal. The boy ran to the shoreline to negotiate for the use of a papyrus canoe owned by a fisherman. Making quick on the haggling, he pushed the canoe off, assisted Jaq and Boz into it, and rowed them down the eastern shore.

Three hours later, they approached a reed-shrouded island where the low water level exposed a narrow isthmus to the mainland. The high stonewall of an ancient monastery rose above them. A barefoot priest in a dirty saffron robe hurried to the water's edge and stood guard there with his staff.

The boy whispered to Jaq: "You must stay here. No women are allowed on Tana Kirkos."

She had heard that nonsense in this country before. Not about to put up with it again, she stood in protest, nearly capsizing the canoe. "That wasn't the arrangement!"

The boy shook his head firmly to indicate that the condition was not negotiable. "I do not make the laws of God. The abbot here fears the sight of women will cause his monks to go crazy."

In the corner of her eye, she caught a glimpse of the far shore of the mainland and saw a village that had been burned to the ground. "What happened over there?"

"The Falashas are gone," the boy said.

"What are Falashas?" Boz asked him.

"Hebrews."

Boz leaned closer to the boy. "Jews live *here?*"

The boy nodded. "Most went back to Palestine thirty years ago. The government of Israel agreed to take them. But a few remained behind, until this week."

"What happened this week?" Jaq asked.

The boy pointed to the east. "The police came and transported them by trucks to Addis Ababa. In the past, some Falashas could not pay their way out of the country because the police demanded baksheesh under the palm. The Hebrews are poor. Now none are left in Tana."

Boz slumped against the canoe's frame. With a sigh of defeat, he ordered the boy to halt before they reached the beach.

His abrupt abandonment of the search bewildered Jaq. "Shouldn't we at least check out the monastery? We've come all this way. There's a remote chance it might be hidden up there."

"We're too late. Now I understand why Covilha brought the Mercy Seat here."

"Easy enough to hide on one of these islands," she agreed.

"And to transport it up the Nile. The Portuguese could have carried it by camel to a prearranged meeting point on the Red Sea. But that's not the real reason he hid it here."

"Then what was?"

"The Templars and the Ethiopian Jews were working together," he said. "Covilha knew the Falashas would protect the Mercy Seat for him."

She suddenly understood his reasoning. "And the Jews wouldn't have left Ethiopia without it. But why, after centuries of delay, would the government allow the last of them to depart this week?"

Boz signaled for the boy to take them back to Bahir Dar. "We need to pay a visit to an old friend."

Addis Ababa, Ethiopia
February 21, Present Day

Brehane Dese hung up the phone in his office and almost danced down the five flights of stairs in the headquarters of Ethiopia's National Directorate of Police. He had just received some unexpected good news. Another Falasha village, this one a few kilometers north of Gondar, had been cleared by the Israeli government to proceed through customs under the Jewish Law of Return. Not that he gave a damn about the Hebrews, but now he would be receiving a new payment of twenty thousand *birr* to expedite the paperwork.

As he sauntered into the busy street, he thought about that new Renault sedan he had been eyeing. The Falashas were potters and weavers mostly, no great loss to the country. No one knew how they had arrived in Ethiopia, anyway. Some said they were descendants of the lost tribe of Dan that had migrated from Egypt over 2,000 years ago. Others believed they came with Menelik, the son of King Solomon and Queen Sheba. He couldn't care less.

Bottom line, they were funding his retirement.

He checked his gold-plated Bulgari watch, confirming that he had fifteen minutes to make it to the Piazza district. He held these clandestine meetings at Club Damu, a seedy bar that was always empty this time of afternoon. There he would handle the exchange of documents for money with one of the middlemen from the Jewish Board for Resettlement, the agency delegated by the Knesset to identify those qualified for repatriation.

He hailed a cab, climbed in the back seat, and lit up a cigarillo. Perhaps he would celebrate his good fortune tonight with a thick beefsteak and one of Madam Zehru's new whores. He rolled down the window, and every head in the Piazza turned as the cab passed. He quite enjoyed being feared. When the cab arrived in front of the bar, he reached for his wallet, but the driver waved off his money. Smiling, he nodded—one of the perks of the job.

He got out, buttoned the jacket of his white gabardine suit, and walked into a deserted lounge cooled by an overhead fan. A television hovering high in the corner blared the BBC news of the day. The bar owner angled his head toward the rear rooms to confirm that his Israeli contact was waiting with the payoff. He picked up his usual complimentary beer from the bar and savored a sip as he sauntered back through the narrow hallway. Another couple of payoffs like this one and he could—

The bottle was knocked from his grasp.

A hand slammed him against the wall and then dragged him into the women's bathroom. He heard the lock click as his arm was twisted behind his back. Another inch higher and his shoulder would wrench from its socket. He reached with his free hand for the gun in his back holster, but it was gone. "Bastaaard!" he screeched. "I will have you hunted down!"

When his arm was released, the inspector turned to find his pistol aimed at his nose. He cursed—it was that Lalibela grave robber and the incompetent U.S. State Department woman who had escaped his detention! Had *they* faked the call from the Israeli resettlement agency?

Boz traced the barrel up the bridge of Dese's nose and dug it into his forehead. "Who's been paying you to let the Falashas leave?"

While Boz pressed the interrogation, Jaq glanced at the loudspeaker above the washbasin, which was piping in the BBC report from the television in the lounge. She hoped that even if this asshole managed to yell for help before being knocked unconscious, his friend behind the bar would not hear him. Dese refused to answer, so Boz took a hand towel from the hook above the washbasin and wrapped the barrel of his pistol with it.

The cop gave a scornful laugh, confident that these two petty thieves were over their heads. "My men expect me back at the office in ten minutes!"

Boz fired a silenced round into Dese's foot.

Dese fell howling and clutching at his bleeding shoe. "Son-of-a-beeech!" He ripped off his expensive loafer and stared at the mangled clump of flesh that once held his toe.

Jaq pressed a hand against his mouth to stifle his cries. As a Christian, she usually protested any form of violence, but even Christ had become righteously angered at the moneychangers in the Temple. And if anybody had it coming, it was this lowlife cop who had tried to lock her up. They were running out of time, so she bit her lip at Boz's accelerated method of persuasion.

Boz raised the pant on Dese's other leg for the next shot. He motioned for Jaq to let up on the pressure, just enough for Dese to speak.

"A charity!" Dese cried, rocking frenetically on his haunches.

"Which charity?" Jaq demanded.

"Bilqis! That is all I know!"

Bilqis Media, she remembered, was the front name Hosaam's fake television crew had used to break into the tower at Gisors. But why would Hosaam provide the funding to bring Ethiopian Jews to Israel? She grasped Dese's chin to force him to look at her. "Who was your contact at Bilqis?"

Dese tried to delay, until Boz, impressed by Jaq's bedside manner, stepped on the cop's wounded foot to speed his responses.

"He called himself Yahya!"

"The night that priest was tortured," Jaq said. "You were there."

Dese refused to confess—Boz fired a bullet into his other foot.

"Gaaawwwdaaaamn!" Dese writhed on the floor like a speared carp. "Yes! I was with them! Okay? I was with them!"

Jaq pressed her hand harder over Dese's mouth, waiting for him to stop screaming. "Who helped you?" She let up to hear his answer.

"A stooge from Yemen. I was not told his name."

"Did he have a tattoo in Arabic on his forearm?"

"A *hadith* verse," Dese admitted between moans.

Boz jabbed the pistol into the inspector's knee to indicate his next target. "You were looking for the Mercy Seat of the Ark."

Dese managed a pained nod. "Yahya and his Yemenite goon offered me fifty thousand dollars for its delivery. The American was working with them."

Jaq got closer in his face. "The American?"

Dese was on the verge of passing out, until her slap brought him back. Cursing, he cried, "Merion!"

She clasped the cop's nose between her thumb and forefinger to punish the slander. "Paul Merion? You lying bastard!"

Dese nasaled, "He took orders from Yahya! I can prove it!"

Jaq glanced at Boz, wondering why Paul would have been working for Hosaam. Was it possible that he had been running drugs for the Pakistani warlord instead of working the illicit trade on his own, as Mayfield and Ochley had surmised?

Boz prodded Dese with the gun again. "The Mercy Seat wasn't in Lalibela, was it? It was taken to Lake Tana centuries ago and hidden with the Falashas."

Dese grasped at his bloodied toes, trying to count how many were left. "The high priest swore it was in Bet Golgota. He said the holy books had been falsified in their claim that the relic was removed to Axum. The priest lied—"

The loudspeaker blared a BBC special report on the television in the bar:

> "A strange development today. Hundreds of thousands of evangelical Christians are rushing to sports stadiums around the world convinced that the Rapture—the End Times heralding the return of Jesus Christ—will occur within forty-eight hours. Many have sold their homes and are gathering with families after Internet stories reporting signs of the Apocalypse. We have yet to trace the source for these reports, but many evangelical pastors having been taking to their pulpits to confirm the authenticity of such claims."

While Boz worked the cop over, Jaq listened to the report and tried to focus her racing thoughts. Was Hosaam now spreading rumors of the Apocalypse through Western news channels to create panic and prepare the Arab street for his Mahdi announcement? If so, the Pakistani scumbag had likely already made a deal with the emigrated Ethiopian Falashas, offering them the expatriation money in exchange for the Mercy Seat. Her fellow evangelicals had been waiting years for the signs that the End Times were approaching. Hosaam was cynically playing on the faith of her own people. The slimy son-of-a-bitch! If Hosaam could fool Christians into believing that the Apocalypse was only hours away, then his plan to delude Muslims into accepting him as the Mahdi would be much easier to accomplish.

Grinning despite the throbbing pain, Dese shouted at them: "Allah will crush you Crusaders!"

Jaq was about to violate the Lord's commandment for meekness by slapping the mouthy cop, but his curse stopped her short. "I thought you were Christian."

Dese snarled at her. "I tell the government that just to keep my job! I am Muslim! And I pray for the day the Mahdi sweeps the world of filth like you! Your judgment is coming!"

"You mean seven judgments," she corrected him. "You *jihadists* believe in seven judgments."

"I mean what I say! The hadith is clear! The Mahdi will bring one judgment and one judgment only!"

Having heard enough lip, Boz was about to fire a bullet into Dese's knee when Jaq restrained him long enough to ask the cop another question. "Who carved the Mahdi's message into the dead priest's chest?"

"I do not know!"

From the corner of his eye, Boz saw Jaq retreat into an inward gaze, as if trying to make sense of what she'd just heard. "What's wrong?"

"I'm not sure." After another hesitation, she shook off her doubt and recovered to the danger of the moment. "Let's get out of here."

Boz circled the pistol under Dese's chin in a warning. "Where in Israel are the Falashas being taken?"

Staring at the cocked trigger, the cop finally muttered "Jerusalem" under his breath.

Boz gave Jaq the pistol to aim. Then he tore a strip from Dese's pant leg and tied a tourniquet above the Ethiopian's mangled knee. He ordered the cop: "Hand over your cell phone."

Dese squirmed while Jaq reached into his jacket and found it. Boz cracked open the phone's casing and wedged out the tiny chip and the gear mechanism that caused it to vibrate. He opened a stick of chewing gum, popped it into his mouth, and removed the juicy wad. He pulled two hospital gloves from his pocket and slid them over his hands. Carefully, he reached into his jacket and brought out a small cardboard box. He lifted its lid to reveal a clear capsule filled with a green powder. He placed the capsule inside the wad of gum with the phone chip and vibrating unit.

"Hurry up!" Jaq pleaded. "That bartender may come looking for him."

Boz rolled the masticated gum into a ball and clamped open Dese's jaw. He whispered to the shaking cop's ear: "I'm going to say this once, so listen up. This capsule has two plastic halves. Have you heard of the Baker tree?"

Dese's eyes dilated with fright.

"I've been told your countrymen grind its bark and use it to poison fish," Boz said. "I just happened to find some for sale in the *merkato* today. There's enough powder in this capsule to kill a herd of cows. If it makes contact with your stomach lining, your muscles will lose control and you'll strangle slowly."

Dese wailed an impotent protest, "No!"

Boz stuffed the gum wad into Dese's throat and held his nose until the cop swallowed. Dese trembled from the thought of the deadly poison sloshing around in his stomach, but finally he gulped it down.

Snapping open the pistol's chamber, Boz removed the remaining bullets and put the handle into Dese's hand to make it appear that he had shot himself. "I wouldn't get too agitated if I were you. You're in no condition to move, especially after your botched suicide attempt."

Dese didn't dare make a move, afraid of setting off the poison.

"Now here's the schedule," Boz said. "That capsule should take about twenty-four hours to pass through your intestines. Don't even think of going to a hospital to have your stomach pumped. The trauma would be too risky."

Still as a mummy, Dese muttered through gritting teeth: "May your children be stricken dead!"

Boz shook his head. "That wasn't exactly the attitude I was hoping for." He pulled out a second disposable cell phone, which he had purchased with five minutes of airtime, and slipped it into Dese's jacket. "A soon as we leave, you're going to call the airport at Addis Ababa and order flight clearance for us. Then you're going to call your contacts with the Israeli government and make arrangements for us to land in Tel Aviv. If we encounter even light turbulence on the flight over, I'm going to dial your cell number. Do you know what will happen?"

Eyes bulging, Dese shook his head slowly to avoid jostling the capsule.

Fed up with Hosaam's taunts and the repeated attempts on her life, Jaq was now filled with such holy fury that Boz regarded her with a mixture of alarm and admiration. She grabbed the Ethiopian by his throat and to make it clear what was happening. "I may be just a stupid—what was it you called me when we first met? Oh yeah, a *demoiselle* from the typing pool. But my guess is that what he's telling you, that chip worming its way toward your ass will instruct the gear mechanism to vibrate and the plastic halves of the capsule will break. Of course, we can't know for sure. I'm almost hoping you give us a reason to test it."

She slammed him back to the floor and followed Boz out the back door.

THIRTY-EIGHT

THE SOUTH ATLANTIC
MAY, 1500

Dias and the crew of the *São Cristóvão* watched in horror as a finned serpent crawled from the mouth of a giant whitefish that had washed onto the deck. While the larger predator squirmed in its death throes, the resurrected serpent slithered back down a drain slit to the sea again. The men had witnessed other such ominous portents since leaving Brasilia; on the morning prior, a gray leviathan with rows of tentacle-rimmed suckers had crushed one of the carpenters who had been lowered overboard to repair the keel.

Dias looked up to study the mast tails. The winds were tranquil, but the sea had turned the color of diluted wine. Were monsters waging a bloody battle below the surface? According to his star charts, the Sun, Earth, and Moon would be in conjunction that night. Such rare meetings were known to produce syzygy tempests that cleansed the Earth of its impurities. Yet the southern horizon appeared languorous, and the distant clouds had the glaze of dusted sugar sprinkled over pastries. It was that kind of lazy late afternoon when an old seaman yearned to lie on his back and gaze wistfully at the crystal blue sky with memories of boyhood adventures.

But this pleasant lull, he knew, was merely the antechamber to Hell.

He signaled for Pedro Alvares Cabral, the commander of the armada, to clew the sails and brace for the coming onslaught. Yet Cabral's flagman answered with an order for the twelve caravels to run hard before the approaching easterlies.

The fool thinks he can outrace a typhoon?

Had it not been humiliation enough to be passed over again for this second India command? Earlier that year, da Gama had returned with nothing to show for his costly voyage but the contempt of the Calicutans. King Manuel was now sending another incompetent diplomat to gain what da Gama had not: a trade pact with the Eastern kingdoms. After jettisoning half of their fresh water supply to increase their speed, Cabral had wasted three weeks on an excursion to promote himself as the discoverer of Brasilia, even though that land across the Atlantic had been located by the Order of Christ two years earlier.

He had agreed to join this voyage for one reason only: Once the fleet reached the Indian Ocean, he intended to split off in this caravel and find Pero. Now, he consulted the journal in which he had drawn the portolans from his last voyage south. The lines confirmed his fear: They were approaching the Cape of Good Hope and its volatile, swirling currents.

To the west, he saw a waterspout forming. And ahead of the bow, the waves from the east were commingling with three meandering lines of seaweed and flotsam. Cabral was leading them into the dangerous confluence where the Atlantic and Indian Oceans merged with the angry waters of the southern pole. On the surface here all seemed placid, but he knew better: Ten fathoms down, in the undercurrents, the three seas were fighting for supremacy.

His restive crew, many of whom had served with him on the first rounding of the Cape, nervously awaited his orders. If he furled the sails and hunkered down, they might survive the ordeal, but then they would be cast adrift. And he would be court-martialed for insubordination. Despite his alarm, he had no choice but to order his pilot abide Cabral's command and run hard before the freshening wind.

The men rushed to their stations like a garrison under attack. Soon enough, the lone spout proved to be the vanguard of the storm. Within minutes, the sky surrendered its brilliant blue for a billowing wall of slate, cold vapors rose up like the plume of a volcano, and the water convulsed with a host of agitated creatures. Flying fish shot into the sails and dropped to the poop as if shot from the sky.

And then he remembered: The year was 1500.

Was he now witnessing the commencement of the terrible marvels of the Apocalypse? He tried to tack north by northeast to reach a port, but Cabral was hell-bent on staying dead center in the path of the whirlwind to reach the Cape. The blackening sky exploded with thunder. Lightning crackled like a whip near the aft. A blast of billowing rain drove the crew to the riggings and hurled three men overboard. The hull groaned and cracked. Each descent from the tumultuous waves poured more water into the holds. Dragged under from the sloshing weight, the caravel threatened to capsize, but Cabral kept sailing southwest.

Why does the admiral not acknowledge his distress cannon?

The flagship disappeared over the horizon. Pelted by hail, Dias fell to his knees spewing sea wash and clinging to the rails. Suddenly, all became silent around him. He was about to offer a prayer of gratitude to St. Erasmus for carrying him through another ferment when he looked up and saw the largest wave he had ever encountered.

God have mercy.

The whitecap hit him like a hammer—a keening sound shot down the deck. He came to consciousness under water. Red streaks curled around his eyes. He reached for his scalp and felt a deep gash. He kicked to the surface. The caravel was gone, disintegrated. Debris heaved and mangled bodies floated past.

This is how it ends.

No mariner ever spoke of drowning. To broach the subject was to court misfortune, and every man who went to sea thus had to come to terms in his own way with the possibility of such a death. He had seen many seamen fall overboard. Some fought to the bitter end. Others surrendered to the futility of struggle. He had long ago decided on what he would do if, as now, he found himself adrift with no hope. He had practiced the ritual a thousand times in his mind, knowing it would go easier if he could forgo the agony of debate.

Backstroking and spewing sea brine, he pulled the dagger from his belt sheath and shouted, "No one may enter the Kingdom of God unless he is first born of the water and wind!"

He listened for the Order's ancient retort. Somewhere, in spirit or in flesh, he felt certain Pero and Zarco were shouting with him: *Water and Wind!*

He cut the veins in his wrists. Floating on his back with arms outstretched, he felt his blood eddying around him. Like the serpent, he would now return to Mother Sea. Slowly, the darkness narrowed in, and he felt himself sinking.

Valladolid, Castile
May, 1506

"Alter not a letter of it! You must promise me!"

Their father's frantic deathbed demand confounded the Colon brothers, Fernando and Diego.

Aged horribly beyond his fifty-four years, the old mariner lay gasping for breath in his spare Franciscan room. "My sigil!" he rasped. "Must be left exactly as I formed it. ... on all of my testaments."

"But why, Father?" Diego asked.

Zarco winced in despair, denied the right to reveal the truth to his own sons, even. His accomplishments in the guise of the Genoan Colon had long been forgotten. In these last months, the Castilians had heaped ridicule on him, calling him the Admiral of the Mosquitoes for having found disease-infected settlements of primitive natives instead of the promised gold and spices of India. To increase the sting of these insults, he had been forced to play the

madman by writing that damnable *Book of Prophecies* and complaining inces-
santly about the loss of commercial profits. To do otherwise would have risked
suspicion. If his subterfuge were ever to be discovered, Spain's diplomats would
petition the Vatican to abrogate the hard-won Treaty of Tordasillas.

He had played the role assigned him by the Old Man to this, the very
end. And he would continue to play it beyond the grave. In bitter reward, he
would never again see Portugal, never again kneel at Filipa's grave, never again
search the horizon from Sagres Point … never again speak with Dias and Pero.
Here, on these thistle-choked vegas of his sworn Castilian enemy, he would lie
rotting forever, his identity hidden even from his own progeny.

Had the sacrifice been worth the gain?

Tortured by the spreading inflammation in his spine, he turned with difficulty toward the window. There, across the street, stood the old archbishop's
house where Isabella had married Ferdinand while the armies of her half-
brother closed in. If only one of those deadly musket balls had found its target
that day, Filipa might be comforting him in her arms this very hour.

He had made four western voyages for Isabella. And how had she repaid
that service? By allowing him to be paraded through Sevilla in manacles. He
shouted at her: "This is how you treat the man who gave you the Indies?"

"Viceroy," whispered Fernando, trying to shake his father from the deliriums.
"You must calm yourself. I have sent for the priest to give you the last rites."

Tears streamed down Zarco's cheeks. Was he to be subjected to *that* final
Christian indignity, as well? Isabella had taken the unction oils a few days after
his return from his last voyage. He had rushed to Medina del Campo demanding
to see her, but the court toadies had denied him permission. He now screamed
to protest that affront. "God has brought me back across the ocean to counsel
the queen!"

"Isabella has been gone for two years," Fernando whispered.

Zarco flailed his arms, trying to rise from the cot. "She schemes to avoid
me! She denies me my rights!"

"You lied to me," said a woman's voice to his ear.

Confused, he turned to find Queen Isabella shrouded in black and laid out
in her coffin aside his cot. Her eyes smoldered with the same fiery passion they
had possessed on the day he first encountered them twenty years ago.

"You did *not* find the Indies," she accused him.

Zarco broke a toothless grin. "I never intended to."

"I gave you everything. Even my virtue."

"You think it was easy conjuring new fantasies to keep your interest stoked?
First gold, then pearls, then an isthmus channel to the Orient. I even told you
I'd found the Garden of Eden. And you *always* believed me."

"Traitorous *bastardo!*" she shouted at him.

He levered to his elbows and came shadowing over her, just as he used to do when he made love to her. Devoid of cosmetics, every furrow in her wasted gray face was nakedly revealed. He taunted her: "On that, dear *Reina*, you speak true enough. I *am* a *bastardo*. A crypto-Jew *bastardo*. *Sim*, it is true. You sent a despicable Hebrew across the ocean while my comrades secured the Temple relics from your clutches. You and Torquemada knew that Our Lord could not return until the Sanctum of Solomon was first restored."

"Cristobal?" Isabella muttered, incredulous.

Zarco grinned at her look of shock. "No, allow me, at last, to properly introduce myself. I am Salvador Fernandes Zarco, a knight of the Order of Christ. We have known everything about you from the day you first suckled your Portuguese mother's teat. The workings of your devious mind and the basest passions of your soul. Our spy overheard your confessions to that Dominican snake that slithered his ambitions through your willing ear and into that black stone you call a heart. Do you know what year it is?"

Caught in the onset of catatonic rigor, Isabella could only shake her trembling head in rage.

"The year is 1504," Zarco reminded her. "Did Torquemada not promise you that the Millennium would arrive four years ago? You prepared for your starring role by burning and exiling thousands of my people. But the End Times did not come, did they? Whore of Babylon! God, it seems, has now abandoned *you*. Instead of raising you to the glory of his Heaven, He struck down your daughter with dementia and took your precious son at the tender age of eighteen. Such a pity. He even left your throne without a male heir. Perhaps it was not God after all who was instilling those visions into your dreams."

Isabella tried to strike at him, but now even her own limbs refused to heed her royal commands.

Laughing at her impotent struggle, Zarco leaned closer to her and, to twist the hilt, spoke his parting words in Portuguese. "You and those Dominican dogs have been duped by the survivors of your terrors."

The queen managed to summon enough strength to shout one last protest. "It cannot be! I am God's instrument!"

Zarco hissed to ridicule that dashed conceit. "How does it feel to be cast from the shores of faith you once held so dear and certain? To learn that you are about to undergo the same suffering endured by those you massacred? The Jews who perished under your pallid thumb wait beyond that veil. Go to them now, sweet Bitch of Revelation! They will escort you to the fires!"

"Viceroy!" Diego Colon dabbed his father's forehead with a cloth. "You are not with the queen. Isabella is dead."

Zarco lurched up, disoriented. Seeing his sons, he was thrust back to the present. He searched for Isabella, but she was gone.

Fernando pleaded with him. "You must hang on and take the sacrament. Do not pass without it, Viceroy!"

Zarco watched in confusion as Fernando's features transformed into those of his old comrade, Bartholomeu Dias. A tunneling darkness closed in on him, and, terrified, he shouted at his friend: "Dias! We are lost!"

"Be quiet, Zarco!" Dias admonished. "Eannes and the knights will hear you. We must not let the Old Man know."

Alarmed that Dias had come to him in spirit, Zarco looked around for a way out of this deepening darkness. "Where is Pero?"

"He is not yet on the other side," Dias said.

Zarco gazed hard into the black depths forming before him. "There are two tunnels here. Which one should we take?"

Dias produced the sewing needle from his belt pouch and stroked the crude navigational instrument against the silk to instill it with the magical magnetism. He floated the needle atop a bowl of water and monitored its gyration.

Zarco watched the preparations as if his salvation depended on the outcome. When the needle finally came to rest, he reported: "The passage to the right leads west. The other one goes south."

"I have always wanted to go south," Dias said.

"South will lead us into the boiling Sea of Darkness," Zarco warned his old classmate. "There are diabolical monsters in those waters. They'll consume us like the whale did Jonah."

"You have been listening to Eannes's wild tales again," Dias scoffed. "The Old Man promised there is nothing to be afraid of in the South."

Zarco was tired of arguing. "Go south, then. I am taking the tunnel to the West. We'll see where we end up."

The two comrades shook hands one last time, and then reluctantly went their separate ways.

Zarco began crawling alone down the dark shaft. After navigating blindly for what seemed like hours, he came to a round iron door. With great effort, he managed to shove the heavy cover aside. A circular stairwell of stone slabs stood before him. He climbed the steps and found himself standing under the charola of Tomar. Eannes and the mariners of the Order surrounded him. They opened a path for a shadowy figure in a hooded robe to appear.

Stepping forward, the Old Man dropped his cowl and beckoned his squire to him. "What took you so long, Salvador?" When Zarco came closer, unsure of what he should do, the Old Man pointed him toward the high platform on the charola. "Go farther, my son."

"To where, my lord?"

"Do you not remember?"

"Remember?"

The Old Man smiled. "You cannot find a peril there so great that the hope of reward will not be greater."

Zarco drew a deep breath for courage. The Old Man had never led him off course. Inspired again by the promise that had driven him his entire life, he climbed the stairs of the charola to find his final reward.

Lake Tana, Ethiopia
October, 1520

Wrapped in saffron robes and shod with reed sandals, Pero tended a herd of goats on his small estate bordering the green waters below Qirqos Monastery. He had just finished refreshing the water trough when he saw his young black servant running up the bushy slope in a state of excitement.

"*Faranji*, master!" cried the breathless boy. "*Faranji!*"

On the near hill, Pero saw his two Ethiopian guards grip their spears, apprehensive that he had sent word for his white rescuers on the far side of the world to come for him. He continued his shearing work, dismissing the boy's claim as just another of his wild fantasies. He had seen only three foreigners in the twenty-seven years that he had been sequestered here in Ethiopia. Two had been Venetians lost on their trek down the Blue Nile, and one, Padre João Gomes, he had sent back to Portugal over fifteen years ago with a message. Having heard nothing from it, he had long assumed that the priest had died in route.

Yet this time the lad was not imagining spirit jinns, for over the horizon appeared a tall, emaciated man in the brown robes and white rope belt of a Franciscan. Approaching warily, the friar asked him: "*Vai aceitar o Senhor Jesus Cristo como seu salvador?*"

Pero's knees buckled; this spectral priest's request that he take the Lord Jesus Christ as his Savior scratched at his brain like a nail. He had not heard his native language spoken in years. "Who are you?"

"Padre Francisco Alvares. I come from across the world in a place you have never heard of. It is called Coimbra."

"I once sold a horse in Coimbra."

"How do you know my tongue?"

"I am Portuguese. My name is Pero da Covilha."

Hearing that revelation, the friar could not have turned whiter if the Holy Ghost Himself had taken on flesh to deliver it. "God be praised! We thought you were long dead."

Pero glanced at his guards on the hill. "Have you brought transport?"

"Transport? For what?"

"Are you not sent by the Order of Christ?"

The friar shook his head. "I am Dom Rodrigo de Lima's chaplain. My captain remains with his caravel at the port of Massawa. I have come here to convert heathens while he trades for spices."

Pero could make no sense of the friar's ignorance of the mission. He had remained here in Ethiopia for nearly three decades, waiting for the Order to send the promised knights to take possession of the treasure. Why had they not come for it? "Do you know Bartholomeu Dias?"

"Of course. Who has not heard of him?"

"Does he command a caravel?"

The friar crossed his breast. "He lies at the bottom of the Sea of Darkness."

Pero sank onto a boulder and fought back tears.

"His caravel sank in a storm years ago, Near the Cape of Good Hope."

"Cape of what?"

"The passage around Africa."

Pero nodded in pride, but he could not understand why Dias had not sailed beyond Africa to reach him. "Then India has been reached by sea?"

"Many times. The first was by da Gama."

"Vasco da Gama? That snot-nosed squire who couldn't bait a hook with a minnow?"

"India is old news," the friar said. "The king has sent Ferdinand Magellan to encompass the entire world."

"King João would never attempt such a feat."

"King Manuel," the friar said, correcting him. "King João went to his heavenly reward twenty-five years ago."

"And Cristobal Colon?"

"Who?"

"The Genoan."

The friar spat at the ground. "That lunatic turned traitor?"

Pero's brows pinched. "He was no traitor! Zarco was—" He caught himself, remembering the vow of secrecy he had taken after those few months he had been allowed to think that Zarco, not the Genoan refugee, had been executed. "What has happened to Colon?"

"The mad Genoan made four voyages to the New World for Spain."

Pero clenched his fists in victory, informed that Isabella had taken the bait. "Does Colon now govern lands there?"

The friar shook his head. "God be praised, the knave met his death a broken and demented failure."

Pero dropped his head to his hands, realizing that both Dias and Zarco had died without knowing that he had gained the object of their quest. All these years, he had watched over God's Mercy Seat, having secretly removed it from Lalibela and hidden it with the Ethiopian Hebrews here. What was he to do with it now? "Many years ago, I sent a message back to Portugal with a priest named Gomes. Did he survive the journey?"

The friar shrugged. "I was only a *menino* then. I know not."

"Are we still at war with Spain?"

The friar smiled and shook his head. "Blessed peace arrived when our king married the daughter of Isabella and Ferdinand."

Pero could not believe his ears. The royal house of Portugal had been yoked to the offspring of that she-devil who persecuted Jews? How could this be? Why had this King Manuel betrayed the Old Man's legacy? He asked, "Isabella agreed to this arrangement?"

"By God's intercession."

"And Portugal and Spain are now one kingdom?"

"Alas, it was not to be," the friar said. "Isabella's daughter died in childbirth. Her grandson, Miguel, would have ascended the thrones of both kingdoms, but he died two years later. Yet one benefice did come from the betrothal."

"Pray, tell me?"

"In return for bartering off her daughter, Isabella demanded the expulsion of all the Jews who had taken refuge in Portugal. Our wise king readily acceded to that salutary demand. If only you had been there, Dom Covilha! The sight of thousands of Jews being driven toward the docks of Lisbon was enough to make Our Lord Himself weep with joy."

Pero gripped his staff with such fury that his knuckles turned white. "And what of the Order's astrologer, Abraham Zacuto? And the royal cabalist, Vizciano?"

"All banished," the friar said. "Praise be to the Almighty."

Pero had to restrain himself from rushing at the friar and throttling his throat. Was this how the saviors of the Portuguese realm were treated? Used for their knowledge and sacrifices only to be thrown to the wolves? Had his own kinsmen in Covilha been exposed and forced into this exodus? Now he understood why the Order never came for him. After the treaty with Spain, this new king must have lost interest in the Old Man's mission to restore the New Jerusalem, if ever he had been informed of it. With Isabella dead, there was now no urgency to prevent Spain from gaining possession of the Temple relics.

"You must come home," the friar said.

That hope was in vain, Pero knew, for he had seen too much. The Ethiopians had never been able to prove that he had taken the Mercy Seat, but they rightly suspected him of knowing its location. They would never let him leave, but at least they would not execute him, for fear of losing the treasure forever. Besides, he was seventy-three years old, too feeble to manage the arduous journey. And even if he were to survive the return to Portugal, the inquisitors of this new King Manuel might discover him to be a Jew and march him to the stake. With a heavy heart, he asked the friar, "My wife, Catrina."

The friar crossed his breast to speed her to Heaven. "She left you a son."

Pero was comforted at least by the promise that his lineage would continue on in Portugal. "I have a son here, as well. I will send him back with you to meet my eldest."

The friar blessed him with a cutting slash of his hand in the air. "Is there anything more I can do for you, Dom Covilha?"

Forced to silently suffer that gesture of worshipped torture, Pero gazed sadly toward the shimmering waters of Lake Tana. "As a *menino*, I made a vow that I have yet to fulfill. I cannot die in peace until I see it accomplished."

The next day, accompanied by his African son and a contingent of royal Ethiopian lancers sent to make sure he did not escape, Pero began his week-long trek on foot with Padre Alvares to the port of Massawa.

There, in the steaming waters of the Red Sea, he was welcomed aboard the *Santo Antonio*. The Portuguese crew, informed that he was one of their kingdom's lost heroes, stood at attention while the captain commissioned him to serve as pilot of the caravel for the afternoon. Provided with a compass and an astrolabe, Pero climbed to the aft loft, and for two hours he tacked up and down the African coast, shouting orders for the handling of the yards and rigging.

When dusk finally settled, the men lowered him into his small currach and rowed him back to African shore. Seeing them off from the beach, Pero fought back tears. No more could he be called the *Ratao*. Surrounded by his Ethiopian captors, the lone survivor of the Brotherhood of the Wind Rose watched as the last Westerners he would ever lay eyes on set sail for Portugal and disappeared over the blue horizon.

THIRTY-NINE

Iaq fought past the hordes of demonstrators shouting slogans and mumbling prayers. Drawn by rumors of an imminent End Times conflagration, thousands of fundamentalist Christian and Muslim believers had rushed to Jerusalem during the night. Palestinian radicals waved black flags to celebrate the imminent victory of the Mahdi, who was reported to be advancing from Tiberias. Christian millennialists, certain they would be Raptured here before sundown, had not even bothered to arrange for lodging; they surged toward the walls of the Old City and the Church of the Holy Sepulchre, falling on their knees in imitation of the *Via Dolorosa* to share for the last time in the sufferings of the crucified Jesus. In the midst of this tumult, armed Jewish extremists lurked in the shadows of the narrow medieval streets, waiting for a chance to seize back all of biblical Israel. Under siege yet again by foreign religious fanatics, many residents had locked themselves inside their homes.

The entire country felt on the verge of levitating from messianic fervor.

She and Boz had flown in that morning, hoping for one last chance to stop Hosaam. When laid over the Canistris map, the remaining unidentified star on the Virgo constellation tracing fell on Jerusalem, and if their theory was right, the Knights Templar would have fulfilled the mission handed down to them by the Knights of the Brazen Serpent by hiding one of the thirteen Temple treasures somewhere in this city. She felt certain that Hosaam had already collected the other twelve artifacts—including the Mercy Seat protected by the Ethiopian Falashas—and was now searching for the last artifact needed to launch his coup. Her best guess as to where the Templars might have secreted the Ark proper? The same underground cavern used by the Israelite priests to protect it during the Babylonian and Roman invasions.

But did *that* hiding spot still exist? And if so, where was it?

She darted into the Cellar Bar at the American Colony Hotel, a subterranean watering hole frequented by foreign-intelligence operatives. There she found Boz sitting at a shadowed corner table under an arch of pink ashlars.

He motioned her over. "The Israeli police are on high alert," he whispered. "The crowds have them spooked. No one is being allowed on the Temple Mount until the prayer service at noon. And then only Muslims."

Her heart was still racing from the crush outside. "Then Hosaam's probably up there already. We have to find a way in."

After making sure no one was watching, Boz reached into his canvas bag and pulled out a map of all the excavations ever conducted in the Old City. He unrolled it across the table and pointed to an 'X' that he had marked. "This finger of rising land here is where the old settlement of King David stood. Here, just beyond the Kidron Valley, is the Mount of Olives, the highest point in the area."

"Where did you get this?"

"I borrowed it from the library at the Israel Antiquities Authority."

She knew she should protest the theft, but he was beyond redemption. "The ground around here looks like Swiss cheese."

"That's because two thousand years of religious nut jobs have been digging into that Mount. The substructure is nothing but layer on layer of rubble left from invasions and destruction. It's a wonder the entire city hasn't caved in."

She studied the map's topography. "Where was Solomon's Temple?"

"No one knows for sure. Nothing remains of it above ground. King Herod doubled the size of the Mount's platform to build the Second Temple, but the Romans destroyed it. All that's left of that structure is the Wailing Wall."

"What's your best estimate of its location?"

"If it actually existed, probably on the southwestern quarter of the Mount. That was the area nearest to King David's settlement."

"What's there now?"

"The Al-Asqa mosque," he said.

"Has anyone ever tunneled under the Mount?"

"In the eighteenth century, a British explorer named Charles Warren mucked around underground near the Wailing Wall. He found an entrance to a tunnel that he believed had been used as a medieval synagogue and cistern. The entrance was sealed off in 1981. A rabbi stumbled onto an extension that led to another hall and created a real shit storm by claiming that it was the forecourt to Solomon's vault below the Holy of Holies."

"What did he find inside?"

"He never went in. Orthodox Jews are forbidden from making contact with the Holy of Holies until the Messiah returns. The Israelis allow the Arab

Waqf to manage the Mount, and the Waqf sealed off the tunnel after the Palestinians rioted to protest the sacrilege."

"I thought Muslims also believed in the Ark."

"They do, but they deny that the Jewish Temple ever sat on the Mount. If any of the Temple relics were to be discovered there, the mullahs would have no choice but admit the obvious."

"So, if Hosaam recently bribed the Waqf authorities ..."

"He could be hiding in the Al-Asqa basements right now."

She stared at the map again. "What's in those basements?"

"Nothing. The Templars used them for stables and storage halls."

Searching for another way to get onto the Temple Mount, she ran a finger across the map toward an area called the Kidron Valley. "Are these graves?"

Boz nodded. "That whole ravine is one giant necropolis. Orthodox Jews believe the Messiah will return for them there on Judgment Day."

"Maybe there was a tunnel leading from one of those graves."

"Sure, makes perfect sense," he said sarcastically. "And which of the hundred and fifty thousand graves do you suggest we plunder first to find out?"

With that idea torpedoed, she searched the map again. She pointed out another landmark that lay south of the Mount. "What's this?"

"The Gihon Spring. The Old City's major water supply since King David."

"Why would the Israelites build their walls to place the springs outside the city? That doesn't make sense."

"The Gihon sits in the lowest ebb of the valley. Archaeologists now think they built towers to extend around the spring to protect against sieges."

"What did the Israelites do for water if they couldn't get to the spring?"

He traced the route for her. "King Hezekiah built a tunnel under his walls from the spring to the Pool of Shalom. He dropped a couple of vertical shafts and lowered men with buckets by ropes to retrieve the water."

"The water ran *away* from the Mount?"

"Yeah, so?"

She thought for a moment. "I remember reading in the Old Testament that the Temple priests used purification pools. How'd they get water up there?"

"Herod brought it in from the south with aqueducts."

"And before Herod?"

He shrugged. "Maybe slaves carried it up from Shalom."

She saw from the blue areas of the map that dozens of reservoirs and basins had been discovered below the surface of the Mount. "Or maybe they ran another tunnel north from Gihon."

"Not unless one of the prophets performed a miracle. That water would have had to flow uphill."

She pulled a pen from her bag and circled Gihon Springs on the map. "Hezekiah dug his tunnel in the shape of an 'S'. Why not in a straight line?"

"Probably easier to follow the natural underground streams."

She opened the digital concordance she had installed on her Blackberry for prayer study. Typing in 'Hezekiah,' she scrolled down all the Old Testament entries that mentioned the king's name. One verse caught her eye: Chronicles 32:30. She read it aloud for Boz, "'This same Hezekiah also stopped the upper watercourse of Gihon, and brought it straight down to the west side of the city of David. And Hezekiah prospered in all his works.'"

"That's just what I told you."

"Hezekiah stopped the *upper watercourse*," she repeated. "That means there was another stream going higher."

"Maybe, but—"

She had that glint in her eyes again, the one she got whenever she was about to propose something outlandish. "The Israelites could have dug a second tunnel running north and dropped a shaft straight down below the Mount."

Before Boz could protest her plan, she was heading for the exit.

The sign on the Gihon Springs archaeological park warned that the fenced dig had been suspended for the Lenten season, but that didn't stop Jaq from climbing over the gate. Boz looked around for guards, then reluctantly followed her. After descending several terraces, each with their own layers of period walls, they found the stone-encased portal that led into the spring. The hole still gushed with the water once used to anoint King Solomon. They walked several hundred feet through the tunnel and came to a gap in the ceiling.

Boz shined his flashlight into the hole. "That must be the shaft drilled by Hezekiah. If there *was* another passage to the Temple Mount, it would have run in the opposite direction."

Jaq backtracked with him, running her hands along the hewn tunnel to search for irregularities. She noticed a row of serried cuts that had been chiseled into the foundation like teeth of a gear wheel. A faint seam ran near the serrations. "Check this out."

Boz hammered at the rock with the small excavating hammer he had brought. Debris came crumbling down around them, revealing an entrance.

She peered inside. "More teeth rows."

Boz cut at the hole until it was large enough to slither through. The trajectory rose slightly, and they found the remnants of an ancient water line.

She ran a hand across torch niches. "Why would they cut these notches?"

"The diggers had to go slightly uphill to prevent the Mount shaft from being too long for their ropes."

"You mean these ridges caused the water to flow *against* gravity?"

He nodded. "I've seen this technique used in magic shows. It's called the Leidenfrost effect. Water can be made to dance uphill by heating the surface. The Israelites must have warmed the tunnel. When the water was propelled forward, the notches caught it and pushed it along like a conveyor belt."

They moved deeper in, until they came to an iron ladder bolted to a vertical shaft. Boz took the lead on the climb up. Two hundred rungs later, they reached a doughnut-shaped ledge bordered by walls covered with ancient graffiti. Above their heads, dozens of stars had been randomly etched into the stone.

Jaq examined a stratum behind her that had been engraved with a table of Roman numerals and Latin words. "Looks like the Israelites weren't the only ones who used this tunnel."

"Roman soldiers?"

"Or Crusaders." She traced the inscription with her finger. "These look like the notations that were on that crucifixion board at Oak Island. It could be another coded message for the square."

"You still have that letter-rotating program on your Blackberry?"

She pulled out her PDA and typed in the turns. She came up with:

$$S \quad E \quad R \quad E \quad T$$
$$A \quad T \quad O \quad R \quad A$$
$$S \quad A \quad N \quad T \quad O$$
$$P \quad E \quad R \quad T \quad E$$
$$P \quad O \quad R \quad A \quad O$$

He watched over her shoulder. "Did you bring your dictionary?"

She rolled her eyes. "I always go spelunking with a full library on my back."

Burned by her sarcasm, he drooped his head in defeat. "Then it's no use."

She countered his hangdog pout with a punishing grin. "But I *did* download the online version with *all* languages."

Reviving, he kissed her in reward. "At least you got brains."

She punched in the graffiti words on the keyboard. "SERET comes from the Latin and Old French word 'serrate.'"

"To cut like a saw. Like they did with those serrated teeth in those ridges."

She typed in the second line. "ATORA is a Spanish derivation for a tight spot, a blockage or passage. It can also mean the Law of Moses."

"SANTO is easy enough," he said. "Sacred, holy, miraculous."

"PERTE is Latin-Old French for 'lost.'"

"Hurry up!" he said, impatient. "Get the last word."

She typed in PORAO, and stared at the results. "From the Latin 'port' for 'carry' and 'pos' for 'to place.' In Portuguese, 'porao' is a 'place of storage.' Like a basement."

Boz cobbled together the possible meanings and wrote the sentence on the wall's charcoal residue: *Cut passage for sacred lost place of underground storage.*

"We've already cut into the passage!" she cried, exasperated. "Hosaam must have gotten here before us. He's just toying with us again."

Boz dropped his hands to his knees, thwarted for certain this time.

Finished with playing Hosaam's perverse game, Jaq began crawling back down the ladder. "Let's get out of here."

"*Atoro!*" Boz shouted.

She clambered back up the rungs. "I told you. It means 'passage.'"

"You also said it can mean the Law of Moses. In Hebrew class, we were taught that '*atoro*' was a variation of '*atarah*.' That's Hebrew for 'crown.'"

"I don't see any crowns lying around, do you? I'm done playing Scrabble. Let's go." She saw him still studying the stars etched into the ceiling. Suddenly she understood what he was about to suggest. "The Woman in Revelations will announce the tribulations—"

"By appearing with a crown of twelve stars."

"The *Stella Maris* ... the Virgin of the Wind Rose." She frantically searched the ceiling and found a cluster of scratched stars that resembled a woman on her back. "That's Virgo!"

The ledge rumbled and shook.

She dived into Boz's arms. "What was *that?*"

Boz placed his hand against the wall, feeling for more tremors. "Probably some construction nearby. The Arabs are building another mosque in the northeastern corner of the Mount."

In a fit of anger, Jaq grabbed the hand pick and pounded at the spot where the representation of the Virgo constellation had been drawn. The ceiling finally gave way, showering them in shards. Lifted into the hole, she gained a foothold and pulled Boz up behind her. Together they stood staring at a vault lined with cedar. On the floor sat a cylindrical device of modern steel and painted drab green. It resembled a giant hotdog bolted to an I-frame.

She backed away. "Is that a ... *bomb?*"

Boz couldn't find an ignition switch. "Definitely not a Temple relic."

The ground rumbled again, this time throwing them against the wall. Recovering, they saw a bronze door over their heads. They pounded on the door until the hinges gave way.

"Whatever this contraption is," Boz said, "it was brought down here through that entrance."

Jaq looked up. "This door must have led to the Holy of Holies."

Boz searched in vain for a contact wire, anything that might disable the device. "Hosaam is definitely here somewhere."

She bent to her knees. "I'm starting to feel sick."

Looking a little pekid himself, Boz asked, "What happens to the Temple Mount when the End Times come?"

Why was he was asking *that* question? "It'll be destroyed."

"Then the Mahdi wouldn't be expected to hang around here when the action starts." Boz circled the cylinder. "Where does the Bible say the Messiah will appear on the Day of Judgment?"

She consulted her digital concordance. "The Mount of Olives."

Boz looked downright spooked. "We need to get across the Kidron Valley."

"You go," she insisted. "If we're wrong and he's still here on the Mount, we may not be able to get back in time. Lift me into that room. Call me if you find anything."

He was reluctant to leave her alone, but she insisted. He was about to retreat into the water tunnel when he stopped. He stared at her sheepishly, digging into his pocket.

"What?" she demanded impatiently.

He stumbled for the words. "Jaq, when this is over—"

"Get going!"

He staggered to a knee. "Will you ..."

She huffed with impatience. Was he losing his nerve? After all the tight spots he had been in during his life of crime? She pushed him off, eager to get into the mosque above.

Boz scrambled over the broken tombstones littering the Kidron Valley and ran as fast as he could up the slope toward the Mount of Olives. This rocky ridge was an outdoor museum of churches erected by rival Christian sects vying to commemorate the many places where Jesus had taught and healed. Behind him, a shattering call to prayer drew thousands of Muslims toward the Temple Mount. In minutes, the two mosques there would be teeming with worshippers. If Hosaam *had* set up his headquarters here in Jerusalem, he was likely hiding in the Arab neighborhood of At-Tur, which crowned the valley and stood eye level with the Old City.

Broiled by the brutal Judean sun, he hurried past the Basilica of the Nations, the traditional site of the Garden of Gethsemane. He was stopped short by a fantastical edifice crowned by golden bulbous spires and onion-shaped cupolas in the Muscovite style. Its front portico was latticed with scaffolding, but no work appeared to have taken place for months. Was this a Russian Orthodox church that had fallen on hard times? A small placard on its door said: *The reconstruction of Saint Mary Magdalene is generously financed by the Bilqis Consortium.*

Bilqis. Hadn't Jaq told him that was the name the Pakistani's front company used to break into the chapel under Gisors? Probably just a coincidence. Still, he stuck his head inside for a peek and asked a long-bearded Orthodox priest dusting the pews, "Excuse me. Do you speak English?"

The priest didn't look up. "Little amount."

"What is this place?"

"Magdelena Convent. Here the whore tells Apostles of Resurrection." The monk pointed to a slot. "Donation box."

Whore? The Russian Orthodox Church still called Mary Magdalene a whore? Boz scanned the empty nave, wondering what was a priest doing in a church for nuns. He dropped in a few coins to buy more time. "The company that is reconstructing the church? Where is it from?"

The priest's face now turned stone hard. "I know nothing."

Pricked by the curt response, Boz walked closer to the altar and saw a stairwell leading to a crypt. "What's below?"

"Tomb of Tsar Alexander's mother. Executed by Bolsheviks."

"Do you mind if I have a look?"

The priest dredged up enough interest to shrug. "God's house is open to all."

Boz descended steps that were bordered by steel bracings. Strange. These modern supports didn't appear designed to restore an ancient elegance. Why was the reconstruction so crude and industrial? He leaned over the tomb of the grand duchess and—a click sounded behind his ear.

"You will take special tour."

He turned to find a revolver aimed at his forehead. The armed priest motioned him into the crypt and pressed a button to open a *faux* stone door. He was shoved into an elevator. Moments later, the box thudded to a stop, and the doors slid apart. Fluorescent ceiling lights flashed, blinding him. When his eyes adjusted, he found himself standing in a high-tech chamber that would have made the White House Situation Room look like an Amish barn.

A clean-cut Caucasian man in a white shirt and blue tie stood at the head of a dozen masked guards armed with rifles. "Mr. Elymas. Welcome to our humble worship service."

The man spoke perfect Ivy League English. He definitely wasn't Russian. Was Hosaam using Western paramilitary mercenaries? That didn't seem in the style of the great Muslim messiah who wanted to make his fellow Arabs think he was crushing the Great Satan. Bracing for a rough pat down or worse, Boz used the magician's trick of misdirection, flippantly twirling his right hand in showman's style as if answering the accusation with bravado. Then, while their eyes were drawn from his free left hand, he reached into his left pocket. He pressed the quick-dial number on the cell phone and switched the speaker on.

The stuffed suit motioned him forward. "Where is your friend?"

"I work alone." He was rewarded for that response with a fist to the gut.

The head creep coolly ordered his guards, "Show our guest to a seat."

One of the human pile drivers shoved Boz into a chair.

Their leader punched a button on a remote to lower a large screen. "I suspect Ms. Quartermane has managed to talk her way onto the Mount by now. Would you like to see what she'll be experiencing in a few minutes?"

Boz watched as real-time surveillance video of the Temple Mount came on the giant screen. The camera zoomed in on a section of its wall that had been buttressed with modern stonework.

"That bulge in the retaining rampart is near the confluence of the southern and eastern walls," the paramilitary executive explained. "The Waqf repaired it a few years ago, but it's becoming more unstable by the month. Do you know what sits below that section?"

Boz's heart sank. "Solomon's Stables."

"You're quite astute, Mr. Elymas. You should have considered intelligence work for a profession instead of larceny."

"Are you Mossad or CIA?" Boz demanded.

The executive merely smiled. "The Arabs have consecrated a new mosque in the caverns under the Temple platform. The al-Marawi is designed to hold forty thousand. The largest place of worship in Israel. My engineers conducted some unauthorized tests on the foundations below that area of the Mount. You know what they found?" Not giving Boz time to hazard a guess, he revealed, "The tensile yield under the stables will fail at one thousand pounds per square inch. That factors out to just about thirty thousand agitated *jihadists*."

Boz figured the odds were pretty long that he'd make it back up that elevator back alive. He had one last chance to tell Jaq what he had tried to say to her earlier. He raised his voice for the hidden phone speaker, "Can you make sure you're finished by six? I'm planning to get married tonight."

The head creep grinned. "I'll send roses. They can double for the funerals."

Boz played unimpressed. "So you'll kill a couple hundred innocent Muslims with a wall implosion. That'll be a little anticlimactic, don't you think? Those fanatics out there are expecting the end of the world."

The executive smiled thinly. "I wouldn't think of disappointing them."

Boz's phone buzzed—the low battery signal had gone off. He fumbled with the damn thing, but it kept screeching.

Two thugs hoisted him from the chair and slammed him into the wall. He groaned, his shoulder blades aching. While one of the guards pinned him with a grip to his throat, the other one ripped open his vest jacket. The muscle-headed flunky found the phone and handed it to his boss.

The executive read the call number on the screen. He tossed the phone to one of his officers. "Trace it and find her."

Boz fought to reach the asshole. "You lay a hand on her and—"

One of the goons hammered his jaw to silence him.

"Now where was I?" the executive asked. "Ah yes, just getting to the *denouement*. The Mount is built on several strata of loose debris. When the southern section fails, a chain of collapses below the platform will be set off."

Forced back into his chair, Boz wiped blood from his mouth. "The Israelis aren't fools. They'll know the bomb wasn't God's work."

The executive laughed as he cued up more footage. "You made it that far into the water chute, did you? What you saw was a teleogeodynamic resonator. It pulses low-frequency electromagnetic waves. We have Nicola Tesla to thank for it. First we steal his radio patents. Now, posthumously, he's going to help us destroy the most revered square mile in the world. I'm surprised you didn't get a little woozy. Its emissions tend to irritate the pineal gland."

The screen showed a tsunami hitting the coast of Thailand.

The executive resumed his show-and-Hell demonstration. "Our trial run with the Andaman earthquake caused that little wave in 2004. We've calibrated the resonator to activate when the southern wall collapses from the weight of thirty thousand worshippers. The subsurface is mostly rubble there, so the seismic effects will be magnified. The Mount will implode, section by section. The induced tremor will split the Kidron Valley, just as the Old Testament predicted. Of course, the resonator will be buried deep under the debris, never to be found."

"No one will believe the quake is natural," Boz scoffed.

"I suspect you may be wrong about that, Mr. Elymas. Take the United States, for example. Half of all Americans believe the Rapture will happen in their lifetimes. And you don't think they'll buy into God's earthquake at Armageddon? We're sitting on the Great Rift fault line. The last big quake to hit Jerusalem was just a few years ago, in 1927. A 6.3 in magnitude. And of course there was that little rumbler that brought down Sodom and Gomorrah. I wonder if we'll see fire and brimstone again?"

"You really think this old church is going to survive it?"

"I've bet my life on it," the executive said. "We've reinforced the bunker to withstand the force of a thermonuclear attack."

"What do you have to gain by destroying Jerusalem?"

"My motive is purely altruistic, I assure you. The Middle East card deck needs to be reshuffled. The Muslims will blame the Jews and Christians for bringing down the Mount. Fundamentalist Jews and Christians will believe the Apocalypse is at hand. And the few sane people left in this world will think it was caused by a terrorist attack."

Though he wouldn't admit it, Boz grudgingly admired the ingenuity of the devious plan. "And the Mahdi will fail to make his grand appearance."

The executive, enjoying Boz's consternation, smoothed out the knot on his tie. "We've war-gamed the outcome. When their scimitar-waving Superman fails to fly in to save the day, disillusion and infighting will set in among the *jihadists*. Riots will break out across the Gulf. Pressured by the Arab street, Iran, Syria and Egypt will have no choice but to deploy their forces. Israel will respond, and NATO will fall in step. *Voilà!* We have our Armageddon. With Jerusalem blown to kingdom come, the Arab militants and Jewish settlers will have no cause to feed their lunacies. Best thing that could happen for U.S. security is to be rid of this rock quarry."

"You're a real patriot," Boz muttered.

The executive glanced at his watch. "Almost noon. The Gog and Magog extravaganza is about to begin. The Israelis should be opening the gates for prayer services in the mosques any moment now. But don't worry, Mr. Elymas. We've arranged a special viewing box for you."

Crouching behind a pillar in the Al-Asqa Mosque, Jaq pressed the call button on her Blackberry. The phone had gone dead, right after Boz had mumbled something about getting finished by six. Had Hosaam's henchmen abducted him? Why did that other voice on the line sound so familiar? She'd only been able to make out scratchy snippets of the conversation. Had that been one of Hosaam's men speaking English? Whatever Hosaam had planned seemed to involve getting enough Muslims into the two mosques here cause the walls below the Mount to fail. She couldn't risk being found here. But if she went outside, his thugs might be waiting.

A *burqa* hung in a closet.

Stealing it, she covered her face and torso like a conservative Muslim woman and hurried along the shadows. Hundreds of men streamed toward her through the doors. She cowered behind a corner, remembering that no women were allowed in this section. She waited at the door until a group of robed mothers passed by outside, and then mingled in.

The phone.

Hosaam might be tracking her. Taking advantage of the Muslim practice of charity, she offered the phone to a passing Arab woman. "I have not performed my duty this month."

The woman was elated by the gift. "May Allah bless you!"

Jaq hurried away. The Mount so packed with worshippers now that she had difficulty maneuvering. They all seemed to be chattering excitedly about the Mahdi's appearance in Tiberias that morning.

She had to find a way to warn them away from that end of the platform.

The guard shoved Boz with the butt end of his Israeli Micro-Tavor rifle toward an empty cave below the Mount of Olives. Hovering over the brow was a giant stone, once used for blocking ancient tombs. Boz suddenly saw what was in store for him: If the implosion from the earthquake didn't crush him, he'd starve to death.

"Get in," the guard ordered.

"I'll see you in three days," Boz cracked.

"Move it, wiseass."

Boz backed into the cave. "At least untie my hands. What am I going to do? Claw my way out?"

The guard grinned. "Maybe you can eat your fingers." He leaned his Tavor against a stone, making sure to keep himself between the weapon and Boz. He cut the tethers on Boz's wrists.

"Now that's strange. Your B-B gun just moved on its own."

The guard turned and saw that his rifle had somehow levitated and come to rest on a stone inside the tomb. "Bloody hell. Are there ghosts around here?"

"Just leave it. Maybe I'll shoot myself."

"You aren't going to be that lucky."

Spooked, the guard inched into the tomb to retrieve his weapon. Boz pulled out his right hand from behind his back and threw a rock at the log prop holding the blocking stone in place overhead. The dolmen rolled down and slammed into place, trapping the guard inside.

Grateful for the negligence in failing to pat him down, Boz retrieved the small retractable mirror that he always carried and put it back into the hidden pocket sewn into the seam of his shirt. Even with hands bound, he had managed to set the mirror a few feet away when the guard wasn't looking.

He ran down the ravine and saw the crowds streaming toward the mosques. The Israeli guards were checking cards. Even if he managed to fake a Palestinian identity, he didn't have enough time to make it across the valley and leapfrog the queues. On a hill just beyond the Kidron, he saw a helicopter sitting on a landing pad. Above it waved a sign: *Tour the Holy Land by Air.*

On the Temple Mount, Jaq ran from worshipper to worshipper, begging them to turn back, but the Muslims avoided her as if she were deranged.

A tall man, in an ankle-length *thwab* and checkered red scarf, rushed past her, hurrying for the Mughrabi Gate, the only Mount ramp accessible to believers of all faiths.

She caught up with him. "Please! Tell your people to leave! There's going to be a disaster!"

"Get away from here!"

After so many shouts of banishment in Arabic, she was surprised to hear English spoken, especially in a Southern twang. Confused, she searched the shadowed face under the scarf and blinked the sweat from her rounded eyes. Was her mind cracking from the heat?

But it was true.

Rev. Merry grasped her elbow. "Come with me, Jaqueline. There's not much time left."

"What ... what are you doing here?"

The pastor scanned the chaotic Mount with darting eyes. "We must cross the Kidron Valley at once. The Seven Judgments are fast upon us."

He gave her no chance to make sense of his miraculous arrival. She followed him as she always did—obediently. As he rushed her across the platform, she thanked God for sending him to help her prevent the disaster. The Almighty truly worked in mysterious ways.

Wait ... *seven* judgments?

Hadn't that been the warning carved into the priest's flesh in Lalibela? But that Ethiopian detective had been adamant that the Mahdi *hadith* prophesied just *one* judgment. She knew only one theological source that promised seven judgments in the End Times.

The Scofield Bible ... the translation used by her fellow Darbyites.

She gasped, slammed by the discovery. But no, it couldn't be. A millennial Christian—not a Muslim—had left that message in the priest's flesh at Bet Golgota? It wasn't possible. She wouldn't believe it. But she couldn't think of any other explanation. Suddenly she remembered the reverend's gift of his ministry-school Bible. She fixed onto his nervous gaze. "*You* are working with Hosaam?"

Rev. Merry hustled her toward the gate. "I'll explain later."

She fought to escape his clutches. "You lied to me?"

"For your protection."

The pastor dragged her into an alcove near the Dome of the Rock, the octagonal shrine that had been constructed over the site of the Second Jewish Temple. He took her frightened face into his strong hands and locked onto her eyes. "Listen to me, Jaqueline. Have I ever failed you?"

"No, but—"

"We are God's instruments. Join us and be Raptured to see Paul this very day."

"Us?"

"Christian brothers and sisters all over the world have come together this hour in holy union to see the End Times brought to bear. Two years ago, I founded the Third Temple Alliance. God-fearing officials in the highest levels of the Western governments and the Vatican have been working covertly with us. We have the precious artifacts of the Holy of Holies in hand. The Ark and its accessories are now ready to be installed in the Millennium Temple."

"The thieves in Lalibela … the bombers at Chartres. … They all worked for *you?*"

The pastor tried to calm her. "They were unwitting accomplices recruited by our missionary arm, Muslims for Christ. The Bible says unbelievers are to be used for the greater glory of God. The Jews will also soon fulfill their destiny by building the Third Temple before they too must suffer the travails of Hell. I was going to tell you about all of this, but you went and got yourself mixed up with that atheist con man. I couldn't risk having our plans exposed to Satan's agents."

She thought back to the incidents of the past weeks in light of this revelation. How could she not have seen his hand in them? "You're not following God! You're *playing* Him!"

Rev. Merry imprisoned her in his embrace. "We have waited too long, darling. The Lord spoke to me in a dream. He wishes our assistance in bringing forth the Last Days. The night my father died a broken man, I vowed to see him vindicated. Now I will finally raise him before the world and reveal him to be the true prophet that he was."

"But you said no one could know the hour!"

The pastor's eyes glowed with God's radiant truth—or was it insanity?

"We are merely laying the fuse," he said. "Our Lord will light the match. Everything is in place. I have positioned dozens of Tribulation Saints across the city to harvest the conversions. The families of the Saints are camped on the Mount of Olives, as was foretold. It will be a glorious devastation of evil. Now come. We must hurry across the Kidron before the trials commence."

She was paralyzed by the choice; he was asking her to give up everything she had fought for in this world. "I love Boz. I don't want to leave him."

"Have you convinced him to take Our Lord as his Savior?"

"No, but—"

"Then you must release him to God's judgment."

Tears streamed down her cheeks. Finally, she surrendered to his reassuring arms, no longer knowing what to believe. She was so exhausted. To be done with it all and rest in the bosom of the Lord this day would be wonderful. Never to have another ...

Alyssa's bloodied face flashed before her eyes.

A cascade of other images and sounds threaded through her memory. The hit-and-run in Rome. The chase in the catacombs. The explosion in the Monsignor's laboratory. The flooding at the Millennium Museum. The NSA meeting when Mayfield humiliated—

That had been *Josh Mayfield's* voice on the phone with Boz.

She gasped. Mayfield was working with Rev. Merry?

That NSA dog-and-pony show Mayfield put on in Washington must have been a front for this pseudo-Apocalypse operation. Of course! Mayfield ordered that Arab man killed in the Oak Island shaft. He also left her that taunting message on the crucifix, thinking she'd be drowned before she could act on it. He'd been perversely enjoying her near misses on this chase all along. After failing to get rid of her in Europe, he must have gotten her transferred to the NSA to throw her off his tracks and keep a close watch on her. She turned toward the one man she had always trusted. "There is no Hosaam, is there?"

The pastor's cold silence confirmed her accusation.

"And Paul?"

The pastor firmed his grasp on her arms. "Paul was our first Tribulation Saint. He willingly chose his duty to the Almighty."

She slowly comprehended the horrid truth; the reverend had done nothing to stop Mayfield from trying to kill her. "Mayfield is Yahya ... and you"—she choked it out—"*you* are the Mahdi."

"Jaqueline, do not question the ways of the Lord."

Her world crumbled under her feet. She froze, blind with fear. In the next instant, she fought off his grasp and staggered through the throngs. *Tell me, God! What am I to do?* As she ran sobbing across the Mount, she saw an Ethiopian monk pass the Wailing Wall below on his way to his monastery. He was carrying a staff crowned with a copy of the Cross of Lalibela. That image reminded her of those three Portuguese knights who had sacrificed their lives to save the world from Isabella and her Dominican millennialists.

She stopped, thunderstruck. This race that she and Boz had been launched upon to prevent the world from being destroyed in God's name ...

It had all happened once before. Even this.

That day in the Coimbra library, she had read how the inquisitor Torquemada filled young Isabella's impressionable mind with delusions of apocalyptic grandeur. Only now did she understand why that discovery had unsettled her. Like Isabella, she had placed her trust in the empty promises of a self-proclaimed holy man. And like Isabella of Castile, she had discovered her fatal error too late.

Or was it?

She glanced back again at Rev. Merry. He was threading the crowds in a desperate attempt to reach her. All the men in her life—the pastor, her father, Paul, her bosses at State, even the God who had promised the Rapture—all of them had ultimately betrayed her.

No, there was one exception. The man who seemed most treacherous from the start had in fact been the one always there for her.

She had created a false idol. Now she had to tear it down.

Boz ran up the ridge to the small wooden shack near the Seven Arches Hotel on the Mount of Olives. Out of breath, he dropped his hands to his knees and finally managed to huff, "I want to take a ride over the Temple Mount!"

The owner of the helicopter tour company looked up from his lounge chair and pointed to a sign in Hebrew above his head. "No flights to the Mount are allowed today. I take you to Masada or Bethlehem or Dead Sea. Four hundred American dollars."

Boz stole a glance over his shoulder toward the Dome of the Rock, where the chanting was getting louder. He pulled out a wad of bills and counted out the fare in front of the pilot. "Let's go."

The pilot didn't move his feet from their perch on the sill. "We wait for three more people."

"I don't have time to wait."

The pilot shrugged, not giving a damn. "Come back tomorrow."

Boz looked up at the sun. He slipped the folding mirror from his pocket and held it behind his back, angling it toward an open gas can that sat near the wooden kiosk. "Very hot today."

Snorting his indifference, the pilot continued reading *The Jerusalem Post.* Minutes later, he turned the page—and found its corner aflame. He jumped up, threw the paper down, and stomped out the flames. He looked around him and sniffed. To his horror, the shack's roof was dropping cinders. He shouted curses in Hebrew and rushed out coughing from the smoke to enlist the aid of the tourist in putting out the fire engulfing the shack. He let loose with another volley of damnations.

His helicopter was airborne.

Jaq clawed a path toward an Israeli police officer monitoring the crowd at the ramp's gate. Wiping her tears, she flashed her State Department ID at him. "In a few seconds, people are going to be running out those doors. When they do, you can't allow them back inside. They'll all die if you do."

The officer merely snorted, no doubt thinking that nothing so fortunate could happen to him this day.

With all of the crazies running around in this country, she couldn't blame him for ignoring her. He probably suspected her of being a Jewish extremist trying to sabotage the services. The Israeli police, she knew, were always on high alert here for trouble between Muslim and Jewish factions. Praying he would sense her sanity, she begged, "Do you understand what I'm saying?"

The officer was about to arrest her before she could cause trouble, but something dissuaded him from following through on the threat, and he motioned her away. Blessed with the reprieve, she covered her face with the hem of her burqa as she ran toward the Al-Asqa Mosque. She elbowed past the throngs and slithered inside, making her way along the wall to the crowded male section. Rows of worshippers lay prostrate on their knees, bowing and praying.

She stationed herself at the rear door. Whispering a prayer for courage, she stepped forward and, with a breaking voice, shouted at the top of her lungs, "They are digging into the Mount!"

The mosque fell silent.

Then, a Muslim man who understood English translated her warning for the congregation. The worshippers exploded with shouts for vengeance. Just as she had hoped, the ambiguous accusation, so charged with political memory, was at once collectively interpreted to mean that Jewish archaeologists and right-wing activists were secretly ignoring the ban against excavations on the Mount imposed after several riots in the past.

She elbowed past the incoming arrivals and ran toward the Golden Gate. The walled-up entry sat at the far corner of the platform, the farthest point from the bulging wall. Word of the excavation sacrilege was spreading faster than the fires of Sodom. Enraged Muslims poured out of the two mosques and followed her to stop the Jews who were violating their holy ground. They converged at the northwestern end of the platform and circled in confusion. Unable to find the desecrators, they turned on her.

"The woman is a liar!" shouted a man in the mob. "She schemes to deny the Mahdi his glory!"

An elderly imam with a kind face raised his hands to calm the crowd. "Ours is a religion of peace! Let us take the woman to the authorities and allow them to deliver justice!"

Ignoring the imam's pleas, the mob surrounded Jaq before she could escape. Several frenzied worshippers ripped off her burqa and revealed her wearing a Western shirt and blue jeans. Finding what they thought was yet another Jewish extremist bent on disrupting their services, they began screaming, "Zionist occupier! No Jew destroys the Haram-esh-Sharif!"

A storm of stones drove her toward the wall.

Rev. Merry fought to reach her in the melee, but he was swept aside.

In the bunker below St. Mary Magdalene, Josh Mayfield washed up in his lavatory and changed into a crisp new shirt. The media would soon be descending on him, and it would be important to appear the very definition of cool assurance for a world in panic. His plan was proceeding like clockwork. That rube preacher Merry had been played right into his hands, stirring up his Rapture nut jobs to help set off the holy war. He couldn't wait to see the look of shock on their faces when Jesus didn't show up to raise them into the sky like hot-air balloons.

Fred Darden rushed in. "We have a problem."

Mayfield sauntered back to the conference room, certain that the State Department official—and his colleague in the Third Temple Alliance—was overreacting. He looked up at the screen, where the real-time video cameras showed a sea of Muslims streaming away from the mosques. He lost his confident smirk. "What the hell's going on down there?"

"We don't know," Darden said. "The Israeli Defense Forces are deploying a unit on the Mount to restore order. And there's a helicopter in the air."

Mayfield pushed a dashboard button, and when the camera zoomed in, he turned another shade purple. "Call that goddamn tent evangelist and tell him to do something to get those goddamn Arabs back to the south end!"

"Like what?" asked Darden.

"I don't give a damn! Start preaching if he has to!"

Boz circled the copter above the Mount, staying high enough to avoid gunfire. He searched for Jaq in the mayhem below. A lone speck broke through the throngs and ran toward the northwest corner of the platform.

Why was half the Middle East chasing her?

He gunned the throttle to speed toward the Mount. Reaching an arm behind his seat, he found a coiled rescue line tethered to an electrical winch. When he came above the eastern corner of the platform, he lowered the copter and hit the switch to unleash the rope and harness.

"Come on, Jaq!"

The thrum of the rotors drowned out his shouts.

He dropped low enough to make eye contact with her. She leapt to reach the rope, but it dangled just beyond her grasp. The copter rocked and pinged. Were the Israelis firing at him? He spun around and went in again. The engine sputtered against the wind. Below him, the platform was a gyre of confusion. Hundreds of Muslims ran for the whipping rope. They caught the harness and tried to prevent the rescue attempt by tethering it to an iron ring on the ashlars.

The copter flailed wildly. Seconds from crashing, he veered hard, angling the propeller blades into the rope. Freed, he spun the copter three-sixty and searched for an open space to land. He took aim for a corner near the Dome of the Rock and dove in for one more run.

My God!

They were carrying Jaq toward the wall.

He pitched the copter down. "No!"

The rioters heaved her over the precipice.

He froze at the controls, unable to push the throttle. Finally, he roused and circled in search of a patch of flat surface to land, but the slope below the walls was riddled with large stones. He searched the ridge in desperation, but there was no way to reach her. If he crashed here, he'd be stoned or arrested, so he sped off under an assault of stones and ricocheting bullets, hoping to land somewhere else and reach her in time.

Having dutifully protected their holy ground, the worshippers—some celebrating, others distraught by the sudden spasm of violence—surged back toward the mosques to await the Mahdi's triumphant arrival.

He took the copter up fast and stole another look down at the Mount.

A phalanx of Israeli Defense Forces armored in riot gear blocked the entrances to the Al Asqa and Al Marawi mosques. An officer—the one Jaq had pleaded with minutes earlier—stood in front of his ranks, prepared to issue the order to fire if the mob tried to breach his lines.

Below them, surrounded by ancient gravestones, Jaq lay motionless in the Valley of Jehosaphat, her head haloing in a pool of blood.

FORTY

A s Boz drove up the dirt lane on the ridge overlooking Strawner's Gap, he spun the radio dial until he found a news update in progress:

"... *the woman, identified as Jaqueline Quartermane, was a State Department lawyer on leave for psychiatric reasons, a Foggy Bottom spokesman said. Quartermane had been receiving treatment in a Rhode Island facility when she escaped to join the thousands of fundamentalist Christians and Muslims drawn to Israel by Internet-fueled rumors of the unfolding End Times.*

William Bratton, director of the Godspring Center in Newport, said Ms. Quartermane had been diagnosed with a delusional illness known as the Jerusalem Syndrome, which causes people to believe that they are characters from the Bible.

Secretary of State McCrozier praised the Israeli Defense Forces for diffusing the dangerous situation. He assured the world that calm has been restored in Jerusalem, and most of the Christians and Muslims who flooded into the country expecting the Rapture or the arrival of the Islamic messiah have returned home disappointed.

In a related development, Israeli authorities say they have found significant structural weaknesses in the southern wall of the Temple Mount. Engineers said a bulge there became worse due to the recent increase in foot traffic. Both the al-Marawi and al-Asqa mosques will remain closed until the Mount's foundations can be strengthened."

He turned into the cemetery and saw a cluster of mourners in black over-coats standing over an open grave. He got out and walked up in time to hear the end of the eulogy. His approach drew suspicious stares. Several of the faces in the gathering reminded him of the Melungeon families that he had seen in the old photographs at the local Masonic lodge here.

"I'll never forget that awful moment when I received the tragic news," the minister said, his voice cracking. "I had just opened my Bible to prepare for Sunday's sermon. There before me lay the passage from Isaiah: 'Then it will happen on that day that the Lord will again gather the second time with His hand the remnant of His people.'" The minister, seeing Boz for the first time, stole a questioning glance at him before finishing his eulogy. "Tears came to my eyes, for I knew then in my heart that God was taking our dearest Jaqueline from us. She is now in a better place. Let us commend her to the Lord and leave assured that we will be with her very soon, when He brings us to His bosom. Amen."

As the mourners departed the gravesite, Jaq's grandmother was rolled past Boz in a wheelchair. She looked up at him and complained: "Daniel, you still ain't shooed those chickens into the coop."

Boz nodded a concession of negligence to humor her delusion.

After dispensing condolences, the minister stopped to offer him a belated welcome. "Did you know Jaqueline well?"

"We used to hunt varmints together."

The minister took Boz's hand into his own clammy palms. "Have you found Jesus, my son?"

"I didn't know He was lost."

The minister maintained his reverential smile, evidently inured to such blasphemy from secularists. "There is still time. I hope your acquaintance with Jaqueline will yet bring you to Christ. We wouldn't want you to be one of those left behind."

The preacher's syrupy unctuousness made Boz want to kick his righteous ass. "Where I come from, we have a saying."

The pastor drew closer to him in brotherly fellowship. "And what would that be?"

"Next year in Jerusalem."

The pastor stared at him blankly, as if weighing whether a threat had been veiled behind that traditional Jewish prayer of hope. Recovering, he turned and walked briskly to his black Cadillac Eldorado, and drove off.

Boz remained behind to spend a few moments alone with Jaq.

One of the mourners, a tall, elderly gentleman in suspenders, waited in his pickup truck until the other vehicles trailed off over the ridge. Then, he got out again and, relying on a cane, returned to the grave. "My eyes aren't what it used to be. Do I know you?"

Boz recognized him as Jaq's childhood physician. "We met a couple of weeks ago."

"Ah, yes," Doc Hopkins said. "How good of you to come back for Jaqie."

Boz watched the Cadillac leave a cloud of dust as it sped down the dirt road. "Who was that preacher?"

The doctor seemed surprised by the question. "Why Cal Merry, of course."

"The televangelist?"

"Jaqie never introduced you?"

Boz shook his head. "I thought he'd be someone more …"

"Godly?"

Boz found that an odd thing for a doctor here in the Bible-Belt South to say. He debated telling him what had really happened to Jaq, but he knew it would be futile. If he went to Interpol or the U.S. Attorney's office, he would just be arrested on his outstanding warrants. No one would believe him anyway. After all, what evidence could he offer to prove that the Mahdi imposter and his Bilqis conspirators had nearly plunged the world into an apocalyptic war? He didn't even know the identity of the mercenary executive who had been hired by Hosaam to install the earthquake resonator under the Temple Mount.

For now, he would stay in the shadows and bide his time. But one day, he vowed, he would hunt down Hosaam and those murderous thugs and send them castrated to their forty virgins. Shrugging off his plans for revenge, he came closer to the small stone to read the inscription:

Jaqueline Quartermane

1989 — 2014

God's Mercy Has Been Found.

God's Mercy? Waving it off as just a coincidence, he circled the stone to see what had been written on the other side:

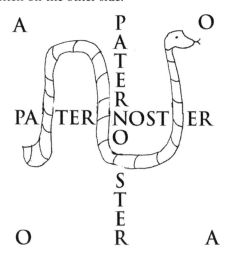

IN HER MEMORY
SNEEDSVILLE MASONIC LODGE

Puzzled by the odd epitaph, he asked the country doctor: "A preacher at that church down there told Jaq and me that snakes like this were only carved on the tombstones of charmers."

Smiling, Doc Hopkins offered an evasive reply. "I always said Jaqie could charm the skin off a copperhead."

Boz studied the stone again. Something about the Latin words PATER NOSTER seemed oddly familiar. The 'A's and 'O's in the corners, he knew, were the traditional Christian signs for the Alpha and Omega, the Beginning and the End. He counted twenty-five letters: Four each of A, E, O, T, and R; two each of S and P; and one serpentine N in the center.

SATORAREPOTENETOPERAROTAS.

Those were all the letters of the Templar-SATOR square. Another translation of the original palindrome suddenly came to him: *God's servants save the eternal cause by working the wheels.*

Did the Knights of the Brazen Serpent still exist?

He glanced over at the doctor, wondering if he knew anything about this word square being passed down through the centuries as a cryptographic device to be used against millennialists bent on igniting the Apocalypse. Now that he thought about it ... no, he was starting to imagine things, just like those religious fanatics. He shook his head, chastising himself for giving a second thought to the ridiculous notion that a covert brotherhood had been guiding him and Jaq in their duel against the modern End Times fanatics.

The doctor glimpsed the darkening sky and tightened the collar of his coat. "Feels like rain brewing in that *ostro* to the west. I'd better get down the road before it muddies up."

Boz turned again with a start, hearing the doctor mention the Portuguese direction on the Wind Rose. He was about to ask him if he knew about the initiation wheel in Portugal when two gravediggers approached, eager to fill the hole before the rains came. He decided to say nothing about it. After all, the very idea of a perpetual war between the spiritual forces of Darkness and Light was just a fantasy. Jaq had always been the one seeing connections and patterns where none existed, not him. Coughing, he whispered a vow over her casket. "This is not over, Jaq."

The doctor, lingering a few steps behind him, came back and shook his hand with a firmness that suggested more than just a passing goodbye. "Never has been over. Never will be. You take care of yourself, Mr. Elymas."

Before Boz could ask him how he had learned of his alias, the grand master of the Sneedville Masonic Lodge limped back to his pickup and drove off into the thickening mists of Melungeon country.

SOURCES
AND
ACKNOWLEDGEMETS

N ovelists who sift the past for their stories owe a debt of gratitude to the historians and researchers who devote painstaking hours poring over primary documents. Of the many sources that I consulted, a few deserve special mention.

One does not tread lightly into the minefield of Columbus studies. Since 1915, several scholars have championed the controversial claim for the explorer's Portuguese background. In 1930, G.L. dos Santos Ferreira and Antonio Ferreira de Serpa proposed Columbus's true identity to be Salvador Gonsalves Zarco. In 1988, Mascarenhas Barreto published an extensive treatment of the subject with his *The Portuguese Columbus: Secret Agent of King John II*. More recently, the Portuguese hypothesis has been advanced by Manuel Luciano da Silva (*Christopher Columbus was Portuguese!*), Manuel da Silva Rosa (*O Mistério Colombo Revelado*), and Alredo F. de Mello (*The Real Colon: Columbus is a Misnomer*). The Portuguese genealogist Luis Paulo Manuel de Meneses de Melo Vaz de São Paio offered a counterargument in his *Primeira Carta Aberta a Mascarenhas Barreto*. Also, in 1973, Simon Wiesenthal made the case for Columbus being a Jew in his *Sails of Hope: Secret Mission of Christopher Columbus*.

I drew extensively from the arguments and evidence set forth by these advocates of the Portuguese hypothesis—in particular, Barreto's evaluation of the elusive Zarco, Da Silva's insights into the origins of the name Colon, and Mello's analysis of the Columbus sigil. But I also grafted onto their theories my own suppositions, tangents, and possibilities. I encourage readers to consult the works of these authors to discover the variances between their scholarship and my flights of imagination.

Louis Charpentier deserves again to be recognized for identifying the possible connection between the constellation of Virgo and the Notre Dame cathedrals in northern France.

In *The Sign and the Seal*, Graham Hancock explored the possible connection between Ethiopia and the Ark of the Covenant, including the tantalizing suggestion offered to him by a priest in Lalibela that the SATOR square contained the Name of God.

I am indebted to John Jeter and Alicia Rasley for their editing assistance and to Lorrene Black in the cryptology department at California State University Channel Islands for her patient assistance in helping me arrive at a combinatrics formula for the SATOR square. Thanks also to David Martin, Michelle Millar, and Stewart Matthew for their invaluable suggestions and encouragement.

Sources for other quotes, illustrations, and maps include:

The map of Lalibela is from *Lalibela: The Monolithic Churches of Ethiopia* by Irmgard Bidder (Thames and Hudson London 1958).

The Vatican: Its History–Its Treasures by Ernesto Begni, James Grey and Thomas Kennedy (Letters and Arts Publishing, 1914).

The plan of Chartres crypt is from *The City of Chartres: Its Cathedral and Churches* by H.J.L.J. Masse (London George Bells and Sons 1905).

The reproductions of the Chartres labyrinth and south transept are from the MEDART database at the University of Pittsburgh Digital Research Library.

Le Mystere des Catherales by Fulcanelli (American Edition reprint by Brotherhood of Life, 1984).

The Templar Treasure at Gisors by Jean Markale (Inner Traditions 1986), quoting the Dorival poem from the 1898 newspaper, *Le Vexin*.

Les Mysteres de la cathedrale de Chartres by Louis Charpentier (Avon 1980).

The Dighton Rock tracing is from *Picture-Writing of the American Indians* by Garrick Mallery, Volume Two, 1972 Dover Reprint of the *Tenth Annual Report of the Bureau of Ethnology to the Secretary of the Smithsonian Institution, 1888-1889.*

The center of the Lullian Circle is from the *Enciclopedia universal ilustrada* (Barcelona, 1923)

Gnosis: The Secret of Solomon's Temple Revealed by Philip Gardiner (Radikal Phase 2006)

Gnosis and their Remains by Charles W. King (David Nutt London 1887)

Encyclopedia of Freemasonry and its Kindred Sciences by Albert C. Mackey (The Masonic History Company 1914).

The wind rose is from Pedro de Medina's *Libro de Cosmographica* (1545).

The Canestris Map is from *Maps of the Ancient Sea Kings* by Charles H. Hapgood (Adventures Unlimited Press 1977)

The NSA seal is from *Code Breaking: A History and Exploration* by Rudolf Kippenhahn (Overlook Press 1999).

The seal of King Alfonso and the stele of Gualdhim Pais are from *viagen-snotempo.com.*

The Mendocas coat of arms is from *The Portuguese Columbus: Secret Agent of King John II* by Mascarenhas Barreto (St. Martin's 1992).

About the Author

A graduate of Indiana University School of Law and Columbia University Graduate School of Journalism, **Glen Craney** practiced trial law before joining the Washington press corps to cover national politics and the Iran-contra trial for *Congressional Quarterly* magazine. The Academy of Motion Pictures, Arts and Sciences awarded him the Nicholl Fellowship prize for best new screenwriting. His debut novel, *The Fire and the Light,* was named Best New Fiction by the National Indie Excellence Awards. He is a three-time Finalist/Honorable Mention winner of *Foreword Magazine's* Book of the Year and a Chaucer Award winner for Category Historical Fiction. His books have taken readers to Occitania during the Albigensian Crusade, to the Scotland of Robert Bruce, to Portugal during the Age of Discovery, to the trenches of France during World War I, and to the American Hoovervilles of the Great Depression He lives in Malibu, California.

Also by Glen Craney

The Fire and the Light
A Novel of the Cathars

As the 13th century dawns, Cathar heretics in southern France guard an ancient scroll that holds shattering revelations about Jesus Christ. Esclarmonde de Foix, a beloved Occitan countess, must defy Rome to preserve the true path to salvation. Christianity suffers its darkest hour in this epic saga of troubadour love, monastic intrigue, and esoteric mystery set during the first years of the French Inquisition.

The Spider and the Stone
A Novel of Scotland's Black Douglas

With the 14th century approaching, the brutal Edward Longshanks of England schemes to steal Scotland. But inspired by a headstrong lass, a frail, dark-skinned boy named James Douglas defies three Plantagenet kings and champions the cause of his wavering friend, Robert the Bruce, leading the armies to the bloody field of Bannockburn. Here is the thrilling saga of star-crossed love and heroic sacrifice that saved Scotland and set the stage for the founding of the United States.

The Yanks Are Starving
A Novel of the Bonus Army

Mired in the Great Depression, the United States teeters on the brink of revolution. And as the summer of 1932 approaches, a charismatic hobo leads twenty thousand homeless World War I veterans into the nation's capital to demand their service compensation. Here is the epic story of political intrigue and betrayal that culminated in the only violent clash ever waged between two American armies under the same flag.

The Lucifer Genome
A Conspiracy Thriller (John Jeter and Glen Craney)

Someone with a lot of money and guns is trying to corner the market on the world's oldest human DNA. And retired Defense Intelligence agent Cas Fielding believes the mystery lies deep inside the core of a precious shard that fell to earth thousands of years ago. Teamed with a sultry geophysics expert, he descends into the global underground meteorite market, only to find himself caught between a rock and an Apocalyptic hard place.

More information at www.glencraney.com.

Manufactured by Amazon.ca
Bolton, ON

18449540R00236